A Simple Scandal

MILLIONAIRES OF MAYFAIR

JANNA MACGREGOR

Disclaimer: This is a work of fiction. Names, characters, places, and incidents are products of the author's imagination, or the author has used them fictitiously.

Prologue

~~~

Amesbury
Nine years prior
At the summer home of the Late Earl of Webster-Harnly

Knowing precisely what David faced when he entered the lion's den, Lady Grace Webster lifted her chin a defiant inch as she stepped inside her father's study. Her brother-in-law, Stewart Arnold, rose from her late father's desk chair and regarded her with a benevolent smile. Meanwhile, Grace's younger sister, Hope, who had married the insidious man, stood beside him.

Their father, the previous Earl of Webster-Harnly, had been buried six months before, and now, her brother-in-law acted as if he were the new earl instead of their third cousin, Raphael Sullivan.

To say Stewart was subtle and underhanded was not an exaggeration. He reminded Grace of a cunning fox lurking near a henhouse, waiting for an opportunity to pillage and plunder the unsuspecting fowl. That was how her former best friend, not to mention former fiancé, Dane Ardeerton, the Marquess of Merrick and heir to the Duke of Pelham, described Stewart. Dane should know, as he had attended

Eton alongside Stewart. Her brother-in-law had cultivated a reputation for cheating his way through Eton while ingratiating himself with the provosts through excessive flattery, another unforgivable trait as deceitful as cheating in Dane's eyes.

Regardless of the outcome of today's visit, Grace would soon be free from having to deal with Stewart. Unfortunately, that also meant she wouldn't be seeing Hope much either. Hope had decided to forgo a Season to marry Stewart, who belonged to the wealthy gentry in their county. Her life was stuck in Amesbury along with Stewart.

Well, Grace would not allow herself to make the same mistake.

London called to her like a long-lost lover serenading his beloved. Grace intended to respond to that call as soon as today's business was complete. She fully anticipated staying with Raphael, the new earl, at her father's former home in London while she immersed herself in all the activities the Season had to offer. She had become somewhat of a celebrity after helping her friend, Annabelle Ernst, find the perfect husband. Since then, everyone had clamored for Grace's help in finding their ideal partner.

"My dear sister, please come in," Stewart drawled, gesturing toward a chair in front of her father's desk. Hope slowly settled into the chair to his right.

Though she was attired in appropriate half-mourning clothing as her brother-in-law and sister, there was a slight difference. Both of them resembled ravens who were holding court for all their lowly subjects. They wore expressions as dark as a twilight sky.

"Thank you," she murmured demurely.

"As you must be aware, my husband is now head of the family." Hope darted an adoring gaze at Stewart. "He made the sacrifice and attended the reading of Father's will in London. He just returned yesterday." She tutted as she picked a piece of lint off his sleeve and then patted his arm. "You must be exhausted, dear."

Stewart preened under Hope's ministrations. "Wife, not at all. You always know how best to take care of me."

Get on with it. Grace wanted to roll her eyes, but by some miracle, she sat there as still as stone. Hope was the one who had found her father's will in a box of discarded papers, which was odd since her father was meticulous with anything important.

"I'm afraid there's no way to ease the shock of what I'm about to say." Her brother-in-law sniffed as he shuffled the papers in front of him. Slowly, he raised his gaze to hers. "So, I shall simply be blunt. Your father died destitute."

The words hovered in the air, eluding her grasp as she grappled for a response. Grace tilted her head, wishing for the words to become clear. "Pardon?"

When Hope scooted her chair closer to him in solidarity, Stewart smiled down at her before fixing his gaze on Grace.

"Destitute. Insolvent. Impoverished." Stewart's eyes gleamed with every word he spoke.

Grace shook her head in denial. "That can't be. Papa was excellent in managing the estate and his funds."

"That might have been the case in the past," Stewart murmured. "But it's highly doubtful. Not when he gambled recklessly with his fortune and the extra estate monies."

"There must be some mistake or misunderstanding," Grace whispered to no one. Her body grew instantly numb as if encased in ice. She couldn't move and could barely breathe. *Destitute.* What did that mean?

"There's no money," Hope snapped. "You have no dowry, inheritance, or trust. Simply put, you have nothing." By then, she was practically screeching at Grace. "Sometimes I wonder how you can be older than me. You act like a child."

"Darling," Stewart admonished gently.

"I'll not be quiet." Hope pointed her finger in Grace's direction. "All your extravagant clothing orders have been canceled, including anything you've ordered at the village seamstress or haberdashery, not to mention the cobbler and hatmakers."

Grace's hand flew to her chest. She'd never heard Hope sound so hateful. It was hard to believe that only months ago, they held each other in their arms as they grieved the loss of their beloved father. He'd been ill for quite some time with a weak heart, but Grace had never imagined that he'd die so quickly.

As she struggled with the news, it suddenly dawned on her that she had no money outside of the small amount of pin money she had saved from her father's generous allowances. She had maybe ten or fifteen pounds at most in her reticule. She gasped as she understood what it all meant. For the love of heaven, she would soon be indebted to her sister and brother-in-law.

Desperate to find another solution, she turned her attention to Stewart. "I have an inheritance from my Aunt Polly."

"No, you don't." Her brother-in-law regarded her with a look of feigned empathy. "Your father gambled that away as well."

None of this made sense. She narrowed her eyes. "How could this have occurred? Father had been ill for several months before he passed. He never left the house."

Stewart poured himself a cup of tea without offering any to Hope, much less Grace. He took a sip and sighed in satisfaction. "He juggled those debts like balls in the air. Somehow, he kept them afloat until his passing, and then the creditors came calling." He shrugged. "I successfully convinced them to accept less than what was owed. Now, the new earl doesn't have to worry about paying off your father's debts." He turned to Hope. "Do you think your father was feeble-minded at the end?"

Hope nodded twice. "Undoubtedly. The father I knew would never have gambled away everything."

"Papa was not feeble-minded." Grace stood so abruptly that her chair screeched in protest. "He was still managing the estate books the day before he died."

Hope hmphed.

"All is not lost," Stewart offered. "If you like, I have enough for a trip to Northumberland, where you can stay with my Great-Aunt Pearl. She wrote with news that one of the local farmers, Mr. Jones, is looking for a wife. He's in his fifth decade. He'll make a fine husband but probably won't live too long. He won't mind that you're in mourning." He smiled as if that solved all her problems. "And if he doesn't suit you, his son might. He'll inherit the farm after Mr. Jones dies."

"Northumberland?" Grace cried, then slowly lowered herself into the chair. "I know no one in Northumberland."

"Never fear. I'll write a letter of introduction to Great-Aunt Pearl.

She would be delighted to host you for a brief visit to see how well you and Mr. Jones get along and if you can find an accord." His smile melted from his face. "You should try to please him. My great-aunt will not spend the coach fare necessary for you to return. You'll have to find your way back...to whatever relative agrees to take you."

Grace swallowed the brick lodged in her throat. She turned her gaze to her sister, seeking some empathy for her plight. They'd never been close as sisters. Grace had always been her parents' favorite, but was it any wonder? Hope was as sour as unsweetened lemonade.

Her sister pointed the same finger in Grace's direction again, flicking it up and down as if finding her lacking. "This is your own fault." She planted her hands on her hips and leaned in Grace's direction. "You're an idiot for turning down the Marquess of Merrick and then thinking yourself fancy enough for a London Season. If you'd married him, there would have been money in the coffers. He would have forgiven our father's debts. All of them," she seethed. "And you would have been rich beyond your wildest dreams."

Grace straightened her back. Her sister didn't know everything that had occurred between her and Dane. Only her father had known, and he'd taken the secret to his grave. Under no circumstances would she share it. Though Dane had walked away from her, she still loved him.

Hope's lips pursed in repulsion. "What a waste of money London was. The Marquess of West Essex wrote a letter inquiring about your hand in marriage."

Grace scooted to the edge of her chair. Perhaps things weren't as dire as she had once thought. The marquess was a tad young but pleasant enough. She had danced with him several times last Season. He seemed to enjoy her company. As a way out of this nightmare, she could marry him. Though she didn't love him, friendship could forge a strong foundation for a *ton* marriage.

"Unfortunately, he needs an heiress." Stewart frowned as if aggrieved on her behalf. "When I explained your situation, he immediately withdrew his interest."

Her heart stuttered in its beat. Stewart was as subtle and refined as a wild boar. If he told everyone in London that she was destitute, no one would have anything to do with her. "What did you say to him? Did you tell him we're impoverished?"

"You are impoverished, not we," Stewart pointed out unhelpfully. "I simply told him you would also need to make an excellent match."

"Another example of a wasted effort in London." Hope scowled.

Grace ignored her. Who would have ever thought she'd prefer to talk to her brother-in-law instead of her sister with such unsettling news? She offered a meek smile to him, all the while praying her stomach would cease roiling. "I'll ask the new earl for his assistance. We've always enjoyed each other's company, and I am his blood relative."

Stewart wrinkled his nose as if smelling something horrid. "Unfortunately, the new earl is not a fan of gamblers and wastrels. He doesn't accept it as his duty to help his poor kindred, and that includes you."

"Don't come to us expecting charity." Hope slashed her hand through the air. "You should have married like me and forgone London. Thank goodness I married before all this nastiness started." Her sister smiled at Stewart like he was the King of England who had granted her the title of Queen Consort. "At least I'm secure and have a husband who will provide for me through sickness and health."

"Those were our vows to one another, darling," Stewart said smugly, then patted her hand. "Let us not be too harsh. She is your sister, after all."

"God help us all," Hope muttered under her breath.

He turned to Grace. "Perhaps you should find gainful and respectable employment. Have you ever considered being a governess?"

Hope smiled, but it didn't reach her eyes as her gaze shot to Grace. "You can stay here until we're out of mourning, but not a day more. You'll be on your own."

Without acknowledging them, Grace turned and, with her most regal walk, she escaped their presence. Governess, indeed. Though the tears burned in her eyes, she would not let them fall. Only when she found the sanctity of her room would she allow herself to grieve. It was unfathomable that her father would have left her in such destitute circumstances. Her father would be appalled if he knew she would be forced to work in someone's household.

Once she closed the door to her room, she flopped onto her bed. Her back bounced from the effort as she closed her eyes when she could no longer contain the hot tears.

Her father had never been a gambler, had he? He went to the Jolly Rooster, the local coaching inn, to dine and spend time with his friends. He never mentioned card games until he'd told her about Dane wagering ungodly amounts of money at a card game with Lord Scoville.

But how would he have known Dane was gambling unless he was participating in such games himself? When he'd told her that he'd seen Dane there with other women, her father tried to convince her not to marry him. Perhaps her father was trying to hide his own gambling habits.

If this had happened a year ago, she would have asked Dane for money until she found suitable employment in London. Under no circumstances would she be indebted to him now or in the future. Frankly, their last conversation made her doubt whether they were even friends anymore.

She blew out a ragged breath and dried her tears. It made little difference at this point. She had nothing except her own intelligence and ability to work. She would survive this setback.

She vowed then and there that she would never allow herself to be in a position where she didn't have the means to have her own household. She would do whatever was necessary to have a home that would always provide her with the security to stand on her own.

Whatever it took, she would not be beholden to her family.

Nor would she ever rely on any man, especially Dane Ardeerton, the Marquess of Merrick.

One

ine years later
London

N

If Dane Ardeerton, the Fifth Duke of Pelham, faced the misery of seeking a wife, he would ensure that Lady Grace Webster would be miserable alongside him. Choosing a suitable woman to marry was the definition of tedious. While it should be one of the most joyous times of his life, it had turned into drudgery.

The coach turned down a thoroughfare that Dane recognized as the edge of Mayfair.

"Flowers for sale!"

The call of a young girl caught his attention. Quickly, he knocked on the carriage's roof, signaling the coachman to stop.

"Whoa," William Fergus, his coachman, shouted as he pulled the coach and four to a stop. "What can I do for you, Your Grace."

Dane leaned out the window. "I'd like to buy a bouquet." He pointed toward the flower girl.

By then, John, his footman dressed in the customary gray and gold livery of the Duke of Pelham, opened the carriage door and leaned in. "Allow me to get the flowers for you, Your Grace." A pensive smile tugged at his mouth. "We're entering a part of town that caters to merchants and several unsavory pubs that draw the riffraff."

"Then I shall be right at home." Dane stepped out of the carriage. "It'll feel like I'm at the Jolly Rooster."

As soon as he walked toward the flower girl, her eyes grew to the size of dinner plates.

"That a righ' fancy coach. You a nob?" Her grin revealed that she'd lost her front two teeth.

"No. I'm a duke." He gave her his most charming smile. "What is the prettiest and biggest bouquet you have?"

She excitedly bounced on her toes as she pulled out a slightly wilted bouquet of roses. "Me mum and me picked these this mornin. Are these for your trouble and strife?" She stared straight at him as if she conversed with a duke every day.

"Trouble and strife?" He lifted a single eyebrow.

She frowned as she nodded. "Trouble and strife. Means your missus."

For a moment, he didn't know what to say. "I don't have a wife. The flowers are for a special lady." He didn't add that he meant special in that the woman who would receive the bouquet was the bane of his existence. But he knew how to calculate odds, and with Grace, it never hurt to have a bit of goodwill insurance. He pulled a guinea from his waistcoat pocket and gave it to the girl.

"*Lud*," the girl exclaimed as she examined the coin. "I've never 'eld one of these before." She scowled slightly. "I don't 'ave any coins to make change."

"There's no need." He took the flowers from her. "Perhaps you can buy your mother dinner this evening."

"I will, Duke." She grinned at him again. "I'm at this corner every day. In case you need more flowers."

"Then I undoubtedly shall see you again." Dane nodded and returned to the carriage. He planned to see the flower girl regularly and was determined to visit Grace daily if only to aggravate her. It wasn't revenge for her jilting him or anything so plebian—more like she needed to prioritize him.

John opened the door, and Dane vaulted into the carriage. Within seconds, the carriage lurched forward, heading to Grace's home. He admired the vivid ruby hue of the roses, which reminded him of Grace's cheeks the last time he had kissed her. It had been over nine years ago, but he could still recall the taste of her lips. He could easily envision her cheeks flaming that same color when he presented her with the bouquet. The only question was whether the cause would be joy or unbridled fury when he offered her such a gift.

He straightened as he glanced out the window. A slight smile tugged at his lips. It didn't matter to him what caused that color as long as the *Governess's* cheeks reddened.

It was one of the most beautiful sights he'd ever seen.

Dane had given Lady Grace Webster the moniker *Governess* when she'd first helped her friend, Lady Annabelle Ernst, land a husband after being on the marriage market for five long years. The poor girl had the confidence of a slug and couldn't carry a conversation past hello. But Grace had come to Annabelle's rescue like a governess with her awkward charges and had practically turned Annabelle into an overnight sensation along with herself. Desperate men and women of the *ton* approached her, seeking assistance. If Grace could help Lady Annabelle find a spouse, then the rest were confident that Grace could work her magic for them.

She'd been one of his closest friends when they were growing up. Her London family home had been directly across the square from his father's ducal mansion, Ardeerton House. In addition, her father owned a summer estate next to the ducal seat. The old duke had never cared for Grace's father, the Earl of Webster-Harnly. They'd been bitter rivals during the sessions of Parliament. Thankfully, their sires' dislike of one another didn't affect their friendship when they were younger.

When they turned into adults, that was another story.

He rubbed his forehead. It was best not to rehash their past. He needed to look toward his future. That's why he was on his way to call on Grace and retain her services. Today, he'd watched his youngest sister marry his best friend. Since his oldest sister had married his other best friend several months ago, Dane had found himself walking around Ardeerton House completely rudderless. He'd never felt so lost and lonely in his life.

Of course, he could always *do the pretty* and attend societal events, but his stomach roiled at the whole notion of flirting, not to mention courting and sweet-talking young ladies. He did not care for insipid females or ones who molded themselves into someone they thought he'd desire. He preferred real women who had the intelligence, self-assurance, and drive to make something of themselves. His sisters were of that ilk, along with his female employees at the Jolly Rooster, his private gambling hell and coaching inn located next to the duchy's seat in Amesbury.

As a duke, he was well aware of his responsibilities to his title. Since he was newly in his third decade, the time had come for him to choose a bride and secure an heir and a spare. He would be delighted if a daughter or two were in his brood. He loved all women, and growing up with his two opinionated and independent sisters had been a joy. They'd given him purpose, happiness, and a sense of family.

He exhaled as he watched the buildings fly by. Recently, he had thought that he and Grace were getting along wonderfully, especially since Grace had helped his sisters navigate society during their introductions. Grace made sure they wouldn't fall victim to the gossipmongers who thrived on stirring up trouble, whether it was true or not. When his youngest sister married Hugh Calthorpe, the Marquess of Ravenscroft, earlier that day, Grace was eager to distance herself from his company.

As the carriage came to a slow halt, Dane peered out the window. A modest townhouse stood nestled between several others, the surrounding homes having seen better days. Their windows were grimy, and the shutters framing them hung askew. It reminded him of all the disheveled patrons at the Jolly Rooster, who couldn't sit straight in their chairs after indulging in too much whisky.

However, the charming house in the center was clearly Grace's home. Everything looked prim and proper. The brass doorknocker shone as though it had just been polished. Everything was in its rightful place.

Proper was a perfect word to describe Grace. She was a prim and proper lady unless she felt her trust had been misplaced.

Then, she turned into a Scottish wildcat who refused to be tamed.

He should know. He had firsthand experience with that wildcat.

Grace's heart lurched in its beat as she gazed at the beautiful ivory brocade dress her friend Lady Pippa Ravenscroft had made for her. It had been a birthday present, and it was one of Grace's most prized possessions.

Not to mention that it was one of her most *valuable* possessions. The gown was a masterpiece with ornate silver buttons, matching trim, and gauze netting so fine you could see through it. To make the dress even more beautiful, it was adorned with tiny, perfectly matched pearl beads that possessed a luster that glowed from within.

Grace rested her head in her hands as she turned to stare out the window at the small garden in the back of her humble home. Though she usually loved to sit at her miniature Louis XV desk as she worked, today was the exception. Before her, the household account book laid open, once again telling a story she had grown quite weary of reading.

She didn't have enough money to pay her bills this month. The butcher and coalman had already sent two overdue invoices. It was only a matter of time before her rent would come due.

She'd always prided herself on her quick ability to make hard decisions and never second-guess herself. However, the decision to sell the dress hurt. She'd only been able to wear the lovely gown once to Pippa's wedding that had occurred earlier in the day at the Duke of Pelham's London home, Ardeerton House. Lady Pippa Ardeerton and the Marquess of Ravenscroft's wedding ceremony had been beautiful, and Grace had felt like a queen in the gown. Alas, she had hoped to wear it at least three more times before she'd have to sell it.

Even if she wasn't running out of gowns to sell, her situation was dire. She stared at the parchment in front of her. If she didn't find a solution quickly, she would be forced to write her brother-in-law and ask if he could loan her some money to tide her over. No doubt he'd make an appearance and start lecturing her about her spendthrift ways. She clenched her fist so tightly that she could feel her nails digging into her palm. She would do anything to avoid that fate. The man thrived on pointing out how she had failed in every aspect of her life.

"My lady?" Her only servant, Theodore Tinniswood, peeked his head around the corner. "I'm about to head to the market." He pointed to the dress across the sofa. "Is that the garment you'd like for me to take?"

Grace hesitated for a moment. This would impact her livelihood. How could she navigate society as an accepted *ton* member if she didn't appear the part?

Everyone called her *Governess* for her ability to lead her clients out of scandal while keeping them from the jaws of society's machinations. She taught them manners and deportment and quizzed them on titles and precedence. If it was essential to the *ton*, she taught it to her charges. She also helped them find their perfect matches in the dizzying world of the marriage mart. However, her current list of clients had dwindled. It seemed that no one was in a rush to marry this year, and there weren't many *ton* members embroiled in a scandal or misbehaving. Not an ideal situation when one was trying to save money to buy a home. It was a disaster if you were trying to pay your monthly bills.

"How much money do you think you can sell it for?" She gazed at the account books. If heaven had any mercy for women like her who lived independently, then the gown should fetch a pretty penny. Every inch of her skin crawled as she waited for her elderly servant to answer.

"I can't rightly say, my lady." Theodore, who preferred to be called Theo, scratched his nearly bald head as he examined the dress. "It's a beautiful gown, but Lady Eskridge had her lady's maid bring ten ballgowns to the market last week. Mrs. Martin still had them for sale at her stall yesterday."

Grace nodded once. She would not cower when forced to make hard decisions. "Would you fetch my blue velvet heels and take those as well? Only sell the dress and shoes together if you can get three pounds or more."

Theo smiled slightly.

Grace hated that smile as she knew what would come next.

"I have a little money saved for a rainy day, my lady. You are more than welcome to borrow it."

She shook her head. Though she was desperate, she had never accepted Theo's offer. She might not have riches, but she still had her pride.

"I would never take any of your savings." She forced herself to hold her servant's sympathetic gaze. "It means the world to me that you're so generous."

"Of course, ma'am. The offer is always open." Reverently, he picked up the dress. "I'll take good care of this for you."

"Thank you, Theo."

"Are you accepting callers?"

Grace nodded. Both she and her loyal servant knew she couldn't afford not to. Her father had ensured that Theo had a pension for all his years as the family's butler, and thank goodness for Grace, her servant had told her he would never consider retirement as long as Grace needed him.

Heaven knew she needed him. She'd been left almost penniless after her father's passing. Her third cousin had inherited her father's title and never showed interest in her well-being. Undoubtedly, the new Earl of Webster-Harnly had thought that Grace's sister and brother-by-marriage would provide for her.

How wrong he would be.

After Theo left the room, Grace pulled a piece of parchment from her desk and dipped her quill into the inkwell. She would take matters into her own hands and contact her former clients, who had daughters and sons on the marriage mart. It wouldn't hurt to drop a brief letter stating she just happened to have found an opening in her schedule if they needed her assistance. If business wasn't seeking her, she'd pursue her own opportunities.

"Ma'am," Theo drawled as he entered the room. He stood straight as an arrow with his nose tilted slightly toward the ceiling in his most regal English butler pose.

She bit her lip to keep from laughing at his charming antics when they had visitors. She blinked slowly and then said a silent prayer. *Please let it be a client who needed her services.*

"The Duke of Pelham is here." Theo straightened his waistcoat, winked, and stepped away from the door.

When Dane Ardeerton, the Duke of Pelham, swept through her doorway, she sat still though her heart galloped like a favored racehorse at the Royal Ascot. *What the devil was he doing there?* He'd asked her to spend time with him after his sister married earlier today, and she'd answered him with a polite but firm no. Were all dukes immune to the words *not interested*, or was this particular one unable to take a hint?

Knowing him, he probably just chose to ignore it.

Slowly, she stood. There was no nod, smile, or "*What a pleasure, Your Grace*" greeting for the man who stood before her.

"That will be all," she said to Theo.

"A moment, if you please," Pelham addressed her butler, who immediately stopped. "How long has it been since we've seen each other, Mr. Tinniswood? At least nine years, by my recollection. I hope your family is well?"

Theo broke out into a wide grin. "Oh, Your Grace, I can't believe you remembered my name."

Pelham tilted his head with a slight smile. "How could I forget the man who rescued me from Princess?"

She promised herself not to be charmed by the duke's antics. Yet, she *failed* not to smile at the memories. As a child, she had a pug dog named Princess, who always bit Dane whenever she saw him. It wasn't because Princess hated him. On the contrary, Princess adored him because he was the only one who would lie on the floor and engage in endless horseplay until they were both exhausted.

Dane always had allowed Princess to win.

Though she was loathed to admit it, it was somewhat of an endearing trait.

Her servant chuckled. "My family is excellent, sir. Thank you for asking." He turned to Grace with a wide smile. "Shall I bring a tea tray, ma'am?"

"Thank you, but not for me," Pelham answered before Grace could speak.

Grace smoothed her hands down her skirt to keep from fisting them. She would not dwell on the fact that Pelham had answered for her in her own household. She had more important problems at the moment.

"Very well. Ma'am, I'm off to the market." Theo took his leave.

When they were alone, Dane's gaze swept across the room. An immediate heat marched up her cheeks. No doubt, he saw the shabbiness of her furnishings, including the threadbare carpets and misshapen pillows. At least everything was clean, neat, and in its proper place.

This was ridiculous. He was *simply a man,* and she would not doubt herself.

"These are for you." He smiled as he extended a slightly wilted bouquet. "They look slightly ragged, but I couldn't resist the flower girl."

The Duke of Pelham would certainly be kind to a little girl hoping to make a few coins selling flowers. She inhaled, and the scent of roses greeted her like a long-lost friend. "Thank you. They're my favorite."

"I remember." As he said the words, he didn't look at her. Instead, he glanced around the room again before his brilliant blue gaze met hers.

"Would you care to sit?" she motioned toward the matching sofas that framed the hearth. Since it was warm, a fireplace screen shaped like a floral fan concealed the grill. It was feminine and pleasing to the eye. Perhaps she'd focus on that instead of the handsome, irascible duke.

He waited for her to sit on a sofa, then claimed a seat opposite and stared at her as she stared at him, neither saying a word.

For the love of heaven, he was as handsome as ever. Perhaps even more so. Tall with broad shoulders that only emphasized his height, Dane made Adonis look like a mere mortal. He was the most beautiful man she'd ever seen, with hair that appeared to have been spun from gold and sunshine. His keen eyes were clear blue, reminding her of the Mediterranean Sea. His bespoke morning coat and matching breeches fit him perfectly. She could stare at him all day and never tire of the sight.

It was as true today as it was when she was a foolish girl who believed she'd found the love of her life. Even after all those years, she couldn't look away if she wanted. The familiar magic still sparked between them and had her leaning in his direction as she waited with bated breath for him to speak. Every part of her practically hummed in anticipation of why he was there.

Which begged the question, would her body ever learn to ignore him?

The obvious answer of no reverberated through her. For heaven's sake, he was the Duke of Pelham, the most captivating, charming, and *infuriating man* she had ever met.

"I'm lonely, Grace."

His soft words enveloped her and, for a moment, stole her voice. How could someone so influential and well-regarded in society be lonely? Everyone begged for him to attend their events, and he refused. He preferred spending time at the Jolly Rooster, his coaching inn and gambling hell, the place where everything had unraveled for them all those years past.

She fought the urge to comfort him and put distance between them by leaning as far away as possible. Yet, the forlorn look he wore tugged at her heartstrings.

She was well-acquainted with loneliness. Though she had many friends and acquaintances, no one except Theo waited for her to arrive home. He didn't count since she paid him to stay with her.

Or at least she did when she had the funds.

"I can certainly understand," she murmured. "Ardeerton House must feel empty. Since both of your sisters have married and are starting new lives with their husbands."

"Then you understand why I'm here." A rare, awkward, half-hearted grin pulled at his full lips. "It's time for me to marry."

Grace froze as she grappled with what he was saying. "Surely, you are not asking me." A wayward frog singing for its mate sounded more harmonious than she did. She cleared her throat before she continued, "Are you?"

"I'll wait for you to close your mouth before I answer," Dane drawled, then threw back his head and laughed as if she'd said something hysterical. After the last chuckles faded, he took out a handkerchief and wiped his eyes. "For a moment, I thought you'd been struck by lightning. I've never seen you speechless. But to answer your question, *no, darling,* I'm not asking you to marry me. *You* only get one bite of the apple with me."

What a pompous arse. "Well, *darling,* one bite is all I need, particularly when the apple is rotten to the core," she snapped.

He laughed again, and she felt ridiculously pleased with herself for a moment.

"Dear, dear Grace, some things never change. I always enjoy your spirit when you forget to be prim and proper. You remind me of pepper. A perfect amount of spice makes a dish extraordinary. Too much?" His good humor turned into a wide grin. "You get burned."

"You remind me of garlic. Too much, and no one can stand your company." Though he smiled, his eyes grew distant. Immediately, she regretted the insult. It was cruel what she'd said. Over the years, she had developed a nasty habit of becoming a shrew with a sharp tongue. "Please forgive me."

Pelham arched one ducal eyebrow. "There's nothing to forgive. Such repartee is another language we uniquely share to express our deepest feelings for one another."

She lowered her voice. "I'm certain you're not here to spar with me verbally."

"No," he replied tersely, then momentarily turned away as if he couldn't bear to look at her. He released a labored breath and directed his royal blue gaze back to her. "I'll come straight to the point. I'm here because I want to hire you. Schedule a few events and select several suitable women for me to meet. Notify my secretary of my request and send him the details." He stood up to leave.

She stood as well. "Dane, wait."

He stopped immediately and stared at her, his gaze penetrating. It was almost as if he could see inside of her and had a front-row view of her unease. "*Dane?*"

"I meant Pelham." The confounded man could always put her on the defensive. She clasped her hands, needing to address their awkwardness or at least her awkwardness. "What about...our past?"

He grimaced slightly. "Consider it erased unless you've changed your mind." A faint glimmer shone in his eyes.

For a moment, she thought it might be a desire to change their pasts and futures. Then she recognized it for what it was. Simply a silly musing best left unexplored.

There had been many a day when she'd dreamt about her life if she had married him. But that was water under the bridge.

She offered a tender smile as a peace offering. "It's best we go on with our lives."

He dipped his chin in agreement. "Very well. I want you to attend the events and introduce me to the women you think would make a suitable duchess. Also, send me an invoice for your services. I'll inform my secretary to pay it immediately."

Then, the dastardly man winked at her before strolling out of her home as if he owned the entire street.

The galling, not to mention vexing, thing was that *he probably did own it*.

Two

"You simply cannot sit in the middle of my desk and stare at me. I have work to finish," Dane murmured as he scratched Dancer's neck.

The irascible black feline twitched its tail and then delivered a cut direct to Dane. He ran a hand over his face as a half-hearted smile tugged at his lips. One thing he could say about his cat, it always entertained him. He'd received the pet from his good friend and fellow millionaire, Malcom Hollandale.

Dane started his millionaire club when he was at Eton. Malcolm was one of the first members. The club was a place where like-minded entrepreneurs could meet and discuss how they made money and what they did with it. Members, both men and women, came from all walks of life. The only requirements were that each member be honest, possess at least a million pounds, and act honorably.

Obviously tired of Dane, Dancer jumped to the floor without a look back and strolled to Emmy, Dane's beloved retriever, who was resting beside his chair. Emmy was Dane's constant companion, and she wagged her tail whenever Dane entered the room. She was a reminder that at least one creature on this massive planet found his company enjoyable, unlike a particular confidant female he couldn't get out of his thoughts. Dancer, however, ignored him unless it suited his purpose, like seeking a scratch or two on its head or perhaps being served a morsel from Dane's uneaten meal.

On its way by the dog, Dancer took the opportunity to express his displeasure by whacking Emmy's nose. With a yelp, the poor dog scampered out of the cat's way, which caused the cat to arch its back with a hiss and prepare for battle.

"Cease," Dane admonished. "Bad form even for you, Dancer."

"Your Grace?" Ritson, his loyal butler, entered the room with a sly grin. It wasn't the first time he'd caught Dane talking to his pets, nor would it be the last. "Lord Trafford and Lord Ravenscroft are here to see you."

"Send them in." He stood and waited for his two best friends, who happened to be his brothers-in-law, to enter the room.

Tall with dark hair and masculine features, Trafford strolled into the room wearing his ever-present smile. He had married Dane's eldest sister, Honoria after Dane had caught them both in *flagrante delicto* at a hunting lodge on Trafford's Amesbury estate. Even though Dane had challenged him to a duel, there was no need. Marcus Kirkland, the Earl of Trafford, was head over heels in love with Honoria.

And she felt the same about him.

Hugh Calthorpe, the Marquess of Ravenscroft, followed, twirling his walking stick as he approached. With his dark coloring, muscular build, and attractive countenance, people took notice when the marquess entered the room. But it was his mischievous grin that drew people to his side. He'd married Dane's youngest sister, Pippa, just yesterday. He was as besotted with Pippa as she was with him.

As was his luck, Dane had caught him in dishabille after Ravenscroft had taken Pippa to bed before marrying her. Naturally, Dane had challenged him to a duel as well.

He had to treat both of his best friends equally.

Tender affection flooded his chest. His precious sisters were married and loved by two honorable gentlemen. Dane had known them most of his life and considered them his brothers long before they'd married his sisters.

However, he still had to goad his friends a tad. Otherwise, they'd think him ill.

"So, the honeymoon is over, I take it. Pippa has come to her senses and thrown you out of your home." Dane arched an eyebrow as he regarded his friend.

"Hardly. She's still as smitten with me as she was yesterday." Ravenscroft settled into one of the chairs in front of Dane's desk with a smile that softened his face. "And I...let's just say she's completely and utterly bewitched me."

"I know exactly how you feel," Trafford agreed with the same dreamy smile.

"Well, I don't know how that feels," Dane growled.

Ritson cleared his throat, indicating that he was still there. "Your Grace, the errand that you requested has been completed. The dress and shoes are prepared for delivery."

"Thank you. I need them sent anonymously."

Ritson nodded, then exited the room.

"What's this?" Ravenscroft rubbed his hands together. "Intrigue?"

"You haven't acquired a mistress, have you?" Trafford frowned his disapproval.

"Not that it's any of your business, but it's nothing of the sort." He poured three cups of tea and served his guests. He slid into his chair and faced his best friends. "I'm glad you're here. There's something I want to discuss. It's Grace."

Instantly, Trafford straightened in his chair.

Ravenscroft glanced at Trafford before he slid his gaze to Dane. "Do tell all, and don't leave a thing out."

Dane sighed as Dancer jumped onto his lap and started to purr. The cat was a menace, but he knew when Dane needed comfort and was never selfish with his affection then.

"After the wedding, I asked Grace to stay, but she refused. So, I took it upon myself to visit her after she left Ardeerton House." Without jostling his cat, he took a sip of his tea. The hot liquid slid down his throat.

"Are...things progressing romantically between the two of you?" Trafford sat on the edge of his seat and leaned forward.

"No." He took another sip of his tea, then set the cup down. Dancer kneaded his breeches, reminding Dane he still wanted his attention. With a slight grin, he obliged his prickly pet and stroked his soft fur. "I secured her services to help me...find a wife."

"You are ready to marry?" Ravenscroft asked incredulously. "Has the world stopped rotating?"

"No. But the oceans may have grown still." Trafford's brow furrowed into lines that reminded Dane of his ducal seat's neatly plowed fields.

Ravenscroft nodded in agreement. "Consider this. Has gravity stopped mid-air?"

Trafford scowled slightly. "No, old man. That one is ridiculous." Then he grinned. "Pelham is looking for a wife. Has the day refused to break?"

"Enough. You both are ridiculous, and might I add, you suffer from a poor sense of humor." Dane chuckled as he shook his head. "Nothing that bleak." He regarded his two friends. "It's time I marry."

Ravenscroft stared at the ceiling as his shoulders shook. "This should be high-brow entertainment."

"Ravenscroft," Trafford admonished with a shake of his head. "This is our friend you're making sport of."

"You're quite right." Ravenscroft grew serious. "Grace is our friend, and it was wrong of me to say such a thing."

His friends started to laugh uproariously as if they were actually amusing. In his most arrogant ducal move, he flicked his wrist as if warding off an aggravating gnat.

"Are you finished?" he asked once the laughter died.

"Come now," Trafford coaxed with a smile. "Surely you see the hilarity in this. Why would *you*, the great Duke of Pelham, need assistance securing a bride? You're the original millionaire in your millionaires' club." He took a long gander at his person. "You're pleasant enough to look at. You could have any person you wanted."

"I don't know about that," Ravenscroft said. "My mother always said that animals' affections are a good harbinger of a person's worth. His cat doesn't even like him."

Both men snickered at the insult.

Dancer took the opportunity to hiss at his friends.

"Thank you," Dane crooned to his cat. "At least I have one ally in the room." Emmy strolled to his side and nudged his elbow with her wet nose. "I stand corrected. I have two."

Ravenscroft shook his head with a smile. "Let's be serious here. Why do you need Lady Grace's help? Trafford is right. You could have anyone."

"Why not? She knows the *ton* along with all my faults, or at least, she thinks she knows my faults." He shrugged. "This is what she does for a living."

Ravenscroft narrowed his eyes in disbelief. "What is your end game?"

"I do want to marry, but I think Grace is in some sort of financial trouble," he confided, then lowered his voice. "What I have to say cannot leave this room."

Ravenscroft and Trafford turned to one another, then regarded him.

"What about our wives?" Trafford asked as Ravenscroft nodded.

"Of course, you can tell them." Only when both of his friends nodded did he continue, "When I called upon Grace, there was a dress and a pair of shoes in her entry. It was what she wore to the wedding. Her butler announced he was going to the market and left immediately. I glanced out the window and saw him carrying a bag with what I swear were puffs of ivory lace spilling out of it. I left shortly after that and couldn't help but notice that the dress and shoes were gone. He must have taken them to sell at the market."

"Perhaps her maid took them upstairs after cleaning them." Ravenscroft glanced at Dane.

Dane shook his head. "She doesn't have one."

"My wife made her that dress for her birthday. In my humble opinion, it was one of Pippa's finest creations," Ravenscroft said with unabashed pride. "Pippa shared that Grace cried when she saw it and said it was the finest gift she'd ever received. Grace couldn't have sold it."

Trafford nodded in agreement. "When Honor came to London to announce our engagement, Grace was the one who chose Honor's fashions to wear to events. She wouldn't sell a beautiful gown, particularly if it were a gift from Pippa." His brow furrowed slightly. "She wouldn't discard a token of that friendship without good reason."

"I agree with your reasoning and would conclude the same...if I didn't send a footman to investigate the market. I described the dress and shoes with instructions to purchase both items if he found them. The footman was back within the hour. I'm having it sent to her today without a note. I only pray she doesn't try to sell it again." Dane thumped a knuckle on the desk twice, signaling his decision. "We should have a family dinner tomorrow. I'll engage Pippa's services for a few new gowns for Grace."

"Won't she become suspicious if new clothing starts appearing on her doorstep?" Ravenscroft asked. "Especially Pippa's gowns?"

Dane shook his head once. "No. This will be from me since I've retained her services to introduce me to potential wives. I'll explain that I don't want her to incur any extra expenses on my account. I'll order several gowns for her to wear to the various social events we'll attend. In addition, I'll say the order was to promote Pippa's modiste shop."

Ravenscroft ran a hand down his face. "*Ton* events are my idea of torture." He shuddered slightly. "Don't ask me to host an engagement ball for you."

Trafford laughed. "He won't. He'll ask Pippa." When his friend's lightheartedness melted in an intense scrutiny, Dane notched his chin slightly upward.

"Why go through all of this?" Trafford asked as he tilted his head and examined Dane. "You obviously have feelings for the woman. Why not ask her?"

Dane's mouth tugged into a sneer. "Ask her what?"

"Don't be dense." Ravenscroft thrummed his fingers against the arm of his chair. "Ask Grace to marry you. You've done it once. You've even courted the woman."

Dane closed his eyes briefly as that familiar ache stabbed him in the chest. He still remembered the day he first met Grace. Tall, gangly, and missing two teeth, she was the same age as he. Her dark blonde hair reminded him of spring's first honey. It was always the sweetest. She and her family had purchased a small summer estate next to Pelham Hall, the ducal mansion in Amesbury. She'd shared her basket of freshly baked biscuits and tarts. From that day forward, he and she became best friends.

There was only one woman who would keep him enthralled. She'd done it the very first time he'd laid eyes on her. When they were twenty-one, he courted her. It was time to marry. He approached courting Grace as a military campaign, each romantic move planned in advance. He brought her flowers and took her on picnics and boat rides. She seemed as enchanted with him as he was with her. She'd even sneak out at night to go on midnight strolls where they'd share kisses that drove him wild with need.

When she'd agreed to marry him, it had been the happiest day of his life. She was his.

Until his father had forbidden it.

That was the fateful night he'd gone to the Jolly Rooster and wagered in a high-stakes card game. Lord Scoville, a wealthy viscount, had played deep. Dane had won big that night.

But the next day, he'd learned how fickle lady luck could be as he lost the most important person in his life.

Grace.

"I'll be blunt as I answer your question." He lowered his voice, but the words were clear as day. "When I hired her, she asked me if I was there to ask her to marry me. Just from her facial expression, I believe she would have considered such an offer." Dane stared at his two friends.

His friends were leaning forward as they rested their elbows on their knees.

"Go on. Tell us what happened. Whatever it is, I'm certain you both will find a way to mend your differences. You are adults. Years have passed," Trafford encouraged with a single nod.

"There's not much else to tell. I'm not certain I'm even interested in marrying her now." He feigned disinterest as he slid his fingers through Dancer's fur and stared out the window to his courtyard. "She jilted me the next day after accepting my proposal."

"You never shared much of this courtship. Why did she jilt you?" Ravenscroft asked.

"After I asked her to marry me, I was with two other women that night."

"You did what?" Trafford bellowed while Ravenscroft shook his head in disbelief.

"I had two of the demi-monde sitting on my lap. Both were...shall we say...in a state of undress." He blew out a ragged breath. "Grace's father came into the Jolly Rooster and saw me with them. He told Grace."

"Pelham, what were you thinking?" Ravenscroft challenged.

"*I was thinking of Grace and our future,*" Dane growled.

Three

Grace sipped her tea and closed her eyes. This time of the morning was her absolute favorite. The whole of London was on the verge of waking and preparing for the day. But she'd already had a head start since the neighbor's rooster had been crowing since five o'clock this morning. It was strange that she never experienced the daily ritual of waking to a loud, obnoxious fowl when she lived in Amesbury at her father's summer estate. But in the city, she seemed to hear every sound. Perhaps it was because she was alone. She dismissed the thought. She wasn't scared of anything.

Except being on the streets.

Theo knocked on the door of the small dining room. "Ma'am, several letters have arrived, along with a package and a new bouquet."

She quickly replaced her teacup on its saucer. She never received much mail unless it was a bill. But those usually came at the end of the month.

Her butler set a large package and several letters on the table before placing the flowers on her desk. It was a beautiful bouquet of deep red roses.

"Who are they from?"

"The flower girl on the corner. When I asked her, she said, and I quote, 'a friendly nob.'" Theo shook his head with a grin.

"Perhaps she has the wrong house." Grace frowned slightly. "And the package?" She pulled it closer. From the feel of it, it had to be fabric of some sort.

"It doesn't say." Theo rocked back on his heels. "A delivery boy dropped it off. When I asked him who it was from, he scampered off."

A bell clanged at the back of the house.

"That must be the coal man." Her butler nodded once, then turned to answer the back door.

She closed her eyes and offered a silent prayer of thanks. At least she had paid his bill that morning with the three pounds Theo managed to acquire from selling her gown and shoes. They would have fuel for the coming month. Thankfully, Dane's generous payment for her services should cover a year's rent unless some sort of catastrophe occurred. She turned her attention to the package in front of her.

With little fanfare, Grace untied the bow of twine, her hands unusually steady despite the turmoil swirling inside her. The paper crinkled as she pulled it apart, the sound sharp in the otherwise silent room. She bit her lower lip, a nervous habit she hadn't indulged in years, as the contents were revealed.

She blinked slowly, her eyes widening as if trying to convince herself that what she saw was real. The world around her seemed to blur and quiet, the soft ticking of the mantel clock and the faint rustle of leaves outside the window faded to nothing. It was as if time had paused to let her absorb the shock of seeing her shoes and dress before her.

This had to have been the work of Theo. He'd offered to loan her money, and when she'd refused, perhaps this was his way of trying to help. Her throat tightened as she thought of his lovely gesture. It meant the world to her, but it couldn't stand. She was a grown woman and would not allow her elderly servant to take on the burden of providing for her.

She stood with her dress and held it up. It was still as gorgeous as ever without a mark on it. When she glanced at her shoes, she saw a note sticking out of one of them.

A beautiful dress and a beautiful lady should never be apart.

She smiled slightly at the compliment. Perhaps Theo never sold it in the first place.

Her smile grew into a frown as she studied the note. The handwriting wasn't Theo's typical scrawl. The words before her were elegant and bold.

Still thinking about the dress, Grace picked up another missive without looking at the address and broke the seal. Suddenly all the air was sucked out of the room. It was a letter on E. Cavensham Commerce stationery informing her that she was now the owner of a banking account with a thousand pounds available.

Grace exhaled softly, dislodging a lock of hair that had escaped her chignon. This wasn't Theo's doing; he hadn't saved enough from his meager earnings for such extravagance. Still clutching the letter, she sank into her chair. Nor could this be her brother-in-law's handiwork, as he would never part with his money. If it had been him, he would've handed it to her while boasting about his generosity to anyone who would listen. Then he would have bragged about helping his wife's spinster older sister. Her sister would undoubtedly hang on to his every word, scolding Grace to be more grateful and reminding her that her husband didn't have to be so generous.

If it wasn't them, then who? She rested her forehead in the palm of her hand.

It couldn't be *him*.

But who else would it be? Dane had the funds and had been present when Theo announced that he was off to the market. The dress and shoes were in the entry when Dane arrived. When it was time to leave, she had escorted him to the door, where he must have noticed that the dress was gone. Then he'd put two and two together.

That was the problem with a man like Dane Ardeerton, the Duke of Pelham. He was too wily for his own good. There was only one thing to do. If she kept the dress, she'd have to find three pounds to reimburse him and return the letter from E. Cavensham Commerce.

She shook her head as a smile tugged at her lips. Perhaps the man thought he was too clever by half. She should return the dress and shoes to him, then ask if he'd like to purchase her lilac evening gown. It was the perfect color to match his complexion, but she'd have to warn him that it would be a tad short, but a lovely lace ruffle at the bottom would make the gown appropriate for him to wear.

Then she would offer to sell him her entire wardrobe if he wanted to acquire more.

What she wouldn't give to see his expression if she offered to sell some of her favorite reticules to match the dresses.

She should be angry, but she couldn't be. Not when her heartbeat accelerated, knowing he'd been thinking about her and perhaps worried on her behalf.

Frankly, she was worried about herself, too. It was comforting to know someone thought to look out for her well-being. But such generosity would make it appear as if she were his mistress.

She opened another missive. This one was from Adam Howard, Dane's secretary. She scanned the note as her brow furrowed. He wanted to meet with her at her earliest convenience to review the duke's social calendar. He'd suggested they meet at one o'clock today as the duke was anxious to attend to the matters at hand.

She didn't have to look at her own calendar to know she was available. She didn't have any other clients. She recognized the Earl of Marbury's crest when she picked up the final missive to break the seal.

She read the first paragraph, then tipped her head to the ceiling and smiled as she said a silent thank you. *There was a heaven after all.* The earl wanted her assistance in helping his ward, Lady Athena Westcott, make her introduction to society. He also wanted to secure the girl a husband as quickly as possible since she was on her own after her parents had passed away last year.

Grace quickly picked up her dress, shoes, and letters and made her way to her study to answer the missives.

Finally, her financial wherewithal was starting to look upward.

That meant she could be more discriminating in her work and dismiss the beguiling, not to mention irritating, Duke of Pelham.

Grace took Theo's hand as she stepped out of the carriage. Thank heavens for her butler's many and varied accomplishments. He was not only an excellent butler, cook, and footman but also a safe carriage driver. "I don't know how long I shall be, but it shouldn't be more than an hour."

"Take your time, my lady. The horses will be fine. We'll be waiting for you." Theo smiled as he clasped his hands in front of him. He never seemed to be out of sorts with her unpredictable schedule, and she appreciated his good humor.

"Thank you." She smoothed her pelisse as she strolled to the Earl of Marbury's front door. Even though money was always a worry, this was her forte. No one was better prepared than she to discuss possible matrimonial matches with a concerned father or, in this case, a father figure.

Before she could knock, a footman opened the door and bowed. "Lady Grace?"

She nodded. "Yes. I'm here to see the earl. I have an appointment."

"Lord Marbury is expecting you." He ushered her inside the formal atrium, where a massive wooden table sat with a vase filled with hothouse flowers. Their cloying scent filled the air. Only wealthy peers had a conservatory in their London homes. Hopefully, the earl would not balk at the fees for her services. The footman escorted her down a passageway tiled in black and white marble, then stopped outside an open double door.

"My lord? Lady Grace Webster is here." The footman bowed again, then waved her inside.

Expecting a middle-aged peer with a paunchy midriff, Grace was taken aback by the young lord who rose from his desk. Jasper Elliot, the Earl of Marbury, stood tall with dark hair and a slim build. The handsome earl couldn't be much older than five and twenty. His hair was cut in the latest fashion, giving him an air of maturity.

She wondered if perhaps he needed her services as well. The day was already starting to look brighter.

"Come in, my lady," he murmured. He came around his desk, took Grace's hand, and bent at the waist. "It's lovely to meet you."

"For me as well," Grace answered.

He waved a hand to a chair in front of his desk. "Please sit. Would you care for something to drink?"

"No, thank you."

He nodded, then took his seat behind the desk. "Lady Athena will be joining us shortly, but I wanted to have a moment to speak with you privately."

"Of course." With an elegance instilled in her since childhood, she sat and gave the young earl her undivided attention.

The earl rested his elbows on his desk and solemnly regarded her. "I want Athena engaged and married as soon as possible. It does neither of our reputations any good for her to be under my roof. I'm young, and she's younger. Yet, I'm responsible for her." He sighed, clearly burdened by the weight of his responsibilities. "I'm her guardian because our fathers were the best of friends. I'm five years older than Athena."

"My deepest condolences to you and Lady Athena." Grace bowed her head demurely.

"Thank you." The earl nodded in acknowledgment, then arched an eyebrow. "I don't think you'll have any issues with her. She's a beauty, attended finishing school, and has impeccable manners. She's accomplished at the piano and needlework. She attended finishing school, which helped prepare her for the world. She could step into a household as mistress this very day and manage it successfully."

"Are you in need of a chaperone for her while she's living under your roof?" Grace smiled sweetly. The man was nervous if the sweat dotting his brow was any indication.

He shook his head. "Athena's aunt on her mother's side is traveling from York to stay with us."

"I understand. If you need my services until her aunt arrives, I'll be more than happy to stay here—"

"That won't be necessary. I expect her aunt any day."

"Fine." Grace pulled out her journal and a newly sharpened pencil from her reticule. "Would you like to know my fees before we start to plan which events would be the most suitable for Lady Athena?"

"Money is no object. I just want her married to an acceptable man and quickly." He pulled a handkerchief from his waistcoat pocket and wiped his forehead. "Bloody hot in here." He stopped and stared at her with wide eyes. "I do apologize for my choice of words. I'm normally not so flustered, but it's been a vexing ordeal since Athena came to live here."

Grace smelled a rat or at least a large mouse. Why was he so nervous? Perhaps Athena wasn't the paragon of perfection Lord Marbury had represented. "I'll be anxious to make her acquaintance."

A knock sounded on the door. "And I am anxious to meet you. I've heard marvelous things about you, Lady Grace."

When Grace looked up, she stilled in her chair. A beautiful young woman entered the room with a shy smile. She glanced at the earl, then immediately blushed.

"Come in, Athena." Lord Marbury's voice cracked, and he cleared his throat. "Come meet Lady Grace, and we'll discuss your future."

"I already know my future, my lord." She sat in the seat indicated and turned her full attention to Grace. "He wants to marry me off to the first man who even sneezes in my direction. I make Marbury uncomfortable living here. He won't admit his feelings where I am an open book."

"I've asked you to cease saying such things," Lord Marbury hissed.

The young lady pointed at the earl as she smiled in Grace's direction. "And there's your evidence that what I'm saying is the truth."

"Do you think you can help me?" Lord Marbury shook his head. "I meant, do you think you can help her."

Grace bowed her head to hide her smile. There was definitely something afoot, but it wasn't anything foul. On the contrary, it was love. The couple before her felt it, but only one would acknowledge it.

"I think I can help both of you." Grace smiled politely. "But you both must attend the events together. Since you're her guardian, I think it worthwhile for you to see your ward interact with the gentlemen I introduce her to." She turned to Athena. "I assume since you've newly arrived in London, you haven't had a chance to prepare a wardrobe for the Season."

Athena nodded.

"I have the perfect modiste you must see. She's a friend of mine who recently married."

"You're friends with a mantua-maker?" the young lord asked incredulously.

"Indeed. I'm friends with the haberdashery owner, the baker, the muffin man, and the night watchman, not to mention various peers and their family members. It's good business to have a wide variety of friends." She turned his way. "The mantua-maker you refer to is the Marchioness of Ravenscroft and the Duke of Pelham's sister."

"Oh, the duke is dreamy," Athena sighed as she relaxed in her chair. "All the girls from boarding school laud his virtues and how handsome he is."

"What balderdash," Lord Marbury mumbled. "He's a gambler."

Grace whipped her head to stare at the young lord. "The Duke of Pelham is a highly respected peer who happens to be one of the wealthiest men in the entire kingdom. He's known for his generosity to charities and foundling homes. He just so happens to also own a coaching inn where *men of similar ilk as you* like to wager on games of chance."

She bit the inside of her cheek. She was all but ensuring that she'd lose Lord Marbury and his ward as clients the way she was speaking to him.

"I stand by what I said." He puffed out his chest. "Lady Grace, only men possessing high morals and honor should have the privilege of meeting Athena."

"Marbury, please," Athena cajoled. You make me sound like the Virgin Mary, which we both know is hardly the case."

"You must cease such chatter. That is not polite conversation," Marbury retorted.

As the two bickered, Grace sat back in her chair. What the devil was she doing defending Dane?

Her father had shared the same opinion about Dane as Marbury. Her father had said he was a rake, a gambler, and a man not to be trusted. He'd seen Dane completely foxed and surrounded by all those women at the Jolly Rooster playing high-stakes card games.

It was the same day that Dane had asked her to marry him.

Four

Dane replaced his quill in its stand and rose from his desk when he heard Grace's mellifluous voice carrying through the air. She'd sent word to his secretary, Adam Howard, that she would call that afternoon. Their visit must have been short since she'd only been there for a quarter of an hour.

Thank heavens Adam met with her first. Hopefully, Grace would be a bit more receptive to Dane. Adam had a way of quietly charming most people. When Dane had hired him, he was an overworked and underpaid clerk at one of the many solicitors serving the duchy. The solicitor never truly recognized Adam's worth, but Dane did. So, he snatched Adam from the bowels of the law practice and presented him an offer of employment.

Adam accepted on the spot and moved into Ardeerton House. He had saved enough money to buy a small home just a few streets away from Dane's London home. When he told Dane he was leaving, he shared that he was about to ask the love of his life to marry him and sought his advice.

Dane had wanted to say *whatever you do, don't have any ladies sitting on your lap in a gambling hell where your soon-to-be father-in-law could see you*. But Adam didn't need that kind of advice. Instead, Dane suggested that marriages should be based upon mutual respect with a keen sense of understanding. A heaping dose of patience should also be added to the mix.

What a farce that he was giving marital advice.

"Mr. Howard, please accompany me. It would behoove you to hear what I have to say to the duke."

Dane chuckled at Grace's directness. He knew it well as he'd heard it over a thousand times before. She used it when she wanted to admonish you but didn't want you to understand the rebuke until she was out of sight.

When the knock sounded on the door, Dane bit his lip to keep from smiling. Otherwise, the woman might believe he was pleased to see her.

It was a secret he intended to keep all to himself.

"Pardon me, sir. Lady Grace is seeking a moment of your time." His secretary stopped and furrowed his brow.

When Grace came forward, her back was turned to Adam. He caught Dane's attention and mouthed, "She's not very happy."

Dane barely nodded in acknowledgment of his secretary's warning. When it came to the *Governess*, to be forewarned was forearmed.

"My lady, what an unexpected pleasure." In three strides, he was by her side. "Let us sit at the table overlooking the courtyard. It's one of my favorite views and the flowers this time of year will take your breath away." He held out his arm for Grace to take and shot a look at his secretary. "Adam, will you ask Cook to prepare a tea tray? See if there are any cream cakes. They're Lady Grace's favorites."

"Yes, sir." Adam nodded solemnly, then turned as if the hounds of hell were nipping at his heels.

"I'm not here for flowers or tea cakes," she grumbled.

"You may not be, but if cream cakes were served, they would put a smile on your face." As he pulled out the chair for her like any gentleman would, her familiar fragrance of roses greeted him. As she sat down, he closed his eyes and deeply inhaled. The scent reminded him of how long they'd been friends before he realized he wanted to marry her. She hadn't changed in all in the years they had been apart. She was still the most attractive woman he had ever met. It wasn't just her silken hair or her expressive brown eyes that glimmered like topaz.

Nor was it the fact that she was tall and voluptuous that swayed his feelings.

Her features were like a bow on a pretty package. It caught your attention, but it was the treasure inside that counted. Her intelligence, quick wit, and effervescent humor always had kept him enthralled. It always had and still did.

"Have there been any juicy scandals to keep you busy?" His smile widened gleefully, and he probably looked like a child in front of a candy shop. "I know you love gossip."

"Why did you do that?" Grace ignored him as she huffed slightly, then blew a piece of her dark blonde hair out of her eyes.

"Do what? Ask about gossip? It's not one of my favorite subjects, but you like it. I'm just trying to be a good host."

"No. No. No." Grace locked her gaze with his. "You should have kept Mr. Howard here."

"Did you think I need a chaperone?" He winked. Instead of sitting across from her, he took the chair beside her.

"Chaperon," she huffed with a grin. "Both of us are too..."

"Do not say old," he reprimanded with a chuckle.

She dipped her head to hide her laugh, but he could still see it. He wanted to crow like a rooster. It was a rare sight, and he missed it. There was nothing like one of Grace's authentic smiles directed his way. That was especially true if it came from the heart.

"How about if I say we do as we please?" She tugged off her gloves.

"That's definitely true," he murmured.

"Now to the matters at hand. We must speak about retaining my services to assist you in finding a suitable duchess."

He kept his face frozen with a slight smile. He'd spoken with Adam earlier and given him several alternative arguments for dissuading Grace from withdrawing her services as his match-making *Governess*. That had to have been why she was out of sorts.

"I told your secretary that it would be more efficient if he could handle your social schedule. I'm not certain it's a good idea to have me involved"—she waved her hand between them—"with whatever it is you plan to do this social Season. You and I will only argue. That won't do either of us any good." She sighed painfully. "You don't need me."

"Grace, I thought we'd settled this." He leaned forward and took one of her hands in both of his. Gently, he rubbed a thumb over her soft skin. "The reason I need you is simple. You know all my faults." He lowered his voice. "Or at least, you think you know my faults."

She narrowed her eyes. "See? This is what I mean."

"You know all, Grace," he teased. But when her face resembled a marble statue, he schooled his features. "Seriously, you know everyone's strengths and weaknesses." He locked his gaze with hers, then lowered his voice. "We've known each other for years. Hence, you certainly know me well enough to know mine."

Thankfully, the stubborn set of her jaw softened. In its place was an openness that made him almost believe they were the same two people who'd practically grown up with one another and had been each other's confidant.

"Perhaps." She huffed another breath of air.

"Spend time with me. Help me." He was practically pleading, and he didn't care. After Trafford and Ravenscroft had left, he'd contemplated his future. He wanted what they had. He wanted what he had shared in the past with Grace. He wanted a best friend, a partner, and a lover who would always stand by his side. In return, he would stand by hers.

She searched his face briefly, then offered him a tender smile. "I was going to storm in here and tell you in no uncertain terms that I wouldn't help you. Once again, you completely disarmed me." She pursed her lips.

"Darling, don't think of it as disarming but enchanting you." He squeezed her hand.

"I know about the dress and the shoes. Is the one thousand pounds from you as well?"

He didn't move a muscle in his face.

Her good humor quickly melted. "You dastardly man," she seethed quietly. "You had my dress and shoes delivered to my home after I had Theo take them to the market."

She pulled her hand from his, and immediately, he sensed the loss of heat—the loss of her. He wanted to reach across the distance and take her hand again, proclaiming it was his.

"I stopped by E. Cavensham Commerce on my way here. I told them to return the money to its rightful owner. If it was you, as I suspect, let me clarify one thing. My financial situation is not something I will share with you. Please do not interfere again." She turned her head and stared out the window.

"I see someone woke up on the wrong side of the bed."

She shot a scowl his way.

"I can only surmise you didn't care for Pippa's creation."

Her gaze flew to his. "No. It was the most beautiful dress I ever..." She turned away.

"Grace," he coaxed softly. "Look at me."

The woman possessed the tenacity of a donkey when riled. By her stillness, he knew she wasn't having any part of him.

"People will think I'm your mistress." She lifted her chin an inch.

"Grace, no." He shook his head vehemently. "They won't. How would they ever discover such?"

Her cheeks turned the color of ripe autumn apples. "You don't give money to a woman without people thinking she's your paramour."

"Perhaps I wanted to give money to a friend. Call it a loan even," he murmured.

She fisted her hand on the table. "I don't need a loan. Just today, the Earl of Marbury secured my services for his ward." She swallowed, and instantly, his focus turned to her long, elegant neck. "You can't interfere in my life, Dane."

He gently clasped her chin and urged her to turn his way. What he saw nearly brought him to his knees. Her beautiful brown eyes glistened with unshed tears. "You have my sincerest apology."

She closed her eyes, but one solitary tear slid down her cheek in defiance of her efforts to keep them at bay.

"Pippa thought you adored that dress. I did the same." As he gently wiped away the tear, another fell on her opposite cheek. He wiped that one away as well. It didn't make any difference to him if they didn't move from his study for the next week. As long as she was upset, he would stay with her.

Comfort her.

"She gave it to me for my birthday," she confessed, then blew out a breath. "I should thank you for giving it back to me."

"Why did you sell it?" He lowered his hand but leaned near her until only two inches separated them.

"I needed the funds." She sniffed but didn't turn away from him. "There were bills to pay." She laughed, but the sound held little humor. "I'll receive the funds from Lord Marbury next week. I can repay you then."

"Repay me?" His voice turned incredulous. "You know how I hate to see you cry. If you stop, that's more than enough payment." He arched a brow. "A fair exchange, in my humble opinion."

"Dane, don't. You're the one who caused them in the first place with your kindness," she warned with a real laugh. "It's just like the one thousand pounds. I have to repay you. Otherwise, people will think I'm your kept woman."

If those same people only knew the truth. He couldn't keep her even if their wrists were tied together. She'd find a way to break free.

"Nonsense. As I said before, how would they ever find out?" He forced himself to remain calm. "They never would. Why are you living in that townhouse? I understand why you wouldn't want to live with your sister or her husband. I've met them before," he drawled.

When she laughed, one side of his lips tugged upward.

"You should be living closer to me in this part of Mayfair. What happened to your inheritance? Couldn't your sister's husband give you part of that? I assume he's in charge of your dowry and inheritance."

She shook her head as if exasperated. "Let me be blunt, *Your Grace. It's none of your business.*"

"You are angry." He lifted his hands in surrender. "Let me make amends. Come to dinner tonight. Honor, Trafford, Pippa, and Ravenscroft will be here." He lowered his head until their eyes met. "Please? For me? I don't want to be the odd man out again." He took her hand once again, then leaned back in his chair. "Those four are always mooning at each other. Seeing my sisters in such a state over their husbands is unsettling. Besides, it's infuriating." He sniffed slightly as if offended. "I'm the duke here. They should pay attention to me."

"What makes you think I'll listen to you."

"Oh, you won't. You never have, but at least I can pretend you'll hang on my every word. Especially when you scowl at me." He winked, and she shook her head at his antics.

"I don't know if that is a good idea, especially since we will work together."

Excellent. He wanted to smile in satisfaction at her answer. Grace would not fire him as a client.

At least, not yet.

She bit her lower lip.

He practically groaned at the sight. Her lips were the color of ripe strawberries, his favorite fruit. The irresistible urge to kiss her right there roared through him. He closed his eyes. He could not and would not fall under her spell again. If she walked away again, he didn't think he could survive it a second time. He barely survived the first time.

"It's a simple dinner invitation." *Why was he trying to convince her?*

Because he wanted her company. No one could infuriate him one minute and then charm him the next as she did. He was never bored or lonely when Grace was nearby.

"It sounds lovely. I would like to see your sisters. I miss them terribly."

Do you miss me? He tightened his jaw, so he didn't speak the words aloud. "It's settled then. You'll dine here tonight."

"Your power of persuasion never worked with me." She stood from her seat. "However, I would like to see your sisters. To answer your earlier question, no scandals are erupting in London this week. I predict that the next time London is up in arms over something, it will be a scandal you create." She bent her head and stared at the carpet. Grace cleared her throat gently, then lifted her gaze to his. Before he could say a word, she continued, "Forgive me. That wasn't fair. I misspoke." She peeked at him and then grinned. "I meant to say that scandal is your constant companion whether you're in town or not."

He rolled his eyes.

"I see you haven't lost any of your renowned charm," she countered.

"I learned it from you," he retorted.

Trading insults meant that things were finally back on an even keel.

"There you are," the former Lady Honoria Ardeerton, now the Countess of Trafford, exclaimed as she took Grace's hands in hers and kissed her on the cheek. "When Pelham told me you were coming to dinner, Marcus and I were overjoyed."

With genuine joy, Grace hugged her friend in return. It didn't escape her notice that Honor's grin was a tad brighter than usual. Grace had seen that smile dozens of times when Honor participated in the Season with her soon-to-be husband, Marcus Kirkland, the Earl of Trafford. Her friend wore it when she didn't want people to know what was truly on her mind.

Lord Trafford wrapped his arm around his wife's waist and tugged her close to his side. "It's lovely to see you, Grace. I can never thank you enough for everything you did for me and Honoria. I wouldn't have convinced this wonderful woman to marry me otherwise."

"Stop," Honor cooed as she playfully batted at her husband's chest. "You're going to make me blush."

He kissed the crown of his wife's head and whispered, "It's true."

Forgetting that Grace or any other family members were in the room, Honoria lifted her gaze to his as they stared into each other's eyes. Their love for one another kept them locked in a cocoon of their own making.

Grace's heart clanged like a rusty church bell, going through the motions. The effort wasn't pretty. The truth was that while she was happy for Honoria and Trafford, it would be naïve to think these feelings of jubilation would last forever.

What was the matter with her tonight? Honoria was one of her true friends, and she deserved this happiness with Marcus. The same held true for him. Neither had experienced ideal childhoods, but they'd found each other as adults and were a family, one devoted and cherished by the other. They were utterly in love and deserved the happiness they now shared.

"Grace, it's our good fortune that you've joined us." The former Lady Pippa Ardeerton, now the Marchioness of Ravenscroft, beamed her way. "Besides seeing you tonight, I look forward to tomorrow. Your new protégé, Lady Athena Wescott, sent a note stating that you both will stop by the shop and pick out a few dresses."

She shook her head, coming out of the daze. Quickly, she leaned in and kissed Pippa on the cheek. "I forgot about that, but yes, we'll be there. Her guardian will join us."

Honoria and Trafford shifted slightly so Lord Ravenscroft could join them. He slid next to his wife and wrapped his arm around her.

"Who's that?" Lord Ravenscroft asked.

"Lady Athena Wescott and her guardian, the Earl of Marbury." Grace clasped her hands demurely in front of her. "They're clients of mine. Lady Athena has newly arrived in town for the Season. Lord Marbury is anxious for her introduction into society."

"How could he be her guardian?" Ravenscroft asked innocently as his eyes flashed with amusement. "He's a pup."

"Lady Athena lost her parents recently," Trafford said. "Honoria and I invited her to stay with us. Lord Marbury insisted she stay with him. He thought it inappropriate for her to be associated with our charity since she would be introduced into society."

Honoria and Trafford had started a charity for orphans of peers who had no one to look after them except for the court-appointed guardians and conservators. Trafford had lost his parents at an early age and had been a terror when he was younger. He attributed it to not having anyone who cared enough for him to teach him how a man behaves. That was the case until he met Pelham and Ravenscroft. They'd taken him under their wings at university and had saved him from a life of debauchery, gambling, and drinking.

Ravenscroft shot a side-eyed glance to Trafford. "Now, why would a young lord want the responsibility of a ward who will be introduced to society?"

"Perhaps his sense of honor dictates it," Pippa offered.

"Yet, why would he insist she stay under his roof? I would think the gossips would swarm at such news with stingers ready to wound." Ravenscroft's face softened as he looked at his wife and winked. "Unless he's hoping to find his own lovely wife this Season."

Pippa returned his gaze. Her face practically glowed with happiness.

Grace forced herself to take a deep breath. If anyone in the world deserved happiness, it was the Ardeerton sisters. She was happy and proud that her efforts had helped them find their happiness. That had to be the reason for the dull beat in her chest.

It certainly wasn't envy. The Ardeerton sisters' happiness didn't mean Grace wouldn't find the same. She just didn't believe that it was her path in life.

The last to join their group was Pelham. His elegance seemed to float around him. He looked like a prince who had decided to grace everyone with his presence. His fitted blue silk evening coat, gold and blue brocade waistcoat, and blue silk breeches accented his blond hair and deep blue eyes. Her breath caught at the sight, and every hair on her arms stood at attention because he was near. If angels looked at him, they'd sigh in pleasure. His hair was slightly mussed as if his halo had fallen to the side and caused his silken blond locks to go awry.

When he came near, she stepped back to create a space for him. Pelham surprised her. Instead of stepping away from her, he moved closer.

Which was tortuous as she could smell his fragrance. Pine, leather, and sandalwood combined into a scent that was uniquely his. Whenever she inhaled, her traitorous body throbbed in recognition. His scent was like an aphrodisiac. It tied you up in knots, and you never wanted to escape.

Perhaps she was falling ill. There was no other reasonable explanation for her thoughts. She shouldn't be attracted to Dane, especially not after the insults they'd heaved at one another when she'd visited earlier.

That wasn't accurate. She was the one who had hurled them. He'd been on his best behavior.

"Your Grace, dinner is served," one of the gray and gold liveried footmen announced.

"Thank you, John," Pelham called out, then held his arm for her. "My lady, if you'd allow me to escort you into the formal dining room, it would be an honor."

Grace nodded politely and took his arm. Just as they were about to head to the formal dining room, she caught Trafford and Ravenscroft smirking at one another. At the same time, Honoria and Pippa, in unison, uttered a small sigh as they offered an affectionate smile.

"It feels as if everything is right in the universe, doesn't it?" Pippa winked at Honoria. "You're with Trafford. I'm with Ravenscroft."

Honoria's enthusiastic nod would likely destroy her simple chignon. "And our darling brother is with—"

"Sorry to interrupt such overly sentimental rubbish, but I'm hungry." Pelham pulled Grace his way, then lowered his voice. "Don't mind my sisters. Since they found their true loves, they can become a bit overbearing. They want everyone to be as happy as they are with their husbands." He patted Grace's arm. "Seriously, this is all I ever wanted for them. Thank you for all your help."

"I thought you believed that money equaled happiness." She glanced up with a teasing smile.

He chuckled slightly, then lowered his voice. "I'm surprised at you, Grace. You know me better than that. I'm a true romantic when it comes to matters of the heart. Love is the only true path to finding ever-lasting happiness."

She bit the inside of her cheek to keep from informing him how ridiculous he sounded. Soft laughter rose behind them as Pelham's sisters cooed sweet nothings to their husbands. It had to be intimate since she couldn't hear a single word. "Some might say that material possessions are the key to one's happiness. They're certainly tangible."

"Since when have you become such a doubting Thomas about romance? Too many unsuccessful matches for the Governess?" Pelham teased.

By then, they all entered the small formal dining room. The table was dressed in a white tablecloth, and the family silver glittered in welcome. The place settings consisted of fine china with the crest of the Duke of Pelham in the middle. At least, that was one positive thing about Dane. He took his time with his family seriously and always insisted his sisters partake weekly in an evening meal with him.

She wasn't being fair. He had many good traits. Protective, dedicated, and driven. He also possessed masculine beauty, charm, and money. He was the catch of the Season. A duke was a rare creature, and one as rich and handsome as Dane was even rarer.

"Grace, when you and Lady Athena visit tomorrow, I have several dresses pulled aside for you. Most will only take minor alterations."

She shook her head. "There must be some mistake. I'm accompanying Lady Athena to your shop. I'm not purchasing any gowns."

"But there's a red satin that will simply be stunning on you," Pippa offered.

"Is it the one you showed me the last time I was in the shop?" Honor played with her cod in mornay sauce. "Grace, you'll be the talk of the *ton*."

Pippa nodded. "Dane insisted that you have several new gowns for the upcoming events you are attending with him."

As Honoria and Pippa continued discussing dresses, Grace's temper began to bubble like a potion in a cauldron, and when mixed with embarrassment, the result was explosive. She let her gaze drift in Dane's direction. That familiar pang of skating on financial ice thudded in her chest. She overlooked the fine china, the stemware, and the compotes that adorned the magnificent table. She could only focus on the arrogant duke seated across from her. The blasted man wasn't even looking at her. But he must have sensed the anger in her stare. His eyes rose to meet hers, and he wore a half smile. The smile vanished as he realized the unbridled fury she displayed on her face. How dare he arrange for new dresses? She might not have a vast wardrobe like she once did, but she still had enough dresses to accompany him to the various events she and his secretary had agreed upon. If he didn't consider her dresses suitable or fashionable enough for him, he could find his own wife.

She was not a charity case. One side of her mouth lifted in a slight sneer. By God, she was an independent woman.

Slowly, his infuriating half-smile reappeared, mocking her, along with a tic in his jaw.

In response, she stared at him with a countenance that could have been mistaken for marble. She dotted her serviette to her mouth with as much poise as she could muster. "If you'll excuse me?"

Honoria and Pippa nodded, and the gentlemen, including Pelham, rose from the chairs in a show of respect and manners.

Without saying another word, she left the dining room and proceeded down the passageway, gaining speed with each step. She would not stay another moment under his roof. Yes, her circumstances had fallen. But she had more pride than to accept handouts. She was almost to the entry, determined to leave before a large, warm hand clasped one of her elbows.

"Grace." Pelham's deep voice vibrated against her.

She stopped but refused to look at him.

"Where are you going?" His words were a caress against her skin. He stood so close that the warmth of his body enveloped hers.

"Home." Grace wanted to stomp her foot in frustration. Instead, she forced herself to turn around and face him. If there was a heaven, then her displeasure would be apparent even to a duke who thought himself the reason the earth rotated on its axis. "You cannot manipulate and force your will on me."

"I wasn't. I promise," he soothed.

"Then I can only think it was to humiliate me by reminding me that I can't purchase new gowns," she hissed softly so no one could overhear.

"Is that what you think?" He narrowed his eyes, then huffed a breath. He opened a door directly across them without tearing his gaze from hers and dragged her through the doorway into the music room.

She'd always wanted such a room where she could spend an afternoon just playing and singing to her heart's content. Why did she even allow herself such thoughts? Envy led to heartbreak. Why couldn't she accept her circumstances without complaint?

Because she had a right to be disappointed, this had not been the future she thought she'd have. She imagined having a loving husband, her own home, and a joyful life just like her parents.

As a child, she always looked forward to the Sunday meal. Her parents were always in high spirits whenever the vicar and his wife were their guests. Her mother had a way of steering the conversation toward something pleasant, especially when the vicar and his wife argued. Grace's father always winked at her mother when she started a new topic.

That was the thing about her father and mother. They were the most loving and nurturing people, particularly with friends and family. That could explain why there was no money when both of her parents died. They probably gave it to the vicarage to help those less fortunate than their family. Once privately, she'd asked Hope if she had ever wondered if there was another reason there was no family fortune. She dismissed Grace's questions, arguing that their father was a known gambler. Hope then praised her husband as the savior of the family.

The back of Grace's throat burned as she fought the tears that threatened. Savior of the family, indeed. Stewart Arnold had never seen to Grace's welfare without expecting her to grovel in gratitude.

Now, Dane thought to help her. Would he want her undying gratitude as well? She would not permit that to happen.

He was a walking scandal.

Or at least, he used to be.

Five

After hesitating, Grace let Dane pull her into the music room. If her glare was any indication, she was furious beyond measure. He only hoped that whatever persuasive powers he possessed would convince her to return to dinner. "Is the beef not to your liking? If not, I'll have Cook prepare one of your favorites. You can't leave."

He felt at peace for the first time since Pippa had packed her belongings. His home was filled with laughter and love. Frankly, having Grace be a part of it was as natural as writing with his right hand. God as his witness, he wished he could leave her alone for both their sakes, but it was a losing battle.

After he'd closed the music room door behind her, she faced him with her arms crossed, ready for a verbal battle. He had seen this side of Grace a million times before, especially since they'd parted ways. "It's not the food. I am not one of the charities that you support. You can throw all the money you want my way, and I will not accept it."

He raked his fingers through his hair, feeling an urgent need to justify his request for Pippa to create a few dresses for her. Beneath it all, he felt a deep yearning to provide Grace with everything that would ease her life.

"Grace, you are not a charity case to me." He stepped nearer, and she stepped back, her body resting against the wooden door. "I thought it would help Pippa." He shrugged, then gave her a sheepish smile. "You know how I am toward my sisters."

She studied him with narrow eyes. "I don't believe you."

"May I remind you that I challenged Ravenscroft to a duel after I found him and Pippa with their disheveled appearances? That's being protective."

Her lips puckered in annoyance.

"You were there shortly after I discovered Honor and Trafford at his hunting lodge." He offered his most innocent smile. "Another perfect example of me being protective."

"Don't use your sisters as an excuse." She reached behind her and twisted the handle to open the door. "Good evening."

A ludicrous, almost primal urge to roar rose in his chest. He would not allow her to leave. Not again, and not when she was this angry with him. It reeked of all those years before when they'd parted for good. Since then, he could have cared less about whether she was angry at his antics or not. It was almost a game to him, and he suspected she enjoyed it as much as he did. But at this moment, this time of his life, he didn't want to argue with her. He didn't want to trade barbs back and forth; he just wanted things to be simple.

He stepped forward until only two inches separated them, resting his arms against the door. Without touching her, he had essentially framed her in his embrace. Grace tilted her head to meet his gaze. "I wasn't using my sisters or you as a tool, or as an implement, or as an instrument."

She narrowed her eyes again, but the beginnings of a grin tugged at her lips.

"There it is. One of those beautiful smiles." Careful, like approaching a wild animal, he rubbed the back of his index finger across her cheek. Her skin was still as soft as down feathers.

He could easily see Grace at Ardeerton House working in her study, then moving to the music room. He'd find her, tease her, then seduce her. Once they were married, he had always planned to have her in every room of this house within the first two weeks. He'd always been a high achiever. And Grace, as competitive as she was, would have been game for such a challenge. She never turned away from any dare. That's why he'd always thought they were a perfect match. They were alike in so many ways. He released a breath through his nostrils.

Yet, it was a mistake to caress her. But he couldn't force his fingers to obey. It seemed as if the world had grown quiet so they could enjoy this rare peace between them. He could practically feel their hearts beating in rhythm. They hadn't been this intimate since the day she had agreed to marry him. They had been perfect for each other back then.

"Grace?" When she opened her eyes, he smiled slightly. "I didn't want you to feel obligated to purchase a new wardrobe as we attended events." He still caressed her softness as his eyes searched hers, begging her to understand what he was saying. "And I did want to help Pippa. She would never carry tales that would embarrass you."

He slid his gaze down her body and then up before he met her eyes. He willed her to see how desirable he thought she was. She had changed over the years. Before, when they courted, she'd been a winsome young woman, and he had been barely a man. But now, her allure was a hundred times more potent than before.

She licked her bottom lip as she held his gaze.

He wanted to groan slightly as his cock thickened at the sight. He didn't have to look to know that his breeches were tented. If she glanced at his body, she'd know what kind of effect she had on him.

And he didn't care. All he cared about was taking her in a kiss that they'd remember for the rest of their lives. Perhaps she would finally regret leaving him.

He was a fool and lying to himself. He didn't want to kiss her so she'd feel remorse. Certainly not for revenge. He wanted to kiss her because she was Grace. *His Grace.*

"I'm protective of my sisters," he murmured, closing the distance between them. He could feel her warm breath skate against his chin. "I'm protective of you."

"Does that mean that you think of me as your sister?" The breathlessness in her voice practically undid him.

"The way I want to kiss you should be against the law. My skin is on fire. If we kiss, London will go up in flames." He didn't breathe as a cavalcade of emotions cascaded through her brilliant brown eyes. Doubt, disbelief, heat, and finally desire.

"I won't kiss you, Grace, unless you tell me that you want it," he murmured in a challenge. "But I'm begging you not to deny either of us this moment."

She leaned near until a hairsbreadth was the only distance between their lips touching.

They were suspended in the air, neither ready to let go. Was it fear?

Perhaps. Most probably, the hesitancy resulted from each knowing that neither would retreat once they crossed this line in the proverbial sand.

It was wicked on his part, but he could not let their standoff continue. He'd never seen Grace back down from a dare.

"Do it, Grace." He lowered his voice until it was practically a deep purr, one designed to subdue an unsuspecting prey, and cupped her cheek with his hand. The softness beckoned him to never let go. "I dare you. Kiss me."

Damnation. Her heart fluttered wildly in her chest. Dane Ardeerton, the Duke of Pelham, could always get her to rise to the occasion much like a fish after bait, especially when he looked like a forbidden treat that would be so satisfying and delicious.

That is until the guilt for imbibing would crash through a person's conscience.

"Do it, Grace," he urged. "I dare you. Kiss me."

She had expected a wicked half-grin, but instead, his blue eyes burned hot with desire. She'd seen that look countless times before they'd parted ways.

She gripped his wrist, but it was so large that her fingers couldn't meet. Neither of them moved. "What are we doing?"

"We're waiting for you to decide how you'll answer the dare." He moved closer until their chests pressed against one another. "Will you be brave enough to kiss me or not? That's the question of the hour, isn't it?"

She didn't have to look between them to know that her heart was pounding, and her chest heaved like a fireplace bellows. Every nerve was on edge ready to react. It would be so easy to kiss him, but where would that leave things between them?

In a befuddled mess.

She waited while keeping her body practically still. Of course, he excelled when divining the truth from others. He taught her how to control her body so that others would react first. But tonight, all those lessons had flown out the window.

He chuckled softly. With an endearing smirk, he leaned closer, bringing his mouth to her ear while she still held his wrist. With a breath that teased, he whispered, "I'm a patient man. I can wait until you are ready. But know this, Grace, playing cards has taught me a singleness of purpose over the years. Sometimes, I'll lose a hand. Sometimes, I'll win it." His nose brushed against the tender skin of her neck as he inhaled deeply. "I know how to play the long game better than anyone. The reward of winning satisfies like no other. It takes years of practice, luck, and a natural skill, which—fortunate for us—I possess."

For the love of heaven, if she wasn't mistaken, he pressed his lips to her neck. But she couldn't be certain. It almost felt like butterfly wings brushing against her skin.

He drew his lips against the tender skin of her neck until they rested against the lobe of her ear. "You still smell as divine as you always have. It's rose water, isn't it?" Without waiting for her answer, he continued, "I wonder if your kisses are still as sweet?"

She sucked in a breath at the seductive words.

He leaned away to look at her face. For a moment, she wanted to moan her disappointment and pull him to her again. Hoping to find her lost indignation that had somehow left the room without her notice, she blinked and swallowed.

Like a bird of prey, he watched the slight movement of her neck— *bloody hell.*

Why was she reacting to him like this? He was someone from her past. She'd dismissed Dane from her life ages ago.

"Grace," he murmured. "I know you're scared, but you have nothing to fear, especially from me."

"Said the spider to the fly."

The brilliance in his eyes made him even more attractive than ever before. The laugh lines that framed his azure eyes told the story of a man who was accustomed to laughter in his life. As a duke, he could always put someone in their place, but as a friend, he'd always let a person know how much he cared for them.

Until there was a card game. Games of chance called to him like the powerful sirens who sang to those poor, misguided sailors and lured them into the seas. But he was never one to gamble excessively, or so she'd heard. He almost always won at games of chance. And when he was losing? He had an uncanny ability to walk away from the gaming table when it suited his interests. Who knew if any of it was true?

Yet, one time she'd seen his remarkable talent with her own eyes. Without a look back, he had walked away from her when the odds were against him.

"Well, this spider is using his keen eyesight to see the apprehension in your gaze."

Dratted man.

He always could see right through her as if she were a web of gossamer threads.

That same infuriating yet all-consuming, indescribable force that connected her to Dane slowly flooded her senses and entire body, rising inch by inch. It was as if the proverbial water had transformed her into a buoy. Grace effortlessly lifted herself onto her tiptoes, almost as though she could float. Her gaze locked with his, and his captivating eyes coaxed her closer until she brushed her lips against his with the faintest of touches. For a moment, she felt like she was home. The comfort in that touch became all-consuming.

"Yes, Grace," he encouraged gently. "It's only you and me in this moment." As he said the words, he wrapped one arm around her waist and the other around her back and pulled her near. "I need to feel you. I need you. Tell me you want this as much as I do."

She nodded, then tangled her fingers in the silken strands of his blond hair. As he pressed his mouth to hers, a deep growl escaped him.

How she had missed that sound. Good heavens, it had been years since she kissed anyone. She'd probably forgotten how. The last man she kissed had been Dane.

When he deepened the kiss, their tongues slid against each other.

A long, throaty moan escaped her. At that moment, she wanted to bare everything. How lonely she was. How unsure of herself and her future. She wanted to reveal every weakness and failure she had experienced and lay them at his feet. "I want..."

"Tell me," he soothed.

"Dane?" Banging on the door jolted her out of her passion-infused fog. "Are you in there?"

His arms tightened around her, the move protective and intimate at the same time.

He rested his forehead against hers, his ragged breath brushing against her mouth. In many ways, it was as if he were still kissing her.

"Honoria," he murmured.

"Are you all right?" Honoria called through the door, then knocked again. "We wondered where you escaped to. Is Grace with you?"

"Is she playing for you?" His other sister, Pippa, called out. "Let us in, Dane."

"A concert?" Honoria's voice rang with glee as she clapped her hands.

"The rest of us would like to hear Grace play," Pippa admonished.

"Younger sisters are the bane of my existence," he chuckled, still resting his forehead against hers.

"Trafford and I have always enjoyed music. It's unfair of you to keep her away from us." Ravenscroft chortled through the door.

"I've never heard her play," Trafford added unhelpfully.

"I forgot to mention that best friends are the bane of my existence as well. Also, meddlesome."

"Then, it's a good thing that I'm not in either of those categories." She smoothed a hand down his chest as she straightened his cravat. She nodded once when she was satisfied with how he looked. "I suppose I'll be giving an impromptu concert."

"If you wouldn't mind," he drawled. "It'll keep them from asking nonsensical questions about why we were in here with the door closed."

She stepped away from the door and straightened her dress. When he didn't open the door, she arched an eyebrow as she caught his gaze.

"One more thing before we let those heathens in here." His voice deepened, making every part of her body vibrate. "Just so you are aware. Your lips are swollen and red like a bee stung them." His finger caressed her lower lip. "I have an answer to my earlier question."

"What's that?" Her voice had turned into a whisper. It was difficult to concentrate with him so near.

"How sweet your lips taste. I'd like to discover if you're as sweet everywhere else." Then the handsome, dastardly man smiled with a slight smirk as if he were letting you in on his most profound and darkest secrets. He would charm the sourest matron in all of London with that look.

She had no defense against it either.

"If you're wondering, your lips are still as sweet as honeysuckle nectar. My favorite."

Grace peered through the window of Lord Marbury's carriage, still burning at the comment he had delivered when he'd told Grace that his morning schedule had changed, and he could not accompany Athena and her to Pippa's dress shop.

Since you are a respected matron, it would be acceptable for Athena to travel alone with you.

Respected matron, indeed. She hmphed silently to herself. She could still turn a man's head if she set her mind to it.

Dane didn't think she was a matron last night when he dared her to kiss him. She hid her smile from Athena, sitting across from her in the carriage. The man was ravenous for her and had utterly captivated her.

It was quite a compliment that Dane still desired her even after all these years.

Her smile evaporated. What if he wasn't besotted with her? What if he was attempting to woo her so that he could jilt her just like all those years ago?

Grace inhaled a determined breath. She had to be overthinking this. It made little difference if the improper, not to mention indecorous, Duke of Pelham wanted her. All she wanted and needed was her own home. She would have a contented life with a deed and excellent savings put away after she'd worked all these years as the *Governess*.

The coach driver called, "Whoa." Instantly, the carriage rolled to a slow stop in front of Pippa's dress shop, which Lord Ravenscroft had purchased for her before they'd agreed to be married.

"My word, Lady Grace, would you look at that red gown in the window." Athena pressed her nose against the carriage window and stared longingly at the dress. "Do you suppose it's for sale?"

"We must ask." Grace smiled at the young lady's enthusiasm. "It is a beautiful gown. Is red one of your favorite colors?"

"It is. But everyone expects me to dress in gold since that's the color associated with the goddess Athena." The young lady smiled sheepishly. "I hope it doesn't sound as if I'm ungrateful for my wardrobe, but it does get a little tiring wearing various shades of ivory and gold all the time."

Everything Marbury had said about Athena had been the truth. She was a beauty, who possessed lovely manners, not to mention she was an heiress. She would have no trouble finding a worthy match this Season.

Grace patted the young woman's arm. "Come, Athena. With her experience and talent, Lady Ravenscroft will help you choose other colors that are becoming on you."

Before they arrived at the shop door, it swung open. Completely oblivious to everyone else, Pippa wrapped her arms around Grace. "You're finally here. Honoria and I have been waiting all morning."

"Honoria? She is here as well?"

Pippa nodded, then turned her smile toward Grace's charge. "You must be Lady Athena."

The young lady dipped a proper curtsey and smiled. "It's lovely to meet you, Lady Ravenscroft. I've heard so much about your dresses. I'm hopeful that I might be able to acquire a few of your designs."

Pippa grinned, her pleasure obvious to all. "I'm certain we can create a wardrobe that will make society declare you the incomparable of the Season."

Athena answered her with a wide smile that made her entire face glow. "I would like that very much."

"Let's not tarry. Come inside." Pippa waved them through the doorway. As soon as Athena passed her, Pippa wrapped her arm around Grace's waist and tugged her in a different direction. "Mary will assist Athena in selecting fabrics and starting the measurements." Her blue eyes twinkled, and her cheeks had reddened. "Come with me. I have a surprise."

For a moment, Grace couldn't say anything. "A surprise?" Grace narrowed her eyes, but she continued to smile. "What mischief is this, Pippa?"

Pippa brought her to a corner of the store reserved for her worktable. The corner provided the best light to sew, as windows surrounded it, allowing Pippa and her staff to see who was coming into the store.

Her friend waved her hand at the table. "Behold."

Three of the most stunning gowns Grace had ever seen were meticulously draped across the table. The first gown was a classic morning dress in pale blue with peacock-colored trim and a coordinating ribbon. It even featured a matching pelisse in the same peacock blue and trim. It was both demure and elegant, a sophisticated gown that enhanced a lady's confidence. The second morning gown consisted of black satin with white trim and jet buttons running down the back. A bright red reticule, trimmed in the same black ribbon and jet buttons, accompanied the ensemble. Only a lady of wealth could afford such accessories as buttons and matching reticules.

But the evening gown demanded everyone's attention. It was an iridescent pink reminiscent of the inside of a seashell. It shimmered and twinkled, with tiny clear jewels sewn into the bodice and trim around the waist and sleeves. A train of gossamer silk in the same pink shade was attached.

They were all beautiful, but the evening gown took her breath away. She would feel like a princess if she ever wore such a creation. Even a *dowdy matron* like *her* would feel as if she were the belle of the ball.

She had to forget the young lord's insult. Based on Athena's comments, he was shy and awkward in social settings. Thankfully,

Athena had Grace to steer her through the Season. A young lord with a young ward would be eaten alive by the gossips.

"Pippa, these are gorgeous." Grace reached out to touch the evening gown but then thought better of it. "I don't want to risk soiling them."

"Go ahead and look to your heart's content," Pippa murmured.

"Who are they for?"

Just then, Honoria came around the corner with her arms laden with shoes, fans, chemises, and even a hat. "Did you start the party without me?"

"Never, dearest," Pippa cooed. "I didn't have time to hide these before Grace and Lady Athena arrived."

Honoria nodded, then looked around the store. "Where is she?"

"Athena is over there with Mary," Pippa answered.

All three of them turned in the direction of Athena, who was not only talking to Mary but also had several young ladies gathered around her.

For a moment, Grace's protective instincts rose. As a new face in society, Athena could easily become a target to the young ladies who thought themselves better than anyone else. In many ways, such women reminded Grace of squawking hens who were the bullies of the barnyard. They were always loud and overthought their own importance.

Just as she took a step forward to go to Athena's side, the young woman laughed and glanced at Grace with a warm smile. She wasn't intimidated and seemed to relish the young women around her. They were laughing, whispering, and then laughing again. All four of them wore smiles.

Grace relaxed.

"They seem friendly enough," Honoria commented as she regarded the women.

Pippa grinned. "They are. They met at finishing school and have recently arrived in town. They visit the shop daily and inspect the fabric and the gowns." She lowered her voice. "Which is wonderful for me. I do not doubt that these intrepid young ladies will find a way to convince their parents that they require one of my gowns."

"You're very generous to allow them to spend time here," Grace added softly so as not to be overheard.

"Truthfully, I like having them here. They have an entirely different perspective on fashion than their mothers or other family members. I think the melding of such tastes will ensure that my gowns are unconventional and highly sought-after fashion." She grinned and waggled her eyebrows.

"You are incorrigible," Honoria said with a smile. "But I like the way you think."

"I learned it all from you." Pippa turned back to Grace. "Before I help your young charge, I wanted you to try these on. If any adjustments need to be made, we can do it here. But I think they'll fit as I used your measurements from your other—"

Before Pippa finished her sentence, Grace was shaking her head. "I can't," she murmured. "I don't have the money to buy these gowns. And if your brother is funding this purchase, it's all the more reason I cannot accept these." She placed her hand on Pippa's arm and squeezed. "You understand that it's not appropriate."

Honoria frowned. "But Grace, we're friends. Practically family. Why can't the Ardeerton family help you?"

"We shall be discreet." Pippa nodded in agreement. "It's no different than if Dane bought us a gown."

Grace bit the inside of her cheek. "It is. I'm not his sister."

"No, but you're..." Honoria trailed off and then looked to Pippa.

Both sisters blushed at the inference. The question on their faces was easy to interpret. If Grace wasn't his sister, then what was she?

His Governess. The person who would teach him all about the marriage mart and help him find the perfect mate. Grace didn't confide that information to Honoria or Pippa. It was Dane's prerogative whether to share that he was hunting for a wife. Not hers.

Honoria smiled sheepishly. "Well, we feel as if you are our sister. Therefore, this is our gift to you."

Pippa nodded in agreement. "I made these dresses specifically for you. When you wear them, every man and woman will have their eyes on you. You'll be magnificent."

"Now, try these on for us. We also have reticules, shoes, chemises, and everything else you'll need for the gowns." Honoria swept two of the gowns into her hands. "Shall we try these on first?"

Pippa pointed to the back. "Why don't you go to my private study? I have a full-length mirror and a pedestal that Grace may stand on. I'll go see about Lady Athena, then I'll join you."

As Grace opened her mouth to say no, Honoria wrapped her in a hug. "Please, Grace," she whispered. "You've done so much for me and Marcus. I know that Pippa feels the same about your efforts on her and Hugh's behalf." When she pulled back, her eyes were filled with emotion. "I don't know what my life would be like if you hadn't helped me."

"I feel the same," Pippa said as she wrapped her arms around both of them. "You're going to make me cry."

Tears welled in her eyes as they broke apart. The Ardeerton sisters always treated her like a true friend, making her feel special to them.

She slowly nodded her agreement. "I have a condition."

Both sisters leaned in.

"Allow me to concentrate on Lady Athena first." Grace's charge was currently picking out fabric with the help of her friends. "She's my first priority. I can come back later in the day or tomorrow."

"Well, I'm not leaving until you are properly fitted with these gowns." Honoria propped her hands on her hips as if issuing a challenge.

"Me as well," Pippa said.

"All right, you two. You're acting like your brother right now."

"We consider that a high compliment," Pippa retorted.

"He knows how to get things done," Honoria agreed, then lowered her voice. "He also knows how to be protective and love fiercely."

Grace did her best to hide her melancholy smile. There was once a time in her life when Dane had loved her ardently, and she'd loved him with that same fervor. Since then, she couldn't help but worry in the darkest part of the night that she had made a mistake all those years ago. Yet, he'd been the one who had insisted that they should break their betrothal.

The bolts of fabric before her faded into the background. Everything had been so clear all those years ago when she'd confronted him in that meadow.

Slinging mud behind them, Dane's horse galloped at breakneck speed

63

across the field. Like her thoughts, the morning rain had left everything wet and muddled. In seconds, Dane dismounted and stormed toward her.

His long legs ate the distance between them. By the set of his jaw, he was furious. Well, so was she. Grace tilted her chin slightly, ready to confront him.

By the time he reached her side, he was panting. "What is the meaning of this?" He waved her note in the air.

"How could you?" she asked at the same time.

His nostrils flared as he stared at her. "Grace, explain."

She narrowed her eyes slightly as she regarded him. The blond stubble of his beard indicated that he hadn't shaved that morning, and it didn't hide the bruising on one cheek. Her eyes widened at the black and blue marks. "What happened?"

"Nothing," he snapped.

She reached to cup his cheek, but he drew his head back.

"It looks like it is painful. Did you get into a fisticuffs match last night?"

"No. It happened after I asked you to marry me." He pursed his lips and narrowed his eyes. "I don't want to discuss my face."

"Fine then. I'm sure it has something to do with where you were last night. Father told me he saw you at the Jolly Rooster gaming tables." She crossed her arms. "With two women who were undressed sitting on your lap. You were completely foxed."

"No, I wasn't, and they weren't undressed."

"Their bosoms were on full display," she countered.

"Well, yes." His familiar, roguish grin appeared. It normally always charmed her, but not today. "I can explain."

"Oh, this should be titillating. Unfortunately, I don't have a pencil and paper to write it down. I'm sure your explanation will be memorable enough that I'll want it as a keepsake."

"If it's memorable, then why would you need to write it down?" he countered, then dipped his head and rubbed the back of his neck. "Let us not do this. I apologize."

"For the girls or your sarcasm?"

"Grace." His voice dropped into a soothing lilt to placate her. "It's not what you think."

"What am I supposed to think when you had two naked women on your lap the same day you asked me to marry you?"

"It's bloody unfortunate that your father saw me—"

"Unfortunate for whom? I think it is a godsend."

"I should have told you what I was doing. Forgive me," he crooned softly. He stepped forward and held out his hands to take hers.

Instantly, she took a step backward. If she touched him, she might fall apart.

"I didn't have much time. Scoville was there looking for a high-stakes game. He's known for running a high table and leaving when he wins a hand. That's why I didn't have a chance to tell you."

"Why should I care about that?" She was practically spitting at this point. Never had she been so livid in her life. Nor had she ever been so hurt. "Did I even cross your mind as you sat there? Did you consider what I would think..." She gasped as the emotion threatened to overwhelm her. "Did you consider how I would feel knowing you'd been with other women?"

"Grace?" Pippa's voice broke her out of her reverie.

"Forgive me. I was woolgathering." She smiled slightly.

Pippa pointed at the window. "Lady Athena asked about the dress in the window. I told her it wasn't for sale."

"Why?" Hopefully, Athena would not be too disappointed.

"Because I made it for you."

Grace turned her attention to the striking gown in the window. If she wore that to Lord and Lady St. Albers' soiree, every man in the ballroom would ask her to dance. If only she could find a way to pay for it. She wanted that gown, and what was more, she wanted to see Dane's expression when she wore it.

Respected matron, indeed.

Six

"The Duke of Pelham." The footman's deep voice echoed throughout Lord and Lady St. Albers' ballroom.

Lord St. Albers flinched at the boisterous announcement. "I don't think I'll ever become accustomed to his voice."

"He does have quite the range," Dane answered diplomatically.

Lady St. Albers tutted. "Edward, you're being as dramatic as Charles." She glanced at the footman, then playfully tapped her husband with her fan before smiling Dane's way. "Your Grace, it's an honor to have you this evening. When I received the note from your secretary, I reread it twice."

"I do not attend many events, but how could I miss this one if you're the hostess?" He bowed, then took the elderly countess's gloved hand in his and brought it toward his mouth without his lips touching her.

She blushed a deep red. She was an attractive woman despite her small stature and silver hair.

"You're a lucky man to claim Lady St. Albers as your wife," Dane said to the earl.

"Indeed." The man's chest puffed up at the compliment. "When we were first courting, men swarmed around Elizabeth begging for dances.

I knew she was mine the first time I saw her. So, it was in my interest to evade those fops and sweep her onto the dancefloor first. I managed to make my case for why she should marry me."

The countess's blush deepened. "His wooing was successful. I never looked at another since that first night."

The earl smiled affectionately at his wife and brought her close. "You should find yourself a good woman, Pelham. There's never a dull moment to be had. It's what makes life worthwhile."

Dane bent his head in acknowledgment. "Thank you for the advice."

He didn't add that he'd already found a good one, but she wanted nothing to do with him.

As he turned to head down the steps into the ballroom, Grace waited for him at the bottom of the steps as she slowly fanned herself. He stilled for a mere second. It was the fan he'd given her for one of her birthdays.

She'd adored it, and he'd asked if she adored him as much as the fan.

She'd answered almost as much. Then she laughed and reached on her tiptoes to kiss him. But he'd known by the heat in her eyes that she loved him. Back then he had wanted to give her the world. When they courted, he'd prepared a picnic for her enjoyment and had planned to ask her to marry him the next day. If his father wouldn't agree to the marriage, Dane had planned to take Grace to Scotland. Even though it was years ago, it still felt like yesterday.

When Grace's gaze caught his, she smiled slightly.

For a moment, he thought the sun had dropped into the ballroom. She wore one of the gowns he'd had Pippa create for her. It was a beautiful red silk highlighting her warm complexion and barley-colored hair. She glowed with happiness. Like a schoolboy with his first infatuation, he couldn't help but smile in return.

When he reached her side, he took her hand and brought it to his lips. It was a little risqué, but this was Grace. He'd never seen her look so enchanting.

"For a moment, I thought this was one of my masquerade parties. I didn't know that Aphrodite would be invited and standing before me now," he murmured with a smile.

This time, her grin was delightfully genuine. "No need to charm me, but I thank you." She waved her fan around the room. "Remember, it's the beautiful ladies attending this night's event for whom you should save your compliments."

"Don't be a spoilsport," he admonished playfully. "I have a beautiful lady in front of me who deserves all my attention." He pointed to her fan. "I see you still have that. I gave it to you for your birthday."

"Shall we take a stroll around the ballroom?" Grace dismissed his banter without a word, but his compliment hit its mark if the way her blush had deepened was any indication. "I want to point out a few young ladies. You can tell me your thoughts and explain your preferences. I thought it would save you time. I know you detest attending these functions."

"How true." Without a word between them, he wrapped her arm around his.

"There's no need for that," she said slightly, then smiled at an older couple as they passed. "I'm perfectly capable of walking around the room without assistance."

"With you in that gown, I'm not. So be a good Samaritan and hold on to me," he hummed in her ear.

"Your Grace, behave please," she admonished as she discreetly pointed her fan in the general direction of a young woman. "See that young woman in the pink gown? That's Lady Evelyn Banbridge, the Marquess and Marchioness of Winterfield's youngest daughter. This is her first Season. She possesses excellent manners and can converse in any subject, including economics. Her parents will grant her groom a forty thousand pounds settlement on the day of the marriage."

"How lovely," he said in a bored tone. "Her parents must be so proud."

"Well, if she's not to your liking, how about the young woman in the light blue dress? That's Lady Anne Sherwood, the daughter of the Duke of Montrose. This is her second Season, and she's one of the most sought-after heiresses on the marriage mart this year. Besides a forty-five thousand pound settlement, she's well-versed in politics, which would make her a wonderful hostess. She's also an expert in fine art. She helped her father cultivate a collection of works worth a fortune. Two master-pieces will be given to the groom on their wedding day."

He pulled Grace into a small alcove where the guests could still see them, but they could have a private conversation without interruption. "Why are you describing these women and how they will benefit me financially or politically? You sound like a money-grubber or a political opportunist. I must ask, are you always chiefly motivated by avarice?"

By the look of shock on her face, he'd succeeded in making her speechless.

But then, one corner of her delectable mouth curved in a sneer. "I suppose you want me to explain who they are as a person while I describe their character and qualities. Are you seeking a little lamb? Someone who will sit in your study embroidering while you work on the estate books or perhaps the bookkeeping for your precious Jolly Rooster? Perhaps you want a soulmate. The perfect light to your darkness. You definitely want someone willing to warm your bed—"

Dane closed the distance between them. "Nothing is wrong with wanting any of that in my future wife. If I recall correctly, you had no qualms about warming my bed. You couldn't get enough of my kisses."

"Your Grace, your memory is growing foggy in your advanced age. If I didn't know you any better, I would think you were a born romantic." The aggravating woman tilted her chin in defiance. "But I know better. You wouldn't have made the millions sitting in your coffers if you were only concerned with love."

"It's an interesting tactic to insult your clients. Does that help you excel at making matches for people?" He ran a hand down his face. This woman could infuriate him with a single barb or arch of an eyebrow. Yet, in the next moment, she could seduce him with just a glance. He took her hand in his. "Let's not fight. Not tonight. It would be a great honor to dance with you."

"What do you think you're doing?" Her eyes widened as if he'd said something scandalous.

"I believe I'm asking you to dance." He flashed his most seductive smile as he lowered his voice. "Do you know what else was on my mind? I want to waltz with the most beautiful woman in the room tonight."

She grimaced as she swallowed and tried to pull away her hand. Instinctively, he clasped it tighter. "People are staring at us."

"I don't care. Do you?" Slowly, he dropped her hand. "Give me all your waltzes tonight." It was a bold statement as everyone's tongues would waggle if they saw them together for two dances, let alone waltzes.

"This is my livelihood you're toying with." She stepped away and looked over the crowd. "Honoria and Pippa are here. Go greet them, and then I'll find you and introduce you to some appropriate young women."

"The excitement will keep me on pins and needles," he mumbled as he rolled his eyes. "You're like a dog with a bone." He turned to leave.

"I heard that," she answered.

"You were supposed to." He glanced over his shoulder as one side of his mouth tugged into a lop-sided grin. "Good thing I adore dogs."

Grace felt like she'd run a mile as her heart raced, and she struggled for breath. Even walking away from her, Dane Ardeerton, the Duke of Pelham, was irresistible. The sooner, the better she found a woman for him to marry. It would be good fortune for them both if it were tonight.

"Lady Grace?" Athena strolled to her side with two other young ladies by her side. "May I introduce Lady Alice Markham and Lady Candace Kent?" A smile of affection softened her eyes. "These two ladies are my best friends and kept my loneliness at bay when we were at finishing school together."

"It's lovely to meet you both," Grace said with a genuine smile.

"We've heard so much about you from Athena." Lady Candace rested her hand on Athena's arm. "She says you made her shopping excursion the highlight of her week."

Grace smiled at Athena. "I enjoyed it very much."

"As did I," Athena answered.

"Are you friends with the Duke of Pelham?" Lady Alice asked.

"I've known His Grace and his family for years," Grace was rather proud of herself. She shared that information without a hint of emotion.

"So, you are old family friends?" Athena looked at her friends and winked.

"Yes," she answered and tapped her toe in time with the lively tune the orchestra was playing. When she looked out over the crowd, her gaze immediately found Dane. He was dancing with Lord Ravenscroft's mother. By the amusement on Lady Ravenscroft's face, Dane must have been charming her with some quip or sharing a secret. He was the perfect gentleman, keeping his attention on his dance partner. He was always respectful of women, particularly with his friend's sisters and mothers.

Several other young ladies joined their group. Everyone's attention was on the Duke of Pelham.

"He's so divine," Lady Candace sighed. Her father, Lord Aston, was engaged with another peer on the other side of the ballroom. The earl was one of the wealthiest men in all the British Isles. Her dowry was worth a fortune.

"Divine and a duke. What a perfect combination." Miss Elsie Engels, who had just joined them, tilted her head with a faraway look in her eyes.

As the young ladies greeted Elsie, Grace observed the young woman. She would have been a catch of the Season with her looks and the favorable settlement attached to her name. However, she was known for being flighty and foolish. At an event last year, she'd been found swimming with two other young ladies in nothing but her chemise in the Duke of Edgerton's courtyard fountain. Dane would never tolerate such behavior.

Athena caught Grace's attention and winked. "Everyone seems to be taken with the duke."

"I understand he's looking for a wife this Season," Miss Adeline Powers, who also had joined their group, chortled as she looked at her friends.

Her father was an up-and-coming political leader in the House of Commons. Dane could make a match with her, as his political agenda aligned with her father's.

"He's gorgeous. I adore pretty things. Perhaps I should marry him," Adeline added with a bold laugh.

"Wouldn't it be easier to buy a posy? They're pretty and much more attainable," Lady Candace offered. "I understand he has rather strict requirements for the woman who will be his duchess. He abhors sycophants."

"Lady Grace, would you introduce me to the Duke of Pelham?" Adeline asked.

"No fair, Addy," Elsie warbled. "I want to meet him. Lady Grace, could you introduce me?"

"Lady Grace has a select few she helps." Candace sniffed with her nose in the air. "My lady, I will ask my father to call on you. I would like to be one of your clients."

"Excellent plan," Adeline agreed with an overabundance of enthusiasm. "My father will call on you as well."

"Mine too," Lady Elsie chimed in.

Grace stood there in astonishment. She had not been this popular since her first Season. If these ladies could convince their fathers to secure her services, she would be well on her way to purchasing her home. The young women were lovely, rich, and, for the most part possessed elegant manners and deportment. All would make fine matches. Even Dane would be fortunate to marry one of them.

A weight of dread settled in her stomach as tendrils of jealousy wrapped around her heart, squeezing tight. She hated even imagining the thought. Yet she was responsible for finding him the perfect mate along with Lady Athena.

The more clients she had, the more money she would make. The more money she made, the faster she would achieve financial security. It had been her priority since leaving Amesbury. Soon, she would have enough to buy her own house. No one would ever be able to take that away from her. She could read, garden, and indulge in her hobbies without worrying about how to pay another bill again.

It would be Grace's refuge as she grew older, with only her memories keeping her warm at night. An image of Dane holding her near after they'd made love the first time skittered through her thoughts. They'd been young and foolish. They'd been fortunate that a child hadn't resulted from their earlier intimacies. Otherwise, they would have had no choice but to marry. She bit the inside of her cheek. Nothing good would come from remembering how much they cared for one another back then. Neither knew what kind of person they would become when they reached adulthood.

"Would the Duke of Pelham abhor a sycophant if the flattery was true?" Athena asked absently as her attention roamed the ballroom. She stiffened suddenly.

Lord Marbury was talking with a young widow, Lady Mary Eastman, who had just come out of mourning. Athena flinched slightly as the earl threw his head back in laughter at something the young widow had said.

Grace recognized the hurt on Athena's face immediately. She'd experienced it herself whenever she saw Dane at a social event. "Let's take a walk, shall we?" She wrapped her arm around Athena's and turned to the other women. "If you'll excuse us? I need some air." Without waiting for their permission, Grace led the young woman away. "You look like you've seen a ghost."

"It's nothing," Athena said stiffly.

"Nothing looks like something to me." She glanced at Marbury, who was still in conversation with Lady Easton. As if he sensed they were near, his gaze found Athena's, and he frowned.

She leaned near Grace. "Marbury told me he didn't want a wife. I should have believed him. He must be looking for a mistress."

Grace slowed her steps. "Athena," she scolded softly so that no one would hear. "I must counsel you not to speak like that. If someone hears what you said, *you* would be the talk of the *ton* tomorrow—and certainly not in a good way."

"You're right, my lady." Athena shook her head. "That was horrible of me. I should have empathy for Lady Easton. I understand she and her late husband had a love match." She turned to Grace and offered an awkward smile. "Forgive me?"

"Of course." Grace continued walking and squeezed Athena's arm in a show of affection. "I've felt that same jealousy before. It's like a plague that eats you from the inside out. But I learned early on that you can't control what others do or feel. But you can control your own emotions. And your own decisions."

Athena glanced at Marbury again. She slowed her step until she stopped. "I'm going to take your counsel. I need to move forward with my life. If the Duke of Pelham is looking for a wife, I'd like to be one of the women he considers. Let us find Marbury. I'm certain he'll want to be there for the introduction to ensure I don't make a fool of myself."

"I don't think you would ever make a fool of yourself," Grace said with a smile as her heartbeat stumbled. "It would be my pleasure to introduce you to him."

As much pleasure as if she were eating nails.

Seven

〰️

"**D**on't look now, but my great aunt is making a beeline for you, Pelham." Ravenscroft ran a hand down his face. "You were always one of her favorites. No telling what the old bird has up her sleeve tonight." He winked Pelham's way. "Or should I say *under her wing*?"

Lady Edith Nelson, Ravenscroft's great-aunt, strolled toward them, swinging her cane like a scepter with the magical power to part the throng of guests as she crossed the dance floor. The ostrich feathers on her ruby turban bobbed up and down like royal subjects trailing their monarch.

"She either wants to play cards or have you escort her around the ballroom all night as she plays matchmaker." Trafford nodded in Honoria's direction. "I'll take this opportunity to dance with my darling wife. I don't want to stand in Lady Edith's way as she makes you the object of her attention."

Ravenscroft winked. "Excellent advice. Pippa is with Honoria. Perhaps I can convince her that one dance is enough to make an appearance, and then we can leave. I can imagine a more enjoyable way to enjoy the evening than staying at the soiree."

"Oh, the allure of a new marriage," Trafford teased. "I shall follow your example."

Both of his friends abandoned him, but Dane didn't care. He adored Lady Edith, and if anyone could make him laugh, it was her.

When she came to his side, Dane delivered a deep bow in a show of respect. Then he took her hand and squeezed. "Lady Edith, what an honor."

"Duke," she acknowledged with a bob of her head. "Where is my nephew off to?" She narrowed her eyes as her gaze caught Trafford and Ravenscroft fleeing like mice who had spotted a cat.

"He decided to seek out Pippa and ask for a dance," Dane explained.

"Your two friends are cowards not to face me," Lady Edith declared, then smiled Dane's way. "But I didn't want to talk to either of them anyway."

"Would you care to dance?" Dane offered with another bow.

Lady Edith tilted her head back and laughed. "Dear boy, aren't you sweet?" She leaned near. "I'd much rather play a game of vingt-te-un and win some of your millions."

"As long as I had your delightful company, I wouldn't mind." He winked in the old dame's direction.

"Charmer." She threw back her head with a laugh. "But you shouldn't be wasting your talents on me." Edith rested her hands on the brass lion's head at the top of her cane. "You should be trying to win the affections of one of the young ladies here." She waved her hand across the room.

"Should I? What if I'm not interested?"

Lady Edith turned her hawk-eyed gaze to him. "Time is precious, and unfortunately, no matter how powerful or rich you are, it's only finite. You can't buy more. Even you, Pelham."

"I shall take your wise advice under consideration." Dane clasped his hands behind his back and smiled. She was correct. He didn't want to waste any more of his precious days without a wife. "Do you have any suggestions?"

"Yes." She nodded her head once, sending her ostrich feathers flying again. "Quit standing here with Trafford and Ravenscroft. Even though I'm entertaining, a divine conversationalist, and politically, not to mention socially savvy, you cannot pin your hopes on me." She took the crook of her cane and discreetly pointed it across the room. "However, make tonight worth your while. See Lord Marbury over there? He's talking with Lady Grace and keeping her enthralled. I've been watching them for the last fifteen minutes. He hasn't left her side."

Dane followed the direction of Edith's cane, which led him to Grace. She had her head tipped back, laughing at something the young earl had said. Even from this distance, the sight of her delicate skin sent a wave of heat through his body. Grace always loved it when he kissed her there. She also adored when he whispered in her ear, just like Marbury was doing at the moment.

Dane frowned as he fisted one hand. The sudden urge to march across the dancefloor and pull Grace away became almost unbearable to ignore. However, he would not look like a heathen at a *ton* event, no matter how much he desired to throw Grace over his shoulder and leave.

"Perhaps she should be the one you ask for a dance?" A sly smile pulled at Lady Edith's lips.

"I would, madame, but Lady Grace can barely tolerate me," Dane confided.

"Nonsense, my boy," Edith exclaimed, then reached a bony hand and placed it on his arm. "I've seen the way she argues with you. She wouldn't do it unless she felt something." The grand dame leaned closer and lowered her voice. "As the old saying goes, there is a thin line between love and hate."

Dane stood silent as he watched Grace. Another woman had come to her side. Hopefully, she was the object of Marbury's affection and not Grace.

"Go ask her," Lady Edith encouraged as she gently pushed him. "What are you waiting for?"

"For her to come to me," Dane said. It wasn't that he was bashful. He didn't possess a shy bone in his body, but Grace was making her way in his direction, accompanied by Marbury and the young woman.

When Grace and her entourage reached them, he couldn't help but grin like a fool. She'd actually sought him out without him having to summon her. "My lady, are you enjoying yourself?"

"Indeed, Your Grace." She smiled politely. "May I introduce Lord Marbury and his ward, Lady Athena Wescott."

Dane straightened to his full height, which meant he towered over the young earl. "Of course. I've had the honor of making Marbury's acquaintance before." He inclined his head. "It's good to see you."

Marbury bowed slightly. "It's been a year or so if recollection serves me."

"Indeed," Dane answered, but he'd turned his attention to Grace and the young woman beside him.

Instead of blushing and sputtering like a typical debutante, the young woman met his gaze directly.

Grace nodded approvingly, but there was something odd in her demeanor. It was almost as if she were purposely holding herself back or perhaps wishing she was somewhere else. "Your Grace, this is Lady Athena Wescott."

"And to think I almost didn't come tonight." Dane took the young woman's hand and leaned over it. "It would have been the most tragic mistake of my life, as I wouldn't have met you."

Lady Athena hadn't dropped her gaze. Dane admired that. She was a beautiful young woman.

Young being the operative word.

Grace stood off to the side, and if he hadn't had his peripheral vision trained on her, he would have missed her slight flinch. He stood and directed his attention to her. "Lady Grace, is anything amiss?"

She rolled her eyes. Since the others had their back to her, they didn't see the gesture. "Absolutely fine."

Suddenly, Marbury, Lady Athena, and Lady Edith turned to face Grace.

She quickly smiled and shook her head. "Truly. I'm perfectly fine."

If he were a betting man, which he was, he'd say that his *Governess* was jealous. Perhaps he should let her taste how bitter jealousy could be. He'd been choking on it earlier.

"Good," he said dismissively, then turned to Lady Athena. "It would be my greatest honor if you danced with me?" He was laying it on thick, but it was all for Grace's benefit so her clients would be pleased.

"Thank you, Your Grace." Lady Athena smiled as if he'd given her the keys to his kingdom. Funny, she wore a gorgeous smile, but it didn't make his heart pound or create a need to step closer. That only happened with Grace.

"Athena, stay where I can see you." Marbury frowned.

Now, it was Dane's turn to scowl. Did the young earl think he would compromise his ward in the middle of the dancefloor? Anyone who knew Dane would know that he had excellent manners.

At least, he always did, except when it came to Grace.

"No need to worry, Marbury," Dane drawled. "I want everyone to see me dancing with Lady Athena. They'll be jealous of my good fortune."

Marbury's stern expression turned into exasperation. "May I have a word, Your Grace?"

"Of course," Dane answered politely and followed Marbury, who walked to an area far enough from the ladies that they couldn't hear. He could still keep his eye on Athena, and Dane could watch Grace.

"I know of your reputation," Marbury said bluntly.

"Which is?" Dane lifted a brow and stood as if bored. It was his most arrogant stance, and it reminded everyone that he was a duke.

"That gambling is your number one priority. The man lucky enough to win Athena's hand will be of excellent moral character whom no one would question."

Dane chuckled and shook his head. "I think you misheard. I asked Lady Athena to dance. Not to marry me."

Marbury narrowed his eyes.

"But you did hear correctly that I love gambling. I even own a gambling hell and coaching inn next to my ducal estate. You should visit sometime. And bring Lady Athena. My sisters practically live next door to me. I think she'd enjoy them. If you'll excuse me? The orchestra is playing." He tilted his head and grinned in Marbury's direction. "Luck is with me tonight. It's a waltz." Without a look back, he turned on his heel and made his way to the ladies. He could only imagine the steam that had to be bellowing around the pompous young pup of an earl.

Lady Edith commanded him to her side. "Jealousy doesn't appear to be his color. The green doesn't suit him."

"Very astute, madam," Dane answered softly.

"Hopefully, I'll see you in the card room. I'll be the one with all the markers on the table before me." With that, Lady Edith deftly spun around, defying her age.

Dane turned his attention to Athena and held out his hand. "My lady?"

Without hesitating, she placed her hand in his and led her onto the dancefloor. Keeping the proper distance between them, Dane took her in his arms and swept her into the familiar routine. They were silent for the first several moments.

"You're an excellent dancer," Lady Athena said as she gazed into his eyes.

"Thank you." Dane expertly turned her to avoid colliding with another couple who were having difficulty with the steps. "It came from teaching my sisters how to waltz."

"I've met them. I understand they are your only siblings?"

Athena was tall enough that he didn't have to strain his neck to make eye contact. "That's correct. They're the most provocative, intelligent, not to mention enchanting women you'll ever meet."

She blinked several times. "The way you talk about them is lovely, Your Grace."

"I'm lucky to have them." He turned her again.

"I understand that Lady Grace's assistance was invaluable when they were seeking to marry."

"In a way," he explained. "My eldest sister didn't care for London, but Grace helped her take her place in society, and Honoria married my best friend. With my youngest sister, Pippa, Grace stayed with her during the Season while I had to travel to my ducal seat. Pippa married my other best friend."

"I see. Lady Grace must be like a sister to you."

He caught himself before his dance partner noticed his slight stumble. "Pardon?"

"Forgive me if I'm too bold, but she seems to be integral to your family's happiness. I also understand that you're looking for a duchess," Athena said.

A bubble of laughter escaped. "I'd forgotten how quickly rumors spread when you make a rare appearance in society."

She frowned slightly. "It isn't true?"

"It is," he answered.

"Have you found her yet?"

"Perhaps." Dane smiled slightly, but he didn't offer anymore.

An enigmatic smile drew across the young woman's lips. She didn't say another word but glanced at the other couples. She turned her attention back to him. "Everyone is looking at us."

"They see me dancing with a beautiful young lady." Dane glanced at the crowd. Indeed, people were watching them—except for the one person he wanted to. From his brief glance, Grace was nowhere in sight.

"Are you dancing with anyone else this evening?" Athena asked.

"No. I think I'll head to my club." Just then, he caught Ravenscroft and Trafford standing on the edge of the dancefloor wearing sly smiles as they watched him. They were worse than an assembly of busybody matrons who thought it their duty to insert their noses where they didn't belong. Standing beside his best friends were his sisters, Honor and Pippa, who were frowning at him.

He would ensure they realized this was just a dance, not a declaration of impending nuptials. Thankfully, the music slowed, indicating that the dance was over. When it stopped, Dane let go of Athena, and they applauded in appreciation for the orchestra's effort.

"I shall return you to Lord Marbury. Thank you for the dance." He offered his arm, and Athena wrapped hers around him. "You're an enchanting dance partner."

"As are you." She leaned near and lowered her voice. "Your Grace, do you think it matters if there's a difference in age between a husband and a wife?"

The young lady had to be at least a decade younger than him. Was that too young? Was he too old? Surely, she wasn't declaring herself interested in marrying him.

"I think it depends on the individuals," he offered without any explanation. He had to nip her interest in him quickly in the bud.

"Excellent answer," Athena said with a laugh. "You and I are of like minds."

"Wonderful." He could only force a tepid smile. Discreetly, he evaluated her. She was undoubtedly beautiful, but she was barely out of the nursery.

He shook his head slightly. He knew what he wanted in a wife, and Lady Athena was not it.

A relieved breath escaped when he found Grace standing next to Marbury. He frowned at the brittleness of her smile. It reminded him of an emerald, easily shattered with the right amount of force. With her caramel-colored eyes and dark blonde locks, Grace would look stunning in the Pelham parure of emeralds. Every Duchess of Pelham had worn them when they'd hosted their first ball.

He'd never considered it before. The brilliant green jewels would also match the jealousy that radiated around her.

Who knew this matchmaking business could be so intriguing?

Eight

It took every ounce of Grace's willpower not to react to Dane
flirting with Athena. She forced herself to inhale deeply five times.
That was usually enough to calm her thoughts, but every nerve
seemed to be on edge tonight. Once she had Athena safely back with
Marbury, she'd take a walk. She would clear her mind if she could be
alone.

She forced her expression to stay pleasant. It was easy to infer that
they enjoyed their dance together based on the many smiles and grins
they shared. They made a striking couple. Everyone in the ballroom
noticed them on the dance floor. Dane's movements to the orchestra's
music resembled a premier ballet in Paris. Every step perfectly synchronized to the music.

Grace turned to Marbury before Athena reached his side. "My lord,
I have an emergency I need to attend to." It wasn't a lie per se. He didn't
need to know that she was desperate for a quiet place where she could
take a moment and lick her wounds, which begged the question of why
she was upset. She had no hold on Dane. Her job was to help him and
nothing more. "I shan't be gone from the ballroom for over a quarter of
an hour. Will you keep Lady Athena company? Perhaps you could ask
her to dance."

"Of course." Marbury's gaze never strayed from his ward, who was making her way to his side. He watched her like a hawk about to pounce on an unsuspecting rabbit. "It would be my honor to attend to Athena while you're gone."

Dane let go of Athena's arm as soon as they had reached Marbury's side. "Thank you for the lovely dance." He bowed politely.

"I hope the future allows us to share another." Athena dipped a deep curtsey.

"If you'll excuse me." Grace didn't wait another minute as she turned and found the quickest exit to the ballroom.

A footman stood by the doorway. "My lady, may I offer you my assistance?"

Grace smiled politely, but it felt like having a tooth pulled. Or, at least, she imagined. If only she were alone, she wouldn't have to play the Governess tonight. "Thank you, but I only need some air."

He nodded. "If you walk to the long gallery, there's an exit to a private terrace that overlooks the formal gardens. It's quiet and cool."

Grace nodded her appreciation and walked straight ahead. The din of the ballroom grew softer as she entered the long gallery. It was a large rectangular room that ran the length of the home. It was more like a library than a portrait gallery. Bookshelves lined the wall opposite the bank of windows. For the first time all night, the knot of tension in her neck relaxed. She rolled her head and took a deep breath.

Dane had hired her to find him a wife. Lady Athena Webster would make a perfect partner and duchess. Even still, it felt like she was stabbing herself in the chest every time she looked at them. It was childish and petty, but when she gazed upon them, she couldn't help but think that she could have easily been Athena if only things had turned out differently.

It was no use crying over something that might have been. She had to look toward her future. This was her life now. She also had to accept that her earlier life had been built on a façade of untruths and illusions.

As she turned the latch to one of the French doors that led to the terrace, a hand reached out and grabbed her arm. "Come with me."

She would recognize that deep voice as smooth as whiskey anywhere. "What are you doing?"

"Having a private conversation with you." Dane opened a door to a small anteroom and then waved her inside.

As soon as she entered, he closed the door. The glow from the lanterns of the formal gardens and terrace bathed the small room in soft light, giving everything an ethereal glimmer. As she glanced around the room, it was apparent it was a game room with a gaming table and four chairs. A large clock shaped like a birdhouse hung from the ceiling. Pink and green striped wallpaper covered the walls. Struck by the feminine beauty in the room, she sighed softly. This was a haven for Lady St. Albers. Then and there, she would sketch the room when she returned home. Though she'd never be able to afford such a luxury, she could appreciate its beauty by drawing it and then painting it.

"That sounded like a sigh of pleasure." Dane stood so close she could feel his warmth surround her. "I'm glad I have that effect on you."

"That wasn't about you. I like the room." She clasped her hands in front of her.

He used his acting abilities and stumbled as he brought his hand to the middle of his chest. "You wound me, Grace."

"Are all men's self-esteem this fragile, or is it only yours?" she quipped.

He chuckled and stepped closer. He lifted his hand to stroke her cheek, then slowly lowered it. "I like your smile. It's real and makes your beauty shine," he said softly.

"Thank you," she murmured as she turned to look out over the formal gardens.

"Where were you going?"

"I needed a bit of fresh air. Things were growing stagnant in the ballroom." She didn't add that her life was also growing stale.

"Are you happy, Grace?"

The deep timber of his voice vibrated in her chest. Would her body ever quit reacting to him? Probably not. The sooner she found him a wife, the better for all of them.

"Well, my happiness isn't what's important tonight. It's yours. How did you find Lady Athena? Is she someone you might desire as your duchess?" She practically choked on her words, but she faced him. Her breath caught at the sight before her. The lantern's light caressed one side of his face while the other was cast in shadows, much like her life. She always considered herself a happy person. She experienced joy in her days, but sorrow and worry were her constant companions during the long nights when hours felt like days.

Nor did those constant companions warm her bed.

He tilted his head as if she were a puzzle he was trying to solve. "She's pleasant. But honestly, these young ladies remind me of children."

"You're not answering my question," she pressed. "You hired me to help you, but I can't if I don't know what you want. These women, especially Lady Athena, are the most highly sought-after in society."

"Hmm, these highly sought-after women are like sweets," he murmured as he bent toward her and lowered his voice. "Boys prefer sweets. Men prefer something more substantial and succulent with a boldness that will stay with them long after the meal."

"They're not wine, Dane."

He laughed, and she smiled in response.

"Here's my answer." He lifted his hand again and cupped her cheek. "I'm happy if you are. Your happiness is important to me." He leaned near until the distance between them was a hair's breadth. "Tell me what would make you happy."

To keep from whispering *you*, she chewed on her lower lip. His gaze locked on her mouth. She swallowed hard as he lowered his lips to hers. She closed her eyes, waiting for his touch, waiting for his kiss, waiting for him. Hadn't she been waiting for him her whole life?

When his lips barely touched hers, she shivered in anticipation. Without thinking, she clasped his evening coat and pulled him near.

His mouth trailed up her neck, kissing her gently, almost reverently, as if she were something precious. He trailed his lips across her cheek. Careful of the pearl drops she wore, he nipped the soft skin of her ears. "It pleases me that you still have the jewelry I gave you. I'd shower you with jewels if you let me."

Without any shame, she pushed closer. Where she was soft, he was hard. His arms wrapped around her, and he held her tight. Her skin felt as if it were on fire. Her breasts were heavy, and her nipples yearned for his touch. The hard length of his erection prodded her stomach where she ached for him. All of him.

She sucked in a breath when he pulled her tighter. "Shall I continue? Tell me yes, Grace," he begged softly. "Holding you in my arms like this is all I've thought about."

"Yes." It was the only word she could utter. When his mouth met hers, she wanted to weep. Little did he know, he was all she thought about as well. He deepened the kiss, and she moaned in pleasure. This is what she'd craved over the years. Him. And only him.

A knock sounded on the door. Instantly, Dane pushed Grace behind him, shielding her from whoever interrupted them. Stunned, she couldn't think or act. But Dane reached for her hand and held it.

"Who is it?" he called out.

"Your Grace, pardon the interruption, but Lord Ravenscroft and Lord Trafford were looking for you. They asked me to find you so they could say goodbye."

Grace's heart pounded with such force that she thought it would break through her ribs.

"Only I would have bloody knaves as brothers-in-law." Dane pulled her into his arms, and she buried her head into his chest. His embrace offered comfort and protection. "No harm has been done, Grace," he whispered, then kissed the top of her head. He lifted his head and raised his voice, never letting go of her. "Tell them I'm busy. They can call on me tomorrow."

"Very well, Your Grace. I'm sorry I interrupted you."

"I'm sorry too," he murmured. "It's not every day that I have Grace Webster in my arms begging for my kisses."

She pushed away from him and straightened her dress. "If memory serves me correctly, you were begging me."

He winked like an utter and absolute rogue. "I'm not ashamed to say it either." He shrugged and offered the telltale smirk that made him look like a boy who emptied the biscuit jar.

What was she thinking? She couldn't be meeting Dane alone. She was supposed to be finding him a wife, not allowing him to kiss her senselessly. "You leave first. Then I'll leave."

"What are you going to do?" he asked.

The air still shimmered between them with the energy they'd created from the kiss. "I'll say goodbye to Marbury and Athena, then I'll have one of the footmen call for Theo."

He flinched slightly. "You can't. I sent Theo home. I thought you...could come home with me."

"What?" she asked incredulously. "Have you forgotten all sense of propriety?"

He stared at the floor and rubbed the back of his neck as if seeking the answers to her questions in the rug beneath them.

"Even though it appears that way, I haven't." He raised his gaze to hers and smiled sheepishly. "You visit Ardeerton House alone, and there's no scandal."

"Society knows I'm friends with your family and aware of my position. Nothing is scandalous about visiting in broad daylight and arriving in my carriage."

"But in my defense..."

This was beyond the pale even for him. He'd made a unilateral decision while deciding to do something scandalous without considering the ramifications. If anyone saw her leave with him, they would likely assume Dane and she were stealing away for an assignation or something equally outrageous.

"Grace." He let out a long, painful sigh. "I merely wanted your company tonight."

She wanted to laugh and cry simultaneously because the sad part was that deep down, she wanted that, too. But she had to think of her livelihood and desire for her future. She could not jeopardize that for Dane's kisses, no matter how devastatingly sinful and seductive they were.

Even if she was desperate to be held by him once more before she let him go forever.

Dane stared out the carriage window, not noticing anything. It was a better view than facing a bewildered Honor and a livid Grace. Trafford sat beside him, shoulder to shoulder.

What an abysmal end to a surprising yet enjoyable evening. Somewhere along the way, Dane misplaced his sense of honor and decency. What was he thinking when he'd decided to take Grace home with him? His blasted cock thought it was in charge and not his rational mind, which seemed to have taken a holiday without giving proper notice. He didn't realize that his solitude had become so dire that he'd made reckless and irrational decisions. Perhaps the footman he had fired for spreading gossip about him hadn't exaggerated when he had divulged that Dane had been careless in business because he had been distracted. But it wasn't true except for one caveat. He was distracted by Grace.

This was entirely unlike him. He'd always prided himself on making decisions based on logic, not emotion. But ever since Grace had come back into his life, he hadn't been himself. After Pippa had moved out, he'd become worse. What was he thinking when he had asked Grace to help him find a wife?

He feared if he examined his reasons too closely, he'd discover something appalling. He couldn't control himself around her. All he could think about was making love to her.

"Whoa," the coachman called out as the carriage slowed to a halt.

As soon as the carriage door was open, Grace took her leave of Honor and Trafford and didn't spare a glance his way. She took the footman's hand and exited. Dane sat for a moment, paralyzed with inaction. At the sound of her voice thanking the footman, he stood and exited the carriage as well.

"Allow me to see you to the door," he murmured as he took her arm.

"That won't be necessary, Your Grace." She tried to tug her arm free, but he held firm and leaned close.

"Show me some of your renowned grace and mercy before you rip my heart in two," he whispered in her ear.

With a frown, she reached for the front door latch.

He stilled her hand. "Grace…" He maneuvered his body so no one could hear or see her.

"Good night, Pelham." She kept her gaze glued to his chest. "Thank you for the escort."

"You have my deepest apology and remorse," he blurted out. "I behaved abominably."

"I accept your apology." She still wouldn't look at him. "Don't blame yourself exclusively. I was a willing partner."

He tilted her chin until their gazes met. "I want to help you. For instance, about your dowry—"

"Is none of your business." Fire and fury flashed in her eyes.

"It seems I'm making a habit of offending you by asking about your dowry and asking you to come home with me." He softened his voice with affection and offered her his biggest smile, hoping to defuse the situation between them. For the world, he didn't want to upset her. But he had, and his chest ached with that knowledge. "Please let me help."

"Let me make this perfectly and utterly clear. Firstly," she said primly, just like a governess, as she held up one finger. "My dowry and inheritance are not your concern."

He narrowed his eyes. Unfortunately, he would make it his business whether she wanted him involved or not. The overwhelming need to protect her wasn't new to him. He'd always felt this way about her until that bloody day they met on the field. Afterward, he'd purposely kept his distance until Pippa invited Grace to Pelham Hall to help Honoria navigate London. Then, his need to protect roared back to life. Yet that instinct wasn't anything like what he felt for his sisters; they were family.

But Grace? *She was his.*

"Secondly,"—she held up two fingers as she swallowed hard—"we both agreed our pasts stayed in our past." Her voice wobbled on the end.

His chest swelled with hope and a bit of pride, just like any man would when he discovered that the woman he wanted and found undeniably attractive was affected by him.

She let out a breath as if her lecture was exhausting.

"Is that all?" he drawled as he winged an eyebrow.

"You arrogant man, no, it isn't," she hissed as she lifted three fingers. "Thirdly, we're not courting." She hmphed, emphasizing her point. "We're not together."

He couldn't resist sending another volley her way. In the most dramatic fashion he could muster, he perused the area around her and the entry of her house. He looked behind him at the carriage. Honor and Trafford were nowhere in sight, and the coachman tended to the horses.

"Darling," he murmured with a chuckle. "There's no one else in the vicinity, so I surmise we're together." He leaned near. "And you are fully aware of that fact."

"Dane," she said with exasperation. "You employed me to find you a wife. You've gone out of your way to impede my efforts." She bit her bottom lip, the same one he'd been sucking on at the soiree. "Why are you trying to make our working arrangement something different?"

He opened his mouth to respond, but no thought came to his rescue.

She glanced at her feet as she shook her head. "I don't know if we can continue this way." Gradually, she lifted her gaze to his. "I plan to reflect on tonight's events, and you should also. We'll see if we can find a path forward."

"I shall, Grace. Is it naughty to say that I cannot wait to hear your thoughts...when we're alone again?" He took her hand and brought it to his lips. "Good night, and dream of me."

He descended the steps with a lightness that he hadn't felt in years. At the bottom step, he turned around. "Grace?" He waited until she faced him. "Just so you understand me, I shall be dreaming of you."

He didn't wait for her reply so he could escape whatever barb she'd wing his way. As soon as he ascended the carriage steps and knocked on the roof, the carriage lurched forward.

"What was that about?" Honor said as she scooted closer to Trafford, who had his arm around her.

"Nothing. Merely a difference of opinion on how the night went," he replied. "Trafford, are you interested in going to the club?"

His friend shook his head. "I'm interested in going home with my wife."

Dane smiled slightly. Both of his friends preferred to spend their time with their wives. Who wouldn't? His sisters were two of the most brilliant and vivacious women he knew.

He was intimately acquainted with another who was equally brilliant and vivacious.

Lady Grace Webster.

When his coach pulled up to Honor and Trafford's home, he said good night and leaned back in the carriage as it returned to Ardeerton House. What exactly did Grace mean that he needed to reflect on what they were doing? He could reflect on a specific truth all night. He wasn't the only one lost in their kiss. The way she moaned and pressed herself against him displayed the same type of hunger he experienced. He hadn't felt this way about a woman since...*her*.

"For the love of heaven," he murmured to himself. He bent forward and rested his head in his hands. Whatever this was, whether it be a headache or an epiphany or something else, he knew his life would never be the same.

And the reason was Grace Webster.

There was only one woman he wanted to spend time with.

There was only one woman he wanted to warm his bed.

The only one he wanted as his wife and his duchess.

The best way to convince her was to get her alone at Pelham Hall. She had always loved Amesbury. But how could he convince her to leave her charges in London?

The carriage halted in front of the door of Ardeerton House. His loyal butler, Ritson, was waiting for him to arrive home.

"Good evening, Your Grace." Ritson bowed. "And how was the evening?"

"Enlightening," Dane said as he gave his hat and clothes to the footman inside the door. "Will you have my valet come find me? We're headed to Pelham Hall."

"Oh?" Ritson's eyebrows nearly touched the top of his head. "You're not going to finish the Season here?"

"It won't be necessary," Dane said confidently. "Everything I need is in Amesbury."

He only had to find a way to whisk Grace away from all the distractions of London.

Nine

Grace took another sip of tea for fortitude. As soon as she finished the cup, she would have Theo take her to Dane's home. It was best if they parted ways permanently. She could not afford to be seduced by his kisses. Nothing good would come from it except her own demise and destruction.

Last night in bed, she'd relived that kiss over and over until she was hot and had thrown off all the covers. That's exactly what he did to her. He made her hot all over, and he was an expert in making her want things that she couldn't trust.

Things such as his steadfast and resolute devotion to her.

When they'd had the confrontation on that field in Amesbury, Grace had been convinced he would return to her and beg forgiveness. But he hadn't. He'd been as stubborn as she had been. Both thought they had the moral high ground. She was convinced hers possessed the highest peak. Yet, she'd learned over the years that the view might be spectacular, but it was a desolate place to exist alone. Meanwhile, he had found comfort in his gambling and millionaires' club.

Yet, she had been determined to show him she could be a success in London. But, of course, Dane had never been there to see her triumphs. Nor her failures. Thank God.

There was no inheritance or dowry. Everything she'd thought about herself and her family was an illusion. Why didn't her parents provide for her future? She'd asked herself the question a thousand times before and still had no answer. The truth was that she was still practically destitute.

"My lady, your carriage is ready." Theo stood at her study door with his hat and gloves, ready to take her to the Duke of Pelham. "Again, I apologize for leaving the soiree last night early. The duke tried to be helpful and kind when he said I should return home. He thought it would be tiresome for me to put the horses up and prepare for the night if we arrived home after midnight. It was thoughtful of him." In the darkness, his eyes twinkled. "He promised to see you home safely."

"No need to apologize again, Theo," she said curtly as she stood and walked to Theo's side. "I've spoken to the duke about his behavior. It's one of the reasons I need to see him this morning." She stood from the desk and walked to the door. As they say, it was best to lance the wound. The quicker she finished the task, the clearer her future would be. She could go back to work without any distractions.

Distractions such as a handsome duke with wicked lips, a sharp and acerbic wit, and a roguish gleam in his eyes when he looked your way. Most thought him arrogant. And he was, but he was also playful and full of vigor. He was a joy to be around, but he wasn't for her.

Grace pulled on her gloves and stepped outside. She pivoted on her foot as a commotion erupted. A man shouted as two others pulled him from the townhouse next door.

"Is that Mr. Hanson?" Grace stopped as she tried to understand what was happening to her elderly neighbor. "Who are those men?"

"They're hired hands to evict him." Theo frowned. "They posted the eviction several days ago."

Grace's hand flew to her mouth in shock. "Eviction?"

Theo nodded. "He told me that he would fight it." Her butler shook his head as they watched the hired men throw Mr. Hanson's clothing and personal belongings onto the street. "His rent is three months late, and his landlord won't give him another chance."

A chill slithered down her spine, a cold, creeping terror that tightened its grip with each passing second. Her steady hands began to tremble as the severity of the situation enveloped her like a heavy fog. The truth was starkly evident—she could end up exactly where she had been before, a place she had fought so desperately to escape.

Her mind reeled back to that awful night in London, the memory clawing its way to the surface. The shame had been suffocating, far too great to ask a friend for shelter. Pride had sealed her lips, making it impossible to seek out Dane for help, no matter how much she needed it. So, she wandered the streets, cold and hungry, with nowhere to go.

She remembered discovering a dilapidated church, its doors cracked open as if beckoning her to safety. Once inside, with her heart pounding, she found that safety was merely an illusion. The hard, wooden pew provided no comfort, and while she tried to sleep, every creak of the building and every distant bump and murmur jolted her back into raw, unyielding fear. The darkness enveloped her, thick and suffocating, as she lay there wide-eyed, muscles coiled tight. It became the longest, most harrowing night of her life. She was terrified she would be kidnapped or worse. Even now, the memory made her skin crawl.

She had promised herself, vowing with every ounce of her resolve, that she would never again fall into such a vulnerable position. Yet, fear sliced through her, threatening to drag her back into that same pit of hopelessness. It was a horror she couldn't bear to relive, and the very thought of it twisted her stomach into a painful knot.

If she hadn't managed to engage Dane and Lord Marbury as clients, she'd have not been able to pay this month's rent. Slowly, she raised her hand to the center of her chest. If she were ever evicted, where would she go? Her sister's husband had made it crystal clear that she could not stay with them.

She had never approached her third cousin. Her brother-in-law had been the one to assure her that no love was lost between her father and the new earl. She couldn't go to Honoria and Pippa. The shame would drown her.

Two men held Mr. Hanson by the arms as he cursed and then tried to take a swing with his fist.

"The Duke of Pelham won't give him another chance? I didn't think he'd be that cruel," she murmured in shock.

"The duke doesn't own that property. It belongs to Lord Grolier."

This fact brought her some relief. A short, staccato breath escaped her lungs. The Dane she knew would never treat another person this way. Lord Grolier was a cruel man with little empathy for others. If she thought Dane was arrogant, Grolier occupied a realm of haughtiness all his own. He had delivered a direct cut to his mother when she joined the Women's Literary Society, a group for women who loved reading and discussing politics. Unfortunately for his mother, Grolier deemed her political views unacceptable, and he considered the people she associated with to be beneath her.

He even refused to contribute to the new foundling home that Trafford and Honoria had established for the poor children of London.

Grace swallowed the thickness in her throat. She'd seen people like Mr. Hanson struggle before. Her father's tenants had sometimes asked for leniency when the crops had a dismal season. Her father had always been generous to them.

Thank heavens for Dane's generosity when he had come to her for help. He'd paid all her fees in advance, and that money had been a lifeline, a beacon of hope in a sea of uncertainty. Even though she had Lord Marbury and others as clients, it would never be enough to extinguish the fear that gripped her chest like a vise. She swallowed, her throat dry, but it did nothing to ease the knot of anxiety tightening in her gut. She *couldn't* lose Dane as a client—not now. She needed that income and the safety it provided like she needed air to breathe. If she had to let him go, everything she'd built would crash into a pile of rubbish. The mere thought sent a tremor through her, a cold reminder of how close she was to losing it all.

She opened her reticule and took out whatever she had in her coin purse. "Will you give this to Mr. Hanson? Perhaps it'll help in some way."

Theo nodded. "I will, ma'am. I'll ensure he has enough to pay for passage to his daughter in Essex."

Grace returned to her study and didn't even look at the garden, which provided solace when troubled. Instead, she looked at her account books. Perhaps there were more extravagances that she could eliminate from her monthly budget. It was unlikely, but after what she'd seen today, she would do everything in her power to stay in her home.

Before she could scour the pages, Theo returned and placed her money on the desk. "He thanked you for the offer, but he said that he didn't accept handouts."

Graced nodded solemnly.

A knock sounded on the front door.

"I'll see who it is, my lady." Theo's gait was a little heavy as if seeing Mr. Hanson's eviction had also affected him.

Grace shimmied her shoulders. She could not let fear overtake her. There were too many things she had to accomplish.

With a flourish of hellos, Honoria and Pippa entered her study wearing smiles brighter than the summer's midday sun.

"Grace, we told Theo that you wouldn't mind us seeing ourselves in," Pippa volunteered as she embraced Grace.

When Pippa released her, Grace found herself in Honoria's embrace. "We couldn't stay away. We had to see you."

Grace hoped the sisters didn't sense her unease when she held on to them a little longer than usual. She stepped back and smoothed her skirt. "No doubt to see what shenanigans your brother got into last night, I presume?" Both sisters wore a sheepish grin. Thank heavens her friends were here. They would ease her troubles, at least for a while. She'd take any reprieve from worrying about her future whenever she could. "I take your expressions to mean you'll not deny it."

"Well, of course, we wanted to see how you fared last night," Honoria chided.

Ever efficient and kind, Theo entered with a tea tray and a plate of cherry tarts.

"Are those what I think they are?" Pippa sat on the edge of her seat.

Honoria placed her hands in a prayer pose. "Theo's superb cherry tarts, I hope?"

Theo blushed at the praise. "Yes, my ladies, they were just baked this morning."

Grace stilled for a second as her guests continued to discuss the tarts with her butler. Perhaps that was an area she could trim in her budget. Sweets and baked goods of all kinds meant extra flour and eggs. She sighed because the truth was she adored Theo's tarts, and he loved to make them. She knew how much it meant to him when he served them to her friends and clients.

"Now, about last night?" Pippa took a bite of her tart, then moaned. "They're still warm."

Honoria moaned in tandem with her sister as she chewed and then swallowed. "May I ask Theo to teach our cook how to bake these?"

"Brilliant idea," Pippa cried, then slid a sly look Grace's way. "Perhaps...we can steal Theo for a day and have him teach our cook as well."

"As long as Theo agrees, I see no harm in it." Grace feigned a look of concern. "But you know he is more than a cook. He's my footman, coachman, gardener—"

"He's every woman's dream, you mean." Pippa placed her hands over her heart and stared at the ceiling.

Honoria picked up a pillow and threw it at her sister. "Theo's mine, or I'll tell Ravenscroft that you've found a new man to fancy."

All three broke into fits of laughter.

There was no denying how right it felt to spend the morning with Pippa and Honoria. She felt closer to them than she did her own sister. If she had married Dane, then they would be sisters in truth. Her laughter died as she shook her head. She couldn't dwell on such thoughts. This was precisely why she had plans to visit Ardeerton House in the first place and terminate their agreement. Even thinking about marriage to Pelham would lead to nothing but heartache.

"So..." Honoria placed her empty plate on the table beside her. "What exactly happened last night? Our brother was uncharacteristically quiet after we left your home."

Pippa nodded in agreement. "We know that Dane hired you to help him secure a wife. But something more is going on between the two of you."

Grace was shaking her head before the words were out of Pippa's mouth. "There is nothing between your brother and me. It's simply a business transaction that requires me to be pleasant to him and introduce him to eligible young ladies out in society."

Honoria nodded her head. "That explains why you and he were alone...together...locked in an anteroom near the St. Albers ballroom."

"That is the definition of being pleasant," Pippa added unhelpfully.

Grace bit her tongue as she thought of a suitable riposte. But the women before her had been true friends to her over the years. If she couldn't be honest with them, then who could she confide in?

"Actually," she began.

Pippa and Honoria leaned forward as if Grace was about to impart some great wisdom.

"He and I argued."

Pippa smirked.

"Typical Dane," Honoria agreed. "Argued about what?"

"He sent Theo home and then said I should leave with him." Grace blew out a breath, upsetting several loose hairs that surrounded her face. "I told him he was being highhanded and—"

"Impervious to you." Pippa turned to Honoria.

Her sister smiled tenderly. "He's arrogant, overly confident..."

"Hugh believes he's overly protective of Honoria and me," Pippa shared.

Honoria nodded once, but her gaze never left Grace's face. "Yes. Overly protective but also excessively affectionate." She reached over and grabbed Grace's hand. "He loves deeply. Once he gives you his heart, he's true."

Grace offered a small smile. Dane's sisters thought the world of him, and they should. He had always put his sister's welfare and future before himself for all the years she had known him. He always wanted what was best for them.

However, that same loyalty and love wasn't for Grace. Perhaps because last night's romantic dalliance hadn't meant as much to him as it did to her, but she would never tarnish the pedestal his sisters had placed him on.

"That's why I'm hoping your brother will find the match of the Season. It will solidify my position as the person people turn to when their daughters and sons are ready to marry." If she could reach around her back, she'd give it a pat. Honoria's passionate speech about her brother conjured memories of last night's fiery kiss with Dane, but she had avoided addressing her response. She sounded remarkably calm even after changing her mind about ending her agreement with Dane. Witnessing a neighbor's eviction makes a person think more clearly.

There was no denying that passion had never been a problem for her and Dane. Their fervor was so hot that they could set a barn on fire with only a glance.

Unfortunately, it also seemed to blaze between Dane and every other woman walking within his vicinity.

"Grace," Pippa chided. "You're more astute than that. He cares for you."

"Deeply," Honoria offered. "Only you."

"I think you're both seeing things that aren't there." Grace set her teacup and saucer on the table and clasped her hands in her lap as she regarded her two friends. "It's my wish that he make a match." She couldn't believe that she was about to utter the words. "A match with Lady Athena would be in his best interests."

Honoria and Pippa stared at her. The surprise was evident on their faces.

"Oh, Grace, no," A glint of Honoria's earlier humor returned. "Trust me on this."

Pippa took Honoria's hand in hers and squeezed. "Honor is correct." Then, with a seriousness that belied her usual good mood, Pippa turned her attention to Grace. "He deserves true love. Just as you do."

"I'm sure he would consider her a suitable match." Grace examined her clasped hands before looking at the two beautiful sisters. Their features resembled those of their handsome brother. Despite enduring unimaginable trials and tribulations with their parents, the siblings remained steadfast in their devotion to one another. "He hasn't mentioned that he wouldn't consider her. However, if he did, I'd find him another suitable woman."

"Oh, Grace," Pippa murmured, shaking her head. "Perhaps you should ask him about that this evening."

"Yes, we came today to ask if you'd come to dinner at my house this evening." Honoria stood and walked to Grace's sofa and sat beside her.

Pippa did the same, only on Grace's other side. "Please."

"Marcus wants to host a family dinner for once." Honoria blushed slightly. "You know how much family means to him. And we consider you family."

Before Grace could refuse, Theo knocked on the open door to get her attention. "My lady, Lord Aston and Mr. Powers are here to see you."

"I wasn't expecting them," Grace said.

"They're most anxious to see you," Theo said.

"We should depart. We have business to attend to." Honoria stood. "Come at seven, please. That will give us time to finish our conversation before dinner."

"I can't wait," Pippa said. She leaned toward Grace and pressed a kiss on her cheek.

Honoria did the same.

Like two whirlwinds that appeared out of nowhere, they departed from her study, quickly saying their goodbyes. Grace could hear the sisters greeting the two men and then the front door closing.

"If you'll see them in," Grace said to Theo, then walked to her desk and waited for her visitors.

Her butler bowed, and in seconds, two distinguished men entered her study.

"Lady Grace, my name is Mr. Alfred Powers." Dressed in a black morning coat and matching breeches, a tall, thin man approached her desk and took Grace's hand.

"How do you do," Grace answered as she evaluated him. His black hair was liberally peppered with gray. Yet, he was still handsome. It was easy to see that his daughter Adeline favored him.

"My daughter met you last night and was determined that I call on you today." He chuckled as affection warmed his features. "She reminds me of myself at that age. Adeline knows what she wants and goes after it. She hoped you could introduce her to eligible bachelors, including a certain duke." He cleared his throat, clearly embarrassed.

The other gentleman approached her desk and took her hand. "Allow me to introduce myself as well. I'm Lord Aston." He bent over her hand and then released it.

Grace was reminded of Lady Candace by his features. While Mr. Powers was tall and thin, Lord Aston was slightly rounder and shorter. But even with his white locks, he was also a handsome man.

"Lord Aston, it's a pleasure." Grace came around from her desk and gestured toward the sofas where she had previously sat with Honoria and Pippa. "We'll be more comfortable there. I believe the tea is still hot, and I'll ask my butler to bring more tarts."

Both men declined her offer.

Lord Aston cleared his throat. "My Candace asked if I would come today. She would like the same introduction to the duke and wanted me to enquire if you were interested in retaining more charges...I mean clients for the Season."

Grace laughed at the word charges. "No need to say clients. I am the *Governess*, after all. However, you both should understand that a certain duke makes his own decisions. I can introduce your daughters to the Duke of Pelham, but he can only marry one person. That means someone or both will be disappointed." Her stomach roiled slightly. Never before had she had so many young women interested in the same man. "Part of my services are introductions, but I will also introduce them to others."

She had to push aside the thought that they were discussing Pelham and her access to him. No matter how uncomfortable providing access to the Duke of Pelham made her feel, she had to remember that this was her work, and everyone in the *ton* knew it, including Dane. She would be discreet so it wouldn't appear as though she was violating Dane's privacy. Her clients were paying for her services, and she would ensure she performed her duties to the best of her ability.

During the next half hour, Grace explained her services, which included introducing her clients to suitable men, matchmaking behind the scenes, and making social calls to the most influential *ton* members. All this was done to ensure her clients made suitable matches during the Season.

Both gentlemen readily agreed and promised to send the monies to Grace's account as soon as they returned home.

After they both left, Grace pushed her unease about Pelham aside and walked to the bookshelf at the end of her study, picking up a new Minerva Press novel she had secured from the circulating subscription library. She deserved a little entertainment after the week she had. She hadn't had time to read it yet, and it was due next week. Thankfully, she wouldn't have to cancel her membership to the subscription library.

Theo knocked on the door and cleared his throat. "Ma'am, Lord Marbury is here to see you."

"Will you please bring him into the study?" Longingly, she smiled as she placed her book on the small drum table next to her favorite chair near the fireplace. Her reading time would have to wait.

"Lord Marbury, ma'am," Theo said as he ushered in her guest.

"Good day, my lord." Grace motioned for him to take a seat in front of her desk. "To what do I owe this pleasure?"

Marbury waited until Grace sat before he flicked the tails of his morning coat and sat down where she had previously directed. Grace clasped her hands in front of her, ready for business. She pasted a smile and waited, fully expecting the earl to berate her for allowing Athena to spend time with Dane.

The earl leaned back in his chair and regarded her with a smug smile. "I wanted to see how you managed the invite."

"The invite, sir?" She was momentarily caught off-guard by the absolute glee in his voice.

"The invitation to attend the small house party hosted by the Duke of Pelham." Marbury scooted forward in the chair.

He was so close to her that he could have rested his hands on her desk. She'd never seen the earl so happily animated before.

"Athena is over the moon. And so am I."

Grace wasn't enthralled in the least. In fact, she felt as if a coach and four had just run over her. The Duke of Pelham had invited Lady Athena Wescott to a house party at Pelham Hall but didn't bother to consult her, let alone invite her.

Was it any wonder she was bemused? It felt like a betrayal. All that talk last night of kisses between them and their shared intimacy meant nothing to him.

She offered a smile as joyful as a melted blancmange.

"I don't know how you secured the invitation or if it was your idea, but I'm pleased. Very pleased," he reiterated. "I'm here to add a little incentive so the courtship moves forward quickly and with a resolution that will make everyone happy."

Her smile faded. Marbury was overjoyed even though he was about to come to blows with Dane for simply flirting with Athena last night.

But when she studied him, there was a sense that his exhilaration did not quite ring true. His eyes had a haunted look about them. Perhaps he was starting to realize his true feelings for Athena.

She drew her attention back to the conversation with a pleasant smile. "When did you receive the invitation?" Thoughts swirled in her mind as she waited for the earl to respond. Under no circumstances would she allow the earl to see that the news had devastated her.

Why had Dane not invited her? He'd hired her for this very purpose. Honoria and Pippa made no mention of a house party. Perhaps they didn't know, and this was Dane's way of taking control of his courtship.

"The invitation arrived by messenger while we were at breakfast. It was addressed to me, and the duke had included a brief note that he'd enjoyed Athena's company last night."

It felt like the same coach and four had run over her again to ensure she was utterly deflated. She had not received any posts today, including a note from Dane.

"Forgive me for being blunt, but I thought you didn't care for the Duke of Pelham." She leaned back in her chair and placed her hands in her lap to avoid drumming her fingers on the chair's arm.

Marbury took out his handkerchief and wiped his brow. It was a sign of nervousness, or he was lying.

"You were correct when you said that the duke was a man of good standing in the *ton*. I made assumptions and formed opinions that I had no right to." He studied his hands in his lap. "May I be honest?"

Grace nodded.

"I need Athena married as soon as possible. I know she has feelings for me. But I can't return them. I don't want to be married this young." He swallowed, his discomfort readily apparent.

"Let me be honest with you," Grace countered softly. "I wonder if you might have feelings for her as well."

"I can't marry. I promised my father I wouldn't rush into an endeavor without considering all the ramifications." He fisted one hand. "What I feel for Athena has the makings of a disaster. Neither of us has much experience with society, or London, for that matter."

"I see," she said softly in hopes of comforting him. "I'm sure your father meant well in securing your promise. But in my experience, the heart does what the heart wants to do."

"Only if we allow it, my lady." He studied his fisted hand and stretched his fingers as if he'd clasped it so hard that it hurt. He feigned a smile. "Here's what I want to offer you. If you can persuade the duke to offer for Athena's hand during the house party, I'll pay you an extra five thousand pounds. If you can have them married by the end of the social Season, I'll pay you an additional five thousand pounds. Ten thousand in total."

"I can't take that offer. I haven't been invited to the duke's party." She cleared her throat at the confession.

The earl waved his hand in the air. "That is not a concern. The duke mentioned to bring you. Athena needs a chaperone. You are a respected matron. This works well for all of us."

Now, she was the one who fisted a hand. After the kisses and sweet words Dane had given her last night, it was inconceivable that he was throwing a house party and, as if an afterthought, suggesting Marbury bring her as a chaperone. She fought not to allow her lip to curl at the moniker of *respected matron*. "What about Lady Athena's aunt?"

"Unfortunately, when the poor woman climbed into the coach to come to London, she fell. The surgeon believes that she broke her ankle. She's bedridden." He picked up his hat from the chair beside him and stood. "I hope you'll consider my offer. We can accomplish everything we want if we work together. I plan on leaving in the morning."

With that, he nodded, then left her there with all her thoughts tossed about as if lost in a whirlwind.

She swallowed hard. Obviously, Dane was considering a match with Athena, which was fine with her, especially since five thousand pounds was a fortune. That was practically half the amount she needed for a lovely house on the outskirts of Mayfair that would be hers. Ten thousand pounds, and she wouldn't have to scrimp and save anymore. She could buy a home immediately for her and Theo and be content.

There would be no rent ever again to worry about.

There would be no more evictions to worry about either.

She would concentrate on investing for her old age. She wouldn't feel the burden of accepting every client who wanted to secure her services. Did she even want to work anymore? How much money would she need to walk away from being the *Governess*?

These were all questions that had to be answered.

She closed her eyes and inhaled deeply. For a moment, she imagined she smelled the briny waves of the ocean. She and Theo should move to the Cornish seaside. Warm weather, sandy beaches, and long walks would be theirs any time of the day. They could eat fresh fish and make new friends. The ocean would be a comfort in and of itself. She and Theo would be safe and secure for the rest of their lives.

Yet, she couldn't walk away from Honoria and Pippa. They were her friends. In many ways, they were her only family.

Rationally, she couldn't refuse Marbury's proposal. He and Pelham were paying her, so why not accept Marbury's offer? If it worked, then she'd be the richer for it. If it didn't, then she would continue to help Pelham and Athena with others.

Her throat burned, a raw ache rising as tears threatened to spill. How could it have come to this? She would lose Dane forever. The thought hit her like a punch to the stomach, leaving her dizzy with pain. He would belong to Athena or another, and the image clawed at her heart, leaving it bloody, bruised, and aching.

In her work, she helped each person find their perfect mate. She might push someone in a particular direction but never interfere with or hinder their interests. A deep, hollow dread settled in her bones. She wanted Dane more than she'd ever admit, but she did need him as well if she wanted security for her future. Perhaps she should feel guilty for pushing him toward Athena. However, he did invite the young woman. This was what he wanted. Grace had to remember she wanted this as well...until last night's kisses.

She took a deep breath as she closed her eyes. She'd always prided herself on her common sense.

The truth was Grace had lost him nearly ten years ago, and now, she wondered if she wasn't partly to blame.

Ten

Dane pushed aside his morning coat and propped his hands on his hips. The harlequin pattern of the marble tiles glistened in the sunlight. Every conceivable tabletop was decorated with fresh-cut flowers from the garden. The cut glass of the chandelier above the entry sparkled, casting rainbow prisms across the floor. After one final but critical study of the entry, he nodded his approval. The house was prepared for Marbury, Lady Athena, and, most importantly, Grace.

Dane had suggested that Marbury should also ask Grace to attend. When the young Earl had bemoaned that he didn't have a suitable chaperone, Dane immediately recommended Grace as the perfect choice. Yesterday's note from the earl confirmed it. Lady Grace Webster would accompany the earl and his young ward to Pelham Hall.

If he knew Grace, she undoubtedly would deduce that Dane was behind the invitation. He had purposely not invited her for fear that she'd refuse his request. But with the request coming from Marbury, Dane knew she wouldn't refuse. She would do everything in her power to ensure that Marbury was happy with her services.

"Your Grace?" The housekeeper, Mrs. Madsen, dipped her head in greeting.

His gaze drifted to the family wing of his home. "Did you place Lady Grace in her usual bedroom?"

Mrs. Madsen nodded. "The rose bedroom next to Lady Honoria's—" She shook her head. "I meant Lady Trafford's old bedroom."

Dane smiled at the slip. Honoria had been married for several months, yet he still thought of her as his little sister rather than the wife of one of his best friends.

"Excellent," Dane murmured, then wiped his brow of sweat. "Are the blush roses in her room?"

"Indeed, Your Grace. The color matches the bedding perfectly."

When he kissed Grace again, the roses would match the perfect blush of her cheeks.

The housekeeper clasped her hands in front of her. "Three large bouquets. Just as you requested. The gardening staff are aware that they must replace her flowers every day."

"That's perfect." Before Dane could say any more, a footman stood by Mrs. Madsen's side asking about the formal salon.

Even though there were only three guests expected for the next two weeks, the activity in the house buzzed with the excitement of a holiday house party with seventy-five guests. But Dane wanted everything perfect for Grace. Every floor in the house had been cleaned at least twice. The silver had been polished, and the formal china with the Pelham crest had been cleaned and placed on the formal dining room table. At tonight's dinner, Cook would prepare all of Grace's favorites: pheasant in truffle and wine sauce, buttered spinach, lobster with fried parsley, and mushroom tarts. Dane hoped the rose ice would please her, especially since he had directed Cook to use the petals from roses that matched the blush roses in Grace's room.

"Your Grace." An upstairs maid dipped an abbreviated curtsey his way, but her attention was directed at his housekeeper. "Mrs. Madsen, the guest rooms have been aired, and the beds made with fresh linens."

As the two walked toward the guest wing of Pelham Hall, Dane took a final look at the entry and nodded to himself. He was ready for Grace.

And everything this house party entailed.

When his butler, Winston, entered the room, Dane raised his chin.

Immediately, the butler moved closer to him. He had been the butler at Pelham Hall longer than Dane had been alive. Winston's cousin, Ritson, was the butler at Dane's London home, Ardeerton House. Both had witnessed the havoc the previous duke and duchess had wreaked upon their children. They had been there to protect Dane and his sisters as much as they could without incurring the wrath of Dane's father.

"Thank you and the staff for all your efforts in preparing for my guests."

"No need to thank me, Your Grace. It's our pleasure to serve you." His craggy face broke into a grin. "If I may be so bold, sir, I've never seen you this invested in your guests' visit before."

Dane laughed. "You know me so well. I want this to be memorable for all my guests, but especially the one whom I'll be asking to marry me."

Winston's eyebrows practically flew to the top of his head. "I had no idea, Your Grace."

"I would be much obliged if you keep that information to yourself." Dane grinned when Winston nodded his understanding. "Also, I want the footmen to wear their black and gold livery this evening for the dinner."

"Of course, Your Grace." Winston didn't bat an eye at the unusual request. The black and gold livery was only used on special occasions, such as when the king, heads of state, dignitaries, or other special guests visited.

Dane wanted Grace to feel special. He wanted her to see that this visit was significant to him and his whole staff.

"I'm going upstairs to change." He nodded to Winston, but before he could walk toward the steps to the family quarters, the front door opened.

The majordomo of the Jolly Rooster, William Atwater, stepped inside. With a stoic nod of greeting to Winston, the man made his way to Dane's side.

"Come with me to my study," Dane said as he continued down the hallway.

Neither he nor William said a word to each other in the hallway. They never discussed the Jolly Rooster's business unless they were alone. Too many secrets could ruin a patron if discussed in front of others. Though he trusted his staff, Dane was always careful to keep the Jolly Rooster's business separate from the duchy. But if William rode here, then that meant trouble was afoot. William was the eyes and ears of the coaching inn and gambling hell when Dane couldn't be there himself.

Dane shut the door and proceeded to his desk. "Something amiss at the Jolly Rooster?"

William nodded as he sat in one of the chairs that framed Dane's desk. "Your Grace, I have been informed that you have guests arriving any minute. However, I did not think this could wait." He took off his hat and nervously twirled it in his hands. "Lord Brixworth just arrived at the Jolly Rooster."

Dane carefully placed his palms on the desk and took a deep breath. It didn't help calm his anger. *"Bloody hell."*

"We both know his reputation. I need your advice before I ask him to leave."

Dane slowly shifted to the edge of his seat. Brixworth had a bit too much affection for his liquor. He also had an unpleasant habit of approaching young women inappropriately. Brixworth was a reckless card player, losing money hand over fist. He showed no regard for making women feel uncomfortable and expected them to meet his desires, regardless of their interest in his advances. As a trusted friend of the king, the viscount believed himself to be above the law.

"I don't have time for Brixworth." Dane thumped his desk once. "Throw the man out."

"He has the deed to the estate next to Pelham Hall and plans to gamble with it." William leaned forward. "He knows you want it."

Dane pulled a handkerchief from his waistcoat pocket and wiped his forehead. He had wanted the old earl's summer estate for years. It included the field where he and Grace had always met. It was a part of their past. "Did you see it?"

William nodded once. "I rode over here as soon as he presented it. He asked if you were at the Jolly Rooster to play. I told my assistant to keep him occupied until I returned. The viscount said he wanted to play cards first, then go to bed. He pointed to Sarah and said that he picked her to sleep with him."

Dane looked out the formal garden windows, but all he could see was a drunken lout about to upset the staff at the Jolly Rooster. It would not stand. He was close to the men and women who worked at the Jolly Rooster. In many ways, they became a part of his family when they accepted him without any judgment. When Dane had enough funds to buy the inn, he'd spoken with every employee and asked them to continue working there. Everyone congratulated him and said they would be honored to work for him. The Jolly Rooster would not be as successful as it was without the hard work of his staff. There was no bloody way that he'd allow Brixworth to maul and accost his employees.

William was built like a prizefighter and could handle any man who wore out their welcome at the Jolly Rooster. But such physical violence wouldn't be necessary. "I think the solution to our problem is for me to have a quick game or two with the man, then divest him of his fortune and that deed. Then I want you to escort him from the premises."

William grinned and rubbed his hands together. "I was hoping you would say that. You've wanted that estate since I've known you."

"I have." Finally, he'd have that part of Grace that had shaped him into the man he was today. Dane pulled a piece of parchment from his desk, then dipped his quill pen into the inkwell. "I'll give Brixworth a welcome that I only reserve for special friends."

Dane didn't need to elaborate that those special friends meant ones he planned to ruin financially through card games.

"We'll ride together. Would you ask the groomsman to saddle Hercules for me? I need to write a note for someone in case I'm late returning."

Thankfully, the trip from London to Pelham Hall had been pleasant. Grace had not minded being in a carriage the entire day since Athena had entertained her as they traveled. Even Marbury was charmed by her conversation.

Grace peeked out the window as the coach and four came to a slow stop in the circular drive of Pelham Hall. The grand Palladium home never ceased to amaze her. All three levels of the grand house were majestic.

Marbury was the first to exit. He helped Athena down, then offered his assistance to Grace.

She smiled at the awe on Athena's face as she took in the grandeur before her and studied the mansion. "Impressive, isn't it?"

Athena pulled her attention away and regarded Grace with her eyes wide open in surprise. "I've never seen anything like this. This makes my father's estate look like a cottage."

Marbury laughed and offered his arm to Athena. "If that's the case, then what would you call my ancestral estate?"

She bent her head near him until she almost rested it on his shoulder. "A home."

Grace exhaled but didn't say a word. She should not encourage any romance between them at the request of her guardian. It was in Athena's best interest to have Dane propose to her while they were here.

It was also in Grace's best interest. The money Marbury promised to pay her upon the successful engagement of Dane and Athena was a small fortune. Yet, such an outcome made her hands clammy. She'd purposefully pushed such thoughts out of her mind as she walked up the steps. She would have plenty of time to compartmentalize everything she felt in the weeks to come. Yet, her conscience had refused to be quiet since Marbury had approached her about the house party. She had made herself weary as she contemplated how Dane would react to the news that Grace had accepted the payment of additional funds if there was a betrothal within two weeks. She slowed her steps. Perhaps he wouldn't care since it was just like gambling. She was wagering on Dane to win her a fortune.

If she were in the same position, she'd be livid. Her future and her happiness were hers to govern. But didn't Dane secure her assistance to help him find a wife? He trusted her, and there was nothing wrong with being rewarded for a job well done.

Perhaps if she kept repeating that mantra, her conscience would ease.

When the door opened, Winston stepped onto the portico. "Welcome, Lord Marbury. I'm Winston, the butler here at Pelham Hall. If you need any assistance, please feel free to ask me or any of the duke's staff. It's our pleasure to serve you." He nodded to Athena. "Welcome, my lady." His familiar face broke into a genuine smile when he turned to Grace. "It's so lovely to see you again, Lady Grace."

"Thank you, Winston," Grace murmured as she squeezed his forearm in greeting. "I'm certain that his lordship and Lady Athena are ready for refreshments, then a rest."

"My thinking exactly, ma'am." Winston turned to Marbury and nodded. "If you'll come inside. I've taken the liberty of having a small repast served in the Duke's salon."

As a footman escorted Marbury and Athena to the formal salon, Grace hung back and whispered to the butler. "Speaking of the duke, why didn't he greet his guests? Is Matthew with him? He always greets me when I arrive. I hope he's not ill."

Winston's face turned the color of cooked cod. He swallowed hard and immediately transformed into a proper butler, his expression reflecting his loyalty to the Duke of Pelham. "I apologize, ma'am, but His Grace was called away on an urgent matter. I expect he'll return within the hour."

Something was amiss if Winston's reaction to her questions was any indication.

"Regarding Matthew, his services were no longer needed." He leaned close and lowered his voice. "He sold information about the duke's personal life to a London gossip rag." Winston shook his head in disgust. "When His Grace discovered what he had done, he...he was relieved of his duties as a footman and paid his wages along with an amount to tide him over for two months until he found other employment." Winston stuck his nose in the air as if smelling something foul. "His Grace expects loyalty. To make money off his private life is the purest form of betrayal. If I had known, I'd have fired him myself."

Her heartbeat pounded in her chest. She cleared her throat. "How did the duke find out?"

"Another footman saw Matthew in the village with a man who happened to be the assistant to the editor of the gossip rag."

She couldn't believe what she was hearing. "I'm sure there's an explanation. Perhaps he needed the money."

Winston smirked. "His Grace said the betrayal was worse because Matthew didn't come to him first. His Grace would have helped him. He's most generous." Winston nodded toward the salon. "May I escort you?"

"Yes," she said faintly.

At this point, there wasn't much difference between her and Matthew. She smiled slightly to conceal her reaction.

She was overreacting. Undoubtedly, Dane would be thrilled about a match between him and Athena. He wouldn't care that she had earned money from her arrangement with him while she earned money from Marbury.

However, an irritating niggle burrowed into her thoughts.

Such news only reinforced that she should have excused herself from working for Dane when she had the opportunity.

Eleven

The ugly sneer on Marbury's face contrasted with the formal dining room's beauty. Their dinner had been served on the duke's best china and silver service. The footmen's black and gold formal livery was only used for the most honored guests. Yet, they had sat in the dining room for over two hours after finishing the meal in the first hour. Marbury was on his second port and becoming angrier by the moment.

Dane had undoubtedly planned to impress his guests if appearances were any indication. Marbury's aggravated sigh once again broke the eerie quiet in the dining room. Even Grace would admit that it set her on edge. She clasped her shaking hands in her lap to hide her nervousness. She didn't want to take a sip of wine, fearing it would spill. The young earl was certainly not happy with the welcome they'd received so far. Even Grace would admit that it was an affront that Dane hadn't appeared or left them another message.

If Dane was trying to woo Athena, he was off to a poor showing with her guardian.

At the direction of Winston's wave, the footmen cleared off the remaining plates and dishes on the table.

With a daintiness that any finishing school matron would be proud of, Athena gently patted the edges of her mouth. With an inherent elegance, she placed her serviette in her lap and regarded her guardian. "I'm sure the duke will be here directly."

Winston cleared his throat. "If I may, tea will be served in the music room." His kind smile didn't crack under the strain of having one angry earl in his presence. "Perhaps a little music would—"

"I don't want any *bloody* tea or music," the earl growled, then stood abruptly. "I'm going for a ride."

"A ride?" Athena stood abruptly, almost knocking over her chair. "It's dark. What if you fall or the horse throws you?"

"Worried for me?" He tilted his head and studied her. "Save your concerns for your duke."

"He's not my duke," she hissed.

"Shall I have one of His Grace's mounts readied for you?" Always the consummate butler, Winston interrupted to nip the squabble that was set to erupt between Dane's two guests.

"An excellent idea." Grace stood and reached for Athena's hand. "The duke's grounds are well-lit when he has guests."

"How do you know that?" Athena asked as she took Grace's outstretched hand.

"I've visited Pelham Hall several times at the invitation of the duke's sisters. We have spent many evenings enjoying the formal gardens at night." She turned to Marbury. "If you'll excuse us, we'll adjourn to the music room."

The earl didn't acknowledge her comment as he turned on the ball of his foot and practically stomped down the hallway.

"Come, let's you and I have a cup of tea. I'll play for you if you'd like." Grace gently tugged Athena in the opposite direction from where the earl had headed.

As they entered the music room, the footman set a tea service on the table and nodded at Grace. Discreetly, he closed the door behind him.

"May I pour?" Grace stopped instantly when she spied a lone tear skate down Athena's cheek. "Oh, my dear, what is it?"

"I just do not understand Jasper or his moods. Sometimes, he treats me as if I am his favorite person. The next minute, it's as if he cannot leave my sight fast enough." Her eyes reddened with tears. "Are all men like that, or just him?"

"I think Lord Marbury is a complicated man with complicated feelings," Grace murmured diplomatically.

"What does that mean?"

"May I be frank?" Grace pulled Athena into a sofa that faced the formal courtyard, which was bathed in an ethereal glow from the outside lanterns. "Perhaps he has feelings that he either doesn't recognize or refuses to admit."

Athena's brow furrowed into neat lines. "Feelings for what?"

"Not what but whom," Grace nudged. "Do you not see the way he looks at you? He couldn't keep from stealing glances at you in the carriage ride." She retrieved a handkerchief from the hidden pocket sewn into her gown and slipped it into Athena's hand.

"Thank you." Athena wiped her tears. "But I've known this man since I was in leading strings. He teased me unmercifully then, and now, he can't bear to look at me. I have lived under his roof ever since my parents passed, and I can confidently say that you're mistaken."

"Darling, I recognize when two people love each other across a crowded ballroom. A slim distance between carriage benches makes it even easier to see."

For a moment, she wanted to withdraw the words. She was supposed to be helping Athena secure a marriage proposal from Dane. But every time she thought upon the task, it curdled her stomach. Inside, a voice cried that he was hers and would always be hers. Yet, logic said she needed security in this world and could only attain that through the monies she'd earn by ensuring this match succeeded.

It wasn't like she was doing something against Dane's best interests. Lady Athena was a prize; any man would be proud to claim her as his wife. Truthfully, it would be easy for the right man to fall in love with her. She was vivacious and intelligent and had a way about her that appealed to people. She was open and would be a loving partner to a husband. Grace did not doubt that.

Which belied the question of where Grace's loyalties should lie?

Should it be with Athena, the young charge she was helping, or with Marbury, who was paying for her services? Bringing up Marbury's obvious deep feelings for Athena muddied the answer. But Grace's feelings for an infuriatingly handsome and arrogant duke churned the waters even more. She couldn't deny what she felt but tried to ignore the protests from her heart.

The door burst open before she could say more, and an incensed Marbury stood before them. "Athena, we shall leave at the first break of dawn. We will not accept any further hospitality from the duke." His voice dripped with venom.

"But—" Athena stood and wrung her hands.

"Now is not the time to question me." He took a deep breath, which seemed to calm him. "Please. For me," he said gently. "Will you go to your room and pack?"

Athena nodded and quietly left the room.

Marbury watched Athena leave before he turned to Grace.

"What happened?" she asked, sitting on the sofa's edge.

"I rode the short distance to the Jolly Rooster on the suspicion that Pelham was there."

As soon as he said the words, Grace sucked in a breath as if she'd been punched in the stomach.

"I hate to share this with you as I know you have a high opinion of His Grace. But that man"—Marbury pointed in the general direction of the Jolly Rooster in the nearby village—"is sitting at a card table with three other men. Gambling and carousing." He laughed, but it held little humor. "Not only that, but he has two almost naked women surrounding him at the table. They're hanging on him like barnacles on a ship."

Grace stood stock still. His words shot straight through her heart. It was the exact same thing he'd done all those years ago after he'd asked her to marry him.

"Surely, you are mistaken," she murmured, bringing her hand to her chest, hoping to calm her runaway heartbeat.

"No, my lady." Marbury walked to a table where several bottles of whisky, port, brandy, and glasses stood. He poured himself a glass of whisky.

Dane had never abided by the dictates of society that said women should drink tea while the men imbibe in liquor. He believed that if you served whisky to one, you served it to all. Right then, she had never been so glad that he bucked society's expectations as it related to serving liquor to females. She needed the liquid strength. "Would you pour me one, please?"

Marbury didn't move as he slowly glanced her way.

"A whisky," Grace added with a lift of an eyebrow. If Marbury thought she was a *respected matron*, then he could damn well serve her a glass.

"Of course, my lady." He poured her a fingerful and brought it to her side.

Grace thanked him with a nod, then took a sip of the liquor and concentrated on the smooth burn as it slid down her throat.

"Obviously, if the duke doesn't hold enough regard to welcome us after he invited Athena and me to visit, then we shall no longer intrude upon his hospitality." Marbury downed his glass and set it on the table in front of Grace. "You're invited to leave with us on the morrow as well. I see that your rooms are on the family floor while Athena's is in the guest wing." Before Grace could respond, he continued, "May I escort you to the stairs that lead to your chambers?"

Grace cleared her throat. "No, thank you, my lord. I shall discuss our leaving with Winston. He'll ensure that everything is ready for our departure, with footmen ready to assist in loading the carriage."

"Excellent idea." Marbury smiled, though his expression looked more like a grimace. "As you can surmise, I'm not fit company for anyone right now." He clenched his fists. "I will not allow anyone, including the Duke of Pelham, to disrespect Athena. We'll discuss how to proceed with your bonuses since the Duke of Pelham will no longer be considered a suitor worthy of Athena's hand. I'm a fair man. You shouldn't suffer financially because the duke is an absolute buffoon. Honestly, I view this as good fortune. I would blame myself if they'd made a match and Athena was unhappy." He glanced out at the court-yard. "There's a full moon. I'm tempted to leave tonight, but I'm afraid it would upset Athena even more."

Grace didn't add that it would be a *fool moon* if Marbury tried to leave this evening. "I think that's wise advice, my lord."

He dipped his head. "Good night, Lady Grace.

"Good night." Grace stood and placed her glass on the desk next to Marbury's empty one.

"Ma'am?" Winston peeked his head around the corner. "I wondered if you needed anything before you retired."

A certain duke to reprimand came to mind. What had Dane been thinking? Obviously, he hadn't. His cock had. She bit her cheek to avoid saying anything she'd regret.

"Do you know why the duke is at the Jolly Rooster gambling right now?" She astonished herself with the calmness in her voice. "You mentioned that he was expected to return within the hour after we arrived. It's been over six hours."

Winston's cheeks turned cherry red as he quickly ducked his head to stare at the floor. "My lady, he was called away on business."

"Winston," she softly cajoled. "Marbury saw him at the Jolly Rooster." She didn't add that Marbury also saw Dane with naked women hanging around his neck. "Do you know what he is doing?"

With cheeks still burnished red, Winston raised his gaze to hers. "I cannot say, Lady Grace."

His silence just infuriated her more. "While I admire your loyalty, I must find out the answers. Pelham invited these people here for a stay and has shown himself to be a complete arse—" She took a deep breath. "Forgive my crudeness."

"I understand how it must appear, but I believe His Grace will be able to explain everything when he arrives in the morning." Winston rocked back on his feet.

"Morning," Grace cried. "His guests are leaving at the first break of dawn, and I plan to return to London with them."

At that moment, everything became crystal clear. Dane might be a duke, but his behavior was more akin to a naughty boy. No, it was more akin to an arrogant schoolboy who thought he owned the world.

Well, she was finished with him and his abhorrent behavior. Just like all those years ago, he only thought of his own needs and pleasures.

"Would you ask that a carriage be brought around?"

"Ma'am?" Winston asked, clearly shocked.

"A carriage," she reiterated.

She understood what she needed to do to move beyond her regret of investing so much attention on Dane.

She would visit the Jolly Rooster and inform the duke that she would return his money as soon as she arrived in London. After tonight, her worry about hurting his feelings for accepting Marbury's additional funds was moot.

She would no longer work for Dane Ardeerton, the Duke of Pelham.

And she would not spare another thought on him after tonight.

"Ma'am, I'm sure the duke would not want you to be out this late."

Winston's persuasive voice and wringing hands did not deter Grace from her mission.

"His Grace will be most displeased," the butler added unhelpfully.

Grace took the coachman's extended hand as she exited the carriage. As soon as she stepped onto the ground, the bustling sounds of the inn's coachyard greeted her. Horses neighed while coachmen and groomsmen called out for assistance from the Jolly Rooster staff. From the looks of the activity, the inn was successful on its own, which allowed Dane to make his fortunes with his cards while entertaining *his women*.

Grace didn't care what *His High and Mighty* did anymore. The Duke of Pelham wasn't her concern.

Honestly, what was the allure of gambling? First, her father, and now Dane. She'd never realized that they were so much alike.

"If His Grace is displeased, it has nothing to do with me. I'm here for business reasons only. He understands business." She headed toward the entrance.

Winston hurried to her side. "Ma'am, please."

Grace stopped suddenly, causing her skirts to slap against her legs. "I can assure you that I'll inform him that you tried to dissuade me from coming." She pointed in the direction of Pelham Hall. "Winston," she said softly. "He has two guests who are bewildered and upset about how the duke has ignored them. Such behavior reminds me of a misbehaving toddler and wouldn't be tolerated by any rational person." She turned on the ball of her foot and walked the short entrance to the inn.

As soon as she entered, she was greeted by a man.

"Good evening, ma'am." The middle-aged man with a full head of gray hair regarded her. "I'm Jack James, the innkeeper of the Jolly Rooster. Are you looking for a room? Is your husband with you?"

The innkeeper was dressed in a fine black broadcloth coat and wool pants. He could easily have been mistaken for a wealthy landowner instead of an employee of the Jolly Rooster.

If Pippa were here, she'd be in awe of the craftsmanship and the high quality of the material. A brass plaque hung on the wall behind the innkeeper. With a high polish, it seemed to glisten. For a moment, she thought she caught a glimpse of the inscription of an intertwined "D" and "G." She blinked, and the image transformed into squiggly lines. She leaned in closer.

The Jolly Rooster is dedicated to my future duchess, the very definition of grace.

She wanted to roll her eyes at such a sentiment. Instead, she pasted a demure smile on her lips. "Good evening, Mr. James. I do not need a room, nor am I married. I need to speak to the Duke of Pelham." Grace widened her stance in determination. "If you'll point me in his direction, I will see to my business and leave."

Mr. James glanced at Winston, who nodded slightly.

"Ma'am, His Grace is in the main cardroom with his guests. No one has been allowed in the room for the last two hours." The innkeeper lowered his voice and turned to Winston. "You know the significance of that."

Dane's butler nodded, then turned to Grace. "My lady, he's in the midst of an intense game and cannot be disturbed."

She'd accompanied her father and mother to the Jolly Rooster numerous times when she was younger. She knew where the cardroom was located and was determined to see Pelham. It made little difference what objections Winston or Mr. James had expressed.

The innkeeper nodded in agreement. "I'm sorry, ma'am."

"I'm sorry, too," Grace agreed with a feigned air of disappointment.

"I'll share with His Grace that you wish to speak with him as soon as the game ends," Mr. James added unhelpfully.

"Thank you," she answered in her most demure voice.

Winston turned to escort her out of the inn. Neither man paid attention to her, as several guests had just arrived. It only took her a split second to make her decision. Lifting her skirt slightly, Grace boldly strolled through the inn until she found the cardroom door.

"Ma'am," the innkeeper scolded from behind her. "You can't interrupt him."

"Lady Grace," Winston called out.

The thud of boots and shoes against the wooden floor gave notice that both men were scrambling after her. Thankfully, there wasn't a footman guarding the cardroom entrance. Without hesitating, she depressed the door latch and entered the room.

The cardroom could easily have been mistaken for the formal salon at Pelham Hall. The space was artfully decorated with furniture adorned with rich crimson silks and ivory and black brocades. A massive wooden table glimmering in the candlelight stood front and center. Cards, markers, and liquor glasses sat on the table like chess pieces on a chessboard. The overwhelming scents of cigar smoke, whisky, and perfume swirled around her. She swallowed to suppress a cough.

All the men sitting at the table turned in unison to look when she entered.

"Lady Grace, is that you? Fancy meeting you here of all places," a man called out jovially.

Once her eyes adjusted to the dim lighting, Grace recognized Lord Alton Brixworth immediately. With a dubious reputation, the viscount loitered on the outskirts of polite society. She'd always been wary of him and had never once allowed any of her charges to interact with him.

"Come and sit on my lap. You'll bring me luck," Lord Brixworth chortled. "I'll return the favor afterward. You can come to my room, and we'll both get lucky."

At the insult, the room grew eerily quiet.

Grace smoothed her hand down her gown. "No, thank you. I'm here for—"

"Lady Grace, you need to leave." A rasp, like a hissing snake, sounded from the end of the table. "Now."

Her gaze skidded down the table until her eyes met Dane's. His hardened stare glowed with anger, and his cheeks were unusually red, no doubt from heavy drinking and smoking too many cigars. But when she caught sight of the women, she whimpered slightly.

Two women in various stages of dishabille surrounded him. One had her arm slung around his shoulders. Another appeared to whisper in his ear as her breasts threatened to tumble out of her silk gown.

Fearing she was about to cast up her accounts, Grace turned her head only for her shock to grow even more remarkable. Surrounding the perimeter of the room, other men sat holding other scantily clad women. A few of the women stood facing the men and allowed them to lap at their exposed breasts. Some of the men were content with women sitting on their laps chatting, while others were in the throes of passion, sharing sensuous kisses.

If she didn't know any better, she would have believed she'd stumbled into a bawdy house.

"Winston," Dane barked curtly. "Get *her* out of here."

Grace stared at him, unable to look away. The eerie glow of his reddened eyes and flushed cheeks made him appear like an otherworldly being, a demon from a fiery underworld.

He stared back at her without any trace of emotion. There was no anger, no fury, no shame, or even disappointment on his face. Dane Ardeerton, the Duke of Pelham, had not changed. He was still the same person who had disappointed her all those years ago. Only this time, she witnessed all his debauchery and all his vices for herself.

She turned and fled the inn, not waiting for Winston to follow her. All she wanted was a bath to wash the stench from her skin. No wonder Marbury was livid when he'd arrived home.

She felt the same. Yet, she didn't want to examine her feelings tonight. Otherwise, she would break down into tears. How could she still feel so much for the man when he cared for no one except himself?

Winston hurried to keep up with her rapid pace as she flew out the inn's entrance.

A coachman wearing the ducal livery offered his hand, and she quickly vaulted into the carriage. Winston followed and collapsed onto the bench, out of breath.

"My lady," the butler wheezed. "Allow me to explain."

"No need. I know what I saw, and I know you saw it, too. He was in the middle of a card game, surrounded by half-naked women. You could tell by his coloring that he was in his element." She knocked on the carriage roof. With a jolt, the coach and four began the short journey back to Pelham Hall.

"My lady, please," Winston objected. "It is not what it appears."

"Stop." She raised her hand, her palm directed at the butler. "I saw it with my own eyes. He doesn't need my assistance in finding a wife. He has no trouble attracting the interest of the opposite sex." She crossed her arms while her heart thundered in her chest. "They're welcome to him."

Twelve

mesbury
Nine years ago

With speed like a flying arrow, Dane's eyesight immediately homed in on Grace, who stood adjacent to the willow tree where they always met. The field butted against Pelham Hall land and her father's summer estate on the other. It was where they'd shared their first innocent kiss and intimate embrace. Ack! Dane had to put such thoughts aside. His legs ate up the distance between them. He had never been this furious except yesterday morning when his father had forbidden him from marrying Grace.

And then, to add insult to injury, he'd received her letter saying she thought they should speak about the future of their betrothal.

By the time he reached her side, he was panting. "What is the meaning of this?" He shook the letter before her, demanding her attention.

Her eyes widened as she studied his face. "What happened?" She reached to cup his cheek, but he drew his head back.

"Nothing," he said curtly.

Nothing was that his angry father had pummeled him in the face when Dane had dared to inform him that he was of age and would marry whom he pleased. The duke didn't take kindly to such insolence and had let Dane know when his left fist collided with Dane's right eye.

It hurt like the devil and was already turning black and blue. Yet even though he was angry with Grace, he didn't want to make her worry about his father's beating.

"It looks like it hurts," she said softly.

He didn't answer. He could not be distracted by her gentle words or sweet scent. Both drove him wild.

"Why do you think we should reconsider our betrothal?" He was practically shouting, but he couldn't help it. He hadn't slept in over twenty-four hours since he'd stayed up all night playing against Scoville. It wasn't until the early hours of dawn that he'd managed to win everything, leaving the viscount in a foul mood.

But Dane was a gracious winner. He nodded his goodbye and then exited the Jolly Rooster as quickly as possible. He didn't dawdle as the viscount had a reputation for being dangerously surly when he lost. Only when Dane arrived at Pelham Hall did he allow himself to bask in the glory of his winnings. He had enough money for him and Grace to live a pleasant life in London. They could rent a townhouse there and a small cottage in Amesbury. Even if his father lived to be a ripe old age, Dane didn't need his approval or funds now to make a happy life for his Grace.

But the idea she called off the betrothal only a day after he'd proposed would not stand.

He took a deep, calming breath before he spoke another word.

"Grace, answer me," he urged. Whatever doubts she had, he would assure her she was not making a mistake by marrying him.

She lifted a defiant chin and locked her gaze with his. "My father visited the Jolly Rooster last night. This was after I'd said you would call on him today and ask for my hand in marriage."

She bit her lip, and he practically groaned at the sight. It had just been yesterday morning, but it seemed like a year since he'd sucked on those luscious red lips and tasted her sweetness.

"Why were you with those women? Did you think about me at all last night?

Dane had to be hallucinating. His eyelids felt weighted down by bricks. He closed his eyes and shook his head. When he forced his eyes open, the specter was still there with a gaze that pierced his. Grace stood at the card room's entrance in all her glorious fury.

Winston stood next to her, wringing his hands. This had to be a dream. There was no conceivable way his butler could be there. Dane had instructed the man to keep Grace occupied at Pelham Hall until he returned.

It was a mirage or perhaps a nightmare.

How long had he been here? For the love of all aches to the head, would that military drum corps quit the incessant marching through his brain? He'd never been so foxed before in his life.

Wait. He hadn't had a drop to drink this evening. The glass of amber liquid before him had been poured as soon as he sat down. He'd never picked up the glass. There had to be something wrong with him. He felt as if he'd imbibed in an entire bottle of Scotland's finest whisky, and it was the day after.

An irritating buzzing flitted around the room. He turned to see Brixworth saying something to Grace. Dane tried to get him to repeat it, but he didn't have the energy to open his mouth. Whatever he said, *his Grace* didn't like it. Her face turned the palest shade of white, reminding him of fluffy, cuddly snow. But snow wasn't cuddly. Perhaps that was why he was shivering. Snow was frigid. Yes, that had to be it.

But as he studied Grace's complexion, he decided it wasn't white. It was gray. No, cream. It reminded him of a baby swan's down. What were they called? Cigars? Signets?

Cygnets. How could he forget? He had a hundred of them at Pelham Hall. With twelve breeding pairs, he'd been overrun by baby swans this year. He considered them adorable but dangerous. Emmy had learned never to approach a nesting pair of parents as they were vicious when they thought their babies were in danger.

But Dancer was another story. That cat had already used one of its nine lives when he got too close to a nest. When the male swan had batted him with his powerful wing, Dancer sailed through the air, all the while yowling in protest.

Dane chuckled, but what erupted from his mouth sounded like a honking goose.

What was the matter with him tonight?

Brixworth opened his mouth.

Dane couldn't quite hear the words, but there was no mistake. By the looks of shock on the other players' faces, the man had insulted Grace.

By Zeus, he would challenge the arse to a duel. He'd done it before to his best friends. He wouldn't hesitate to offer one to Brixworth. He dug in his waistcoat to find a glove or a handkerchief. He'd slap the man and challenge him in front of everyone. Grace would see how serious he was about her wellbeing.

Where was his bloody handkerchief? He tried to stand up, but gravity was against him. It wasn't easy to move. The dueling would have to wait. First, he had to get Grace out of the Jolly Rooster. He didn't want her further distressed.

"Winston, get her out of here."

Who was screeching like a cat defending its territory at midnight? *Bloody hell. It was him.*

Well, he was a duke and had every right to screech, bellow, or growl. Besides, they were in his gambling hell. Must abide by his rules.

The apparition, who looked remarkably like *his Grace*, turned and disappeared into thin air. How did she do that? He'd have to ask *his Grace* to show him that trick. It would come in handy when he wanted to escape ballrooms.

He laughed and instantly started to cough.

His beautiful Grace. He should marry her. He'd ask her tonight, right after he won the deed for the estate next to Pelham Hall. He didn't care about the estate; he wanted the field where he and Grace used to meet. Maybe he'd propose to her there. She'd say yes. He'd obtain a special license and marry her tonight at Pelham Hall. That meant he'd need to go to London to secure the license, but he could rest if he slept the entire way there and back. He'd invite Honoria, Pippa, Trafford, and Ravenscroft. His whole family would be there.

First things first. He had to finish this game quickly so he could marry Grace. His lips turned down. She better not leave him again as she had the first time he had asked her to marry him.

Wait. Was she the one who left?

Perhaps he was the one who had left her, but that didn't matter. He could tell by the haughty expression on her face that day when she asked why he'd been gambling that it didn't make any difference how he answered. She was leaving. So, he did what anyone in his position would have done. He left her first. He was accustomed to people leaving him.

Every time someone left him, it felt like being stabbed in the chest. All the people who mattered to him abandoned him. His father had built a dining room for him at Eton to share meals during his visits. But he never traveled to Eton. He had left Dane there and never returned.

Then Grace had left him.

Now they would marry, and she wouldn't leave him again. However, marrying Grace meant he had tasks to accomplish. He had to win that deed and then throw Brixton out.

God, was that him shaking like a leaf? They must be in Antarctica.

When Grace married him, that would make him feel better.

But first, he had to teach Brixworth a lesson.

With a monumental effort, he cleared his throat. "This is the last hand of vingt et un."

"Ready to run after Lady Grace?" Brixworth chided with a feigned grin.

"Yes, as a matter of fact." He was about to add that he would marry her tonight but then thought better of it. "It's time for you to go home." Dane leaned forward and prayed he didn't fall face-first into the table. "If you win this hand, I'll give you the Jolly Rooster."

Gasps spread across the room.

Dane blinked slowly. "If I win, you shall give me the deed to Sommer House and the surrounding land. Then you shall leave tonight and never return to any property that I own."

Brixworth threw his head back and stared at the ceiling as he laughed. The skin on his neck jiggled with each guffaw. No one else dared laugh with him. They all knew what it meant to be thrown out of the Jolly Rooster. No one in polite society would have anything to do with Brixworth again. That's how much influence Dane had over London. Everyone wanted to gamble here. Even the king, who counted Brixworth as a close confidant, had gambled here and declared it was one of his favorite establishments in England. That had only added to its popularity.

"Let's make it interesting. The dealer won't play. It'll be you and me against the other." Dane winged an eyebrow. "You agree?"

"It'll be my pleasure to win the infamous Jolly Rooster from you. Then I shall throw you out." Brixworth took a drink of his brandy.

"We shall see." Dane nodded to the dealer. He placed one card face down in front of each of them, then another card, this time face up, alongside the first.

Brixworth had a ten of diamonds in front of him.

"My lord, would you care for another card?" the dealer politely inquired.

"No." Brixworth turned with a smile and stared at Dane.

Dane's card was the five of hearts. He blew out a silent breath. What was the rule about asking for another card? For the life of him, he couldn't remember. Didn't you ask for another card if you had a card with a five or lower number?

Or was it a card with the number three or below? He wiped the sweat from his brow. When had it gotten so bloody hot in here? He'd speak to his innkeeper about this. Why couldn't they keep the inn at the perfect temperature instead of having it hot one minute, then cold the next? He wiped his face again, hoping to clear the mindless muck cavorting in his thoughts.

He had to find Grace. With a wave of his wrist covered in white lace, he motioned for the dealer to give him another card.

Again, the crowd who had gathered around him gasped. Murmurs started to grow in volume.

"What is wrong with him? Everyone knows you don't ask for a card unless a three or below is dealt."

Hush," someone scolded. "His Grace knows what he's doing."

Whoever that was, he would give the man a raise for his faith in Dane's strategizing abilities. Honestly, he had no idea what he was doing, and he didn't care at that moment.

The dealer flicked a card and placed it next to Dane's five of hearts. It was a six of clubs.

Sighs of relief ricocheted off the walls.

The dealer asked Dane if he wanted another.

Dane frowned as he looked at the cards on the table. He struggled to focus on them but knew then that he'd bloody forgotten how to play the game. Thankfully, fate was looking out for him. He shook his head as he tried to clear the fog from his head.

"Very well," the dealer said before he flipped Brixworth's card and revealed it to be a ten of clubs.

That made twenty.

Dane straightened in his seat and nodded at the dealer. When he flipped his card, it revealed the jack of hearts. The sight of the hearts reminded him of Grace—*his Grace*. He slowly gazed at each of his employees in the room, all cheering him on. Gradually, a welcome rush of euphoria eased the pounding of his headache.

A chorus of shouts filled the room as everyone, including Dane, realized he had beaten Brixworth. He pumped his fist in the air. Sommer House was his. Now, he would throw that bastard Brixworth out of the Jolly Rooster, then take his carriage to Pelham Hall and marry Grace.

Or should he marry Grace first?

Did he have a carriage here, or did he ride his horse? Why couldn't he remember anything?

"Your Grace, no need to concern yourself with cleaning the garbage." William Atwater leaned close and laughed softly. "I'll ensure that his lordship signs the deed and is escorted from here immediately."

Dane would have smiled, but it took too much effort.

His majordomo frowned slightly. "Are you all right, sir? Perhaps you should rest. Shall I have your room prepared for you?"

"No." Dane slowly stood. "I need to marry Grace."

Grace wadded the gown she'd worn to dinner into a ball and stuffed it in her travel bag. She'd be the first in the carriage at dawn if she had her druthers. Lord Marbury had said that they'd leave at first light. Dawn could not break soon enough for her.

How could she have allowed herself to be duped by Dane? Blissfully ignorant, she had allowed her heart to soften toward him. And be trampled once again. She had practically presented it to him on a silver platter. She had been swept away in his arms and lost in his all-consuming kisses. What woman would not? She had always promised herself that she would never allow her heart to become malleable again for a man.

Not after Dane Ardeerton had torn it into a million pieces.

But it was a good thing she'd gone to the Jolly Rooster this evening and seen the evidence for herself. He hadn't changed. He was still the selfish, arrogant man from her youth.

And he still kissed divinely, just like he had nine years ago.

She growled as she fisted her hands by her side. "I cannot and will not think of him or his kisses again."

She stilled when a battering ram pounded on her door.

"Let me in."

A drunk Dane was on the other side of her door.

"Go away." She crossed her arms over her chest. It wasn't ladylike to yell through a door, but she refused to give in to his demands. It had to be well past two o'clock in the morning.

"I know you are in there." He pounded the door again and again. "Let me in, or..."

Everything grew quiet, and she released a sigh of relief.

"I'll break the door down," he roared.

"For the love of all dukes," she murmured as she marched across her room. He would likely wake the entire household if she did not appease him. If Marbury found Dane, he'd probably challenge him to a fisticuffs match. As drunk as Dane was, he wouldn't have a fighting chance. She shouldn't care, but she did, even though he'd hurt her by having those women glued to his side. However, she would not allow history to repeat itself. She would stay strong and determined. She swung open the door. "Really, Dane? What is so important..."

Gripping the doorframe, Dane leaned to one side with his eyes closed, resting his head against one hand. He resembled a statue of

Atlas, balancing the world's weight on his shoulders. He didn't spare her a glance.

He looked as if he'd lost his best friends in the world.

He probably had since the two women from the Jolly Rooster had disappeared.

"Are you all right?" she asked softly.

She still had to fire him as a client. That was why she'd initially gone to see him. She straightened slightly. She had business to take care of, and now was as good a time as any to say everything she needed. "We cannot work with each other anymore. I'm not even certain we should stay friends." She nodded in relief, then scowled slightly. "I'm not even certain we were friends in the first place," she mumbled.

His eyes were still closed. He hadn't moved an inch.

"Dane, did you hear me?"

"Yes." Before he could say another word, he coughed. He was so hoarse that he could have been mistaken for a seal. He cleared his throat and then locked his bloodshot eyes on her face. "I agree that you no longer work for me."

"If you're trying to say that you don't need my services anymore, you're too late. I just dismissed you as a client. I was on my way to the Jolly Rooster tonight to tell you the same." She crossed her arms and squeezed her waist, desperate for some warmth. She'd always thought she would feel jubilation at telling him she was finished with him, but the exact opposite was true. A chilling emptiness filled her.

He waved an arrogant hand in dismissal. "I do not need your services because I found my duchess."

She gulped a breath as her heart galloped at a breakneck speed. "One of those women sitting on your lap this evening?"

"What are you talking about? No. Those women are my employees." He shook his head. The movement caught him off balance, and he swayed for a second before he gripped the door frame tighter. "I found my duchess. *You.*" He tried to grin, but it turned into a scowl. "You're going to be my duchess. That's why I'm here." His words grew louder. "Do you hear me? *You're my Duchess.*"

"Yes, I hear you," she whispered. "Now, keep your voice down. People are sleeping."

"Oh. You said yes." He looked taken aback momentarily, then glanced over his shoulder and bellowed, "Good night, everyone."

"Please, Dane," she hissed.

"You will marry me." He nodded once. "I heard you say yes. I asked you, and you said yes. You're a woman of your word."

This entire conversation was getting out of hand. "I said yes that I heard you. I didn't say yes, I'd marry you. And I won't marry you."

"Yes, you will. I want you." He took a deep breath and slowly released it. "I want you for my duchess."

"Dane, you're repeating yourself."

He arched one eyebrow. "I'm a duke. I can do whatever I want."

She blew out a breath. "We cannot marry. You were with two other women tonight—"

Slowly, he raised his red-rimmed eyes to hers. "I told you that they are my employees. Didn't you hear me?"

She didn't say anything. He sounded exhausted.

"Now, Grace," he admonished. "For the love of God, please end my misery. My literal misery. Just say yes again so you know you have agreed."

"Are you hurting?" For the first time that evening, she truly saw him. Instantly, the urge to comfort him became unbearable. The poor man wasn't drunk; he was unwell. Heat radiated from his body, and his face was flushed. He could barely keep his eyes open.

"I hurt all over." He leaned his entire body against the door and patted the middle of his chest. "Particularly here. My heart hurts. It hurts for you."

"Oh, Dane," she murmured, ignoring what he'd said. "Let me get Winston. You should be abed."

"Don't be stubborn, woman. I'm not leaving until you say yes. But you already said yes." Then, without warning, he fell forward and landed at her feet.

She dropped to her knees and brought his head into her lap. She brushed her hand across his forehead and cheeks. His skin was hotter than a blacksmith's fire.

"Grace," he murmured. "I'm dying."

"*Winston*," she screamed. "It's the duke."

135

Thirteen

 ❧

Grace paced the length of the room and back as she repeated the litany over and over. "Please, please make him well."

Her stomach dropped as if she had taken a jump off the highest fence at Pelham Hall. What would she do if he didn't survive?

No. She would not allow herself to think such thoughts. He was a man in the prime of his life. He was strong, and more than anything, he was determined. He would not let this illness defeat him.

"Dane, do not give up." She huffed at the ridiculousness of her words. He couldn't hear her. Though they were in the same wing, he was in his ducal suites as large as the Prince Regents' royal apartments. Besides, he was half out of his mind with a fever.

"*Grace.*" Another agonizing cry echoed through the house.

How long could she allow him to suffer without going to him? Perhaps if she'd let him see her, it would be enough for him to calm down and rest.

"*Grace, please.*"

She squeezed her eyes closed at the heartbreaking sound of him calling for her. Enough was enough. She would not allow him to suffer if her presence or simple touch would bring him comfort.

Grace cinched the belt of her dressing gown. Just as she was about to take a step toward the door, a rapid knock echoed.

Thinking it could be Dane, she ran to the door and flung it open. Instead, an agitated Winston stood there, wringing his hands.

"My lady, I apologize for disturbing you so late. I hate to ask because I don't want you to become ill yourself, but might you consider seeing His Grace? He's distraught and refuses to rest." Winston turned his gaze down the hallway as another gut-wrenching yell sounded. "He will not retire until he speaks with you. I understand if you don't want to come. But I told him I'd ask."

"Of course. I was about to come to his room." She smiled slightly. "Please, there's no need to apologize. I'm worried about him, also." She stepped out into the hallway, and the two of them made their way to Dane's chambers.

Winston nodded gratefully. "Thank you, ma'am."

"Have you called for the doctor?" She pulled her belt tighter. At least she would see him with her own eyes and could judge his condition.

"Yes, but he's out of town visiting his daughter. She's about to give birth to his first grandchild." His brow furrowed into a worried frown. "I've sent a footman and a groomsman to London to bring back another doctor, but I don't expect them for three days."

"I'll help in any way I can." She patted the butler's arm as they hurried down the hallway.

"Grace, come to me." Dane's bellow grew more agitated. "Please, Grace."

Winston opened the door of the ducal apartments and motioned for Grace to enter. He followed and pointed to a closed door across the private salon. The entire ducal bedchamber was decorated in silver, gray, and black. It was elegant and masculine, like Dane.

Just as she reached for the door latch, the door swung open, and a footman looked straight ahead, neither acknowledging her nor Winston. She entered the room with Winston following a step behind her.

The lavish room was decorated for a king, with a massive four-poster bed with brocade curtains surrounding it. A fireplace held a robust fire, casting the room in a golden warmth.

When Grace realized Dane wasn't in bed, her gaze flew across the room until it landed on the most enormous copper tub she had ever seen. With wet hair and his back to her, Dane lay in the tub with his head resting on the lip. Two other footmen stood beside the tub as if keeping watch.

"Grace," he bellowed again.

Winston cleared his throat. "Lady Grace is here, sir."

"Oh." He sat up slightly as if surprised. "Ah, Gracie," Dane crooned loudly. "Finally, you're heeding my call." He braced his arms against the walls of the oblong tub and looked behind him. It took a moment for him to find her. "Come closer."

Grace took a step back. Not only was it awkward to be in his bedroom, but the man was naked and bathing in a tub. "That's not appropriate, Your Grace."

"Shush," he called out. He pointed to a spot next to his tub. "Come closer. I'm getting hoarse calling for her." He shook his head and laughed. "I mean calling for you."

Grace glanced at Winston, who nodded once. Slowly, she made her way to Dane's side.

"Why were you at the Jolly Rooster this evening?" Dane brought a wet linen towel to his chest. It was long enough to cover his torso. Who knew that Dane was modest?

When she reached his side, he picked up the toweling and twisted it, wringing the excess water from the linen.

Her gaze skimmed over his chest. As a young man, he had always been muscular. When they were younger, she studied his body whenever they swam together in the pond. It was a thing of beauty that always made her feel hot and achy. But as a man, he was incredible. Every defined muscle, sinew, and ligament begged to be touched. Her hand seemed to have a mind of its own as she reached for him, but thankfully, she jerked it away in time before anyone noticed.

"Everyone out except my Gracie."

Winston took a step forward. "No, Your Grace. That's improper."

"No, it's not. Grace is the queen of prim and proper. Or should I say the duchess of prim and proper." He bent his legs. "She'll protect me. Besides, she's marrying me."

"Dane," she murmured. "You're ill."

He grabbed one side of the tub and made his way to stand. He swayed as he stood. Water sluiced across the golden skin of his muscular backside. Unable to look away, she watched the water career in zigzags across his taut skin and muscles. Good lord, she was gawking at him like he was a sweet treat, and she was a starving woman.

"Could you help me, Grace?" He swayed again. "I seem to have lost my balance and can't find it anywhere."

The two footmen by the tub rushed forward and grabbed his arms, helping him out of the water. Winston ran to his side with a linen toweling. Dane batted it away and reached for a gold silk banyan. For a moment, she mourned the loss of viewing his magnificent body. What was wrong with her? The poor man was gravely ill. But even sick and fully covered, Dane was an imposing sight wearing such a garment.

She stared at the plush carpet to avoid seeing something she shouldn't. "Perhaps you should retire. Your body needs rest."

Dane nodded. "You need rest too, so you'll stay with me."

"Your Grace, no." Winston's objection sang through the air. "There are reputations to be considered."

No one moved or said a peep until Dane broke the silence. "Not to worry, Winston. My reputation is safe." He lifted his nose and tried to sniff the air but coughed instead. "Grace is here. She won't let anything happen to me."

Carefully, the footmen escorted him to his bed.

Winston turned to her. "I'm sorry. I don't think he knows what he's saying."

She patted his hand. "I'm sure once he's asleep, you'll be able to get some rest. Don't worry about me. I'll see myself out."

She hadn't taken two steps until Dane bellowed her name. "*Gracie.* Where are you off to? I told you that you must stay here."

Winston let out a pained sigh. "Your Grace, must I remind you that you have house guests who might overhear you?"

Dane sat on the edge of his bed, then waved away the footmen. Always a gentleman, he murmured, "Thank you for your assistance." He turned his attention to Winston. "I don't care. Marbury doesn't care. The only thing he cares about is Lady Athena." He laughed slightly, then turned his fevered gaze to her. "The only thing I care about is you." He swallowed, and the effort was difficult for him. "Will you please not leave me again?"

Grace stared at him for a moment. His eyes glistened with emotion. She'd never seen him this vulnerable in all the years they'd known one another.

"I'll beg if you want me to," Dane said softly. "I don't care if Winston, John, Harry, and Thomas see me. I don't care if all my other footmen see me. Add in all the rest of my staff, here and at the Jolly Rooster, too." He extended his hand. "Please, Grace. I need you."

The entreaty in his gaze almost brought her to her knees. "Do not fret. I will stay by your side as long as you need me to." She turned to Winston. "I'll help him fall asleep, then come find you."

Winston studied Dane and then turned to Grace. "Thank you, my lady." He pointed to the salon next door. "I will be in there with the door open if you need me."

"You will not sleep in there with the door open. Neither will Grace," Dane huffed out a command. "Winston, you shall sleep in your bed. Don't worry about Grace." The most wicked smile pulled at one corner of his mouth. "She's sleeping with me. In my bed." His balance wobbled, but he straightened his back, his arrogance fully displayed. "Where she belongs."

Winston motioned for the footmen to leave, then slid beside her. "Call if you need me." He glanced at Dane, then smiled softly. "He's adamant that you stay with him. He's as weak as a kitten. I've known him since he was a baby. He has a good heart—"

"Winston, I can hear you," Dane growled, then flexed his bicep. "I'm strong as a lion."

"Good night, Your Grace." Dane's butler winked at Grace. "Thank you for taking care of him." He turned and closed the door behind him.

"So, what shall we do?" Dane patted the bed beside him. "Come sit by me. We could play vingt et un, whist, hazard, or loo." He held his head in his hands. "I don't know where the cards are. I probably left them at the Jolly Rooster. I'll fetch them. I could ask Winston to bring more people into my room. We need five players for loo."

"Dane," she said softly. "Why don't you rest? I could read to you."

He wrinkled his nose. "That's boring." He waggled his eyebrows. "If we play hazard, then the loser of each hand must remove an item of clothing. What are you wearing?" He studied her attire. "By my calculations, you are wearing a dressing gown and a chemise. I'm wearing my banyan. You're at an advantage then."

"I never take advantage of a sick man." Grace shook her head with a smile. This was the Dane she knew from long ago. He was always self-assured and included her in every devilment or shenanigan he could think of.

With his eyes half closed, he began to unbutton his banyan. He fumbled with one button, then finally wrestled it open. "Take me off of this." He frowned. "I meant help me take this off. Then we'll take off your clothing."

"I don't think that's wise." She bit her lower lip to stifle a laugh as she pulled the banyan over his shoulders. "You'll catch a chill."

"I'll not suffer such a fate, especially if I see you naked," he murmured. "I'm always hot when you're close to me." With an exaggerated movement, he threw back the covers and then fell against the pillows. "This is the worst luck. I have the most beautiful woman in the world in my bedroom, and I'm ready to fall over."

Her heart swelled in her chest at the compliment. "Careful, Your Grace. I will write everything you say in my journal and read it back to you."

"If you publish it, I wager you'll sell a million copies. Everyone listens to what I say except you." He moved to the middle of the bed and leaned back against the stack of pillows. He closed his eyes and patted the bed. "Will you sit with me?" He opened one eye to peek at her.

Without saying a word, Grace joined him in bed. He was sitting in the bed with his long legs stretched before him. She scooted next to his body and mimicked his pose.

She reached over and felt his forehead. His fever had gone down. No doubt it was due to his bath. "If you become feverish again, I'll call the footman so you can take another bath."

"Thank you." He reached for her hand and entwined their fingers together. "Do you know you're the first woman I've ever had in my bedroom?" He squeezed her hand. "It's only fitting that it's you."

"I think there's a compliment in there, even if I'm acting as your nurse." She laughed softly as her heart pounded at his confession. Perhaps she was special to him.

"There is a compliment," he murmured. Slowly, he turned to her. "Your father loved you. Why do you suppose he didn't leave you an inheritance or even a dowry?"

It was on the tip of her tongue to scold him, but Grace relaxed. She'd never spoken any of it aloud. Perhaps it would ease the pain if she told someone. Plus, with Dane ill, he would never remember their conversation.

"Stewart went to London for the reading of the will. When he returned, he called me into my father's study, where he sat at Father's desk." She swallowed the hurt that had lodged in her throat. "He said that Father had been a reckless gambler and had lost everything. Stewart offered to send me to Northumberland to stay with his great-aunt. There was a farmer who had agreed to marry me."

"Please," he drawled. "You with a farmer in Northumberland? That's like marrying the sun to a rock. All that heat wasted on something that couldn't appreciate how extraordinary its rays are."

"That's a sweet thing to say." She looked at their clasped hands. There was no place else she'd rather be than by Dane's side, particularly when he was ill. She considered it a gift if she brought him comfort. If she had married Dane, how many evenings would they have spent just like this, sharing intimate details? She couldn't think that. It would make her ill, probably more so than Dane was currently. "Stewart told me I couldn't return home if I didn't marry the farmer. Hope agreed."

"You should have lived with me."

She placed her free hand over the middle of her chest. The memories still caused her heart to ache. "Hope told me that I should have married you. That I was a fool to have let you go."

"We all make mistakes, and you're not a fool. You never have been." Dane's eyes were closed. "I shouldn't have let you go."

She stilled for a moment. He was the one who had broken their engagement. Not her. Perhaps the fever impacted his memory.

"Tell me that they didn't turn you out."

"They did." Her voice was barely above a whisper. It hurt to say the words. Her own family did not care that she had no one to help her. Nor did they care that she was frightened. "I went to London and stayed in a church that first night."

"Oh my God, Gracie. Tell me you didn't." The anguish in his voice took her by surprise. "You should have come to me." He sat up and turned to her. "Were you by yourself? I should have never left you that day in our field."

"Dane, hush." She pressed a kiss to his forehead. It was somewhat cooler but still warm. "Here's something you might find amusing. I imagined ghosts rising from the crypts and brushing past me that night." She chuckled softly. "That made me realize I could not stay on my own. I needed help. The next day, I visited a friend from finishing school and stayed with her until I found an acceptable matron from whom I could rent a room. Then I went to a jeweler and sold my mother's pearl necklace for money." It had been the one her father had given her mother to celebrate Grace's birth. "After that, I started my business. Discreetly, of course."

"Of course," he echoed.

The room was silent except for the crackle of the logs in the fireplace.

Out of nowhere, Dane broke the quiet that surrounded them. "The necklace? It was the one with the sapphires?" Dane asked.

"Yes. I'm surprised you remember." She sniffed as tears threatened. "I had planned to give it to my daughter...but that wasn't to be."

Dane let go of her hand and pulled her near. The warmth of his body was a comfort she didn't know she needed.

"I remember everything. As soon as we both feel better, I'm going to wring your brother-in-law's neck. Then I'm going to find that farmer and give him a piece of my mind. The very idea that he thought I would give you up." He huffed a breath. "Then I'll find your necklace for you. You can still give it to our daughter."

She smiled slightly but didn't argue with him. When he was well, he wouldn't remember asking her to marry him or referring to their daughter. But for tonight, she'd pretend that he was still hers.

"I have a confession," he murmured.

"What is it?"

"On that field, I walked away from you before you could walk away from me. You see, I never felt love from my parents. It's more like apathy and rejection. As a young lad, I promised myself I'd never suffer through that again with anyone I loved." He pulled her tighter against him. "I loved you so much, Gracie." He closed his eyes as if in pain. "When you wrote me that letter and asked to meet, I was scared. I knew you were going to leave me. So, I thought if I let you go first, it wouldn't hurt as much." He leaned his head against hers as they stared at the fire. "I was wrong. It hurt more."

Her eyes brimmed with tears. One fell but thankfully, it was on the cheek he couldn't see. She wanted to gather him in her arms and give him everything he'd been denied and had denied for himself. When she remembered that day, there was a wildness, a defensiveness in him that she didn't recognize. It was his fear of losing her. Why hadn't she seen that? They'd always been there for each other ever since they were children. And she let him ride away without even fighting for him or for them. Regret for all their loss of not having each other through the years threatened to crush her.

Quiet descended again.

"I wasn't going to leave you that day." She sniffed and wiped her eyes. "Or at least, that hadn't been my plan."

"Hmm." Dane cleared his throat as if waking up from a cat nap. "The more time we're together, the more I think we can find our way back to each other. That's why I always want to kiss you."

She was instantly wide awake. Dane Ardeerton was a constant mystery. A part of her heart would always belong to him, but she had never dared to hope that he still cared for her the way she cared for him.

Yet, he still was cavorting with women on his lap.

He turned and looked at her. "Did you know that I named my cat after you?"

"No, you didn't. Your cat's name is Dancer." She released her breath. His changing the subject meant either he didn't remember what he'd just said, or he didn't want to delve into the subject any further. That was for the best. She had her own goals, and buying her own home was her first and foremost concern. Dane Ardeerton would never change. He'd proven that tonight. "Honoria told me that your cat is a wild thing that tortures Emmy to no end."

"Ack, Dancer is still a kitten. He's just defining his territory," he murmured. "D-a-n for Dane, and c-e for Grace. I added the 'r' because it fit his personality." He chuckled slightly. "He dances sideways before he attacks.

The room grew quiet again.

Her heart pounded, but she forced herself to ask the question. "What happened to Matthew?"

"I dismissed him." He pried one eye open and regarded her. "I know you enjoyed him. Frankly, I was a bit jealous. I cut a finer leg than he does," he scoffed. "But I didn't dismiss him for his legs. He tried to sell secrets about me to a gossip rag. I paid the editor to keep them quiet. I will not tolerate disloyalty."

"Do you know why he needed money?" She played with the edge of the cover and refused to look at him for fear he'd see the truth on her face.

"It didn't make any difference. I paid his wages, and he, in essence, was selling me. Hence, he betrayed me." He sighed and wrestled with the covers. "I don't want to talk about him anymore."

And neither did she. Her only salvation from earning his disgust would be if he fell in love with Athena. The thought crushed her. What had she been thinking? She should have never agreed to Marbury's proposal.

"Grace?"

"Hmm?"

"I'm done not taking risks for the people I love." His voice faded. "I'm loyal and protective to those I love and who love me."

What balderdash. She fought the tears that threatened to fall. She couldn't forget that he had women hanging all over him that very night.

Dane's soft snores fell into a rhythm that matched her breath. She had never experienced such an intimate yet bittersweet moment before. They could have had the life she had always dreamed of, but from his words, she knew that it was too late to try to find what they had once shared.

"There's one thing you should know, you sweet, aggravating man," she murmured. "Even though I shouldn't, I've loved you always and will forever, even though you have a nasty habit of having naked women on your lap."

Fourteen

Grace's eyes flew open the following day when she couldn't move. She was surrounded, encased, and hemmed in by a large, hot brick. Her eyes flew open when the sweet song of a wren greeted the new day. Panic flared when she couldn't move. It wasn't a brick lying on her but a large male.

Dane had buried his head against her neck, and his chest was atop hers. One long leg was thrown over her hips, pinning her in place.

A soft knock sounded on the door, and Winston entered the room. "Good morning, Your Grace."

Grace tried to roll Dane off her, but he was a dead weight.

Winston peeked around the room. "Lady Grace?"

With a pitiful voice, she called out, "Help."

Winston's eyes widened. "Oh, my dear lady, allow me to lend assistance." He rushed to the bed and pulled Dane toward him, thus freeing Grace.

"I hope you had a restful...night," the butler said with a smile as if it were a common occurrence to pull a duke off her body.

"It's not what you think." Grace scooted off the bed and stood. No doubt, he thought that she'd been intimate with Dane. Well, she had, but not in the manner Winston must have been thinking. "We simply talked, then fell asleep." None of the footmen or the maid even glanced her way. Her eyes locked with Winston's gaze. "You must believe me. Nothing happened."

Dane moaned and reached for her. "Grace, I'm cold."

Winston simply nodded. "Thank you for staying with him. You gave him great comfort yesterday and this morning. How is the patient?"

As soon as he placed his palm on Dane's forehead, another moan sounded. Dane batted it away. "Leave me. I need Grace."

"Yes, sir." Winston turned toward the door and snapped his fingers.

A parade of footmen entered the room carrying steaming buckets of water. Efficient and incredibly stealthy, they poured the water into the copper tub without hardly making a sound. Just as quietly as they entered, they left. Another footman walked in, followed by an upstairs maid. While the footman tended to the fire, the maid opened the drapes. They were greeted by a dreary yet typical English morning.

Winston came to her side. "He is quite hot and clammy. I took the liberty of ordering His Grace a bath. I also ordered one for you in your room."

"Thank you." Grace ran her hands down her dressing gown. "You're a godsend. I'll dress then depart with Lord Marbury and Lady Athena."

From the outside, the call of a coachman filled the room. "Come on, my boys, go to it." The lurch of the carriage and the clomp of horses' hooves signaled a departure.

"Was that Lord Marbury?" She rushed to the window to see a cloud of dust rising from the Pelham Hall drive. "He was supposed to wait for me."

Winston shrugged sheepishly. "I'm sorry, my lady. His lordship was in a high dudgeon this morning and insisted they leave."

"He left without me?" Grace hissed, then turned her gaze back to the window. Marbury's carriage turned out of Pelham Hall's circular drive, then disappeared from sight.

Winston stood beside her. "His lordship was quite peeved with His Grace for monopolizing your time last night. I tried to explain that His Grace was ill, but the man would not listen. He kept interrupting me."

Everything grew still. Slowly, Grace turned to Winston. "You're telling me that Lord Marbury knew I stayed in Dane's chambers last night?"

Winston stared at the floor and nodded sheepishly.

"Did he say anything?"

"No, ma'am. He just grumbled on his way out of the house. He took one of the maids as a chaperon." The butler lifted his gaze to hers. "But not to worry. He'll send her back to Pelham Hall as soon as they arrive in London."

Not to worry? This was an unmitigated disaster. Her reputation teetered on the edge of ruin. Not only was she not there to act as chaperone, but there was no telling what the young lord thought of her helping Dane last night. Knowing Marbury, he would likely think that she and Dane were having a torrid affair. If he had mentioned what had happened to anyone, it would have spread faster than wildfire to every sitting room and salon in London.

Grace squared her shoulders. It didn't matter what Marbury thought. She was helping a friend and nothing more. Her best recourse was to return to London as quickly as possible and try to minimize damage. She could not afford to lose any remaining clients if she wanted security for herself and Theo.

"Lady Athena said she would call on you when you return to London," Winston added. The beleaguered look on his face indicated that he realized the seriousness of the situation. "I'm sorry, Lady Grace, but he was despondent when he was calling for you. I was concerned that..."

Grace released a pent-up breath and placed her hand on the butler's arm. "You were concerned that His Grace might have screamed all night."

Winston nodded.

She glanced over at Dane, who, with the help of the footmen, was making his way to the bathing tub.

"I'll leave you with His Grace." She would bathe, finish packing, and then head to London herself. "I would like a carriage ready within the hour. I'll be heading to London myself."

"You can't stay?" A hint of hysteria sounded in Winton's voice.

Forceful but polite, she answered, "No."

"Do not let her leave," Dane grumbled.

Winston stood beside the tub and regarded him with clasped hands. "It's a bit difficult to explain that no carriages are available when you have ten housed here at Pelham Hall."

Not at all embarrassed about his naked body, Dane leaned forward in the tub and regarded his loyal butler. It wouldn't be the first or the last time that his butler saw him naked and vulnerable. Whenever Dane had been ill as a child, it was always Winston who sat with him so the other servants could rest at night.

"I don't care. Have the groomsmen take a wheel off of every vehicle. He closed his eyes and, with a gingered movement, reclined against the tub. "That will keep her here."

"Are you feeling better, sir?"

Dane lifted one eyelid and regarded his butler. "Only if Grace is here." She could not leave Pelham Hall until she agreed to marry him.

In deep thought, his butler tapped his cheek with one forefinger.

That was the problem with the blasted man. He never listened to Dane. Even though he had Dane's best interests at heart, he'd gone against Dane's plans. If Winston hadn't brought Grace to the Jolly Rooster, Dane could have convinced her with sweet words that she was everything to him. She wouldn't have been able to resist him. Heaven knew he couldn't resist her.

"You should know that I'm going to marry her."

Winston rocked back on his heels with a jubilant smile. "Excellent news, Your Grace. I'm glad things are once again progressing in that matter."

"She said no last night because she saw Sarah and Molly sitting on my lap. She thought I wanted to marry one of them." Dane rolled his eyes. "I told her they were my employees, but I'm not certain she believed me. Perhaps she should chat with them to understand what I was doing."

Dane dipped his head underwater and enjoyed the warmth of the bath. He should stay in the water for the entire day, and he would ask

Grace to bathe him. A sly smile tugged at his lips. Yes, she would never be able to resist him or his proposal if he could kiss her.

That was the thing between them. No matter their differences, there was no denying the heat that ignited between them when they were together. He'd never experienced anything like it, and he had only had it with Grace. He should hold a ball and have it in her honor after they marry.

He rose from the water and shook his head. Water drops flew everywhere. He would plan the ball himself after he took a brief nap.

"Hmph." Winston scowled. "Why wouldn't she believe you?"

Dane pursed his lips as a jolt of shame hit him. "Perhaps because of what her father saw at the Jolly Rooster after I asked her to marry me the first time."

"You never explained it to her?"

Dane shook his head. "An error on my part."

"A major one." Winston stuck his nose in the air, reminding Dane of himself. It was pure dismissal. "My mother always said it's better to clean the entire floor than to sweep the dirt under the rug. The hidden dirt will eventually show up again."

Dane closed his eyes. "I'm too sick for riddles."

Winston blinked like an owl. "Sometimes it's best to confess, ask for forgiveness, and hopefully, start anew. Have you ever considered how Lady Grace must have felt when she told her father you wanted to marry her, and he confided that on that very day, you had other women on your lap while you gambled? She had to have been humiliated and devastated."

"I didn't sleep with those women." Dane's voice rose in anger.

"Does it make a difference?" Winston tilted his head as if contemplating his question, then shook his head. "More importantly, would it make a difference to Lady Grace? You should have talked to her then and begged forgiveness."

"I know." Humiliated, Dane plunged his head into the water. He was hiding like a turtle in its shell. Still, his clever butler was correct. If Winston thought his actions unacceptable, no wonder Grace didn't want to have anything to do with him. A sudden pain erupted in the middle of his chest. He hadn't felt it since that day on the field. He'd broken her heart and, in doing so, had broken his own.

And his had never mended.

He had felt like a coward and hadn't wanted to lose her then. He could only hope he wouldn't lose her after they found peace between them last night.

He came up for air. "You're right. I'll speak to her."

"Good luck, sir." Winston clasped his hands in front of him. "Regarding last night, please allow me to see if I can help. Lord Marbury stopped in the village this morning and was as chatty as he was sour. He told anyone who listened why they were leaving Pelham Hall. I know what to do to sway Lady Grace's opinion."

If Dane wasn't so weak, he would ask his butler more. But if Winston had a plan, Dane was all for it.

Winston had a talent for accomplishing the impossible.

Even if it might be a little underhanded.

But Dane could support his butler's efforts. After all, every advantage was fair in love and war.

But first, he had to explain some things.

Grace munched on a piece of toast as she stared out the window and studied the view. The formal gardens at Pelham Hall were a thing of beauty, and she'd always enjoyed spending time in them. It was such a shame that she was leaving within the hour and couldn't take a walk. However, she had important business in London. Specifically, she had to meet with Marbury and explain what had happened last night.

She took a sip of tea and marveled at how well she felt. The bath rejuvenated her, and she was anxious to travel home.

A footman entered the room and nodded in her direction. "Ma'am, I hate to intrude, but it will be impossible for you to return to London today. The carriages are currently being repaired."

She placed her hands in her lap and smiled at the footman. By the look on his face, she knew that he was telling a falsehood. Well, she'd put him out of his misery. "No need to explain. I am certain His Grace said that I couldn't take one." She lifted her serviette and patted her lips. "It makes little difference if the duke's carriages are unavailable. I'll take a dog cart to London if I have to." She tilted her head and then smiled. "Is His Grace's curricle available for a trip to town? I can manage one of those quite well. My father taught me."

Before the footman could utter an answer, Winston swept into the room. "The parish vicar, Mr. Stephenson, is calling. He's waiting in the family salon. Allow me to escort you."

"He's waiting for me?" she asked. "How would he even know I was here?"

"Lord Marbury shared the news of His Grace's illness. It's spread throughout the village. The vicar wants to hear about His Grace's health this morning." He swept an arm toward the door. "I've told him everything I know. Now, he's asking for you. Come, my lady."

Grace stood and followed the butler up the stairs to the second floor, where the family salon and the private chambers of the Duke of Pelham were. With an efficiency that belied his age, Winston strolled down the passageway and threw open the door.

Chatter filled the air. It wasn't just the vicar present but the entire village from its appearance.

Once Winston cleared his throat, all conversation ceased.

Without hesitating, an older man approached with a genuine smile. "Good morning, Lady Grace. I'm Mr. Stephenson, the village vicar." He smoothed the brim of the hat he was holding in his hand. "We were wondering how the duke is this morning. Lord Marbury said you were nursing the duke back to health."

Grace's heart slowed its rhythm. There was no telling what else Marbury had said that morning. She glanced around the room at all the expectant faces. Remembering her manners, Grace smiled in greeting. She had no idea who these people were since she hadn't lived in the area for years. "Perhaps Winston should be the one to explain."

When she turned to Winston, the blasted man had disappeared, leaving her with all the guests. They looked at her as if she were the mistress of the house and knew all.

"My lady, I'm Mr. Bennett, the muffin man." A middle-aged man with brown hair that glistened with touches of distinguished gray approached her. "The duke is my best customer." The man chortled slightly. "The duke says my muffins are the best he's ever tasted. I've brought some and left them with Cook. I hope he enjoys them. And you, as well. He was a godsend when my family first moved here. We were down to our last shilling. I was fearful that I would have to beg for food. But the duke magnanimously offered us a place to live and set up a shop with the largest oven I'd ever seen."

The vicar frowned. "He knows the meaning of magnanimous?"

"Hush," an elderly lady hissed at the vicar, then turned to the muffin man. "Mr. Bennett, *not yet.*"

"Oh, pardon me," Mr. Bennett said in apology. "I was supposed to say something else." He glanced sheepishly at Grace and cleared his throat. "We're all worried about the duke."

The elderly woman who'd taken the vicar and the muffin man to task turned her way with a delightful smile. "I'm Mrs. Hughes of the lady auxiliary. We must know how the duke is feeling." She looked at her companion and waved a hand. "This is Mrs. Morris."

The elderly woman at Mrs. Hughes's side nodded in greeting, then patted Grace's arm. "Word has it that you spent the night with him. That was a kind gesture. We're all delighted he's in such good hands." She smiled serenely at her companion.

Alarm bells rang in her ears, making her incapable of forming a coherent thought. She was ruined if every villager knew where she slept last night.

"I...I," Grace faltered.

"Lord Marbury said you didn't leave the duke's side all night. Mrs. Hughes and I are forever grateful to you and the Duke of Pelham. He offers us the use of the Jolly Rooster for our meetings."

"As long as he doesn't have any games of chance scheduled," Mrs. Hughes chortled, then swallowed her laughter. "I only meant *if* His Grace didn't have any of those dashing gentlemen visiting from London that day."

Mrs. Morris nodded. "There's nothing uncouth or vulgar about the Duke of Pelham's card games. We assure you, my lady. His Grace takes his games very seriously."

"Indeed," Mr. Bennett agreed.

"Ma'am?" Mr. Stephenson asked. "How is His Grace feeling this morning?"

They all held an expectant expression, waiting for her explanation. Grace blinked slowly. What was she supposed to say? Even acting as if she could relay any information about Dane's condition was a step too far, even if they were in Amesbury.

"I'll tell you how he is," a voice called from behind Grace. "He has a fever."

Grace turned and discovered a disheveled middle-aged woman with long, tangled gray hair that hung loosely about her shoulders.

Without introducing herself, she walked forward with a slight limp. "I apologize for my tardiness. It couldn't be helped. The cat got out." She held a bottle in her hand and gave it to Grace. "Here. Give him a spoonful in the morning and evening. And give him another dose if he wakes up in the middle of the night. That will drive the cough out of his chest."

"Along with the devil," someone murmured behind Grace's back.

Without taking offense, the old woman threw back her head and laughed. She was missing several teeth and didn't care if anyone saw that. When she finished her laughing spell, she winked at Grace. "I'm Mrs. Grimalkin. I'm an apothecary by trade."

"As well as a witch," Mr. Stephenson offered.

Grace whipped her gaze to the vicar, who shrugged.

"Ack," Mrs. Grimalkin snickered. "'Tis true. I used my special cards last night. Someone had to find out about the duke's health. Oh, before I forget, this is for you to hang in the duke's bedroom." She pulled a glass ball with a string attached at the top from her pocket. "Place this witching ball in the window closest to where he sleeps tonight. It'll cast out the evil spirits. Also, it would do the duke some good to gargle salt in his water. Have him spit it out; he should not swallow it." She nodded once. "It's nice to meet you, Lady Grace Webster. I'm sure we will see each other again."

With that cryptic statement, Mrs. Grimalkin turned and left Grace with the rest of the villagers.

"Best do as she says," Mrs. Morris said. "As the village witch, she can predict the future."

"And cure sore throats," Mrs. Hughes added.

"And deliver babies," Mr. Stephenson said. "She's a valuable member of our village. Just as the duke is, he's a man with a heart of gold. He'd give the coat off his back to someone in need."

"He would lay his best morning coat in a mud puddle if one of us were crossing the street." Mrs. Hughes said unashamedly. "He loves dogs, cats, and especially children."

"And spinsters," Mrs. Morris added before her eyes widened. "But not inappropriately. I've never seen him be untoward to any female. Especially a spinster like yourself."

Grace merely blinked at the insult.

"Heavens, no," Mrs. Hughes agreed. "He's dutiful and respectful of all women. But you are not a spinster. You're a very accomplished senior debutant."

Mrs. Morris nodded.

Grace wanted to roll her eyes but smiled instead.

"Rumor has it that he's found his duchess," Mr. Bennett said.

"I only hope I'm the one to perform your ceremony," Mr. Stephenson said boldly. "You'll make a beautiful bride."

The rest of the guests murmured their agreement.

"Well, we best get going so you can give the duke his tonic. Give him our regards." Mr. Bennett nodded at the others, then bowed to Grace. "Thank you for taking care of him, my lady. He's truly a gift to our village and takes care of all of us. He needs you. Be gentle with him."

"Gentle with him?" What in the world was happening with these people? It was almost as if they were trying to convince her that Dane was some virtuous paragon of goodness.

No one answered her as they shuffled from the room. An odd assortment of "thanks" filled the air. After the last guest left the room, Grace collapsed on the nearest brocade club chair. What in the world was that about? It was almost as if they'd known that she was leaving for London and wanted to ensure that she understood Dane's worth to them. It had to have been Dane and Winston's machinations that brought them to Pelham Hall this morning.

She studied the bottle that Mrs. Grimalkin left for her. She lifted the stopper and smelled the pleasant fragrance of witch hazel. The advice to have Dane gargle salt water was also sound. She would find Winston and tell him what had been discussed so he could help Dane after she left for London. He could also decide where to hang the witching ball.

She had other matters to attend to. If need be, she'd go to the Jolly Rooster and see if she could hire a carriage and a driver. Of course, it would cost a fortune, but if she didn't return to London as soon as possible and secure her reputation and business, she wouldn't have any money.

Before she could rise and find Winston, two pretty ladies entered the room. One had a mane of fiery red hair, and the other had glistening dark brown locks. They smoothed their dresses as if they were nervous.

"My lady?" One of the young women stepped forward. "I'm Molly Adams, and this is Sarah Foley." She dipped a curtsey.

The other young woman did the same.

"If you're searching for the other villagers, I'm afraid they just left." Suddenly, like a bolt of lightning, Grace recognized the two women. They were the ones who had been sitting on Dane's lap last night.

"May we have a word with you?" Sarah asked meekly.

Before she could answer, the two women came closer and stood before her.

Molly was the one with red hair. She nodded once at Sarah, who took a deep breath and then turned her full attention to Grace.

"My lady, I don't want you to have the wrong impression of the duke and us. You see, he was—" Sarah bent her head as if she couldn't go on.

Molly patted her on the back and soothed her. "Let me finish, dear." She turned her blue-eyed gaze to Grace. "That rat, Lord Brixworth, wouldn't stop touching Sarah. I told Mr. Atwater, the majordomo, and he came straight to His Grace." Her cheeks matched the color of her hair, betraying her anger. "The duke protects his family, and we're part of his family." She narrowed her eyes and regarded Grace. "His Jolly Rooster family."

Sarah wiped her eyes and took a steadying breath. Her gaze met Grace's. The young woman's determination shone brightly in her eyes.

"I need to tell you a story about the duke. Once, I thought I was in love. He was a coachman who said the same to me. Then he left in the middle of the night after I told him I was carrying. My parents threw me out of their house. With no one else to help me, I went to the duke, who gave me a house without asking for rent and allowed me to earn a living washing the linens for the Jolly Rooster." A tear streaked down her cheek. "He's the best of men." She shook her head adamantly. "He has never been inappropriate with any of his staff."

Molly nodded her agreement. "It was our idea to sit on his lap and stand beside His Grace. We knew that Lord Brixworth"—she sneered when she said his name—"would only have eyes on us. He's a menace with his unwanted advances to women." She was practically spitting with rage. "After the duke won the game and the property last night, he ordered that Brixworth be thrown out and never allowed to return to the Jolly Rooster."

"Property?" Grace narrowed her eyes.

Molly stilled and looked at Sarah. "Do you know what property he won?"

Sarah shook her head. For the first time since she'd entered the room, Sarah smiled. "His Grace wanted you to leave last night because he didn't want you in danger. But he wasn't himself. It was apparent that he was ill when he left the inn. He came straight home to you."

Well, he took his time and ensured that he finished the game and won his property before he came home, even if he was ill. Was this something her mother experienced with her father, a man who loved to gamble to the exclusion of all else?

"He only has eyes for you, my lady." Molly nodded. "He has your initials carved with his in the entry."

Through the roaring din in her ears at the news, she squeaked out, "What?"

"'Tis true, my lady. No one had ever noticed until Molly's son, Tim, saw it one day when he was nine. He was always an observant lad." Affection rang in her voice. "He asked the duke about it, and His Grace said that the initials belonged to the woman he would marry one day."

Grace stood up, completely startled by the news. "I'm not certain I understand."

Molly's slow smile reminded Grace of a sphinx. "He's yours. Always has been."

Maybe she did understand. A sudden warmth slapped her cheeks. *It was their initials* intertwined on the plaque at the Jolly Rooster. Perhaps his time with Molly and Sarah had been well-intentioned. But what about all those years ago?

The longcase clock struck the half hour.

"We must go," Sarah bowed again. "We're preparing for Tim's wedding breakfast tomorrow."

"Wait," Grace said. "I thought you said Tim was nine years old."

"That was nine years ago, my lady," Molly said with a chuckle. "Shortly after the duke bought the Jolly Rooster."

They both took their leave. Grace looked at the bottle still in her hands, then slowly sat in the club chair. Could he have been pining after her for nine long years? She shook her head. It was impossible. Yet, why would Molly and Sarah tell her a falsehood? These people adored Dane. And it wasn't because he was a duke or a handsome man or a prodigal gambler. They loved him because he cared for them and protected them as if they were his own family.

She buried her head in her hands. Slowly, she lifted her head. There was no denying he was a scoundrel, a walking scandal, a rogue, and an altogether infuriating man.

But he was caring, giving, protective, and too handsome for his own good.

He apparently wanted her to stay at Pelham Hall if he had made excuses that all the carriages, carts, and even his curricles were unavailable.

She clasped the bottle to her chest. Perhaps she could stay until his fever broke. This was her chance to ask about that night nine years ago.

Then, she'd leave and take care of her business in London.

Perhaps his fever-induced confession was the truth.

It was hard to fathom that Dane Ardeerton had loved her all these years.

Especially when he called her nothing but a Scottish wildcat.

Fifteen

"Where is she?" Dane's head throbbed from all his bellows.

"She had visitors." Winston held out his palms in an attempt to keep him calm.

"Who called on her? For how long? Where is she now?" He didn't care who heard his rant. He wanted Grace in his bedroom, and the blasted woman had not been to see him in three hours. She couldn't leave him again. "I cannot rest if she isn't here."

"Yes, Your Grace. I will fetch her immediately."

As soon as Winston turned to leave, Grace entered the room. "What is the meaning of all that shouting? You sound like a rooster and one that isn't very jolly."

His butler smiled in relief and went to greet her. Grace held out a bottle, and Winston muttered something before leaving the room.

With another bout of dizziness, Dane collapsed against a pile of pillows. "Finally, you're here."

"You remind me of a petulant child."

"You saw my body. I'm anything but a child." Color painted her cheeks, and he grinned. *Ah yes. His Grace had enjoyed the view.* "Are you blushing?"

"Stop," she scolded, then softened her voice. "Is your fever returning?" Grace came to his side and laid her cool palm against his forehead.

"Yes. I'm fevered because I am burning for you."

She scowled at his flirting.

He took her hand in his and pulled her near. "I've missed you."

She sat on the bed next to him. "I've only been gone a few hours."

"My heart can't tell time. It just knows when you're absent." He waited for her to offer a sarcastic comment as he studied her. Instead, her blush reminded him of rose buds. He scooted over and patted the bed. "Who came to see you?"

"Quite a cast of characters who sang your praises." Composing herself, she narrowed her eyes playfully. "I met the vicar, the muffin man, Mrs. Hughes, Mrs. Morris, and finally Mrs. Grimalkin. Somehow, they were aware that I had spent the night with you. Mrs. Grimalkin brought you this and instructed me that you take a spoonful day and night, as well as when you have a fever." She handed him the bottle, then picked up a spoon from his side table. "Winston says the woman is known for her herbal remedies."

Dane opened the bottle and sniffed. "I've had this before. It's a miracle potion." He took the spoon and poured himself a dose. When finished, he returned the bottle to Grace, who set it on the side table.

"She also brought you a witching ball." Grace grinned as she pulled the glass ball from her pocket. "She will use every weapon in her arsenal to see you well."

Dane took it and carefully placed it on the side table. "She brings one every time she visits." He patted the bed. "Sit with me." He was on his best behavior. Perhaps he was acting juvenile, but he didn't want her far from his side. When Grace rose from the bed and reached for a chair next to the bed, he took her hand. "I meant sitting next to me here."

Grace released a heavy sigh, then scooted next to him. "I was sitting in this exact position last night."

"And this morning, you hugged me in this bed." He turned to view her better, then waggled his eyebrows. "I'd like you to repeat that if you don't mind."

"I was trying to push you off. You are quite heavy, and you had me pinned under you," she protested but smiled. "I'm glad you're feeling better. I was worried about you last night."

"I have an excellent nurse." He brushed a stray lock of hair off her forehead and tucked it behind her ear.

She mimicked his pose. "Molly and Sarah from the Jolly Rooster also visited me. Did you have Winston send them to me?"

"No," he murmured as he stared into her face. From what little he remembered of that night, Grace was livid when she saw him with the women. He slammed his eyes shut as memories flooded his thoughts. For the love of all men, Molly and Sarah had dressed in silk gowns that were split down the middle, revealing their breasts. He remembered playing against Brixworth, and Molly and Sarah thought to distract the man if they showcased their cleavage. The story was even more horrific when he remembered that other women, members of the demimonde, were present as well.

No wonder Grace had been so angry with him.

She scowled as she bit her lip, revealing her apprehension.

"How did you know where to find me?"

She released a painful sigh. "Marbury. When he returned from finding you at the Jolly Rooster, he told Athena to pack and that they were leaving first thing that morning. He told me what he'd discovered as soon as she left us. I was so angry with you that I made Winston send for a carriage. I wanted to find you, give you the devil, then terminate our agreement."

He had to keep his emotions under control. His inn and employees were important to him, but Grace was everything. "And then when you found me?" he asked, spacing the words evenly.

"It reminded me of the last time we'd fought over the Jolly Rooster."

He nodded slowly. "Grace, they were not there with me, and more importantly, I wasn't with them." He took his hand and entwined their fingers together.

"Molly and Sarah told me what you were doing." She glanced at their hands. "You wanted to win a property and then banish him from the Jolly Rooster."

He brought their clasped hands to his mouth and kissed the top of her knuckles. "I lost track of time. I never should have stayed there that long. I think the fever made me dull-witted. But it's more than that. Brixworth had something that didn't belong to him. I'd been trying to win it for years." He wouldn't tell her it was her father's summer estate until he knew the whole story. He didn't want to upset her needlessly. "It was a warning to anyone who dares to treat the people I care about in a demeaning manner. I'll do everything in my power to protect them."

"That's very noble."

"That's me, a knight in shining armor."

"Hmm," she hummed sleepily. "By the looks of you last night, your armor needed a little polishing."

"Are you saying I'm sullied?" He wanted to shout to the heavens when she leaned against his shoulder. But he decided against it since he'd been loud enough last night to wake everyone in Pelham Hall. Instead, he wrapped an arm around her waist and tugged her closer to his chest. He pulled her near, never wanting to let her go. "What happened to your father's summer estate?"

"The earl owns it." Her voice softened. "Ask him."

"I will." It was now or never for him to explain what happened all those years ago. He turned slightly. "I need your forgiveness for what happened nine years ago."

Her slight snore was his answer.

He pressed a kiss to the top of her head. "Rest now, Gracie. I have plans for you this evening. But if you're wondering, I feel much better now that you're where you should always be. In my arms."

Dane didn't know how long they slept, but it had grown dark outside. Grace was still sound asleep beside him when he woke. Careful not to disturb her, he slid across the bed and then walked to the other side. As he peered down at her, he smiled and then bit his lip not to laugh aloud. She resembled his Grace from old. A smattering of freckles frolicked across her nose and cheeks, and a slight smile tugged at her lips. He leaned down, gently pressed his lips to her forehead, and then closed his eyes. He wasn't a religious man, but then and there, he said a silent thank you for having her back in his life. He'd do everything in his power to make her happy. He tucked the bedcovers around her, then quietly entered the attached salon.

Two footmen stood outside his apartment doors.

"Your Grace, how are you feeling," John asked.

"Much better, thank you. I shall take another bath. Would you bring another tub and place it in here?" He glanced at the closed door to his bedroom. "Hmm, Lady Grace is still resting. I don't want to wake her."

Ever efficient, his staff had his bath prepared in record time. Thankfully, Winston had sent several trays of food for them to eat. Dane wanted to stay in the cocoon he and Grace had created over the last day, so he dismissed the footmen.

He slid into the warm water and relaxed as he washed. Tonight, he would take responsibility for his deplorable actions. He only prayed it would be enough to earn Grace's forgiveness. He was no longer that wounded young man who thought to strike first before someone could hurt him. He wanted the life they had planned to share with one another.

He would devote his life to making her happy and ensure that her days were filled with love and laughter. After everything she'd done for his family and him, that was the least he could do for Grace. He just hoped it was enough to make amends for his past.

"I wondered where you were." Grace strolled into the room. She glanced at the tub, and instantly, her cheeks reddened. "Shall I give you privacy?" She walked toward the door.

"Come to me, Grace," he held out his hand. Water sluiced down his arm, some dripping on the carpet below. He could have cared less. His only concern was her. "I need you."

She raised her gaze and studied his chest. He leaned back against the tub and rested his arm against the side, giving her a better view of his body. Her cheeks were even redder, if that was possible when she raised her gaze to his. He wanted to preen like a peacock that his hen was so enthralled with his body. But now was not the time. He needed to say his piece.

After hesitating, she came to his side and sat beside the tub. "The physician should be here soon."

"I'm sending him back to London. I don't need him." He cupped his hands and threw water on his face. "Not when I have you. The best medicine anyone could offer me."

She rolled her eyes and then locked her gaze with his. "Dane, don't be ridiculous."

"I'm not. I'm being truthful."

She clasped her hands around her bent legs and stared at her stockings. "So, you're feeling better."

"As long as you're by my side."

"I need to return to London."

"Not yet," he whispered. "We should discuss our past."

She sighed, the woeful sound tugging at his heart. "I understand what happened last night," she said, blinking twice. "However, I don't understand the time you had naked women on your lap when we parted."

He wrung out the linen toweling, then rested against the back of the copper tub, feeling a devastating shame wash over him. If only he could wash it away. Oh, he could throw out some pithy saying that he was a duke and could do what he wanted, but this was *his Grace*. She deserved the truth, no matter how foolish it sounded.

"I was young and prideful. When I told my father that I was marrying you, he forbade me. He punched me in the face after I said I would defy him. The only thing I could think about was proving to him that I was a man and didn't need him or his approval."

Her eyes widened in shock. "Your father was the one who hit you?"

Dane nodded once.

"No parent should hit their child no matter how old he is or what he said." Her eyes glistened with tears. "I'm so sorry, Dane."

He wanted to lean over and comfort her. But he had to tell her everything before he could earn the right to touch her again.

"I had no idea he thought so ill of me." She shook her head. "But your father should have explained his reasons."

"He didn't think about us. He only wanted control over his heir and the dukedom." Dane waved a hand, sending water splattering against the copper tub. It hit him square in the face. *Fitting.* He sniffed, then wiped his face. But none of that mattered—not his father's schemes, not his wounded pride. Only this. Only her.

"My father is not what's important. My confession is."

His breath shuddered as hot tears burned his eyes and nose. He tilted his head back, blinking furiously at the ceiling, as if the answer to his idiocy might be written there in bold letters: *PELHAM, YOU ARE A COMPLETE AND UTTER FOOL.*

"I wanted to win money so we could marry in Scotland," he rasped. "I wanted to set us up in a modest home and never have to crawl to my father for help. I wanted to care for you, Grace. I wanted to be your hero." His throat thickened with emotion and the sheer foolishness of his past. "And this is the shameful part. I was a damned fool."

His voice turned hoarse, and his hands trembled, but he made himself look at her—really look at her. At the tears shimmering in her beautiful eyes. At the heartbreak he had put there.

"I was flattered, Grace." The admission tasted bitter on his tongue. "Those women...they laughed at my jokes. Which, let us be honest, aren't even that good." He let out a short, humorless laugh. "They sat in my lap. Told me I was charming. And did I send them away like a man with half a brain would do? Of course not. I basked in it like a complete and utter buffoon."

His chest ached with disgust at his arrogance. "And after I won Scoville's money, they wanted to take me to bed to celebrate. And do you know what I said?" His breath hitched. "I told them it was a lovely offer, but I had the woman of my dreams waiting for me."

He dragged a hand through his wet hair. "Which, in my mind, meant I had acted with honor." He let out a sharp, self-mocking laugh. "And yet, somehow, I missed the obvious. Letting them linger, letting them fawn over me, and allowing them to turn me into some prize stallion at Tattersalls made me an absolute arse. All in front of the Jolly Rooster patrons. They saw my stupidity." His voice broke at the next humiliating part. "You were waiting for me, thinking the worst. And why wouldn't you? I gave you every reason to."

A single tear slid down his cheek, and he wiped it with a rough hand. But it wasn't enough—it would never be enough because nothing could erase the hurt he had caused her.

"Know this, Grace." He leaned forward. "If I had known the cost of my vanity, I would have thrown every last guinea at their feet and run like the devil was on my heels because I lost you that night. The most important person in my world."

Tears streamed down her face now, each one slicing through his heart like a blade. He reached out on instinct before catching himself.

Right. He didn't have the right to comfort her. Not yet. Maybe not ever.

"Don't cry, Grace." His voice was wrecked, broken. "I'm not worth it."

She inhaled a shaky breath. "But we were."

His stomach twisted. "God, I know. I know." His shame threatened to suffocate him. "The thought that you would believe I was unfaithful sickens me. Not because I don't deserve your mistrust—but because I hurt you. I witnessed what infidelity did to my parents. I saw the destruction it caused to them, my sisters, and me. I promised I would never be like them, Grace. I would never do that to you, the woman I loved. And I didn't." He let out a sharp breath, shaking his head. "And yet, with my sheer, unmatched stupidity, I committed something just as heinous."

Another tear fell, then another. "There isn't a single day that I don't regret what I did. Though I won Scoville's money, I lost everything that mattered."

He bowed his head, the weight of his failures pressing him down, making breathing impossible. But he forced himself to lift his gaze—to meet hers.

"I hope you can forgive me." The words were barely above a whisper. "And if you can't... it's what I deserve. If you want to throw something at me, I won't even dodge."

She nodded with a grin, then stared at him for an eternity, her tears glistening like tiny, unbearable stars. "I forgive you," she whispered.

The breath left his lungs in a shudder. He had no right to it—no right to hope or redemption. But she had given it to him anyway.

He swallowed hard, his voice rough with solemnity. "For the rest of my life, I will prove that your forgiveness was not in vain."

She held his gaze, and for the first time in years, something fragile and precious flickered between them.

"It's done, Dane," she murmured. "I understand. We were both young and foolish." A tremulous smile curved her lips, soft and bitter-sweet. "Thank you for telling me. Let us look to the future."

He let out a breath he hadn't known he'd been holding.

The future. With her. It was more than he deserved. But God help him, he would spend every moment ensuring he did.

He lowered his voice. "Let's think about tonight as well." He reached for her with a trembling hand, expecting her to pull away, but she didn't. He trailed a knuckle across her cheek, marking her with a glistening water trail on her delicate skin. "And us."

A cloud of doubt darkened her honey-brown eyes. "We should discuss your duchess before we do anything we regret. You haven't even met all the people I had planned to introduce to you."

"I don't want them, Gracie. I told you last night I found her."

"I thought you were hallucinating." A hint of teasing brightened her voice. "You had a high fever when you said that."

"Minx," he growled. "We're talking about our future."

She chuckled softly, then rested her head on her knees while wearing an impudent grin.

But as the seconds ticked by, she grew serious, and her gaze gleamed with wonder and hope. He felt the same.

"Let me show you what I feel for you." He leaned near, the movement jostling the water in the tub.

She halved the distance between them. Their breaths mingled much like a prelude to a kiss. But she didn't move any closer. She simply stared into his eyes.

"I won't kiss you unless you tell me it's what you want." His voice broke with huskiness.

She nodded.

"Say the words," he demanded softly. "Tell me." Inch by inch, he trailed his fingers across the silk of her dressing gown that hid her collarbone. Her pulse pounded in her neck, the movement mimicking her heartbeat.

When he lifted his gaze to hers, the longing in her eyes almost undid him.

Like water breaking from the dike, the words escaped Grace. "Kiss me."

Without hesitation, Dane stood, and she did the same. He stepped out of the bath and wrapped her in his strong embrace. She didn't care that his body was wet; he had her in his arms, and the comfort felt like home, a place she'd missed for so long. But it was new. He'd changed through the years just as she had. She nestled against his strong shoulder, then tilted her head and wrapped her arms around his neck. She could put the past behind her. They had been so young and headstrong back then. She could forgive him and start anew.

With a wicked grin, he studied her for a moment. "I will kiss you, Grace, but know this, tonight—"

She pressed her finger against his lips. "Tonight is for us."

"Tonight is for you." He grinned.

When he brushed his lips against hers, it was the first volley in this newness between them. There was only one thing she could do, and that was willingly surrender everything—her reservations, her thoughts, and her very being—to Dane, the only man she'd ever given her heart to. The world around them faded away as she focused only on the sensation of his touch. She reveled in the sound of his groan against her mouth, a primal noise that ignited a fire that she never thought would extinguish.

His kiss deepened, and he pressed the tip of his tongue against her lips, beckoning for entry. When she opened herself to him, his tongue slid against hers in a movement so familiar that it felt as if they'd done this every day of their lives. Her arms tightened around his neck, pulling him near as he held her against his body. He tasted of mint and something else that reminded her of the sweet air of a summer storm, electrifying her senses. Her heart raced as her head spun from the sensations. At that moment, all thoughts of their pasts disappeared from her mind. She was fully present and blissfully lost in him.

Where she was soft and malleable, he was hard and unyielding. Her skin burned from the heat between them, her breasts heavy and craving his touch. And where his hard cock pressed against her abdomen, she longed for him to take her—all of her.

She let out a small whimper of protest when he pulled away slightly. His presence surrounded her, his arms providing a safe haven as she melted into him. Dane had been correct when he declared that this night was a singular moment they shared. No one would discover what they did in his apartments. A heady feeling gave her the affirmation to take what she wanted tonight without fear of reprisal.

"More?" His gaze was unrelenting as he searched her face.

She nodded.

He pressed a kiss to her nose. "More what?"

"Mmhmm," she hummed softly, her eyes falling shut as his lips pressed kisses against her neck in a feather-light touch, sending shivers down her spine.

He moved his head and brushed his mouth against the shell of her ear, sending tingles through her whole body.

"You have to tell me what you want." His lips gently grazed the shell of her ear again as if he were testing the waters. Then, they moved across her cheek and to her jawline, leaving tiny kisses in their wake. "Because I will never disrespect you again."

"Do tell," she retorted playfully. "So, no more wildcat?"

"Someone is being very witty tonight." He trailed his lips across her cheek. "Or perhaps you're being naughty."

"I don't want to be either. I simply want you."

"To do what?"

She gulped a breath and lifted her gaze to his. "Make love to me," she said softly.

He finally quit teasing her when his lips met hers in a soft, tender kiss that sent warm tingles through her body. His touch was feather-light, and she melted into it, losing herself in the moment. She closed her eyes and inhaled his fresh scent of sandalwood and pine.

His touch was gentle yet powerful, making her feel safe and vulnerable. His lips trailed down her neck, leaving kisses and gentle nibbles, making her shiver with anticipation.

Their faces were inches apart, his warm breath fanning across her cheek. She leaned into him, her chest rising and falling rapidly. The movement tortured her sensitive nipples. As he explored her mouth with his once again, his hand inched higher, stopping just below her neckline.

She moaned into the kiss, her fingers threading through his soft hair as he trailed his thumb over her skin, resting it on the pulse point at the base of her neck.

"I feel your heartbeat thundering. It matches mine." When he kissed her this time, there was an urgency, a hunger that wasn't there before. His hands roamed over her backside, learning every inch of her once again.

"Dane," she murmured.

"I've waited for you and this night for nine years." Without another word, He swept her into his arms and started toward his bedroom.

She squeaked in surprise as she tightened her arms around his neck. "Are you strong enough?"

Dane immediately stopped, his eyes latching on hers. Then, like the arrogant duke he was, he winged a haughty eyebrow.

"I meant, have you recovered enough?" Like a schoolgirl, she blushed.

With a wicked grin, he pinched her bottom. "You will just have to wait and see."

Dane laid Grace on his bed. There was no rush tonight. He planned to savor every inch of her, wanting her to know how precious she was to him. Without breaking her gaze, he climbed over her.

"Touch me," she begged when she pulled his hand to her breast. "Here."

He traced her collarbone, and Grace growled. "Not there."

He nipped her shoulder, then squeezed one breast gently before lowering his hands and untying her dressing gown. He pulled the folds apart. Underneath, she wore a chemise. His breath stilled at the way her breasts pushed against the muslin fabric. Her nipples poked through the thin material.

"Let's get this off you." He helped her remove the garment, then sent it sailing through the air. He stared at her perfection. The last time he'd seen her naked body, she'd been young and lithe. But now, she was a woman with endless curves. And he planned to explore each one tonight, starting with her breasts, which could always send him into a frenzy. They perfectly fit in his palms.

"Grace, what witchery is this?" he murmured, lifting his gaze to meet hers. When her eyes opened wide, he chuckled. "You're more beautiful than ever. You enticed me when we were younger, but now?" He lowered his voice. "You've enchanted me. Perhaps a better description is that you've bewitched me."

When she blushed, he felt rejuvenated in body and spirit. He wanted to fill her with all the compliments he would have given her if they'd married all those years ago. They'd wasted too much time quarreling and bickering over nonsense. He should have begged her forgiveness years ago, but he'd been a damnable fool. Tonight marked a new beginning for them, and he wouldn't waste this opportunity.

His mouth watered to taste the stiff peaks of her peach-colored nipples. He lowered his mouth to one breast and sucked the nipple into his mouth. She took his hand, guiding it to her other breast. She arched into his touch, commanding him for more. He was hers to rule, and she was his to pleasure. He teased her nipple with his tongue, then sucked. The other nipple deserved attention as well, so he rolled it in between his fingers. He smiled when she mewled in pleasure. All he wanted tonight was to please her and re-explore every inch of her glorious body. Every move, touch, and caress was another commitment, a testament to how much he revered her.

He slowed and braced himself on his elbows. By then, she was panting, hungry for more, as their eyes met. No words were exchanged, but he could tell from the swirl of emotion in her gaze she understood how momentous tonight was for both of them. He moved down her body, kissing her every inch of the way, exploring every curve and every soft dip of her body he could find.

After he placed a reverential kiss on each defined hip bone and the soft swell of her abdomen, he lifted himself off the bed and knelt on the floor. He pulled her to the edge of the bed and spread her legs.

"What are you doing?" Grace leaned against her elbows to see him better.

"Touching you," he said nonchalantly. "Your every wish is my command. Now, be a good girl and watch."

"Dane," she protested softly.

"You always remind me that I am a walking scandal." He winked. "Allow me to prove it. I think you will enjoy it."

Gently, he separated her folds, then licked her from her entrance to the bundle of nerves designed for pleasure.

Grace moaned, but her eyes stayed on him. As he swirled his tongue, she let out a long, low moan that echoed through the room. Her taste, sweet and salty with desire, was more intoxicating than his finest whiskey. He slipped one finger inside her, feeling her wet heat and the tightness of her muscles. His hard cock jerked at the thought of her squeezing him. She gasped when he slipped another, then another finger inside her.

With each thrust of his fingers and circle of his tongue, Grace moaned louder. She collapsed on the bed, her hips rising to meet his touch. He wouldn't rest until she had come on his hand, his tongue, and his cock. He wanted to worship her every day for the rest of his life.

"Please," she whispered, her voice shaking. "I can't withstand much more."

"Yes, you can," he murmured against her skin. "Trust me." Without hesitation, he stretched her slowly but firmly. She bit her lip, her nails digging into his scalp. Her panting increased as she bucked her hips against his face as he sucked harder.

"I need you."

He smiled against her skin, then lashed his tongue against the sensitive skin. He thrust his fingers in and out of her as his cock wept for attention. He closed his eyes and fought the need to take it in his hand. His pleasure would come later.

He knew she was close to climaxing as Grace pulled his hair. She screamed his name, and her body squeezed his fingers as her orgasm roared through her. He continued to stroke her with his tongue, but he gentled his movements. Grace moaned his name again and combed her fingers through his hair. Slowly, he rested on his haunches as he watched her catch her breath. Unable to stand it anymore, he trailed kisses up her body, then took her into his arms. He kissed her, then nestled his head against her neck. "Shall I continue to show you how strong I am?"

She giggled and stroked her fingers up and down his back. "I think you should." She pushed her hips against his. "I need you inside me."

"Grace," he murmured. "You're tight."

Another pink blush washed across her cheeks. "I haven't been with anybody since you."

For a moment, he couldn't utter a word. He'd been her first and only. If he had his way, he would be the last man she ever made love to. He squeezed her tighter, then took her hand and wrapped it around his cock, letting her feel the girth and every inch of his hardness.

"I do this to you?" she asked innocently.

"You're a minx and a she-devil combined. With a healthy dose of Scottish wildcat." He laughed against the softest of her neck. He grew serious as he lifted his gaze to hers. "We don't have to do this. We can always be creative and find other ways to pleasure each other."

She smiled gently. "I can't bear it unless we're together."

"Gracie," he murmured, then nipped her chin. "I don't know how gentle I can be. I've wanted this for so long."

"As have I. I don't want you to be gentle." Boldly, she pulled his hair and stole a kiss. "I'll not wait. Think of me as the one who claims you. The one who will make you mine."

Dane lowered his forehead to hers. "Then I shall pray that my strength holds until I give you everything you want." He grinned. When she laughed, he moved his body over hers. He rested his weight on his elbows to watch her. "You're more beautiful than I ever imagined." He slid his cock through her wetness, barely entering her. He closed his eyes, desperate to control his runaway heartbeat.

When he looked at her again, she gifted him with a tender smile as she wrapped her long legs around his body. His heart tumbled into a freefall. He hadn't felt anything like this since their last time together. Ever so slowly, he worked his way inside her. She was tight and hot, and the urge to slam into her grew fierce, but he took his time, letting her adjust to every inch of him.

Another jolt of lust sliced through him as her sultry moans filled the room. He thrust again and circled his hips to stretch her. He had to make this good for her. He wanted her to come undone in his arms. He wanted her to see that no matter what they'd experienced in the past, they were always destined to be together.

He pushed deeper. Her fingers dug into his shoulders. Her breath danced across his chest, and she moaned again. Dane steadily increased his pace, and her body trembled with anticipation.

The scent of their sweat and desire mingled with the night air, making him lightheaded. He gripped one hip and pulled her closer. Soon, his hips met hers in a ruthless rhythm as he moved in and out of her. His movements were rough, and her body met his with equal force. Her inner walls gripped him tightly, her nails digging into his back as he slammed into her, their skin slapping together in a primal rhythm.

Grace's breath grew ragged, and her eyes were half-closed as she seemed to lose herself in the moment. Her breasts bounced enticingly with each thrust, heightening the intensity of his passion.

His free hand found its way to her clitoris, teasing and circling as he moved deeper and faster. Grace shuddered beneath him, her body arching off the bed. Dane lowered his head and nestled against her neck. With a groan, he scraped his teeth against her tender skin marking her skin, marking her as his. She tasted like an intoxicating mix of wine and fresh air. With every breath and moan that filled the room and echoed off the walls, he lost track of time and space as their bodies moved in perfect unison.

Her moans turned into whimpers, and he bit his lip to stifle his own cries of pleasure. Her body tightened, squeezing his cock as she writhed under his touch.

"Dane," she cried.

He picked up the pace, driving into her with a fervor that matched her sultry cries. Their rhythm of movement turned into a dance older than time itself. He could feel the heat rising between them. With each forceful thrust, he drank in the sight of her body. Her hair had turned into a golden halo surrounding her on the bed.

His need to fill and claim his beautiful Grace was too great to go slow as her walls tightened around him. Grace's eyes fluttered open to meet his gaze. He felt every inch of her wet warmth envelop him. Her fingers dug into his back with a desperation that mirrored his own. Sensations from his back to his ballocks ricocheted through his body. With a final groan, he let go. Her tightness gripped him like a vice as he spilled inside her.

He bit into her neck, claiming her, tasting the saltiness of her sweat and the sweetness of her skin. She moaned, her body trembling underneath him as her walls squeezed him over and over again, milking him of every last drop.

Repeating her name like a mantra, Dane praised her softly and cooed soft words of love. As their bodies cooled, he pressed gentle kisses to her neck. He had no idea how long they lay in each other's arms, but he knew one thing. He'd never felt so sated or such contentment. Everything was right in the world.

Grace turned in his arms, her eyes searching his face. "That was…"

"Incredible," he said with a grin.

She frowned in concentration. "I was going to say amazing."

"Again, I'll ask if it is your opinion that I'm strong enough?" He entwined their fingers together, and then he brought her hand to his mouth.

"I'm not certain I have enough information to form an opinion." She kissed his chest. "Perhaps you should demonstrate it again?"

He sucked in a breath. "Give me a moment or two?"

They both laughed, basking in the afterglow of their lovemaking. Time seemed to stand still as their hearts beat in unison and their breaths synchronized.

He sighed in contentment. He thanked the heavens that she forgave him. Once again, he was hers, and she was his. It had always been their destiny.

Sixteen

⟡

G race smoothed the soft strands of Dane's hair from his brow. He nestled his head a little closer to her chest. They still hadn't moved from his bed. They'd made love twice more that night, and he'd been so generous and gentle in his care afterward. He'd brought in a basin and linen toweling to clean her. Then, he'd brought in a tray with bread, cheese, and fruit. He'd said he needed to keep up his strength after their lovemaking.

Tears had filled her eyes when he'd opened a delicious bottle of wine and had toasted the night and them. Every romantic gesture had reminded her of the old Dane from her past in so many ways.

It was hard to believe that just two days prior, he'd been so ill that he collapsed to the floor. She pressed a kiss to his forehead. Thank heavens, his strength and vigor, along with Mrs. Grimalkin's tonic, had propelled his speedy recovery.

She didn't mention her plans last evening, but she had to leave for London today. There was no avoiding it. When Dane followed, hopefully, she would have soothed Marbury's ruffled feathers and ensured he knew she didn't want his money. She would also ask him to keep her confidence about nursing Dane. No good would come from that information coming to light in London.

Hopefully, that would end the matter. It would leave her free to concentrate on her remaining clients. She glanced down at him sleeping next to her. In slumber, he looked like the boy she used to follow everywhere. In their youth, they had been so entangled that she didn't know where he began and where she ended. But then it all changed, and their friendship had grown more profound until he'd walked away.

Grace closed her eyes, willing herself to live in the moment. For the first time in years, loneliness didn't haunt her. Fear didn't threaten to choke her. Perhaps she was too sanguine about her future, especially when the past demanded her attention. For years, she'd watched Dane navigate society, never showing a hint of interest in marriage since he'd asked her. Once, she'd believed in the fairy tales and happy endings that he had once promised. If she committed her heart, she'd again place her happiness into his hands, which terrified her.

He was a gambler, just like her father. Yes, Dane was wealthy. Or was he? How could she trust him with her future if she didn't know? The man she'd trusted most in the world had betrayed her by gambling away her inheritance and dowry. What if Dane gambled as incessantly as her father?

If she lost Dane, she would also risk losing the Ardeerton sisters, the only real family she'd had since she left home. Not to mention that if she walked away, she'd be crushed the first time she saw him with another woman. She doubted if she'd ever be able to put those pieces back together again.

What she needed was a cup of strong tea. Perhaps she'd be able to make sense of it all. Grace made her way across the bed with snail-like speed until Dane tightened his grip on her.

"Where do you think you're going?" His murmur reminded her of buttery leather stretched and repeatedly tanned until you wanted to wrap yourself in it and luxuriate in its decadence.

Before she could answer, the door suddenly opened. Instinctively, Grace drove under the covers. It wasn't Winston because he would have announced himself. The footmen or maids would have knocked. Dane sat up and placed a hand on her hip, anchoring her in place.

"Bloody hell, Pelham." A male voice boomed across the room. "We rode like the devil from London to help you convalesce, and you have a woman in your bed? Were you even ill?"

Dane's grip tightened. "Do not say another word if you value your life."

"He has a woman in his bed," the intruder announced.

"Pelham, this is bad form. Even for you," another male voice called out.

"What have you done?" a female said curtly.

"I'm going to kill him," Another female retorted.

"Calm down," Dane hissed. "You're in my bedroom, and I'll not tolerate all this caterwauling. You're giving me a headache."

"That's the least of your worries," a female hmphed.

"When your footman arrived in London to fetch a doctor, he told Honoria you were gravely ill. We expected to find you on your deathbed."

No. No. No. This couldn't be happening. Though the voices were muffled, she recognized Trafford and Honoria. Even though Grace was under the covers, she slammed her eyes shut. That meant if Honoria was there, then the other woman was Pippa.

"Dane, I think Honoria asked the question of the hour. I don't care who is under those covers. What about Grace?" Pippa huffed.

"Leave this to me," Dane murmured, squeezing her hip.

"I'm just so disappointed in you," Honoria announced.

"Oh, for the love of all sisters everywhere," Dane scoffed.

"It's not a trivial matter, Dane," Pippa said. "Perhaps you should see your guest out of the bedroom so we can chat. I still want to know how you will explain yourself to Grace."

Grace slowly drew the covers from her head but held them close to her chest. She was as guilty as Dane about their night together. "He doesn't have to explain anything to me."

"Grace?" Honoria took a step closer.

Pippa shook her head at her brother. Her nostrils flared, signaling how riled she was. "She's our friend. I will not allow you to treat her this way."

Trafford put his hand around Honoria's arm to stop her from coming closer to the bed. "Let Ravenscroft and I handle it."

"Nonsense," Honoria pulled away from her husband and came right to the side of the bed with her arms crossed. She tipped her chin as she regarded Dane. "I love you to the ends of the earth, but this is unseemly."

"Oh, this is rich," Dane mumbled under his breath.

"Remember when you caught Marcus and me at the hunting lodge and threatened him with a duel?"

"Like it was yesterday." Dane pursed his lips to keep from smiling. "Don't challenge Grace to a duel. This isn't her fault."

"I'm not going to challenge her, *Your Grace*." Honoria's sarcasm rang through the room. "I'm challenging you."

"I'm going to be her second." Pippa cried as she stood next to her sister. "After she finishes, then I'm going to challenge you next." She turned to Ravenscroft. "Do you have your gloves so Honor and I can slap his face, or did you give them to the footman when we arrived?"

As if this couldn't get any more embarrassing, Winston whipped around the corner with a speed that belied his age. "I apologize, Your Grace." He suddenly stopped, then ran his hands through his white hair, putting every wayward strand back in place. Without missing a beat, he straightened his waistcoat, then smoothed his morning coat, immediately donning his proper English butler persona. "I wasn't aware that your family had arrived."

"I don't think you could have stopped them," Dane replied, then arched an eyebrow as he stared at his sisters. "What family challenges its members to a duel?"

"The type who has their friend's best interests at heart," Pippa sniffed.

"Pippa, do you remember when your brother came to your shop and discovered us there?" Ravenscroft chortled. "Then he brought me to my knees the next day in his study?"

"I do." Pippa's gaze softened as she looked at her husband. "I was so proud of you for not retaliating." She turned to her brother and narrowed her gaze. "That was wrong, Dane." She waved her hand palm side up across the bed. "But this, taking advantage of Grace? It's beyond the pale even for you. This is scandalous."

"Ouch," Trafford exclaimed as he raised his shoulders defensively. "Good luck with that, old man."

Dane rolled his eyes. "This is between Grace and me. If it's a scandal, it's a simple one."

Honoria propped her hands on her hips. "There's only one thing to do."

"Tar and feather him?" Ravenscroft offered with a laugh.

"It would depend upon how hot the tar was," Honoria replied. There was no hiding the anger in her voice. "But seriously, you need to acquire a special license. That doesn't give us much time to plan who will attend the ceremony and how many to invite for the wedding breakfast."

"Or create and sew a proper dress that will do Grace's beauty justice," Pippa uttered.

"Exactly, my darling," Ravenscroft agreed. "The only way to define your brother's behavior is—"

"That's enough," Dane bellowed. He turned to Winston. "Would you please escort my family out of my chambers? I don't care where you put them. The barnyard might be an appropriate place for all their braying we've heard this morning."

"Yes, Your Grace." Winston bowed, then turned to Dane's sisters. "Lady Trafford and Lady Ravenscroft, if you'll accompany me?"

"What do they call this?" Ravenscroft tapped his chin as he tilted his head to stare at the ceiling. "Ah ha, I have it." He snapped his fingers. "Karma."

Trafford raised an eyebrow in a manner that reminded Grace of Dane. "And I've heard she can be especially challenging if you have misbehaved."

"*Out.*" Dane pointed to the door.

When Honor and Pippa marched out of the bedroom with their heads held high, their husbands had the good sense to follow them.

When the room quieted, Grace let out a sigh. "What a catastrophe."

Dane smiled as he embraced her. "I think it's rather charming. I'm quite delighted they are concerned for your welfare."

"Even at your expense," she asked incredulously. "And I am supposed to be the definition of..."

"Prim and proper?" Dane finished for her. "I much prefer you like this in my bed and naked. Besides, it's all theatrics, sweetheart. Trafford and Ravenscroft are only trying to return the favor from when I caught them with my sisters in dishabille." He winked, then pressed his lips to hers. "I'm happy to see them, but is it wrong to want you all to myself for a while?"

"No." Heat bludgeoned Grace's cheeks. This man treated her as if she was his entire world. "But we've had our fun and games. Now it's time to face reality again." She leaned up and pressed her lips to his. "I'm thrilled that you're feeling well."

"I'm right as rain." He waggled his eyebrows. "Ready to make love again. Perhaps we'll try for four times today."

She swung her legs off the bed while holding a sheet to her chest.

Before she could stand, Dane wrapped one hand around her waist and pulled her close until her back rested against his chest. He nibbled on her shoulder blade. "This view of you is irresistible. We may not leave this bedroom for a month." He pushed her hair aside and kissed the sensitive skin of her neck.

"I must return to London." She closed her eyes as he continued to kiss and caress her as if it was nothing at all upsetting that his entire family had seen them both naked in bed. "I don't know how we'll face them," she said softly.

"Darling, look at me," he coaxed softly as he cupped her cheek and turned her so their gazes met. "This is between you and me. Not our family."

It was such a sweet sentiment that they were her family. Hot tears threatened, and she tried to blink them away. "I consider your sisters a godsend, but I'm not a part of your family," she protested faintly.

"A matter of differing interpretations. They officially will be your family as soon as we marry," he murmured as he pressed a gentle kiss to her nose.

Before she could discuss his fever-induced proposal, a knock sounded.

"Your Grace, I'm here to help you dress, " a muffled voice called out behind the door.

"That's Kendrick, my valet." He quickly kissed her lips and started to move off the bed. "I shall ask Winston to assign you a maid to help you bathe and dress."

"Dane. Wait." She grabbed his hand. "About marrying. Nothing has changed between us."

He stilled instantly, then blinked slowly. Then he blinked again. "A moment," he called to the door, then turned back to Grace. "I must have not heard you correctly. Would you mind repeating what you just said?"

She dropped his hand and lowered her gaze. "I do not hold you to your promise of marriage." She laughed in an attempt to sound light-hearted, but her heart felt the unbearable weight of her predicament. "You had a fever. Frankly, you can't remember half the things you spouted that evening."

Dane's voice turned into a low growl. "I beg your pardon, but I remember everything I said that night." A muscle twitched in his jaw, betraying his aggravation. "If you're worried about a scandal, I know exactly how to stop it. We'll give people an up close and personal view of us. That's what they want to see. I'll host a ball announcing you're mine."

"What about what I want?" What she needed was a home of her own. She fisted her hands, scraping together every ounce of courage she possessed. "I want security. I want to know that I have a home at the end of the day." She tightened her fist and pounded it softly in the middle of her chest. It was beyond humiliating to say the words aloud, but he needed to hear it. "I want a home that I will never worry about losing. To have that, I need my clients. I need to be the *Governess*. That's why I must return to London and ensure Marbury doesn't say anything. I can't have my livelihood threatened. He told the villagers here. Who knows what he'll say in London."

His nostrils flared. "You don't think I can give you security and ensure your reputation?"

"I honestly don't know." He cringed, but she would not capitulate. "I don't hold you to a promise you made when you were not lucid. Let us not turn this into..." Flustered, she stood with the sheet around her and started to pace. "I'm not the woman you proposed to all those years ago."

"What are you talking about?" He pointed at her, his nostrils flaring again. "I knew exactly who that woman was when I proposed to her all those years ago, and I knew who she was two nights ago. At this very instant, she's standing before me." He lowered his voice. "In my bedroom, I might add. You are right here. You have fought with me since we met in that godforsaken field." He shook his head. "That's not correct. Even before I asked you to marry me, we've bickered. I know what you'll say before you say it." He threw his hands in the air. "What is this, Grace?"

"You hired me to find you a wife."

He propped his hands on his lean hips. "You're not still trying to find me a match on the marriage mart. If you are, let me dispel you of that notion. I don't want any woman you've introduced or will introduce me to."

Desperate to end this discussion, she tilted her head up in defiance.

"There she is," he murmured with a laugh. "*My Governess* in all her glory." He stalked her much like a panther determined to catch its prey. "I can see by the look in your eyes you want to teach me a lesson. I would welcome it. Any time. Any place." His voice dropped to that seductive tone she could never resist.

But this time, she would. She closed her eyes, but she didn't lower her chin. If only she couldn't hear him, she could remain steadfast. Perhaps she should hold her hands over her ears so she couldn't hear him speak, even if it were childish.

"Shall I bend over so you can teach me some obedience?" He was practically purring as he circled her. "Explore your naughty side with me. You could tie me up." He widened his eyes and grinned. "Or I could tie you up. I think you would enjoy it as much—"

"Dane, stop," she hissed.

He shook his head as if trying to shake off his confusion. "If you are worried about my sincerity, I promise that you are at the forefront of my thoughts. Always. What about the letter I left explaining my presence at the Jolly Rooster?"

"What letter?" She straightened her shoulders.

"The one I left for you. I gave it to Winston to give to. . ." He plowed his hands through his hair. "I meant to give it to Winston to give to you. It must still be on my desk."

"You were ill and can be excused for the letter. However, I'm not speaking about that."

"I thought you forgave me." He bowed his head. "Please tell me this isn't about my apology. If it is, tell me what to do, and it's done."

The forlornness in his voice made her heart pound against her ribs, trying to reach him.

"Oh, Dane." She lowered her voice. "You walked away from me once." She closed her eyes and remembered the hurt from all those years ago. Her voice broke. "How do I know it won't happen again?"

What if he lost everything just like her father? He'd have to walk away from her.

Or she would have to walk away from him.

Only after a moment did he slowly raise his gaze to hers. "All I beg is that you allow me to prove that it will never happen again."

Seventeen

⌒◦⌒

Dane adjusted his cravat in the mirror. "Thank you, Kendrick."

"Of course, Your Grace." His valet bowed as Dane exited the dressing room.

He strolled the second-floor hallway and bypassed the family sitting room. Knowing his sisters and brothers-in-law, they would be waiting for him in his study, ready to give him the devil as they peppered him with questions.

Instead of dreading it, he was looking forward to the conversation. He'd planned to explain that he and Grace were meant for each other and had recognized the inevitable.

Or at least, he had until Grace had confided she had doubts about marrying him.

It was just like that irascible woman to complicate everything. It should be so simple. Grace would move in with him, and they would marry immediately. He wanted to host a ball on her behalf and introduce her as his duchess. He despised social events but the thought of having her on his arm as they walked around the ballroom sent a ridiculous thrill through him.

Yet, it was unnerving that she didn't trust him and kept bringing up the past.

He stopped just before he reached the staircase to descend to the main floor. He lifted his head and stared at the ceiling.

Of course, she felt that way.

Why hadn't he seen it before? He had never shown her that he would always protect her. For all that was holy, he never considered that Grace didn't know he would always put her needs before his. He had thought that what happened in that field all those years ago was finally behind them. But he'd abandoned her just like Stewart, her sister, and her father. How could she know? He'd never proven it, demonstrated it, or even discussed such a topic with her.

And he would have to be careful and not upset her again with talk of her dowry and inheritance.

He vowed then and there to do everything in his power to ensure that Grace knew how much he cherished her and how he would protect her. He would prove it by caring for her every single day for the rest of his life. He would do whatever it took to ensure she knew how much he loved her.

And he would tell that as soon as he found her.

She desired security—a place to call her own. This wish was logical, given that her family had forsaken her and ruined her future. What had become of that dowry and any inheritance might hold the key to helping her move on from the past. God, the guilt weighed on his conscience for not recognizing how vulnerable she had felt all those years. Whatever it took, he was determined to uncover exactly what had happened to that money. He suspected her father had provided for her, but something—or *someone*—had stolen it from her. It would be his life's mission to reveal the truth. He paused, imagining all her potential reactions. She could be angry at him for interfering, but she might also finally be ready to put aside that unfortunate chapter of her life and open up her heart and life to him. Heaven knew he was ready.

If she still wanted to be the *Governess* and own her own home, he would find a way to help her secure it. Perhaps he would buy the block she lived on, then lower the price of her home to an amount she'd feel comfortable paying. He'd give her all the security she wanted and more. That's what a man in love does for the woman he adores.

With a newfound determination, Dane started down the marble

staircase, only to abruptly stop. Below him stood Grace with a straight posture that would have made a dance master envious. Beside her, Stewart Arnold stood close, wagging a finger under Grace's nose as if reprimanding her.

Dane's upper lip curled in disgust. Grace was clearly distraught by the telltale blush she wore and the way she twisted her fingers. She had done the exact same thing in his bedroom earlier. He rubbed his hands together as a smile tugged at his lips. He could not wait to rebuke her worthless brother-in-law and then personally escort him from Pelham Hall with explicit instructions never to return.

"Darling, were you expecting this man?" The words were cutting, but his voice's drawl proved that he thought the man beneath his Grace.

"Your Grace, do you remember—"

Before she could finish, Arnold strode forward and bowed from the waist. "Excellent to see you again, Your Grace. I'd heard a rumor in town that you were ill. I hope you are much recovered."

"I am, and it's all because of the excellent care I received." Dane stood there with his feet hip-width apart, ready for battle.

Arnold turned to Grace and frowned. "Is that so?"

Grace's eyes widened.

"Is there a reason for your visit?" Dane asked curtly. "I have family who is waiting for Lady Grace and me."

Arnold narrowed his eyes. "Yes, there's a reason for my visit. I'm quite concerned about that 'excellent care' you speak of and how my sister-in-law is involved in it. Your other house guest mentioned it in the village. I was there when Marbury stopped for supplies." He shook his head. "Grace's sister is bedridden with worry. We're both concerned with her reputation...or lack thereof."

"Watch your tongue," Dane growled.

Arnold's eyes flashed with unbridled anger. "I will not watch my tongue. We both know that you've ruined her."

"Stewart, you need to apologize to His Grace," Grace hissed as her cheeks heated.

Without his gaze leaving Dane, Arnold laughed, but it held little humor. "I will not apologize for defending your honor." Arnold lowered his gaze and lifted it, staring straight into Dane's eyes, taking his measure. "It makes little difference to me if we discuss the matter here. I'm sure your staff will be enthralled when they hear what you've done. London will undoubtedly hear of this before the week is out."

"Are you threatening me?" Dane took two steps forward, towering over the man. "More importantly, are you threatening Grace?"

Arnold took a step back. "It's not a threat, but even you, as well as I, know that rumors can find their way into the salons and sitting rooms of the *ton's* busybodies."

Grace gasped.

Dane instinctively took a step closer to her. Her brother-in-law was more worthless than pond scum. He had little regard for her and didn't care that her livelihood depended on a sterling reputation. Dane couldn't wait to teach him a lesson.

"Come to the library," Dane commanded. He extended his arm for Grace to take. When she did, he leaned near and lowered his voice so that Arnold couldn't hear them. "Would you allow me to handle this?"

She leaned against him, and it took everything in his power not to scoop her into his arms and take her away from the ugliness that her brother-in-law was spewing.

Her throat bobbed slightly as she swallowed. "I don't want to leave you alone with him."

"Protecting me again, *Governess*?" He patted her arm. "Let me protect you for a while, darling. Will you head to my study? You'll find Honor and Pippa there, I'm certain of it. I'll come find you when I finish with the garbage."

"Dane," she murmured. "Don't do anything either of us will regret."

Dane hated negotiating with vermin, but he had no choice if he wanted to protect Grace. "Just speaking the truth, darling." He stopped and took her hand. In a show of respect, he brought it to his mouth and placed a gentle kiss on her knuckles. With a pleasurable sigh, he watched her walk down the passageway.

Of course, he couldn't help but notice the sashay of her hips, the very curves he had held in his hands last night and this morning. She was a magnificent woman, and whatever it took, he would make her his.

Finally, and forever.

He turned and feigned a smile. The sooner he disposed of this riffraff, the sooner he could join his family and make plans with Grace.

"Follow me," Dane ordered. He didn't wait for the man beside him to follow. He strolled to the library but could hear Arnold rushing after him, trying to match his steps. When Dane entered the library, he pointed to a table in the center of the room. He waited for Arnold to sit before he took the chair on the opposite of the table. "What do you want?"

"It should be obvious. As the head of the family, the responsibility of caring for my wife's elder sister falls to me. Since my sister-in-law is a member of polite society, you know that her reputation is paramount." His smile filled with feigned compassion. "Particularly since she finds great joy in helping others find a love match." He shook his head and furrowed his brow. "Imagine how shocked we were to find that our beloved sister was staying with you without anyone chaperoning her."

Dane wanted to roll his eyes at such a pious display of untruths. By Grace's own admission, the man practically threw her out of his household. The longer the man talked, the stronger the urge became to reach across the table and grab Arnold by the throat.

"You do realize that I was ill," Dane challenged.

Arnold smiled slightly. "And I'm delighted you made a full recovery. Unfortunately, you've compromised her. There's only one solution to save Grace."

Dane held up his hand. "Before you continue your trite diatribe, I've already asked her to marry me."

"Excellent." Arnold sat back in his chair with a wide smile, tugging at his lips. "Excellent news," he repeated as he rested his clasped hands on the desk in front of him. "What are your thoughts about the marriage settlements."

Dane pursed his lips. Naturally, that was Arnold's only concern. He'd never once asked how Grace was. He didn't embrace her when he saw her. He didn't offer her comfort. Nor did he try to whisk her out of Pelham Hall. No, his first and foremost concern was money.

How originally banal and clichéd.

What was that old saying...what is sauce for the goose is sauce for the gander.

"Before we discuss settlements or dower, what about the monies Grace's father set aside for her when she married." Dane didn't crack a smile.

"Surely, you're not concerned with that, Your Grace. Everyone knows you are the original Mayfair millionaire." Arnold's face turned serious. "May I be honest?"

Dane nodded once. He already knew Arnold would say that Grace's father was a wastrel. It would give him the opening to grill the man on the specifics.

"Grace's father was a tenacious gambler. He wagered everything that was not entailed to the estate." He shook his head as if this was the saddest story ever written. "When I went to the reading of the will for the family's benefit, that's when the whole sordid story revealed itself."

"Where did he gamble?" Dane softened his voice, trying to disarm the man. "London?"

Arnold shook his head. "The Jolly Rooster. After his wife died, the man's grief couldn't be contained. He went to the Jolly Rooster nightly." He let out a heavy sigh.

"The Jolly Rooster?" Dane leaned forward and placed his elbows on the table. "How much did he lose?"

Arnold shrugged. "Several tens of thousands."

"Were there any funds left?" Dane studied Arnold's eyes as they shifted slightly. Through his years, he'd learned when men were trying to hide something, and Grace's brother-in-law fit the mold exactly.

Arnold shook his head. "There was only enough to pay for the estate's remaining bills before the new earl moved in. When I approached him about Grace, he'd said it wasn't his problem. That left poor Grace without anything. Shortly after I returned from the reading of the old earl's will, the Marquess of West Essex asked for her hand."

Dane had never heard his sisters, brothers-in-law, or members of his various clubs mention such an offer of marriage, and Grace certainly never told him.

"West Essex had to withdraw his offer once he learned there were no monies for settlement purposes." Steward didn't blink. "He had to marry a coal heiress."

Dane's heart stumbled in his chest, stealing his breath. He might have lost Grace forever if her dowry hadn't been lost.

He leaned back in his chair and thumped the table softly with his knuckle. "You are aware that I own the Jolly Rooster?"

Arnold nodded.

"I have all the old account books. In reviewing them, I never saw the earl's name." He didn't blink as he stared at the man.

Arnold stared right back at him. "I can't explain what your records say. I only know what the family solicitor said."

"Didn't the earl's secretary or bookkeeper mention the state of the estate to the solicitor at the time the earl fell ill?" Dane continued to thump the table as Arnold fidgeted in his seat.

"Not that I'm aware of, Your Grace."

"Where are the old earl's estate account books?"

Arnold's Adam's apple bobbled as he struggled to answer. "I assume with the new earl."

"But you don't know for certain?" Dane smiled slightly.

"No, Your Grace."

"What about Grace's father's summer estate, Sommer House, the one next door to Pelham Hall? Who owns that? Perhaps that might be part of the marriage settlements?"

"It belongs to the new earl. Part of the entailed property of the earldom." Stewart pulled at his cravat, another sign that the man was lying. "Back to the matter at hand. What about the marriage settlement?"

Dane threw back his head at the baldfaced lies sputtering from the man and laughed. "All in good time. I need to formally ask Grace to marry me."

"As head of the family—" Stewart puffed out his chest "—I can answer for her."

More like the head arse of the family and a poor example at that.

"The answer will be no. I will not ask you." Dane wanted to add that Grace was now part of his family, not Stewart and Hope Arnold's family. But it wouldn't help Grace if the man became riled. Dane didn't want Grace upset. "Grace is an adult and can make her own decisions."

"But I'm her brother by marriage." He had the audacity to look offended.

It took all of Dane's restraint not to physically throw the man out of Pelham Hall. Instead, he counted to three, smiling serenely. "She mentioned you suggested she marry a farmer. Where was that?" He wrinkled his nose as though he were smelling something foul. "Northumberland, if I remember correctly."

"I was looking out for her welfare." Without success, Arnold tugged his waistcoat to cover his thick middle.

If you were looking after her welfare, wouldn't you have had her become part of your household instead of sending her out into the proverbial streets without even a goodbye?

Dane blinked twice. He'd had enough of the man's foolishness. The man thought to enrich his coffers by acting like he had Grace's best interests in mind. What a farce that was. But he needed to play politely and appear friendly to find out what happened to her dowry. There was no earthly way the story Stewart Arnold told today resembled the truth. Dane had studied all the Jolly Rooster books before purchasing the coaching inn to ensure he knew the operation and the men holding excessive debts.

Grace's father's name was never listed in any of the books that covered the last twenty years. The man may have gambled, but not at the Jolly Rooster. Dane suspected that when the old earl passed away, he had ensured Grace was provided for. He would bet that she had a dowry when her father died.

Which meant that Dane had to find the old earl's solicitor and bookkeeper. The first person he needed to call on was the Earl of Webster-Harnly and find out exactly what happened all those years ago when he inherited the title from Grace's father.

Dane stood, and Arnold had the good manners to stand as well.

"It's been wonderful, but I need to see my family." He chuckled softly. "My sisters probably have Grace hidden away somewhere, planning their activities for the day. I have to make sure I'm on the agenda so I can ask your lovely sister-in-law for her hand in marriage. Once I have the answers, I'll reach out to you, and we can discuss marriage settlements."

Dane waited for the man to ask what he meant when he said, "*Once I have the answers.*"

Smiling, Grace's brother-in-law nodded in agreement.

Thankfully, Winston possessed a keen sense of when guests had worn out their welcome. His wily butler appeared that very instant with a footman. "Mr. Arnold, if you follow Thomas, he'll see you out."

When Arnold bowed, Dane waved a hand as if dismissing him. *What a common toad.*

Thomas didn't crack a smile as the man practically skipped to his side.

Arnold turned and addressed Dane, "Your Grace, you can call on me anytime. I look forward to our next conversation."

"As do I," Dane answered.

As soon as Thomas had the man out of the room, Dane motioned for Winston to shut the door. "If you have a moment?"

"Of course, Your Grace." Winston closed the door with barely a sound, then came to Dane's side.

"Do you remember who Grace's father employed as his personal secretary and the estate manager?"

Winston didn't hesitate. "The estate manager was Edgar Baker. The last I heard, he had retired when the old earl passed away and had gone to live with his son in York. He'd been with the old earl's father as well. Simon Fields worked as the old earl's secretary. He was from Hinton, two villages over. He went to work for the new earl and is at the earl's London home."

"Thank you." Dane's mouth tugged into a smile. "When I need to know the gossip, I know who to come to."

Winston raised one eyebrow. "That's what makes me the perfect butler for you. You can stay above the fray, and I'll provide the information you need."

"Indeed. Thank you." Dane laughed. His butler turned to leave, but Dane stopped him. "Another moment, please."

Winston turned around and clasped his hands in front of him like a dutiful butler.

"Do you know where the earl is spending the Season?"

Winston cracked a smile. "In London. He's decided to take a wife."

Dane shook his head. "How do you know what is happening in London."

"My cousin Ritson always keeps me abreast of the comings and goings of the *ton*. I keep him abreast of everything happening at the Jolly Rooster." He beamed proudly. "Our duty as your butlers is to know everything for you." With that, Winston turned on his heel and left the room.

Dane walked to one of the floor-to-ceiling windows and gazed at the fields and pastures spread before him like a chessboard. He was lucky to have such loyal servants who looked after his wellbeing. Once he married Grace, they would help with anything she desired. Unlike other men, it didn't bother Dane a whit if she wanted to work after they married. His only condition?

She had to save all her dances for him.

He had to make up for all the lost time they'd had apart.

Eighteen

Grace perched on one of the black velvet sofas that ran parallel to the fireplace in Dane's study. Across from her sat Honoria and Pippa, who were serving tea.

"Cook made cream cakes, but they aren't as good as your Mr. Tinniswood's creations." Pippa handed Grace a plate of cakes and then served her sister.

"Indeed," Honoria said with a benevolent smile that betrayed nothing. "Let us change the subject."

Those last words compelled Grace to brace herself for the inquiry that was sure to come. The first question she would likely face was, *"What are your intentions toward our brother?"*

"I'm just wondering why you didn't become ill when you nursed Dane?" Honoria asked, then took a bite of her cream cake.

Grace blew out a silent breath of relief, then shrugged. "I'm not certain. I suffered a mild case of influenza earlier this spring. Dane turned away the doctor before I could ask his thoughts. I think that might have caused his illness. One of the Jolly Rooster footmen also fell ill, but I've heard from Winston that he's on the mend."

"Has anyone taken ill at Pelham Hall?" Pippa set the plate of cream cakes on the table.

"No. Winston and I were careful about who had contact with Dane." Grace took a sip of tea for courage. "It's miraculous that no one else appears to be suffering the same."

"I've heard that sometimes the sickness doesn't spread to others when they've previously suffered from it." Honoria shrugged. "That might be a wives' tale."

Pippa shook her head. "I'm just thankful that everyone is well and happy. Especially you and Dane. Winston said you never left his side."

Both sisters regarded Grace with a questioning look, then turned their gazes to each other with a knowing smile.

"What?" Grace asked in confusion.

"You and Winston seem to be thick as thieves." Honoria smirked.

Pippa bit her bottom lip to keep from laughing.

Grace didn't blink as she knew what was coming. Dane's sisters would start asking about the two of them. And she would be ready for them. "You both are exaggerating. He was mightily worried about Dane's health. It's my understanding that Dane has always been close to him."

Pippa gently set down her tea. "I'm sure Winston understands how much you mean to Dane."

"Oh, my goodness, yes," Honoria gushed. "Along with his cousin, Ritson, who is responsible for Ardeerton House. Winston is wonderful and will quickly become a favorite and confidant."

"I don't know Ritson very well." Heat filled Grace's cheeks as the memory of Winston rescuing her from a sleeping Dane's embrace marched into her thoughts. She had no idea what the butler thought of her. Yet, he'd been kind and protective when she'd come to stay with Dane. She smiled slightly at the memory. Besides Dane, his sisters, and perhaps Theo, there weren't many in her life who thought of her well-being, and she was grateful for Winston and his attention.

The quiet in the room became deafening. Best to lance the wound, as some would say. Grace would face whatever the sisters would ask her. She owed that much to them because of their friendship.

Grace pushed the plate away from her and didn't touch her tea. She forced herself to hold her hands together in her lap. "I'm sure you both have a thousand questions, and I will try to answer them all. But you see, your brother and I—"

"Are in love?" Honoria offered, then grinned. "Both of us couldn't be happier for you and Dane."

Grace could feel her eyes widened. She might love their brother, but they hadn't had much of an opportunity to discuss their feelings, particularly after all these years. She huffed out a breath at the difficulty of navigating her friendship and allegiance to the Ardeerton sisters and her allegiance and love for Dane.

Pippa nodded and leaned slightly toward Grace. "I always knew that something percolated between the two of you. Though, frankly, I thought it was more of an animus than an amorous relationship between you."

"Oh, that's clever," Honoria said with a laugh. "Animus versus amorous."

Pippa dipped her head in acknowledgment. "I try, but my darling husband is a master at such wordplay. Now, about you and our brother."

Grace bit her bottom lip. "I'm sorry that you found us in his bedroom."

"Nonsense," Honoria scolded playfully. "Served Dane right for the way he treated both our husbands."

"Exactly," Pippa added, then took a sip of tea. "Now, shall we discuss the wedding?"

Both sisters turned to her with open expressions, signifying they were determined to plan a wedding.

"I have a lovely ivory silk that would be stunning on you." Pippa's gaze swept over Grace's body.

"What about the burnished gold silk that arrived before we left town?" Honoria tilted her head toward her sister. "Look at Grace's eyes and hair. She would rival Venus in such a color."

"That is simply brilliant, Honor. Our brother won't be able to tear his gaze away from Grace with the dress I'm designing in my head."

"Or his hands off her either." Honoria sighed.

"She could wear a flour sack, and I would think she was stunning."

They all turned to face the entrance to the study, where Dane stood in all his glory. Behind him stood Ravenscroft and Trafford. Even she would admit they were all handsome, there was only one who stole her breath. With his gold hair, he could have been mistaken for the Greek god Helios. She sighed slightly as memories of last night rushed through her.

Without a care in the world, Dane strolled to her side and bent down to kiss her cheek.

"Dane," she scolded. "What are you doing?"

"Greeting my fiancé." Dane lowered his voice so the others could not hear their conversation. "And my lover, whom I've been parted from for way too long."

She inhaled as another bout of heat flooded her cheeks. Really, she was acting like a schoolgirl instead of a grown woman.

"I love to see you blush." Then, the handsome, intriguing cad winked at her as he sat down beside her. "I sent your brother-in law away."

"Everything all right?"

Dane nodded. "He wanted to discuss settlements. I told him that I had to secure your hand first." He winked as he brought her hand to his lips. "We have things to discuss that I think might ease your concerns about marrying me. Let's not tarry. I want us to marry quickly."

Trafford and Ravenscroft sat down beside their wives. Suddenly, the large study seemed to shrink after the three men settled onto the sofas.

"When is the wedding?" Honoria pressed.

"As soon as—"

"I return to London and settle whatever concerns Lord Marbury may have," Grace finished for Dane.

Frowning at her, he tilted his head. "That's not what I was going to say."

"What were you going to say?" Pippa asked innocently.

"That when we return to London, Grace will move her belongings, herself, and Theo into Ardeerton House. Meanwhile, I'll secure the special license." Dane nodded once, the movement ensuring that everyone knew that his word was law in Pelham Hall.

Pippa gleefully clapped her hands. "Grace will be such a beautiful bride. That will give me enough time to design and sew a dress for Grace."

Now, Ravenscroft was the one to frown. "That means you'll be up all night." He shook his head. "I don't like it."

"I don't like it either," Grace parroted. When everyone's attention turned to her, she swallowed that bit of discomfort she experienced when she became the center of attention.

And not in a good way.

"What I mean is...I won't be moving in with Dane." Grace clasped her hands tighter.

Dane swiveled until he was facing her. "Yes, you will."

"No, I won't," Grace defiantly corrected him as her heart pounded in her chest. "We've addressed this before."

"No, we have not," he countered. "We've agreed upon marriage."

"Their first lover's spat," Honoria cooed.

Pippa and Honoria sat on the edge of their seats as their gazes bounced between Dane and herself. For the love of all dukes everywhere, this was not a tennis match. Even Trafford and Ravenscroft were watching them intently.

"Did you quarrel with your wife before you married?" Ravenscroft arched a brow as he regarded Trafford.

"Indeed. To make matters worse, I always seemed to be in the wrong and apologizing." The handsome earl shook his head as he smiled smugly at his wife.

"That's because you were always wrong." Honoria tilted her perfect nose in the air and sniffed.

Ravenscroft tilted his head back and roared with laughter. Pippa turned to him with a slight scowl.

"I don't see what is humorous about this situation." She crossed her arms and stared at her husband. "If memory serves me correctly, you were apologizing to me practically daily because you were always wrong or behaved poorly."

"He still behaves poorly and still is always wrong." A lopsided grin tugged at Dane's lips.

By then, the entire group was in an uproar with laughter. Grace stole a peek at Dane's face, where he wore a blinding smile filled with love and affection for his family. It was marvelous for him and his sisters that they were a family who loved freely and could tease one another without anyone bickering or belittling the others.

This would be her life when she married Dane.

She meant *if and not when* she married him. She would not make any rash decisions about her future.

After the laughter finally died, Dane took her hand and brought it to his lips. "I think you should move in with me."

Grace immediately shook her head. "Don't ask me that. It would be unseemly."

Honoria narrowed her eyes. "Why do you want her to move in before the wedding?"

Pippa's gaze homed in on her brother's face.

Dane waved a hand in dismissal. "Grace and I have wasted enough time not being together. Where's the scandal if we're to be married."

Pippa ignored her brother. "Grace, you could stay with us in London until the ceremony."

Honoria turned to Grace. "I was thinking the same. You could move in with us."

"Nothing has been decided," Grace protested. The Ardeerton siblings ignored her and continued their conversations.

"But it would make the gown fittings easier for Grace and me if she stayed at my house." Pippa looked at her husband. "You wouldn't mind, would you? Your mother and great aunt would relish the extra company."

Ravenscroft bit his lips as his eyes twinkled with mirth. "Not only do I not mind, but I would insist upon it. Then Pelham could visit Grace anytime he'd like." He laughed with glee. "My mother and great aunt could act as chaperons."

Dane rolled his eyes. "Grace and I don't need chaperones."

"You most certainly do. Especially after what we discovered this morning in your bedroom," Trafford pointed out.

"Careful, old man," Dane warned. "You're discussing my future wife. I would hate to call you out for embarrassing her."

Trafford nodded once, then turned to Grace. "Forgive me, my lady.

Pelham is right. Sometimes, our teasing becomes a little ribald. I meant no harm."

"And no offense was taken," Grace said in reassurance. "But you see, what I want Dane to understand is that it is imperative that I return to London as soon as possible."

Honoria sighed in pleasure. "I adore it when I hear Grace say our brother's first name with such affection."

Dane shook his head, feigning annoyance, but they all could see the humor in his gaze. "About Marbury."

"Dane," Grace said a bit more forcefully. "I'm doing it not only for my reputation and business but also for yours. Marbury believes you deliberately ignored us to play a lurid game of chance with Brixworth. It makes little difference whether it's true or not. He could cause real harm."

"I don't care about my reputation. I'm a duke. Once you marry me, you'll be a duchess. All of society will be clamoring for your attention." Dane arched a perfect ducal eyebrow.

"I wish it were that simple." Grace reached over and placed her hand over his. "It's not only us I'm worried about, but also my clients. Every day that I'm away, then it appears as if I've abandoned them and put my interests first." She leaned near and lowered her voice. "You see that, don't you, darling?"

He narrowed the distance between them and lowered his voice. "That's the first time I think I've ever heard you call me darling in years." He grinned. "I like it. You know what else I like?"

She shook her head.

"You." He pressed his lips to her cheek but didn't pull away. Instead, he whispered in her ear. "Yes, I see what you're saying. Let's go back to London." Dane nipped her earlobe.

Thankfully, no one could see what he was doing, or they didn't seem to care. Both couples were involved in another conversation.

"However," he murmured, then pressed a kiss to the tender skin below her ear. "I will use that time to convince you to move in with me. And that means you are riding in the carriage with me...*without a chaperon.*"

"Foolish man," she murmured.

"Difference of opinion between us." He grinned like a rogue determined to charm his way into getting what he wanted. "I believe I'm quite brilliant."

"You always have," she countered with a sly smile.

"What matters most is that you believe it too."

Nineteen

G race buried her head in her hands. She and Dane never had the opportunity to discuss what was happening between them. His siblings insisted that they were in the room whenever she and Dane were together.

Grace rose slowly from her desk, her gaze drifting to the small garden outside her window. It had become a tangle of overgrowth in her absence, the once-pristine beds now choked with weeds and wildflowers that had taken advantage of her neglect. The sight tugged at her heart—a reflection of the chaos she had returned to, both in her garden and her life. Her hands itched to reclaim order, to find some semblance of control amidst the turmoil.

Honor and Trafford had accompanied her and Dane back to London. Throughout the journey, Dane had been beside her, trying to convince her to move into Ardeerton House when they returned. Honor had sided with Grace. Grace had declined Honoria's and Pippa's generous offers of her moving in with one of them. It was out of the question that she should ask Stewart and Hope for their assistance with anything. Dane had agreed with her. Thinking of such a prospect twisted her stomach with dread. The thought of appeasing them was almost unbearable, especially when they looked upon her with complete disdain.

"Ma'am, I've unpacked your bags, and I'm off to the market now."

"Thank you, Theo. Take your time," Grace answered. "I have correspondence to answer."

Theo nodded, a look of mirth flickering across his face before he quietly exited her study. Grace sank back into her chair, the familiar scent of aged leather and ink doing little to soothe the storm within her. She reached for a piece of parchment, its crisp edge biting into her fingertips, and selected her favorite quill from the inkstand, a gift from her father, its shine only enhanced with age. She needed to write to Marbury and ask to meet to discuss what had happened. She would use all of her charm to soothe his concerns while minimizing any damage to reputations.

Dane was correct that it wouldn't do much harm to his reputation, but hers was another concern. She still had other clients to contend with. She also planned to confront the earl about Athena subtly. Poor Athena, sweet and innocent, was caught in Marbury's conflict with Dane, which wasn't an argument at all. Couldn't Marbury see that Athena was in love with him? Everyone else could see it. Perhaps Marbury was too blind or too stubborn to acknowledge the truth?

Grace's thoughts churned with frustration. She had always been attuned to the subtle dance of courtship, the unspoken words and glances exchanged between a man and a woman. But Marbury seemed oblivious, stuck in his own world of pride and fear. He thought he didn't want Athena, yet he couldn't bear the idea of anyone else being with her. Ironically, his close relationship with Athena reminded Grace of Dane and her courtship.

Perhaps Marbury needed to understand her long past with Dane. That might be the nudge he needed to envision a future with Athena. The sooner he recognized his feelings for her, the better it would be for everyone involved.

A soft knock interrupted her thoughts before Grace could put quill to parchment to ask to call on Marbury.

"My lady?" A young woman in a lady's maid uniform and a man in a simple livery stood at the entrance of her study. "Mr. Tinniswood said that it was all right if we came in here and introduced ourselves."

Grace's eyebrows shot up to her hairline, or at least, it felt as if they did. It was highly unusual for Theo to allow visitors to waltz right into her home without announcing them first. Slowly, she stood. "How can I help you?"

The young woman was attractive, with dark brown hair and matching eyes that seemed to fill her face. The man beside her was strikingly handsome, tall, and possessed blond hair a shade darker than Dane's.

"My lady, I'm John Powers." He gazed at the petite woman beside him with an affectionate gaze. "This is Mabel Simmons." He turned to Grace and smiled. "We're your new staff. I'm your footman, and Mabel is—"

Mabel bounced on her toes. "I'm your new lady's maid. My aunt, Alice Roberts, is Lady Ravenscroft's lady's maid. She thought I'd make an excellent lady's maid for you." A delightful pink blush colored her cheeks.

"There must be some mistake." Their enthusiasm was infectious, as she could attest by her own smile. But she had to nip this mistake in the bud. Not only did she not hire any new staff, but she couldn't afford them. She could barely afford Theo.

"No mistake and no worries, my lady. You must want to know more about us. We're from Lavenham. We grew up next to one another." John smiled as if the sun rose and set on Mabel's shoulders. He clasped his hands behind his back. "If it's all right with you, Mabel and I will settle first, then get to work. I'm also acting as your new coachman. Mr. Tinniswood said the old carriage needed to be moved before the new one arrived."

Mabel nodded her head enthusiastically. "Indeed. I have quite a bit to organize myself." She tilted her head toward Grace. "Shall I unpack your new gowns in here so you can see them, or shall I take them to your bedroom?" She closed her eyes and sighed. "Lady Ravenscroft truly outdid herself. I've never seen such beautiful gowns. Each one is like a piece of artwork. And Lady Honoria, I mean Lady Trafford, has exquisite taste in shoes and reticules. She picked those items out for each gown."

"Sorry, I'm late. The crowd at the market was double in size from yesterday." A middle-aged woman with white hair and a kind smile entered the room. "Did you introduce me?"

"No, ma'am," Mabel said.

The older woman nodded once, then stepped forward. "My lady, I'm Ese Fournier. I'm your new cook. My grandfather served in the French court years ago." She cleared her throat. "I learned everything I know from him." She held up her hand to stop Grace from saying a word. "No need to fret about my needs. I've brought my pots and saucepans. Your kitchen will be sufficient."

John nodded once in agreement. "Now, ma'am, your new carriage will arrive in the afternoon." He rocked back on his heels. "If Mr. Tinniswood agrees, I'd be honored to take you on your first ride. After all, his sole responsibility is now serving as your butler."

Grace's head spun with the overwhelming influx of new staff, dresses, accompaniments, carriages, and who knew what else. "I didn't order any carriages or new gowns. While I'm certain"—Grace put her hand to her forehead to fend off the sudden throbbing in her head—"you all are wonderful. I can't afford any new staff. There must be some mistake."

The trio who stood in her room frowned at the same time.

"But, my lady, there's been no mistake," Mabel said softly. "The Duke of Pelham is the one who arranged for us to work for you."

John placed his hand on Mabel's shoulder and patted her gently. "There, there, my girl. You'll still be a fancy lady's maid to a duchess. Lady Grace must not have heard from His Grace yet and what his plans are."

Mrs. Fournier chuckled. "He's a generous man. You are a lucky lady to have captured His Grace's eye."

"I must correct you, Mrs. Fournier. I am the lucky one because this delightful creature has agreed to marry me." As the three servants dipped curtseys and bows, Dane marched up to Grace and brought her hand to his lips. "Darling, I couldn't wait to see you."

Grace shook her head slightly. It was incredulous that Dane was here with all these people. To ensure that she wasn't dreaming, Grace pinched herself and flinched.

Indeed, this was actually happening.

"Mrs. Fournier, would you be a dear and prepare Lady Grace and me a pot of tea."

The cook beamed when Dane's face transformed into a beguiling smile. "Of course, Your Grace. I was just on my way to do that very thing."

"Thank you." He turned to Mabel and John. "Would you fetch the rest of the packages out of the carriage and take them upstairs? The new carriage has arrived, and I'd like to escort Lady Grace to see it and get her thoughts."

"Of course, Your Grace." John nodded once and escorted Mabel from the room.

When they were alone, Grace pirouetted on the ball of her foot and faced Dane. "What have you done?"

"I'm making your life easier." He took her in his arms and brought her near. "Which makes my life easier."

She whipped a hand toward the door. "How does hiring three servants, which we never discussed, make your life easier?" She lowered her voice and glanced toward the door. "I can't afford them."

"Darling, I should have discussed it with you first, but I knew that you would refuse. So—"

"So, you went ahead and hired them to work for me?" She cleared her throat after she realized her voice trembled. It was no wonder as a riot of emotions threatened to overtake her. She was ecstatic for the servants, the dresses, the shoes, and the carriage, even if she couldn't accept them. But why couldn't she? Good heavens, having someone share her burdens would be so easy. Dane could be that person. Perhaps she was too hasty in not agreeing to marry him. It might be selfish on her part, but she was tired, so very tired of worrying over every single shilling.

What if she married him, and things changed? She swallowed the doubt that bubbled from nowhere. She had to be logical. She had never heard rumors that the Duke of Pelham didn't pay his bills or was late in payment. For heaven's sake, he was the original millionaire of Mayfair.

But she'd never heard rumors about her father either.

Suddenly, all her emotions collided, and a pitiful sob wrenched free. God help her but she didn't want Dane to be like her father.

"Darling?" Dane took her into his arms and pulled her close. "Why are you crying?"

Burning hot tears rolled down her cheeks. As soon as she wiped one away, then two others reappeared. "I don't quite understand it myself."

She buried her head against his strong chest. He took her hand and placed it over his heart, where it pounded a strong, sure, and soothing rhythm.

"Do you feel that?" he murmured.

She sniffed as she barely nodded.

He led her to one of the sofas and brought her onto his lap, where he pressed his lips against her temple. "Every beat is yours, Grace. Ever since I first met you when you were a little girl, missing your front teeth, my heart knew." He pressed a kiss to one cheek, then the other. "My heart has always been and will forever be yours." In a reverent kiss, he pressed his mouth to hers.

She whimpered at the soft touch, but he withdrew and studied her. "What has made you so unhappy?"

What was the matter with her? She truly believed Dane was a good man. She had to cast her doubts aside. But then Marbury popped into her thoughts. Now was the time to tell him the truth about the earl. "I think I'm overwhelmed."

"Overwhelmed?" Dane hummed softly.

She pushed back and cupped his cheeks. "I've felt so alone for so long, and you've changed everything. No one but my parents and you have treated me like someone to cherish." She hiccupped as she thought of her ill-advised agreement.

"Oh, my darling Grace," he crooned softly. "You are my beloved. You are the treasure I value most in the world, and I'm thankful for you every day." He pressed a kiss on her forehead. "Once you marry me, you will never be alone again." He tipped her chin until their gazes met. With an affectionate smile, he kissed her tears away. "I'm sorry if I've inundated you and your household with all this. But know this, Grace, you deserve everything."

Being held by him was a comfort she hadn't realized she needed. "You didn't overwhelm me. I'm trying to understand how much my life has changed in the past week. I need to get my business in order," she blurted out.

"Tell me what business?" He scowled slightly. "The Governess?"

She nodded.

"All right, darling." He played with her fingers, then pressed a kiss to her palm. At the gesture, her heart practically broke through her ribs to reach him. "Know this, sweetheart. I've waited so long to have you. As your husband, I plan on spoiling you every chance I get."

"But you're already spoiling me." She played with the buttons on his gold brocade waistcoat. "And we're not even married. The servants and the clothes." She let out a tremulous sigh as she wrestled her emotions into some order. But it was a useless endeavor when his scent wrapped around her and confounded everything.

"Well, the servants all come from Ardeerton House." He leaned close and lowered his voice. "I'll tell you a little secret. Ritson almost had a mutiny at the house. The entire staff wanted to come work here and were quite displeased when they heard that Mabel, John, and Mrs. Fournier had been chosen."

"Why?"

He took her hand and entwined their fingers. "Because you will be my duchess. My staff wants to please you as well as me. When you move in with me, they will be assigned to you. I already discussed it with Mr. Tinniswood. Consider it an engagement gift. There's nothing scandalous about that."

She didn't have a retort. He was being earnest.

"Grace," he whispered. "I want to give you the world."

She straightened to her full height. "But I won't make Ardeerton House my residence—"

His familiar lopsided grin appeared. "You don't want to move in with me until you're married. And you must discuss Marbury's abhorrent behavior with him."

"Dane." She placed her hand on his chest, trying to anchor her resolve. "I have to tell you something."

He winged an eyebrow. "What is it?"

"Marbury," she whispered, trying to gather every speck of courage she possessed.

"He isn't worth your worry," he huffed. "The man didn't have the common sense or courtesy to wait to understand precisely what was happening at the Jolly Rooster. His loose lips allowed your brother-in-law, who was at his Amesbury estate, to hear about my illness when he was in the village, no doubt looking for gossip," he spat. "Furthermore, I have every right to my opinion since Marbury is upsetting the woman I adore. Not another word about the earl."

"But—"

"He's in the past and no part of our future. Now, I have something to tell you. I bought the townhouse next door and have moved in there temporarily."

"What?" she cried softly.

He nodded. "A man has to do whatever is required to be close to the love of his life." He shrugged. "This was the best for both of us. If you refuse to move in with me, then I will do the next best thing and move in next door." He pressed his nose against hers, then lowered his voice. "I can't spend another day, night, or even an hour away from you, so I've decided to live next door. I'll be as close to you as possible. Once we're married, I'm never leaving your side. Society matrons can't fault either of us for living next to each other."

Grace laughed and pulled him into a hug. "Of course, they will. The original millionaire of Mayfair has decided to move out of his palatial home and is now on the outskirts just to be close to—"

"The love of his life? His fiancée?" Dane arched a perfect eyebrow. "They will all understand. I have faith in them. Now, let's stretch our legs and go have a look at your new carriage."

Grace slid off his lap and stood. Overwhelming was putting it mildly. She felt like a fairy princess in her very own story. When Dane held out his hand, she wrapped hers around his.

"You didn't have to do that," she said quietly.

"I wanted to, Grace." His voice deepened in excitement. "Wait until I show it to you. It's a beautifully lacquered bird's eye maple with black trim. The benches and curtains are an ivory velvet."

"It sounds exquisite," she said breathlessly.

"Just like you," he crooned, then pressed his lips to hers. "Come." He tugged her to follow him. In minutes, they were in the alley behind her townhouse, where a small mews stood guard over two carriages. Her old one and then a carriage that could only be called a masterpiece.

"Oh, my goodness." Grace let go of his hand and rushed to get a closer look at the carriage. The side panels gleamed from the high polish of the wood. The glimmer reminded her of diamonds. She ran her hand down the panel in awe. She'd never seen a carriage so exquisite in her life.

Dane rocked back on his heels as he watched her. "Will it suit you?"

"Suit me?" Slowly, she turned around with a smile that she couldn't contain. "It's like a fairytale carriage the handsome prince uses to fetch his princess." She tilted her head and smiled slyly his way.

Dane came to her side. "Perhaps instead of a handsome prince, he's a devastatingly handsome duke."

"Who said dukes were handsome?" She bit her lip to keep from laughing.

"Minx," he growled as he twisted the handle and opened the door. "It's time you were taught a lesson."

"Hmm," she hummed playfully. "That sounds dangerous."

"You'll like it." He took her hand in his for support as she climbed the stairs.

When Grace sat down, the smell of new fabric and polished wood greeted her. She inhaled deeply. By then, Dane had taken the seat across from her.

"I've never sat in a new carriage or even smelled one."

He widened his legs and rested his hands beside her hips. He leaned forward, encasing her. He inhaled sharply. "The only thing I smell is you. Time for your lessons."

"Dane," she whispered as she leaned forward, closing the distance between them. He was her Dane of old, and she wanted to bask in his lightness and warmth—at least for now. "What are you going to teach me?"

"This." He pressed his lips to hers as he wrapped her in his embrace.

What began as an innocent and chaste kiss shared between two lovers smoldered until it burst into an undeniable desire between them. She moaned her approval as he deepened the kiss. His tongue slid along the seam of her lips, and instantly, she parted them. She wrapped her arms around his neck as their kiss became the only thing she could concentrate on. His hands gripped her waist and then slowly traveled the length of her ribcage. She arched her back when one of his hands cupped her breast. When he pulled her close, his hard length pressed against her stomach.

She ran her hand over his hardened cock. She was rewarded for her boldness as it throbbed and thickened in her hand. She slid from his embrace until she was kneeling on the floor. Never taking her eyes from his, she reached and started to unbutton the falls of his breeches.

He placed a hand over hers. "What are you doing?"

"Teaching *you* a lesson. I think you deserve one as well."

He leaned back against the bench and widened his legs even more. "I've been very naughty. I may need several lessons."

"I agree. You've been downright..." She sighed. "Incorrigible, I'd say. And since I am the Governess. I take my duties very seriously." She released another button, then rubbed her hand against his length. The feel of this viral man's evident desire for her made her breath catch.

"That's another thing I'm guilty of." He cupped her neck with his hand as a half-smile tugged at his lips. "I have unpure thoughts about my governess."

By then, she had unbuttoned his falls and had pulled his shirt away from his body. She was rewarded when his thick cock sprang forward. The tip glistened with his arousal, and she licked her lips in anticipation.

Then she froze. What was she doing? She had no idea how to please him.

"This is my fantasy come true." His smile instantly faded. "What is it?"

Though her cheeks heated, she forced herself to hold his gaze. "I've never done this before. I've only ever read about it."

His pupils had grown in size until the blue of his irises had practically disappeared. "You've read about doing this?" His voice broke on the last word.

She bit her lip and nodded. "I've fantasized about you and how you enjoyed it."

He swallowed, and his Adam's apple bobbed in his throat. But his intense stare never strayed from hers. "Did you become aroused?"

Her lower abdomen clenched as everything within her tingled. "Yes."

"Did you touch yourself as you thought of me?"

"Yes."

He cleared his throat. "That proves that there's no wrong way to do this. If you touch me, I'll enjoy it. Just looking at you on your knees before me is enough to make me come."

Never looking away, she grabbed his cock with one hand and lowered her mouth until she pressed a kiss to the crown. His unique smell of musk and evergreen rose to greet her. He groaned as she licked his tip, then ran her tongue up and down his length.

"Give me *grace*," he murmured as he closed his eyes.

She was giving him *grace*. She was giving all of herself to him as she lowered her mouth and tried to swallow his girth. Her eyes watered as she gagged slightly. But she was determined to please him.

He cupped her cheeks. "You don't have to take me deep. It's something we can work on together. The crown is sensitive."

She nodded, then took him in her mouth again and sucked. His hips flexed toward her, an obvious sign that he enjoyed her efforts. She repeated it, but this time she sucked harder and was rewarded with more of his taste. She pumped his length with her hand at the same time she sucked.

"Grace, for the love of heaven," he murmured as he rocked his hips and gripped her tighter.

She took his ballocks in her free hand and squeezed slightly. By then, his hips were in constant motion. She could feel his length swelling in her mouth.

She let go for a moment when he tried to pull her up. "I want this. Give it to me," she demanded.

Without another word, he nodded, then held her head tightly as he moved his length in and out of her mouth. "Grace."

It was the only warning she had before his hot seed erupted in her mouth. She swallowed every bit and didn't move as he orgasmed. He chanted her name over and over like a benediction before collapsing on the bench opposite her. Without a second thought, she licked his length, then kissed the crown.

"Come here, Governess." He pulled her from her knees and sat her on his lap. He kissed her with the fervor of a man well-pleased. "You certainly taught me a lesson. One I'll never forget."

She sighed in pleasure, then tilted her gaze to his. "Did you enjoy it?"

"What do you think?" He pressed a kiss against the tender skin in the hollow of her neck. "Just between you and me, you should teach me that one repeatedly." He took her in another kiss.

When they broke apart this time, she nestled her head under his chin. "I like the way we christened this carriage."

"I'll have to get you another so we can do this again."

She waved a hand in dismissal. "No need. I've taken quite a fancy to this one."

"I've taken a fancy to you." He pressed a kiss to her nose, then put himself to rights. "Now, I shall teach you a lesson." He laid her across the bench seat. "I've been dying to taste you all day."

Just as he lifted her dress, a voice rang out. She cringed and closed her eyes. For the love of all dukes everywhere, they were about to be caught in a state of undress. At least she was, since Dane had already dressed.

"Your Grace?"

"Darling, whoever it is wouldn't dare disturb me," Dane whispered.

"Your Grace? Mrs. Fournier asked me to tell you that dinner is in half an hour and will be served in the courtyard."

Dane's mischievous smile flashed in her direction before he leaned down and pressed a kiss to her lips.

"Dane," she hissed quietly. "John will think that we've done something wicked in here."

"Nonsense. You said we're just christening your carriage, and then you taught me a lesson," he whispered, winking. "Everyone does it, especially a fine pupil like me with his beautiful governess." He sat up and looked out the window. "Thank you, John."

"My pleasure, Your Grace," John called out. "Oh, if you see Lady

Grace, will you tell her that Mabel is ready to assist her in dressing for dinner? She's picked out several gowns for Lady Grace's perusal."

"It would be my pleasure to inform her. Thank you, John."

"Thank you, sir."

"Is he gone?" Grace bit her lip, praying that she wouldn't have to face the footman. Otherwise, her cheeks would burn for the rest of the night if she had to face him.

"Yes." Dane chuckled, then rested his forehead against hers. "Unfortunately, you'll have to wait until after I feed you for me to teach you a lesson." His mouth tugged into a mischievous grin. "Unless you really want to be naughty."

Twenty

"What did you think of your new carriage?" Mabel said as she smoothed the turquoise silk gown and laid out Grace's pearl earrings. "These will match the ribbon trim used for the gown." She sighed dreamily. "Have you seen the exquisite chemise and stockings that Lady Trafford purchased to match this gown? The duke won't be able to resist you tonight when he sees what you are wearing." She clapped a hand over her mouth. "My tongue sometimes runs ahead of my thoughts, my lady. Please forgive me."

Grace couldn't help but like the young woman. She had an effervescence about her that made everything a little brighter. After being alone for so long with only Theo, Grace enjoyed having Dane's servants in her home. Even Theo had welcomed all three without a single quibble. It seemed he quite fancied being solely a butler and managing the household. He'd even taken a liking to Mrs. Fournier, who had invaded his kitchen as if it were her own.

She still blushed at the thought of her boldness in the carriage. Though she'd been on her knees for Dane, she had felt powerful and the one in control, particularly when he was crooning her name as she pleasured him.

And it was all because of Dane, who had given her free rein to pleasure him. She shivered slightly in anticipation of tonight. No telling what Dane had planned for her. But the thought of Marbury hung over her head. Several hours ago, she'd received notice that the earl had made good on his promise and put the amount he promised into her account. She'd already sent word to her bank to return the funds.

She still hadn't received a response to her request to meet him. Tomorrow, she'd call on some acquaintances and clients. The way she was received would indicate if there was gossip about her stay in Amesbury that she needed to be concerned with.

"Ma'am?"

Grace shook her head to clear the fog in her thoughts.

"What about the pale pink gown with the red trim?" Grace fingered the soft silk. It felt decadent and sensual beneath her fingers. Instantly, she wondered what Dane would think of it. She would feel like a seductress in his presence. "Lady Ravenscroft certainly created a masterpiece with this creation."

Mabel tilted her head and regarded Grace. "Lady Ravenscroft did sew these gowns, but His Grace's ideas and thoughts went into every design. Lady Ravenscroft told me when she delivered them to Ardeerton House."

Grace stilled as her thoughts swirled. Ironically, she would have been furious if these gowns had been delivered two weeks ago. Now, she wanted nothing more than to please him. If he wanted to give her dresses, she would gratefully accept them. It was one way he showed his love. Ever since she'd known him, he was always buying gifts for his sisters, and now, he was purchasing them for her.

"Ma'am, I forgot to mention it, but a footman from Lord Marbury's home stopped by earlier with a brief message. He asked if I'd tell you that Lord Marbury would like for you to call upon him the day after tomorrow."

"Thank you, Mabel." As the young maid prepared her bath, Grace released a pent-up breath. She would have preferred to see Marbury as soon as possible, but this would have to do. Once she explained the circumstances to the earl, she could close the chapter on that unfortunate episode, including the extra money, Dane's illness, Athena's broken heart, and the damage to their reputations.

Then, she could concentrate on building her happily ever after with Dane.

Dane paced in front of the round table with two chairs in Grace's courtyard. He wasn't nervous at all; he simply couldn't wait to see Grace again. When he surprised her with the carriage, he never thought she would be so receptive to his gift. His Scottish wildcat had resisted him every step of the way when he had given her gowns and an account at E. Caversham Commerce. Blood rushed to his cock as he thought of Grace and their interlude in her carriage. He had never dreamed she would even know how to do that. He smiled to himself and bit the inside of his cheek. Perhaps his little governess would share her books where she'd read how to pleasure a man. They could study them together.

"Your Grace?" Samuel Wilton, one of his footmen he'd brought over from Ardeerton House, stood before him. "Everything is ready. I informed Lady Grace that you were waiting for her."

"Thank you." Dane took one last look at the table. A stunning bouquet of blush roses from the little flower girl rested there. Candles of various shapes and sizes adorned the smaller tables surrounding the dining area. In the dusk, the flames flickered, reminding him of fairies dancing around in a magical kingdom. Hopefully, Grace would be as enchanted by it as he was. When they settled into Ardeerton House, they would dine outside whenever the weather allowed. He had instructed Harry and John on how to create the setting to make it perfect for his future duchess.

"John and Mr. Tinniswood will serve dinner now," Harry advised.

"I didn't know that your butler duties included serving Lady Grace and me," Dane jested to Theo.

Theo sat down two covered dishes on the table and then lifted the lids. "This butler does, Your Grace," he chortled, then lowered his voice as the two footmen brought even more dishes to the table. "Thank you for sending us John, Mabel, and Mrs. Fournier. I don't know what I would have done without their help." The elderly man's cheeks reddened. "I'm not as spry as I used to be."

Dane stood and patted Theo on the back. "Thank you for taking care of Grace all these years." Emotion threatened to choke him up, but he pushed himself to complete his thought. "I should have been here for her long before now."

Theo's gentle smile shone in the evening light. "Enough of that, Your Grace. It was my pleasure. I'll stand by Lady Grace's side for as long as she needs me." He looked over the work of the two footmen who stood nearby, waiting for his approval. Theo nodded, indicating that the two footmen should wait by the door for Grace.

"Theo, if you ever get tired of working, you'll always have a home at Pelham Hall, Ardeerton House, or wherever Grace and I are." Dane cleared his throat as he met the man's gaze. "I will always be in your debt for the care you've provided for Grace over these past years."

Tears welled in the old man's eyes as he nodded once. "Thank you, Your Grace." He bent his head as he wiped away his tears. "I'll go and escort her to you now."

Without another word, Theo left his side and entered Grace's home.

In what seemed like a matter of seconds, his future and all his hopes and dreams stepped toward him. Grace had wrapped her arm around Theo's as he escorted her to Dane's side. Her eyes glistened with wonder as she took in the scene before her. But the world suddenly stopped on its axis when her gaze met Dane.

He'd never seen Grace more stunning in his life. But, of course, he always thought that when he saw her. Throughout the years, he'd realized that Grace was the type of woman who would always be treated kindly by age. Every day, she became more beautiful. And if fate was kind, he would be the lucky devil by her side through those years.

Without hesitation, he strolled toward her, and Theo bowed to Grace. When Dane reached her side, he took her hand and pressed his lips to her delicate skin. "In this moment, I'd give my fortune to be as eloquent as Byron. I've never seen you so enchanting. It's little wonder the moon is rising over the horizon, and the stars are twinkling in the darkening sky. They all vie for your attention, but I'm the fortunate man who will dine with you tonight."

Even in the twilight, he could see Grace's blush. "I don't think you should worry about matching wits with Byron. If he listened to you tonight, he would envy your imagery."

"It's not imagery if it's the truth." He squeezed her hand and laughed. "Don't tell my sisters about my musings. They'll taunt me to no end."

"They'll never know. This is ours."

Dane rubbed his finger down the soft skin of her cheek. "I feel the same."

Grace waved a hand at the table and the candles. "This is gorgeous. It looks like I stepped into a magic kingdom."

"One that you rule," Dane said as he pulled her chair for her. Once she was seated, he took his seat but ensured it was close to hers. "Allow me to serve you."

She placed her serviette on her lap as he poured them a glass of champagne. He held his in the air as she lifted her glass. Before he could toast her, Grace did the honor. "To the future."

Only after it grew quiet could he speak. *Damnable emotions.* "To the woman who has chosen me and, in doing so, has given me the greatest gift of all, her heart. I raise my glass to a life of shared dreams and a love that will only grow stronger with time."

Dane brought the glass to his lips without breaking his gaze from hers. For the first time, he understood what his best friends felt about their wives.

Where was all of this heady sentiment coming from? If he was this emotional now, he feared he'd be a bawling baby when they finally said their vows. Yet, when he gazed into her eyes, all questions and fears ceased. This woman was his destiny, and their lives had been intertwined for decades.

"Grace, I have something I must say."

She regarded him, and a slight furrow formed between her brows.

He took her hand and squeezed. "No frowning. Not tonight."

She nodded with a slight smile.

"I realized something about myself. Only with you do I have the fortitude and desire to marry. I shall never be alone with you by my side.

Even when we quarreled, it never broke our invisible bond with one another."

A genuine smile of affection pulled at her lips. "Even Byron discussed how love and hate are kindred emotions easily woven together." This time, she was the one who squeezed his hand.

"You have my promise that I will always have your best interests at heart." It was her turn to blink twice, but it didn't hide the glistening of tears in her eyes.

"No tears, darling." Dane speared a deviled quail's egg and placed it on her plate. He added a slice of roasted beef and several buttered potatoes.

"You remind me of a red fox I once saw at Pelham Hall while walking. He was feeding his vixen, who had a litter of pups."

"Where do you think he learned that trait from?"

Grace giggled. "You are incorrigible."

"You love that about me. You also love that I'm wealthy." He waggled his eyebrows. "That may be my most redeeming trait in your eyes."

"Very." She popped a potato in her mouth, then closed her eyes and moaned as she chewed. "Delicious," she pronounced, then dipped her gaze before she met his. "I have a question. Are you truly wealthy?"

"What kind of dinner conversation is that?" He tilted his head and regarded her. He shouldn't be surprised. His Grace was always concerned about money.

"We've never discussed it." Her eyes never left his.

"Yes, I am." He needed to be patient with her. Ever since her father died, she'd had to earn her way in life. "Darling, don't worry about money. We have plenty. Let us concentrate on us tonight."

The brightness in her eyes dulled. "You're right. Forgive me. That was a horrible display of manners."

"There is nothing to forgive." He brought her hand to his lips.

The night continued as they finished their meal and drank their champagne. John and Harry were discreet and unobtrusive when they cleared the table and brought out Dane's bottle of port and two glasses. He poured two glasses and gave one to Grace.

"This is another reason why I adore you," she said as she raised her glass. "You are generous in sharing your port."

"Thank you." He took a sip, then sat his glass down.

Grace did the same. "I'm surprised you moved next door."

"Why? I thought I had made it clear that I refuse to be separated from you. You will compare me to a barnacle clinging to the keel of a ship. I won't disappear easily." When she laughed, he savored the sound. He knew he would never tire of it.

She leaned near him and winked. "I like that."

Her gown highlighted her long neck, and the urge to kiss her soft skin became almost unbearable. His voice turned into a low rumble. "Another reason I moved in next door is so we could make love whenever we desire." When her eyes widened, he continued, "Hear me out, Grace. You made it abundantly clear that we can't live together until marriage, but we've wasted so much time. I know that our actions may result in a child, but we're to be married. Frankly, I don't care because I want children with you. But the most important thing is you. I think of you every hour of the day and night." He shrugged. "If that means I'm a besotted fool, I will gladly claim that title."

Her eyes grew hooded. "I want that too, even if it makes me your match as a lovesick and wanton fool."

"You are never that," he declared softly. "If you're lovesick, then let us be lovesick together." He took her hand and played with her fingers, then brought them to his mouth. "You don't by chance know of a secret passageway in that house of yours that I can sneak through and sleep in your bed?"

"Like Romeo and Juliet?"

"No. We don't have a nurse to help us unless Theo wants to play the role."

"Don't corrupt my butler."

"Spoilsport." He scowled slightly. "I don't care for that play anyway."

"Do tell." Her tongue slid across her lower lip, making it wet. Then the temptress bit the tender skin.

He groaned at the sight and reached for her. He slid his free hand under the table and reached for her thigh. The feel of her tender skin beneath his fingers made him want to bay at the moon.

Instantly, she stilled at his touch before placing her palm over his hand. "What are you doing?"

"I'll combust into flames if I can't touch you," he whispered.

"Well, we can't have that happen." She tangled her fingers with his.

He moved their hands closer to the juncture of her thighs and rubbed his thumb slowly against the silk of her gown. "Your gown is soft, but it feels as coarse as a canvas sail compared to your skin.

She shifted slightly in her seat. He continued his ministrations for a moment, then started a slow slide of her skirt up her leg. "I want to touch you." He brought her forefinger into his mouth and sucked. "I want to make you wet."

"I already am." Her voice fluttered with arousal.

"Will you share?" His hand slipped between her thighs.

"Dane," she protested softly but opened her legs.

"Don't scold me." He slid his fingers into her folds and found the sensitive nub. She sucked in a breath and closed her eyes. The feel of her heat and wetness made his cock thicken and throb. But tonight wasn't about him. It was about his Grace.

The tender skin of her chest grew red as her chest heaved in and out. She placed her hand over his, and instantly, he stopped. "Is this all right? Say the word, and I'll set you back to rights."

Slowly, she twisted and met his gaze with a wicked but playful gleam in her eyes. "Don't stop."

Dane leaned close and rubbed his nose against the tender skin on the side of her neck. "You smell divine. Your scent has always caught my attention, but when mixed with the sweet scent of your arousal?" He pressed his lips, then tasted her with his tongue. "All I can think of is making love to you."

If anyone saw them, they would think that he was sharing secrets. In many ways, he was. But they were sensual secrets.

She loosened her hold but still held her hand on his. "I want more as well."

"That's it," he praised. "You can guide me. Show me where you want me to touch you."

Grace nodded slightly.

He nipped below her ear, acknowledging her. Their chests rose and fell as they breathed in unison. Grace closed her eyes and gasped a soft moan, lost in the heat of the moment. Her chair creaked as she arched her back, pushing further into his hand. She let out a small whimper as he circled her clitoris, his thumb, and forefinger relentless in their teasing.

"Tonight, I think I'll pleasure you with my fingers, mouth, and cock. In that order."

She whimpered and opened her legs even wider until her thigh rested against his. He bit his lip to keep from groaning. Slowly but surely, his middle finger circled her entrance. She was so aroused that his fingers were coated in her wet heat, making his cock thicken even more, if that was possible.

She was like a heavenly body encircling him in her orbit. He would never leave and had no desire to. As he studied the side of her face, her lips were parted. He closed his eyes to keep from coming in his breeches, something he hadn't done since the first time he'd touched Grace when they were curious about each other's bodies.

He inched another finger inside, stretching her. Releasing a groan, Grace threw her head back in pleasure at the contact.

"Darling, we must be quiet. Look at me," he commanded. When she did, he twisted in his chair facing her, then closed his mouth over hers. He removed his hand from her body and wrapped it around her chair.

Grace groaned in disapproval. "Dane."

"I won't leave you," he murmured. He replaced his left hand with his right, his fingers thrusting in a slow rhythm, mimicking what he wanted to do with his cock. Her breath hitched as he rubbed circles around her clitoris, working it faster and harder with each passing moment. All the while, his tongue explored every bit of her sweetness.

Grace grabbed the lapel of his evening jacket and held on for dear life. She moaned into his mouth as her hips rose to meet each thrust of his hand. He could tell she was close to her climax as her muscles tightened around his fingers. Then, in a flash, her body stilled. She closed her legs, entrapping his hand as he slowed his movement. The softest sigh escaped her.

It could have been seconds or minutes. He'd lost track of time. There was nothing more enchanting than having his Grace come apart in his arms.

She rested her head against his shoulder. With deliberate slowness, she moved her hand from underneath the table and palmed his cock through his breeches. It twitched as if it were a dog, and she had petted it. Typical. It was unruly when he tried to control it. But with Grace, it would follow her anywhere.

She moved to unbutton the falls of his breeches.

He placed his hand over hers, stopping her movement.

She lifted her head and met his gaze. "Don't you want me…"

"Grace, you have no idea how much I want you." He murmured as he pressed his lips to hers. "But I just saw Theo peek outside."

"He probably wants to clean the table so he can go to bed," she said dejectedly. "Do you have a secret passage in your house?"

"Unfortunately, I don't." He pulled her closer into his chest. "This is why we should be at Ardeerton House." He stopped as he remembered another entrance to his townhouse. "Wait a moment."

"What is it?" Grace pushed away and faced him.

"I do have a secret passageway. It's next to the backdoor."

If anyone had told Grace earlier in the week that she would have let Dane pleasure her in the courtyard while the servants were in the house, she'd have been horrified at such behavior.

But that would have been because she had never understood the urgency, the need, the hunger to be with your love. Dane was right. They had wasted years. Perhaps they were making up for lost time. She smiled to herself. What smoldered between them could not be extinguished. Why had she even thought she could push him into another woman's arms?

Dane reached under the table and smoothed her dress. "I don't want you to fret that anyone might see something inappropriate."

"That's very gallant, Sir Galahad," she teased.

"Minx, call me simply Galahad, as in the Duke of Galahad," he answered as they both stood.

He took her hand and led her to the back corner of the courtyard, where a wrought iron fence separated their back entrances. The darkness surrounded them, and before they took another step, he swept her into his arms.

"Finally," he murmured before he slammed his mouth against hers.

When Grace melted against him, she sighed softly into his kiss. But the dastardly darling fiend deepened the kiss, reigniting all the passion that had blazed between them.

"Dane," she whispered like a prayer against his lips.

"Come with me," he sighed against her lips, then took her hand and pulled her through the iron gate.

The night swallowed them, and she couldn't see a foot in front of her. She pulled on his hand, slowing their pace.

"What is it, darling?" His voice, smooth as whisky, comforted her.

"I can't see."

"Don't worry. I know where we're going." He kissed her lips and then tugged her hand, encouraging her to follow him.

After leaving the courtyard, Dane led them to the rear of his townhouse. Rather than using the back door, he opened a smaller door to the left of the main entrance. It was concealed by paneling that matched the house's trim.

"Voila! Watch your precious head for me," he murmured as he ducked through the door first.

She followed. "What is this?"

"I discovered it the first time I examined the fireplace in my bedroom. It leads directly here." He opened a tinderbox and lit a piece of tinder with a flint. After lighting a nearby candle, he blew out the fire from the wood. "You first."

When her eyes adjusted to the light, she noticed a steep staircase with handrails on both sides. "It looks like an escape route for when the revenue officers come to steal you from your bed in the dark of night."

When she started up the steps, he followed her and slapped her behind. "What a devious mind you have. I thought the owner built it exactly for the reason we're heading upstairs."

"Ouch." She rubbed the spot. He grabbed her hand and entwined their fingers. "You mean trysts with unmarried women?"

"This is not a tryst. This is catching up for lost time," he murmured in a sinfully dark voice.

When they reached the top of the stairs, he reached around her and opened the door to his chambers. As soon as she stepped in, she was surrounded by the essence of Dane. Candlelight flooded the room, and a massive bed with a wood frame commanded the center. It was richly appointed with luxurious silk and brocade bedding in black and ivory. Matching pillows were strewn around the room and on top of the bed.

Before she could comment on the room, Dane kicked the door closed and pushed her against it. With his arms bracketing her head, he lowered his mouth to hers. He devoured her as if he were a starving man and she was the nourishment he needed.

"Where are Emmy and Dancer?" she asked breathlessly.

"Home at Ardeerton House. In my bed. Which is where you should be."

"Dane."

With an exaggerated huff, he continued, "You can't blame a man for trying. I'll stay as long as you're here." He pulled away, then, as if unable to leave her, he took her in another kiss. "Gown off."

"I'll need your help." She turned and rested her arms toward the door. Dane pressed close against her. It was difficult to determine who was harder—Dane or the wood.

With a slow breath, Dane made quick work of the fastenings on the back of her dress. It slipped from her shoulders in a swoosh. She turned and never took her eyes from his as she untied her stays. It fell next to her dress on the floor.

With a shaky hand revealing everything he felt for her, he gently untied her chemise. It joined the rest of her clothes, leaving her in only her stockings and shoes. He leaned closer and pressed his lips to the spot on her neck where her pulse throbbed. "To think we will always be together without needing to sneak through the night like secret lovers takes my breath away. I beg of you, can we marry tomorrow?"

She untied his cravat and unbuttoned his waistcoat. He shrugged his coat and let it join the rest of their clothes. After a flurry of activity, he stood before her with a tent in his breeches. He wanted her as much as she wanted him.

He swept her into his arms and brought her to his bed, where he sat her on the edge. He dropped to his knees and unbuttoned his falls, freeing his engorged cock. Carefully, he removed her evening slippers and untied her stockings, rolling them down her legs.

He finished undressing and leaned over her as he took his cock in hand. Never taking his eyes from hers, he tugged hard. A longing, or perhaps a new fervor, glowed in his brilliant blue eyes. She'd never seen such intensity before.

After a moment, it became too much. She dared to look at the rest of his body. A bead of arousal shimmered on the crown of his cock. She licked her lips at the sight.

Something was different about tonight. They were ravenous for each other, but a new tenderness had budded between them. Perhaps it was the realization that whatever brought them together was too powerful to ignore.

Dane lowered his body over hers and held her hands above her head. His mouth met hers in a kiss filled with longing and love. She felt him position himself at her entrance. He pushed forward tentatively at first, then more until he was firmly seated in her.

"What I feel for you is more than love." With a languid ease, he moved inside her. "What I feel for you defies the limits of any word I know. I've always thought that love was supposed to be tender and sweet?" He shook his head. "But that is not what I feel for you. What burns in me is far fiercer, more consuming. It is a fire that cannot be quenched, a need that gnaws at my very soul. When I look at you, it's as if the world bends to you, as if time itself pauses, and nothing else exists but the pulse of your presence in my heart. This is not just love; it is something deeper, something wild and untamed. It is a devotion so boundless it terrifies me because, without you, I would be utterly lost, as if the air itself would vanish."

Tears welled in her eyes. "I don't know what to say."

"You don't need to say anything. I'm simply telling you the truth." He buried his head in her neck as his pace increased in tempo. "Promise never to leave, Grace. It would destroy me."

Twenty-One

D ane waited in the study of the Earl of Webster-Harnly. He slowly strolled around the room, examining its contents. One could quickly form an opinion about a man based on how he maintained his inner sanctum. If the desk looked cluttered, then the chances were good that the man wasn't meticulous with his books or had someone else manage them for him.

Of course, that wasn't always the case, but Dane had seen enough in his life to feel confident in the prediction. He'd had too many men in the Jolly Rooster who had gambled over their heads because they didn't realize that they didn't have the money. They were incapable of keeping their finances organized.

He predicted that the earl knew to the exact shilling how much was in his personal and estate coffers. Everything in the study was organized. Even the earl's quills were lined up in a neat line like soldiers in formation.

Dane smirked slightly. If Dancer ever saw such a sight, the cat would knock them over with one swipe of his paw and not even feel an ounce of remorse.

"Your Grace, I apologize for keeping you waiting." Raphael Sullivan, the Earl of Webster-Harnly, entered the room with a slight smile.

Dane could also tell that the man was a no-nonsense sort by the cut of his clothing. His black broadcloth coat fit him like a glove, as did his buckskin breeches. His boots shined as if freshly polished, and his cravat was a simple mathematical knot. There was nothing fancy about his attire except his gray waistcoat. Made from silk, it featured silver buttons that captured the natural light of the day.

"No need to apologize. I enjoyed looking at your study." Dane extended his hand when the earl reached his side.

Webster-Harnly took Dane's hand in a shake, then motioned for him to sit in one of the two chairs that framed his desk. "I must admit that I was a bit curious when I received your card. It's not every day that the duke who is the original Mayfair millionaire calls on me."

"I'm not here as a millionaire. I'm here as a man determined to solve a mystery that frankly has me quite baffled." Dane swept his coattails aside, then sat down and faced the earl.

A footman brought a tea tray and sat it on the desk before the earl. After pouring two cups, the man bowed and then took his leave.

Dane took a sip, then nodded his approval. "It's just the way I like it. Strong and hot."

The earl leaned back in his chair and grinned. "I'm glad you approve. Now, tell me about this mystery."

"It's about your predecessor. Did you ever hear a rumor that the previous earl was a gambler?" Dane took another sip of tea and eyed the earl over the cup.

Webster-Harnly placed his cup on the desk and shook his head. "No. It would be quite out of character for him, I believe. When I inherited the title, everything was in immaculate order." The earl cocked his head. "I'm curious. Why are you interested?"

Careful not to divulge Grace's secrets, he continued, "I had a visit from Stewart Arnold the other day."

Instantly, the earl slapped his desk. "Let me guess. He's demanding money that he believes the old earl lost at your establishment since you own the Jolly Rooster." He shook his head. "The man was here demanding money as well. After all these years, he complained that his wife's inheritance wasn't what they expected from the earl's personal estate." Webster-Harnly sneered slightly. "His wife received everything she was entitled to. I witnessed the disbursement myself when I inherited the title. The man is a greedy opportunist."

Dane sat on the edge of his seat. "That's interesting that his wife received her inheritance, and he was questioning you about it. He came to see me under the brotherly guise that discussing marriage settlements with me was his duty. You see, Grace and I are to be married. He told me that Grace had no dowry. I'm not interested in her dowry or inheritance, but I am interested in what happened to it."

"Congratulations."

Dane nodded his thanks.

The earl smirked. "I never liked the man."

"Why?" Dane asked.

"When I was a young lad, he was overly concerned about money." Webster-Harnly snorted slightly. "It wasn't that he didn't have any. He's gentry with a large profitable estate. But Stewart Arnold makes assumptions about a person's worth based upon their wealth."

"You mean financial worth?" Dane asked. "I could see that."

The earl shook his head. "I mean a person's worthiness. He always would snub the young men on scholarship who attended university." The earl rested his elbows on the desk and entwined his fingers together. "I don't know about Lady Grace's inheritance. My secretary handled that part of the earl's estate. He served the old earl, and I kept him on. He is quite a brilliant fellow who only offers his opinion when asked. The rest of my staff call him the 'Vault.'"

"A valuable employee, then." Dane relaxed slightly. With his experience of running the Jolly Rooster, he had developed an uncanny knack for determining a gentleman's worth. The earl seemed to have the same opinion of Arnold as Dane. Plus, he'd never heard of the earl being one to share in gossip. If he wanted to help Grace, then he would have to share more. "May I have your word as a gentleman not to share anything I say here today."

"Of course." The earl tilted his head. "You've piqued my curiosity."

"It's about Lady Grace."

The earl's mouth tilted in an affectionate smile. "I haven't seen her since we were children at a family Yuletide party, but I've always thought highly of her. She was particularly kind to me at those gatherings. I was an awkward youth, and she always ensured I was included in the various games. How is she?"

This was the same man who Arnold said would not have welcomed Grace into his home after her father died. Dane studied the earl for any hint of insincerity, but there was none. Either he was telling the truth, or he was a marvelous actor.

"She is well, and I agree that she's extremely kind. I've known her since we were children as well."

The earl nodded once. "I can see by the smile on your face that there is true affection. I'm happy for you and her. I was going to call on Lady Grace and see..." He cleared his throat, then pulled his cravat away from his neck. "Bloody thing is too tight." He cleared his throat again as his cheeks reddened. "I was going to ask Grace if she could introduce me to a few young ladies who might be interested in matrimony. I know I'm quiet, but I'd make an excellent husband."

"I have every confidence that she can help you. I'll let her know that you might call on her." Dane exhaled. "I'm quite perplexed. You see, I know for a fact that her father adored her and had provided her with a dowry and an inheritance."

"Just a moment," the earl said, then picked up a handbell and rang it.

In moments, an elderly but distinguished gentleman entered the room. "You rang, my lord?"

The earl nodded and motioned toward Dane. "This is the Duke of Pelham. He has some questions about Stewart Arnold and my predecessor's estate." Webster-Harnly swung his gaze to Dane. "This is Simon Fields. He was the old earl's secretary, and now, he's mine."

Dane stood and shook the secretary's hand. He had a surprisingly powerful grip for a man in his sixth decade. "How do you do? I understand from the earl that Lady Hope Arnold inherited money from her late father, but Lady Grace Webster did not. Did you know the reason why?"

By then, the secretary was shaking his head. "Respectively, that is not correct. Lady Grace received an inheritance as well. Her father was adamant on his deathbed that his eldest daughter receive her money as soon as possible. He also wanted Sommer House to be given to Lady Grace. There was also a small inheritance from an aunt." The man's cheeks colored slightly. "The previous earl passed before he could discuss the matter with Lady Grace. Mr. Stewart Arnold arrived immediately after Earl's death and took both daughters' inheritance directives. He said he would ensure that Lady Grace received her monies and Sommer House."

Dane's eyes widened at the news. "Are you certain there were monies for Lady Grace?"

"Indeed, sir." The secretary didn't blink. "The old earl was meticulous with his accounts and estate matters."

"Did you ever hear of the earl having gambling debts?"

"Absolutely not."

Dane almost cringed at the secretary's umbrage.

The secretary stuck his nose in the air. "The previous earl did not tolerate such behavior and hadn't since..." The old man's voice grew quiet. "I've said too much."

"Continue," Webster-Harnly urged. "No one will judge you here."

The man nodded once and looked out the window toward the sculpture garden that was outside the earl's study.

"I promised the old earl I wouldn't say anything."

Dane nodded and rose to stand beside the man. "You are loyal to him, but you see, I'm loyal to Lady Grace. She never received those funds or that property. She was led to believe that her father was an irresponsible gambler who was practically destitute."

Horror flashed across the secretary's face, and his gaze flew to the current earl.

Webster-Harnly nodded. "The duke is marrying Lady Grace. You can tell him what you know."

After hesitating for a moment, the secretary swept his gaze to Dane. "It wasn't the earl who was the incessant gambler."

Grace plopped on the sofa in her study after a dreadful morning of making social calls. All of her acquaintances weren't receiving callers. When she left Lady Franklin's house, she saw someone who looked remarkably like the lady peeking from an upstairs window.

She couldn't escape the uneasy feeling that everyone had been avoiding her. She rested her elbows against her knees and held her head. Was she being shunned because she was in love with Dane? She didn't want to draw conclusions, but it would make sense if Marbury had spread tales about the Pelham Hall visit. Goosebumps rose on her arms. Everything she'd worked for over the years was in danger of being destroyed. She should have left for London at her first opportunity.

Grace pulled out her stationary and quill to work on her correspondence. She would know the truth when she called on her clients. If they refused to receive her, then her reputation was in tatters.

Theo entered the room with a grin, placing a tray of hot cherry tarts and a fresh pot of tea on her desk.

"Seems you're enjoying the duke's company," Theo said with a small grin.

If he only knew the extent of how much she was enjoying Dane, poor Theo would be aghast at her behavior. "It's been lovely."

"I, too, enjoy the duke's company," Theo beamed. "I also appreciate the staff he sent, especially Mrs. Fournier." He rocked back on his heels. "Neither of us minds having the other in the kitchen."

Grace sipped the hot tea and sighed. If only her life were as perfect as her tea.

"I'm on my way to the kitchen." With a spring in his step, Theo nodded and made his way to Mrs. Fournier.

It was wonderful that her loyal servant was delighted with the changes Dane had instituted within her household. Slowly, the smile on her face disappeared. She still had to confess to Dane what she'd agreed to do for Marbury, namely steer Dane toward Lady Athena. She had little doubt that he would be furious with her. She was furious and disappointed in herself.

Shame, the kind she had never felt before, welled inside her. It was just like gambling. She had gambled on Dane's future along with hers.

No matter how much they had argued and been at odds with one another in the past, she loved him.

She had always loved him, and no matter what, she had to confess and face whatever wrath he directed at her. She deserved it—all of it. She only hoped he could forgive her.

Grace rested her head in her hands as all she had jeopardized came into focus. Tears gathered in her eyes, but she refused to allow them to fall. If she lost him, she doubted if she'd ever recover from it this time. She sniffed back the tears, vowing she would not wallow in her sadness until she spoke to Dane. However, there was no denying that her life was tumbling into a fall that could crush her. If her reputation was sullied, she'd be devastated. If she lost Dane, she'd be destroyed.

"Ma'am?"

She quickly wiped her eyes and regarded her footman. "Come in."

John stepped into the room. "The mail has arrived, and Lady Athena is in the entry." He stepped closer and lowered his voice. "She seems out of sorts, my lady. She's obviously been crying."

"Bring her in, please." She stood and waited. Within seconds, John escorted an obviously distraught Athena into Grace's study.

With the dark circles under her bloodshot eyes, Athena appeared miserable. "Lady Grace." Her voice broke, and she brought a handkerchief to her mouth and slammed her eyes shut.

"Come in, darling," Grace said as she took the young woman's hands and squeezed them. She led her to one of the sofas and sat down, pulling Athena to join her. "Whatever it is, I will help you." If she were a betting woman, she'd wager this had something to do with Marbury.

Athena buried her head in her handkerchief and sobbed quietly. Grace could do nothing except rub the young woman's back in comfort as the young woman's shoulders shook with grief.

"What's happened," Grace asked softly as she held Athena's hand.

She squeezed Grace's fingers and then tilted her head to the ceiling. After a moment, she composed herself and twisted her body so that she faced Grace. "I'm leaving London."

"Why? Don't you want to finish the Season?" Grace kept her voice even and calm.

"I'm leaving for a cottage that my parents left me when they died. It's on the coast of Cornwall. They traveled there yearly to celebrate the day that they married." She smiled slightly as another tear cascaded down her face. "I always thought I'd take my husband there, but now..." She closed her eyes tightly. "I apologize for being so emotional. I just didn't know where to turn."

"Did you quarrel with Marbury?" Grace stood and brought Athena a cup of tea.

"No." Athena shook her head. "Yes." She tilted her gaze to Grace. "Honestly, I don't know." She twisted her fingers together.

Grace had never seen the young woman so unsure of herself. "Whatever has happened, we'll find a solution. Allow me to call on him. I had planned to visit him anyway. He left Pelham Hall in a fury, and he needs to know that His Grace was severely ill—"

"I don't think you should call on him on my behalf. I'm not certain it will help matters."

Grace patted Athena's hand. "What do you mean?"

Athena swallowed, but the movement was obviously difficult for her. She took a deep breath and let it out slowly. "I'm carrying."

"What?" Grace's voice cracked slightly. "Are you sure?"

Athena nodded. "I saw a midwife yesterday."

"What about Marbury?" Grace asked.

Athena lifted her head proudly, "He doesn't love me and acts as if he doesn't want to have a thing to do with me. So, I've decided to leave."

The room turned eerily quiet. Grace didn't move as Athena crushed her hand, as if Grace was the only thing keeping her from flying out the window.

Pregnancy was a common enough occurrence when a couple clearly loved one another and had every expectation of marrying. Grace had seen it throughout her years as the Governess. But the despair on Athena's face and her confession meant that the young woman realized her future.

If news of the pregnancy without the benefit of marriage came to light, Athena would be ruined, and nothing would repair the damage. Even if another man came forward and offered to marry her, it might not quell the rumors or her loss of standing within society. Gossip would spread like wildfire, and speculation would be rampant over who the child's father really was. Marbury and Dane would be the likely suspects.

There was only one solution. If Marbury wouldn't marry her, then Grace had to find a man who would marry Athena and claim that the child was his.

Grace blew out a silent breath.

"What shall I do?" Athena whispered.

"If a suitor could be found, would you marry him?"

"No," Athena said curtly.

Grace's gaze locked on a movement outside her door. Her heart pounded in her chest as she saw Dane standing there with a pained look. He must have heard everything she and Athena had discussed. That was the thing about the man she loved; he hated to see any woman suffer, and she could tell by the stricken look on his face that he was as shocked at the news as she was.

She shook her head slightly at him as Athena buried her head in her hands again and sobbed.

Grace brushed the hair that had fallen against Athena's face behind her ear. "Is the child Marbury's?"

"Yes." Athena nodded.

Dane's face turned the color crimson. He was riled and beyond angry at what he was hearing.

"Did you tell him?"

"I tried, but I couldn't find the words." Athena sobbed quietly as Grace attempted to comfort her. "I told him I was in trouble, but he doesn't understand the truth. He became angry and asked what kind of trouble, then told me he didn't want to know. He said it didn't make any difference. He'd find someone to marry me."

"Don't you think he needs to know," Grace murmured.

She shook her head. "I am humiliated, Grace. I can't tell him. He will hate me even more than he does now. When we returned to London from Pelham Hall, he didn't say a single word to me." Athena wiped her nose and turned to Grace. "I can't raise my child in a home where the father hates me."

"Oh, darling, I'm certain that he doesn't hate you. I think he loves you." Grace took her hands and squeezed. "I'll not make excuses for his behavior, but perhaps he's as lost as you are."

Athena shook her head. "I don't think so, Grace. I told him that I was leaving for Cornwall, and he didn't try to stop me. He said he'd be in contact with me by letter."

"You're going to raise the child yourself?" Grace's heart broke for the young woman before her. She was ensuring that she would never be welcome back into London society with such a decision.

"After the baby is born, I thought I would settle on the continent somewhere. I'll say I'm a widow raising my late husband's child. I have enough money from my parents to live comfortably on my own." She sniffed and smiled at Grace. "I guess I didn't need your help after all." She lowered her voice. "If you're willing, I would cherish your friendship." She sniffed as a woeful chuckle escaped. "I seemed to have lost everyone who I thought loved me."

"Oh, darling," Grace crooned as she rocked her. "I've felt the same way before. But listen to me. Marbury loves you." She wiped away a tear on Athena's face.

"I beg to differ." Another barrage of tears fell.

"Did I ever tell you that I was engaged once and let the man I loved more than life walk out of my life? It was the biggest mistake of my life."

Athena blinked, then blew her nose. "What happened?"

"Let's say our pride and hurt got in the way of hearing each other." Grace pushed several loose strands of hair off the girl's face. "Don't make the same mistake I did."

"I'll consider what you said. Perhaps I'll write him. But not now." She shook her head and closed her eyes. "I just...just cannot," Athena said as she stood. "I must be on my way. I want to make it to the Red Swan Inn before it grows dark."

"Would you like to stay here with me?" Grace asked. She glanced in Dane's direction, but he was gone. She had little doubt that if Athena stayed with her, Dane would involve his sisters in making the young woman comfortable. Knowing Honoria and Pippa, they would offer Athena refuge at their country homes. Honor owned a small cottage in Amesbury where she'd undoubtedly allow Athena to stay.

"Thank you, but no." Athena smoothed her gown and then kissed

Grace on both cheeks. "I need to be somewhere that no one will recognize me."

Grace could only nod at her logic.

Athena took a piece of parchment from her reticule and handed it to Grace. "This is my address. I hope you'll write. I'll send word once I'm settled in Cornwall. There is a couple who are the caretakers of the cottage. I know that they'll help me if Jasper will not." She smiled shyly.

"Think about what I've said."

After they exchanged their heartfelt goodbyes, Athena left. Dane came into the room and took Grace into his arms. "That was very kind of you. Are you all right?"

"Barely." She buried her head against his chest and inhaled his scent. It comforted her when she was a little girl and did the same for her now. "I hate that she's going through this alone."

"What can I do?" He pressed a kiss to her temple. "If you say marry her, I'll throw you over my knee."

"Be serious. I would never subject her to such torture." When she pushed him away, he grabbed her arms and held her close.

"What do you mean by torture?" He arched a perfect ducal eyebrow.

"Marrying you," she quipped. "You would eat her for lunch."

"The only one I would like to eat is you." He waggled his eyebrows.

"If you did that, I could easily find myself in the same position." She stilled as her words hung between them.

Dane pulled away, took her hand, and brought it to his lips as he stared into her eyes. "Nothing would please me more than if you were carrying our child." He pressed a kiss to her lips. "Except you marrying me and each of us pledging our troth to one another for always."

"Thank you," she murmured.

He pressed a kiss to Grace's temple, then stood. "I have business to attend to." He pointed his finger at her playfully. "When I return, you and I should have a private conversation."

Grace nodded and said a silent prayer. That would be her chance to confess all. "I have something to share with you also."

As Dane swept from the room, Grace collapsed against the sofa.

Dane was perfectly attuned to her and would do anything to help her and her friends. What would she do if she lost him?

It was ironic that Athena wanted to live in Cornwall. It had once been Grace's dream, but then the irresistible Duke of Pelham swept into her life again.

Making it doubtful she'd ever be the same again.

Twenty-Two

~

Dane inhaled sharply as he thrummed his fingers on one knee. Waiting for a worm to emerge from the ground was less tedious than waiting for Marbury to attend him. Frankly, with the décor a mud brown and black accents, it looked as if the said worm had decorated the room. Marbury needed a sense of fashion and a dose of good judgment.

He'd been waiting for the *pup* for over a quarter of an hour. By all rights, he should be offended and give the man the cut direct the next time he saw him, but he'd wanted to ease the worry of his darling Gracie.

The young earl was an honorable man, but Dane could understand the temptation of Athena living under his roof. The man was undoubtedly smitten with her if the way he had stared at Dane during their dance was any indication. Perhaps Marbury would see that he couldn't let Athena go if Dane shared his regret over losing Grace all those years ago.

A sly smile tugged at his lips. Even he would admit that the matchmaking business had its perks. It was a worthwhile and somewhat entertaining pursuit. He could understand why Grace enjoyed it. It felt like giving fate a boost. Perhaps she would be gracious and thank him by doubling the Jolly Rooster's profits for the next month.

Dane smirked as images and snips of conversation with Grace rushed through his thoughts. The woman could tie him up in knots, and he'd be willing to stay there as long as he could be in her presence. That's how deep his affection and commitment were to her. Sometimes, he couldn't believe he'd been so lucky to find his way back into her life. He would not dwell on how much time they'd wasted sniping at one another. They were hurting in their own individual ways, but the present offered a perfect opportunity to make amends for lost time.

A thud sounded against the wall, accompanied by the shattering of glass. Instantly, Dane stood to investigate the noise, but Marbury entered the room propped up by his butler.

"No real harm, sir. You never cared for that vase even if King William gave it to your family," the butler tutted as he escorted a wobbly Marbury into the room.

Marbury swayed slightly as he pulled down his waistcoat and regarded Dane.

In return, Dane stared at him. The man reeked of whisky. With a slight sniff, Dane could also detect the odor of brandy. With his scraggly beard, bloodshot eyes, and wrinkled clothes, it didn't take a genius to deduce that Marbury had been utterly foxed last night and didn't bother going to bed.

What a waste of good brandy.

"What do you want?" Marbury sneered.

His butler's eyes grew wide. "Sir," he muttered softly. "It's the Duke of Pelham."

"I don't care if he's King William himself." Marbury stumbled his way to his desk and plopped into the seat.

"It's not what I want but what you want and how I'm going to help you from throwing your future away like rubbish." Dane leaned back in his chair and accepted a cup of tea from the attending footman. "Thank you." Dane waved a hand at Marbury. "He appears to need something a tad stronger."

"Brandy will do me fine," Marbury added.

"It's done you a bit too fine, my friend," Dane admonished. He turned to the footman. "He needs coffee."

The footman looked for direction from the butler, who nodded his agreement with Dane's assessment. Without hesitating, the footman placed a steaming cup of coffee in front of the earl.

"Forgive our lack of expediency in serving you, Your Grace." The butler bowed. "The household has been in an uproar since Lady Athena departed for Cornwall."

"No need to apologize. That's why I'm here." Dane took a sip of tea.

Marbury instantly grew alert. "You're here for Athena? After your debacle with Lady Grace at the house party you invited us to?" He huffed his disapproval. "Naturally, you've come around to put a claim on Athena after you destroyed Lady Grace's reputation."

Dane counted to five, then smiled serenely. It was enough time to get his anger under control before he ripped the man's head off. "Have a care, Marbury. I'm here to keep you from making the biggest mistake of your life. I suggest that you finish that coffee before you speak again." Dane adjusted the lace at his wrists. He'd always loved this shirt design. It reminded him of Grace and the first time they'd kissed. She'd said it was soft against her skin when he held her cheeks and pressed his lips to hers. He'd ordered ten more immediately after that and still did every year.

"Before I give you some much-needed advice, you must correct your thinking about Lady Grace. She and I are to be married, and I will not tolerate anything to be said that might hurt her or her reputation." He didn't miss the slight grin on the butler's face at Dane's admonishment of the young earl. Dane had never really enjoyed giving lectures. But this young pup deserved one. Hopefully, it would clear the cobwebs out of his head so he could see his way clear to Lady Athena. "Lady Grace attended me at Pelham Hall when I was ill. I assume that you didn't know the particular situation, so I won't hold it against you." He wrinkled his nose at the stale smell of alcohol. "Has an animal died in here? Or is that you?"

The butler chortled at the comment, then bit his lip to keep silent.

"Whose side are you on?" Marbury directed at his servant.

"The right and ethical side," Dane drawled, then turned his attention to the butler. "My good man, would you leave us alone? What I have to say to his lordship is private."

The butler nodded. He and the footmen attending them closed the door behind them in seconds.

"You asked why I was here." Dane placed his empty cup on Marbury's desk and leaned against the back of the chair. "Athena came to see Grace. I happened to be there..."

Marbury rolled his bloodshot eyes.

"Careful," Dane growled softly, but the warning was clear. "I will not tolerate any slight to Grace."

Marbury nodded sheepishly. "I apologize."

"As I was saying, I caught the tail end of the discussion, but I heard enough to understand that the young woman is despondent. You know you're the reason she's leaving town for Cornwall?"

Marbury ran both hands through the mess of dark curls on his head. "I was jealous and lost my temper with her." He shook his head and tilted his head to stare at the ceiling. "She's beautiful and kind and—"

"And everything you wanted but didn't know that you needed. Am I correct?" Dane asked softly.

Marbury exhaled painfully and nodded. He directed his gaze to Dane. "I am the real reason that she left. She was distressed when she came to me. I know she's in some kind of trouble." He rested his elbows on the desktop and buried his head in his hands. After a moment of silence, he regarded Dane. His bloodshot eyes had filled with tears. "I didn't want to hear that she'd fallen in love with another man and had somehow found herself compromised."

Dane cocked his head. "Had she fallen in love with someone prior?"

He thickly swallowed as he nodded. "Me. When we were younger, I knew that she'd developed feelings for me that I could not return." He chuckled morosely. "Or, at least, I wouldn't allow myself to return." He lifted his sad gaze to Dane. "But all those efforts were in vain. I thought if I introduced her to gentlemen or had Lady Grace introduce her, she would find someone else, and my own feelings for her would lessen."

"I see." He felt sorry for the young lord for the first time since he'd entered Marbury House. He'd inherited the title and the responsibility of Lady Athena's guardianship before he had come to grips with his place in the world. "So, you were close to Athena."

He nodded. "We practically grew up together. Our parents were close, and so, we became close."

"You and Athena are somewhat similar to Grace and me. We grew up together, and she was my best friend. I always thought we'd marry. I'd asked her to marry me when I finished my studies and returned home. I was ready to start my life, but I knew the only way to do that was with Grace by my side."

Marbury leaned forward. "I thought the two of you were at odds."

Dane laughed. "We were, but we've always loved one another. You see, there is a significant difference between you, Athena, Grace, and me. Your parents would have welcomed the match between the two of you. My father and Grace's father hated one another. They couldn't agree on anything inside the House of Lords or at White's when they happened to be together. Nor could they agree on which side of the street to walk on when they saw one another. My father forbade me from marrying Grace." Dane held the young man's gaze. "I planned to circumvent my father's wishes, but I didn't share them with Grace. I gambled at the Jolly Rooster and made a fortune the night my father refused to allow a match with Grace. I was intent on proving him wrong. This led me to make a bad error of judgment, which hurt Grace." He leaned close and lowered his voice. "I thought she would leave me, so I ran like a coward instead of handling it like a man. She despised me for it." He swallowed as the familiar shame crawled up his throat. "I deserved her loathing and so much more. I lost years with Grace because of my stupidity. I was too headstrong." He cleared his throat and smiled. "I don't want the same thing to happen to you and Athena."

Marbury's brow wrinkled as he considered Dane's words. "I didn't leave. She did."

This time, it was Dane who wanted to roll his eyes. Instead, he took a deep breath, gathered every spec of patience he possessed, and then continued, "But you see, Athena left, and you didn't try to stop her. Why do you think she left London? Why do you think she left this house, the refuge she found after she lost her parents? You were the one common thread that ran through her life. She saw you as her past, present, and future. Do you really think she was about to tell you she'd fallen in love with another man?" He softened his voice. "Especially after what you both shared?"

Marbury slowly lifted his head and held Dane's gaze. "She told you?"

Dane shook his head. "No. But she told Grace, and I overheard. Athena is in love with you. It was apparent the first time I met her. Just as it was that you were in love with her when you demanded that I tell you what my attentions were toward her when I asked her to dance."

"Well, I was trying to protect her reputation." By the slight wobble in his deep voice, his initial reluctance turned into accepting Dane's wisdom. "I know you're a duke, but she deserves the very best of men."

"Of course she does," Dane encouraged. "I feel the same way about Grace. Don't keep yourself from her because you're scared. I was scared too and thought that I'd lost the love of my life."

"But you didn't if you're marrying Lady Grace," Marbury pointed out.

"That's true." Dane grew silent and stared at the design on the carpet but didn't really see it. All he saw was Grace's beautiful visage. "But I did lose years with her that I have lost forever." He raised his gaze to the young lord before him. "But I won't lose anymore. Don't make the same mistake that I did. Go find Athena and tell her how you feel. Give her the chance to share everything with you."

"Even if it hurts?" The vulnerability in Marbury's voice was unmistakable.

"Even if it hurts," Dane repeated, tapping his forefinger on the young man's desk. It wasn't his place to tell Marbury that Athena was expecting a child. That news belonged to her, and Dane would not take that away from either of them. "If it offers comfort, I believe you'll be overjoyed."

Marbury released a breath and smiled. Just as quickly, he frowned. "I don't know where to find her."

"She told Grace she wanted to make the Red Swan before nightfall." He tilted his head and arched one eyebrow. "If you left within the hour, you could meet her at the inn."

"What if she doesn't want to see me?" Marbury sighed with apparent pain in his voice. "I acted abysmally toward her."

"Apologize, take her in your arms, then kiss her. When you do, make certain you pour every feeling you have for her into the kiss. Then tell her in words." He stood with a smile. "It worked for me." He couldn't resist provoking the man. He deserved it for being so aggravating. "Though you only possess half my charm, I'm confident it will also work for you." He scrunched his nose. "But take a bath first before you find her."

Marbury stood as well. "I owe you an apology."

Dane nodded, encouraging the young earl to continue.

"It's about Lady Grace."

Dane's voice dropped as he stared at the earl. "Pray tell, what about her?"

Marbury dipped his head as if struggling to find the words. After a long moment, he lifted his head. "I offered her money to convince you to choose Athena as your duchess." He sniffed and shook his head. "I thought if you married Athena, then I wouldn't be tempted anymore." His soft laugh betrayed his embarrassment. "I'm an absolute idiot for doing it."

"She did what?" This time, it was Dane's turn to struggle. He narrowed his eyes as everything came into focus. That was why Grace had been adamant about Athena being his perfect duchess. "I assume Grace accepted?" He tightened his stomach, preparing for whatever answer Marbury would give him.

He nodded. "Before I left Pelham Hall, I told her I would still pay her. Your snubbing of Athena and me shouldn't reflect poorly on Lady Grace. She tried to bring both of you together. You can lead a horse to water and all that." Sheepishly, he smiled. "Of course, that was before she spent the night with you. Thank heavens you didn't get attached to Athena. But Lady Grace returned the money. I heard from my bank this morning."

It felt as if he had been punched in the stomach. His ears rang as he reflected on Marbury's words. Grace had been uncertain about marrying him for a long time, but he had dismissed her concerns. Fool that he was, he allowed his love to deepen and wrap its tendrils around his heart, a situation he had been thrilled with. He swallowed, but it did nothing to soothe the ache in his heart. She had broken that feeble organ once, but he never thought she would do it again.

Dane closed his eyes. Perhaps Grace didn't want him like he wanted her. Perhaps money was her prime motivation instead of love.

He had to leave before he said or did something he would regret. "I appreciate your time today."

Marbury shook his head. "It's me, Your Grace, who will forever be in your debt." He rang the bell, calling for his butler. "I must prepare to travel so I can meet Athena tonight. May I show you out?"

"No, thank you." Dane took his hat from the chair next to him. "I know my way."

The next several moments were a blur. Somehow, he made it to his carriage without casting up his accounts. He waved off the footman who was there to open the carriage door. He wanted to do the simple task himself.

"Where to, Your Grace?" his coachman called out.

"Ardeerton House," he murmured. He needed distance. He breathed in and out as he settled the riot of emotions. It was the only way he knew how to confront the chaos that Marbury's words had unleashed.

As the coach lurched forward and out of the Earl of Marbury's drive, Dane rested his elbows on his knees and placed his hands over his face. One thing was certain. Too much was at stake to make a half-cocked decision. He'd done that once before, and he'd suffered for such a rash decision. Like he'd advised Marbury with Athena, Dane had to give Grace the benefit of the doubt. In his heart, he and Grace were committed to one another. He still had to tell her everything he'd learned when he'd called upon the Earl of Webster-Harnly. Then he'd ask her about her agreement with Marbury.

As the carriage and four slipped into the London traffic, deep in his heart, Dane knew that Grace was his, and he was hers, which meant one thing. There was only one reason why Grace would make such an arrangement with Marbury, and that was for the security it would provide for her and Theo's future.

The woman that he loved more than life itself constantly worried about security, a basic need that she'd lost because she thought her father had gambled hers away. He took it for granted every day. He vowed then and there. He would not lose Grace again. He would prove to her that she was safe with him—always and forever.

He leaned out the carriage window. "I've changed my mind about Ardeerton House. I need you to take me somewhere else and wait for me."

Twenty-Three

❧

"**M**y lady?" Theo knocked on the door jamb of the small sitting room in the front of the house. "I was asked to inform you that there's been a change of plans. You have been invited to Ardeerton House to dine this evening."

Grace nodded. Dane had said he had business. His appointment must have run late. "Will his sisters be there?"

"I can't say, Ma'am."

It didn't make any difference. It was a simple dinner. No rumors would erupt from that.

"Mabel has several gowns for you to choose for the occasion."

"Indeed, I do," Mabel sang through the hallway. "Each one is gorgeous and utterly enchanting."

Theo rocked on his heels with a sly grin. "I agree." Then he glanced over his shoulder. "But I somehow restrain myself from singing such information through Lady Grace's home."

"Theo," Grace chided.

"She's young and excited as we all are, my lady." Theo held her gaze with a gentleness that revealed his affection. "You deserve all the happiness in the world, and I believe His Grace is of the same mind. Mark my words. His Grace will do everything in his power to make you happy."

Grace bit her lip to hide her smile and glanced at her book. "Thank you, Theo. I don't know what to say."

"You do not have to say anything, my lady. Just enjoy. His Grace's carriage will pick you up in three hours." Theo dipped his head and then left Grace alone.

She pulled her book to her chest and sighed. The man she'd loved since she was a little girl loved her in return. He had continued to love her since they departed. It was hard to fathom that after all these years, he loved her more than he ever did.

Her heartbeat stumbled. Was she being reckless after all these years to feel such jubilation? Nothing had ever been easy for her since Dane had left her on that field that day, and especially not since her father died.

Just as she was about to send for Mabel to discuss her evening schedule, a curt knock sounded on the door.

"Grace."

Before she even looked up from her book, she recognized the voice.

"Hope." She rose from her chair and went to her sister's side. She wrapped her arms around her for a hug, and her sister half-heartedly attempted to return the gesture. "What are you doing here? Is something amiss in Amesbury?"

Grace only saw Hope when she called upon her sister and brother-in-law in London. They split their time between the city and Amesbury. However, they never visited her in the town or invited her to Amesbury. She should be overjoyed that her sister was here for a visit instead of wary. She shook her head slightly. "Forgive me for my lack of manners. You've taken me by surprise. Do come in. Let me ring for a tea tray."

"I don't have time for tea." Hope closed the door behind her. "What I share with you must be kept in the strictest confidence."

"What is it?" Grace took Hope's hand and led her to the adjacent chair where Grace was sitting. Only after Hope settled did Grace take her seat.

Hope's back was straighter than a measuring stick. "I understand you've come to an understanding with the Duke of Pelham."

"Understanding?"

"Marriage," Hope snapped. "Don't be coy."

Grace leaned back in her chair at her sister's sharp tone like she'd been slapped. Of course, Stewart would have shared what happened at Pelham Hall.

"When are you marrying?"

"I don't know." Grace shrugged. It was bizarre that her sister was asking about Grace's future. She'd never been interested in it before.

"If you have any illusions of delaying the marriage, don't." Hope sniffed and lifted her nose in the air. She was out of sorts if the twisting of her fingers was any indication. "You lost him once, and only by divine intervention have you been presented with an opportunity to marry him again. Don't lose him."

"I don't plan to." Grace tilted her head and regarded her sister with a quizzical gaze. Ever since the Northumberland farmer, Hope couldn't have been bothered by Grace's marital prospects.

Hope's forehead was dotted with sweat, and she swallowed repeatedly in an apparent effort to keep herself calm.

"If something is amiss, I'll help you." Even though Grace doubted that Hope had much affection for her, she would always be there for her sister if she needed her.

Hope glanced at her hands and linked her fingers together to keep from fidgeting. "You need to marry the duke as quickly as you can. I need money." Hope's eyes widened. "Don't think it's for me. It's for Stewart. I need fifty thousand pounds."

"What?" Grace cried. "Why does Stewart need that amount of money? That is a fortune."

One tear slid down Hope's cheek. In all their years together, Grace could count on one hand the amount of times she'd seen her cry.

"This is difficult," Hope whispered.

"I'm your sister. I will not judge you." Whatever trouble Stewart Arnold had found, Grace would not put any of the blame on Hope.

Hope studied her entwined fingers. "Stewart has amassed several debts across Amesbury and around London. That's what I need the money for. He doesn't have enough to pay for the gambling debts this time." A gut-wrenching sound erupted, and Hope slapped a hand over her mouth.

"So, this isn't the first time he's amassed gambling debts?" Instantly,

Grace fell to her knees beside her sister and took her in her arms. "I'm sorry you're in such pain. I'll do anything I can to help."

"Anything?" Hope asked with a yearning glint in her eye. "Marry Pelham and ask him for the money."

Grace pulled away and shook her head. "I can't do that."

"Why not?" Her tone was sharp as her eyes narrowed on Grace.

"Why should the duke give you or Stewart any money? It wouldn't feel right to marry Pelham and then ask for a fortune to pay a relative's gambling debt," Grace said softly as she patted Hope's hand.

"And why not?" Her sister pulled her hand from hers. "Pelham owns a gambling hell. He knows how debts accrue and how easily they can be erased the next night." Hope's cheeks burned crimson in indignation.

Grace's eyes must have widened to the size of dinner plates at her sister's outburst. "Pardon me?"

"Don't 'pardon me' with that innocent act of yours. You might have been able to fool Mother and Father with such theatrics, but your wiles never worked on me." Hope pointed a finger in Grace's face. "No matter how much I tried to win their affection, there was never a day that I wasn't reminded that they loved you more than me." Her sister was so angry that spittle flew from her mouth. "But I'd always attempted to do the right thing and never caused them a hint of disgrace." She sneered as she raked her gaze up and down Grace's body. "But you and your high and mighty duke are a walking scandal." She shook her head. "I know that you spent several nights in his bedroom."

Grace shook her head as she leaned away and stood. "You have no idea what privately occurred between Pelham and me." She sat in the chair opposite Hope.

"Just like I do not know that you spurned him all those years ago because of your foolish pride."

Her sister wasn't in her right mind at the moment. Perhaps Stewart had so upset Hope that she didn't know what she was saying. Grace had never heard such bitterness spew from her sister's mouth. Hope had always tried to lecture her even if Grace was older, but this was entirely different.

"Having a few naked women on his lap isn't a reason to not marry him. You should have thought of that all those years ago. Thankfully, it doesn't bother you now. Everyone in London knows that he had naked women hanging all over him at the Jolly Rooster, then he went home and found you in his bed." She huffed her distaste.

It no longer bothered her since Dane had explained everything. There wasn't a thing he would not do for her because that was the type of man he was—a protector.

But it wasn't for her to share with Hope. Nor would she allow Hope to cause her to doubt the man she loved.

"Grace," her sister hissed even more flustered. "Do not cross me on this. Marry Pelham as soon as possible and give me the money."

Time stood still as the unspoken word "or" stood between them.

This time, it was Grace who swallowed her unease. "Or what?"

Hope wrinkled her nose as if smelling something foul. "Or I shall ruin you and Pelham as well."

Grace gripped the chair arms as her pulse pounded. The words her sister spewed were pure malice. "You don't mean that."

Hope rolled her eyes. "Do not play the innocent with me. Imagine what the *ton* would say if they knew that you had slept with Pelham as he was courting Lady Athena. It is an easy explanation for why the young woman fled London."

"That's not true." Grace shook her head. She could not divulge Athena's secret without causing her permanent damage. Yet, Hope sat there, ready to destroy them all.

"It doesn't make any difference if it's true. People love gossip. You would lose your livelihood. No one would trust their daughter's future to you. You slept with a client, for God's sake."

She had not felt this powerless since the day Hope and Stewart practically threw her out of the house. It was ironic. She'd been worried about society turning on her, but it was her own sister who was doing just that.

"Imagine how your duke would take the news that while you were sleeping in his bed, you were taking money from Lord Marbury to persuade him to marry Athena." Hope tapped her forefinger to her chin and stared at the ceiling. "Or perhaps he did know and didn't care as long as he could have you in his bed and marry her."

"How did you hear that?" Needing distance from Hope's vitriol, Grace stepped away from the chair she clutched with a death grip.

"Stewart was at White's last night. Marbury was foxed and crying to anyone who would listen, how he lost the love of his life. Stewart took pity and sat with him. The earl shared your little agreement to convince Pelham to marry Athena."

Grace had never been this angry in her entire life. How dare her sister come into her home and make such insinuations and threats about the man she loved, along with a young woman who had no idea about any of this?

"There's no scandal. You need to leave. Now," Grace growled in a low voice. "I never want to hear another word from you. And in case it isn't clear, you are not welcome anymore."

Both stood at the same time, but Hope wore a smug smile.

"Grace, there's no need to become defensive. Just get Pelham to give you the money, and all will be well." She leaned close and lowered her voice. "You must understand. I love Stewart, and I'll do anything to protect him."

Grace lifted her chin. It was ironic that she and Hope shared the same trait. Grace would do anything to protect Dane. "I don't care."

Hope narrowed her eyes and took a step closer. "You should care because I have no qualms about going to Pelham and telling him the truth about you. Your impending marriage and reputation would be ruined."

Grace shook her head and stared at the floor. Her sister had no idea the lengths she would go to protect Dane, even if it meant giving him up and allowing herself to be ruined in the process. That was the thing when you loved someone with your whole heart. You would sacrifice everything to protect them.

"Or you could see him yourself and secure the money I need."

Grace waved a hand toward the sitting room door. "Oh, I plan to see him. Don't worry, dear sister." Grace nimbly stepped around her. "John, will you escort Mrs. Arnold out and make sure she never returns?"

Her footman's eyes widened, then narrowed in understanding. "Of course, my lady. It would be my pleasure."

"My pleasure as well," Grace murmured so no one could hear. "Thank you, John. If you'll wait by the door for my sister," she said politely. Once John was far enough away that he couldn't hear her next words, she turned to Hope and crossed her arms over her chest. "What if word spread through the *ton* that your husband was an inveterate gambler who doesn't pay his debts?"

Hope laughed as if Grace had said something funny. "I see you do have a backbone." She wiped her eyes. "Then that makes my story all the more truthful. Stewart's name has never been linked to gambling, but rumors are already swirling about what you've done. It's only a matter of time before your precious duke finds out the truth." She picked up her reticule and stood by the door. "Grace, come now. We're family. Just ask him for the money, and all this unpleasantness will be swept under the rug. Send word to me at our London home. We'll be here for a fortnight."

When the door closed, Grace exhaled and took a deep breath, but it did little to alleviate the suffocating feeling of drowning. She collapsed into a chair and buried her head in her hands. Now was the time to finally share everything she had done.

She had lied to Dane by not telling him about the arrangement with Marbury and why she had thought it a godsend. Of course, she loved him then, but she didn't believe he wanted to reconcile.

Grace swallowed the nausea that threatened her as she wrapped her arms around her waist to ward off the sudden chill. She would not allow Dane to become embroiled in her family's tawdry business and their threats.

Now would she allow him to suffer because of her mistakes, such as failing to tell him when she had the chance to explain her actions. She loved him more than her livelihood or reputation. Tonight, she would share everything with him before Stewart or Hope told him first.

Even if it meant losing him forever.

Twenty-Four

Grace nodded at Ritson, Dane's London butler.

"Welcome to Ardeerton House. Please come in, my lady." Ritson beamed as he snapped his finger at the footman dressed in the Pelham gold and silver livery. "We've all been expecting you."

She smiled demurely. They wouldn't be expecting her again after tonight. She swallowed, hoping to dissipate the sadness that hung over her head. She only hoped she would not turn into a blubbering mess this evening and could leave with her head held high.

She smoothed her dress and took a deep breath. She could do this. She had faced worse than this and survived, but nothing would break her heart more than losing Dane. Though she would earn his disdain, and it would feel as if she'd been stabbed in the chest, she had no other course. She had to protect him.

"Thank you." She glanced at the entry table, which was adorned with a crystal vase that seemed to reach the ceiling. It was overflowing with stunning roses and branches of holly. How fitting that both their prickles and thorns were meant to protect against any threats. Perhaps it was a sign of how the night would unfold. She gasped slightly as tears filled her eyes, but she pushed them away. Once she returned home, she could cry her eyes out.

"There you are," Dane called out with a jovial smile as he approached her from his study. Before she could greet him properly, he halted in his stride. He took his time as he allowed his gaze to peruse the length of her. "Ritson, Aphrodite has come to dine with me this evening."

Ritson chuckled, and the footman by his side joined in.

"Indeed, Your Grace," Ritson answered.

By then, Dane was beside her and took her hands in his. "Let me take a good look at you." The smile that tugged at his lips was pure mischief. "That gown is stunning on you. However, it's my opinion that you make the gown stunning."

She couldn't help but smile at his compliment. She'd chosen a simple cream silk that shimmered with every step. Pippa had designed it, especially for Grace, saying the gown would bring Pelham to his knees when he saw it. Perhaps it would allow him to have at least one positive memory of her tonight.

He pulled her close and pressed a chaste kiss to her cheek, then whispered for her ears alone, "It'll be more stunning when it's laying over a chair, and I have you naked in my bed."

"Dane," she scolded, but no real rebuke sounded in her voice. She had no standing to challenge him.

"Come, my little temptress." He offered his arm, and she wrapped hers around his. "I thought we could have a brandy before dinner."

"I would like that." It was precisely what she needed. A brandy would give her the liquid courage to say everything she needed tonight.

"Do you mind if I escort you to my study instead of the salon? I wanted to have a word with you before dinner."

She nodded her agreement. Privacy would allow her to talk to him without his staff overhearing their conversation.

When they crossed the threshold, he closed the door.

Instantly, she found herself pressed against the hardwood.

"I've been dying to do this all day," he murmured, cupping her cheeks and pressing his lips to hers. His body encased hers in heat, and his familiar scent surrounded her, giving her comfort, even if it was just a brief respite. His lips moved softly over hers before his tongue traced the seam of her lips, begging for entry. She could deny him nothing and didn't want to, for that matter. This might be the last time she ever kissed him.

For the love of heaven, she would make herself sick with such thoughts.

As his tongue slowly slid against hers, Grace's body melted against him. She'd never felt such a need and desire for a man as she did with Dane. He was everything good, kind, and protective. The urge to drop to her knees and beg his forgiveness loomed like a rogue wave, a force she couldn't withstand. When she pulled slightly away, he pulled her nearer. Perhaps it was selfish, but she hoped this kiss would last forever so she didn't have to confess everything this evening.

But that wasn't who she was. Whatever came from their discussion, she needed to face it. Living in this constant state of apprehension was unbearable. When she smoothed her hands against the strong breadth of his chest, the muscles under her palms flexed.

Gently, she pushed him away. "Dane, I have something most urgent that I must tell you before you speak."

His brow gathered into neat lines. He leaned in and kissed her once, then nodded. "Sounds ominous, especially when you've interrupted a perfect kiss." He took her hands in his and grinned. "There's that blush that always enchants me."

"Dane," she warned. "Please don't distract me. This is important."

"Come then." Not releasing her hand, he took her to his desk and motioned for her to sit across from him. "But I must do something first." He grinned as he opened a desk drawer and pulled out a long velvet box. Without breaking her gaze, he rounded the desk and leaned against it before her. He extended the velvet-covered box to her. "Open it, darling."

Her heart faltered for a second in its beat. The man wanted to give her a gift, and she was about to divulge how she'd betrayed him. "Perhaps you should hear what I say before you give me this."

"No, Grace. It would give me great pleasure to see you open this." He cupped her cheek and tilted her chin until their gazes met. "I love you and want you to have it. Please open it."

Without tearing her gaze from his, she opened the box slowly. When she glanced down, her breath caught. "Oh, Dane," she murmured breathlessly. She lifted her head and became lost in his dark blue eyes. "It's my mother's necklace." Tears burned her eyes. For a moment, all she could do was shake her head. She couldn't form the words to ask where he found it and how he did it.

"Darling, breathe," he said softly, wiping away an errant tear. "I found it in a small shop just outside of London. The proprietor told me he'd had it for years. He couldn't sell it because no one could afford it."

"But why?" Grace looked at the beautiful pearl and sapphire necklace. Reverently, she ran her fingers gently over the pearls and gems. It was just as she remembered. The pearls glowed with a luster that reminded her of her mother. She'd always worn it as it was her favorite piece. "I don't know what to say." She shook her head as another set of tears fell. "I never thought I'd see it again."

"I promised you that I'd find it, and I did." He picked up the necklace and clasped it around her neck. He leaned back and admired his handiwork. "Beautiful, just like you. I scoured London and the surrounding area until I found it. It's yours, Grace. It's always been yours. Just as my heart has been and always will be yours. One day, it'll be our daughter's necklace. Just as you planned."

She closed her eyes and took a deep breath. She didn't deserve such love or kindness from Dane. Not after what she'd done. "I don't know where to start."

"Tell me. Whatever it is, we can find our way together."

Why did he have to be so kind to her?

Because that was who he was, and she had to trust him.

"I've betrayed you."

Every inch of Dane's body froze as he stared at her. It didn't matter what she was about to confess. He would forgive her and do everything he could to demonstrate how much he loved and needed her.

"Start at the beginning," he coaxed. He took one of her hands in his. It was ice-cold. Instinctively, he rubbed it between his.

"Lord Marbury approached me after you invited him and Athena to Pelham Hall. He made me an offer. He'd give me five thousand pounds if you became engaged to Lady Athena. If you married her before the end of the Season, he'd give me ten thousand pounds." She swallowed thickly, but his brave darling continued, "After leaving Pelham Hall, he gave me the money even though you had no interest in Athena. But I returned it." She bowed as if waiting for the executioner's ax to fall. "I wanted to use the money to purchase a home. I wanted Theo and myself to have security for our futures. It's no excuse. I gambled with your future just as my father gambled with mine."

Though Marbury had told him about the agreement, he'd wondered when she'd tell him. He knew that, eventually, she would. That was Grace. She could never live with herself otherwise. But her confession only confirmed his suspicions as to why she made such an agreement.

But that niggle of doubt wormed his way into his heart. Before he could tamp it down, he asked, "Does that mean that you didn't want me?"

Her gaze snapped to his, almost bringing him to his knees. His Grace was in such pain. He could see the turmoil swirling in her caramel eyes. Tears flowed freely.

"Never think that." She sobbed and brought her hand to her mouth. The wretched sound filled the room.

He did the only thing he could. He took her into his arms and held her. He rocked her slightly as he tried to comfort her.

"I was so frightened." Her head was buried in his chest, but he could hear every word she said. "You see, my neighbor next door was evicted the day that Marbury came to see me with the offer. I had failed to pay my rent on time earlier in the year."

"Hush, darling," he murmured. "I understand. There's no need to fret."

She leaned back slightly but didn't release his lapels. She was holding on for dear life—and she always could. He would do everything in his power to protect her.

"But my heart was broken. If you had made a match with Athena, I had decided that Theo and I would move to Cornwall. I couldn't bear to be near you when you were married to another." She sobbed into his chest again as if utterly defeated. "I was going to tell you earlier, but I was a coward, especially after you told me about firing your footman."

Dane had had enough. He swept her into his arms and walked to the couch. He sat down and settled her on his lap. "My poor darling. Don't cry." He tilted his gaze toward the ceiling and sniffed. *Damnable tears. Who knew they were contagious?* "There's nothing to forgive." Dane kissed her forehead. His shirt was soaked with her tears, but this was the only place he wanted to be—holding her, comforting her.

Forever.

She lifted her head from his chest and wiped her eyes. "I'm no different than my father or your footman Matthew. How can you forgive me that easily?"

"Firstly, you love me. This means that I know in here"—Dane placed his hand over her heart—"you would never hurt me intentionally. Secondly, I love and adore you. I meant what I said. I will not lose you again."

She sniffed. "I never want to lose you."

"Good, because you're stuck with me forever. Now, quit interrupting." He gave her his best ducal expression. "I'm a duke. You can interrupt me anytime you like when you're my duchess." He grunted and rolled his eyes. "That's a falsehood. You interrupt me now all the time. I can't wait to see what you're like when you're my duchess."

She laughed, which was his intention all along.

"Thirdly, my darling, not all betrayals are inexcusable. You were protecting yourself and Theo." He cupped her cheeks and rubbed his thumbs over her tender skin. "Let me tell you a story. My father was a vicious man. When Honoria thought our father had destroyed her favorite pony, she was devastated. It was only until years later that we learned the truth. Winston and Ritson had rescued the pony without the old duke being any wiser. They loved Honoria and wanted to protect her pony. Yet they knew what happened could never be divulged, or the old duke would have dismissed them without any references. They had even hidden it from me."

She blinked several times as she listened to the story. "What an evil man."

"I agree." He pressed a kiss to her lips and pressed his forehead to hers. "What they did was a betrayal. But they had good reasons for doing what they did. I would always forgive them for that because they were protecting our family. Just as you were protecting yours."

Her brow furrowed slightly. It appeared that her sorrow had lessened, but she was still upset.

"You should know that Hope came to see me. She needs fifty thousand pounds. Apparently, Stewart is a gambler and cannot pay his debts. She told me if I didn't ask you for the money, she would come to you and tell you what I did." She grabbed his lapels again. "I would have told you. Please believe that."

"I do, darling," He pulled her close. "But it's not Stewart who has the gambling problem."

"What do you mean?" Her voice quivered as her eyes searched his.

It gave him all the more reason to pull her tighter to him. "It's your sister. Hope is the one who needs fifty thousand pounds."

Grace stared at him. "Hope? No, she said it was Stewart."

"I'm sorry, darling." He gently stroked her cheek. "I had a long conversation with Stewart, but that was only after I found your father's old bookkeeper. He revealed everything to me. Your sister is the one who stole your dowry and inheritance to cover her gambling debts. She also made Stewart sign the Sommer House deed over to Brixworth to settle a debt. Your father wanted you to have it. When your father was sick, she altered his bookkeeping journals and private documents to make it appear that he was the one gambling instead of her."

"Really?" She shook her head. "My father..."

"Your father loved you."

There was no point in saying anything. They both understood that her father hadn't neglected to provide for her future. Her sister took everything from her and forced Grace to find her way without assistance. That changed when Dane came back into her life. Never again would Grace have to worry about her security.

"Stewart told me that Hope has been gambling since before he married her. She's practically bankrupted him. He also came to me and asked for the money."

"Dane, I don't want—"

"Do not fret, darling. It's done. Hope is out of debt. However, she's no longer welcome into any respectable gambling establishments. I've had her banned."

Grace nodded her agreement. "I'll find a way to repay you."

"You will not." Dane's heart pounded against his chest. Grace's actions spoke louder than words. She loved him too much to profit off him, even if it meant she could no longer realize her dream of home and security. "There's no need. Stewart has agreed to return the money to me over time with interest. Let me show you something else." He brought her to his desk and pulled out his bookkeeping journal. He flipped it to the beginning. "See this? This is what I won from Scoville all those years ago. I've invested it. This is the latest entry." He pointed to the page.

"You're worth that much?" She shook her head in disbelief.

He couldn't help but laugh. "Probably more, love. This was two weeks ago." He pulled her close. "Darling, you're not a gambler. Your father wasn't a gambler. But I am. A careful one." He pointed to the amount listed in the last entry. "This is for our family. I would never risk that. I don't gamble with my money or the ducal estate monies—only the profits from the Jolly Rooster. I guess you could say it's my entertainment money." He leaned in closer and winked. "I'll share with you."

She turned her earnest gaze to his. "You are the most honorable man I've had the good fortune to meet. I hope you can forgive me and my treacherous family."

"There's one more thing you should know about your family. Not all of them are scandalous. The Earl of Webster-Harnly had no idea that you needed shelter. Stewart and Hope didn't contact him for fear that you would discover what had happened to the estate and your inheritance. He still employs your father's bookkeeper."

"I guess there's a silver lining there, but it's pretty dull if you ask me." Devastation darkened her eyes as she chewed her bottom lip.

"Stop, darling." He stroked his thumb over the soft skin. "If anyone is going to nibble on your delectable lips, it's me."

She was clearly distracted as she didn't answer or challenge him. "At least he's not the ogre I thought he was. But that doesn't excuse the rest of my family."

"No, he's not an ogre. He's rather a charming fellow. He said he would call upon you and ask for your help securing a suitable bride." Dane kissed her cheek, then lifted Grace and sat her on the sofa facing him as he knelt beside her. "Thank you for telling me all this."

"I couldn't let my shameful family harm your reputation." She clasped her hands in her lap. "Even if you would hate me."

"Let me tell you something about family, darling. I am your family, and I don't want to hear you deny it. Honor, Pippa, and those ham-fisted men they've married are your family."

She frowned. "Ravenscroft and Trafford are your best friends,"

He tapped his chin for a moment. "I suppose you're right." A half-smile tugged at his lips as he winked at her. "As I was saying, it doesn't matter if we share any blood. We share something far more precious— our hopes, dreams, disappointments, and, especially, our hearts. That creates a bond stronger than blood." He kissed the top of her hand. "You might think Hope and Stewart are your true family, but they aren't. They didn't care or shelter you as a family should. But I will if you allow it."

She nodded.

"I will do everything in my power to ensure you feel loved, wanted, and cared for the rest of your life."

Gentle tears fell down her face.

"Now, now, I can't have my bride-to-be shedding tears." He reached into his pocket and found the small wooden box he'd put there earlier. "Speaking of brides..."

Grace gasped when he opened the lid.

"Will you do me the highest honor I will ever receive and marry me?" He reached for her hand and slipped a gold sapphire ring on her finger.

"It's the color of your eyes." Grace smiled through her tears.

But he knew her well enough to know that they were happy ones. "I thought so also. I wanted you to have a reminder that even if I'm not by your side, you will always be in my heart."

"I love you."

He arched an eyebrow. "That wasn't the answer I was looking for, though I cherish every time you say it."

She blushed. "Yes. I'd be honored to marry you." She peeked at him, wearing a grin. "I always said you were a walking scandal, but it was always me."

"It was a simple scandal, Grace. Mine are always much bigger." He contemplated the ring on her finger. "The stone doesn't have quite the same brilliance of my eyes, but it's a good replica."

"You are such a duke," she playfully scolded. "But I wouldn't change a thing about you. But shouldn't you wait to put the ring on my finger?"

"You know me. I'm always impatient when it comes to churches and vicars." He stood and pulled her into his arms. "That's why I have a special license in my pocket and the family vicar waiting for us in the salon." He kissed her with a passion that would leave no doubt how much he wanted her. "Marry me, Grace. Now."

"I've never been able to say no to a handsome, kind, patient, passionate, protective, and, not to mention, efficient man." She laughed and took his hand in hers. "Let us be married."

Twenty-Five

D ane had escorted Grace to a small retiring room off the salon, where she washed her face. When she glanced at the mirror on the wall, her eyes didn't hide anything. She was quite a sight for a bride. She pinched her cheeks and patted the slight puffiness around her eyes. Anyone looking at her would be able to tell she had been crying. It wouldn't surprise her if the vicar thought Dane was marrying her in a sympathetic gesture to stop her tears.

At first, the tears had been born out of the sadness she had felt when she confessed all. But then they quickly turned into tears of happiness. And it was all because of Dane. Her hand reached for her mother's necklace, securely clasped around her neck. She still couldn't believe that he had found it for her.

She braced her hands on the washstand and bowed her head. Her only sister had betrayed her due to an incessant need to gamble. Perhaps she had been desperate and had no other avenue to take. However, Dane's generosity had given Hope a second chance, even though she didn't deserve it. Grace never considered herself vindictive, and there was no denying that Hope deserved sympathy, but Grace could never imagine forgiving Hope for what she had done to her over the years.

Perhaps one day, she might find it in her heart to forgive Hope, but she would never forget her sister's actions, including throwing her out of her own home and telling her lies about her dowry and the current Earl of Webster-Harnly. Perhaps next week, she and Dane could visit the earl. Grace wanted to rekindle her relationship with her cousin.

She sniffed and lifted her head to gaze in the mirror once more. The woman who looked back at her had transformed into someone more confident. And it was all thanks to the extraordinary man she was about to marry. She smiled at her reflection. Tonight, she would marry, and she was determined to savor every moment of it. Her only regret was that Honoria and Pippa weren't there to witness their brother's marriage. Both had wanted him to marry someone deserving of his love, someone who would cherish and love him in return. They would see their wish fulfilled as Grace would always love and adore him.

Murmurs and laughter came from the salon. Grace pinched her cheeks once again, then opened the door. She entered the formal salon and stopped. Honoria and Trafford, along with Pippa and Ravenscroft, stood next to Dane.

As soon as Honoria saw her, she took Pippa's hand. "She's here."

Both sisters made a beeline for Grace. As soon as they were beside her, Honoria hugged her.

Grace wrapped her arms around her friend and squeezed hard. "I can't believe you are standing in front of me."

"Me next," Pippa said and took Grace in her arms.

"Oh, Pippa," Grace exclaimed. "Thank you for being here, and thank you for the dress. I know I look like a fright, but it has been quite a day."

"Nonsense. You are a beautiful bride," Pippa cooed.

"Dane is a lucky man," Honoria added, then pulled Grace into her side. "Welcome to the family, Grace. Pippa and I always wanted another sister."

Pippa leaned near as if sharing a secret. "And we always hoped that sister would be you."

Grace felt another round of tears about to appear, but she swallowed them back. "And I've always wanted you both as my sisters, though I already feel that way."

"Enough, you two. I need my bride by my side," Dane growled.

"Pfft," Pippa snorted. "Someone is anxious to say his vows."

"He's been fidgeting since he entered the room." Honoria studied her brother. "Marcus tried to calm his nerves."

"Hugh has been teasing him relentlessly since we arrived, and Dane has not snapped at him yet," Pippa said confidently. "A sure sign our brother is nervous."

The conversations faded around Grace as her eyes met Dane's. A huge smile tugged at his lips as he came forward. He was so devastatingly handsome that he stole her breath. He'd changed into a white silk formal evening coat that made his blond hair shimmer. But it was his eyes that captivated her. She had never seen them so vibrant and filled with emotion.

Without even glancing at his sisters, he took Grace's hand and held it to his lips. "Your beauty is ethereal."

Honoria and Pippa sighed in unison.

"I believe your husbands are waiting for you," Dane said without looking at his sisters. "I must speak with my bride privately."

Heat blossomed on her cheeks at the intensity of his gaze, but she wasn't shy. It was the warmth and anticipation of saying their vows.

"This is the happiest day of my life." He pulled her near and wrapped his arms around her. "Tell me this is what you want."

"I have wanted you as mine from the first time I saw you."

Dane tilted his head back, sighed, and delivered his best mischievous smile. "Thank heavens."

Grace wrapped her arms around his. "I feel as if we're already married."

"I feel the same. I've had Mabel and John move your things here. My housekeeper has prepared a bedchamber for Theo. I thought he could live here with us. I know how much he means to you."

"Oh, Dane." This time, she did shed a tear. "Thank you."

"You should also know that I bought your townhouse, and I've had my solicitor create a trust for you to hold your property. Your town-house deed is in there, and so is the one I bought next to it." He bent his head and smiled sheepishly. "The property I won from Brixworth when I was sick? It was Sommer House. That deed is in your trust as well. You have complete control over everything, and no one can ever take it away."

She tilted her head and stared at him. "Truly? Why on earth?"

"Because I never want you to feel insecure about where you live. I know how much your own home means to you." He pressed a kiss to her forehead. "I also purchased a cottage in Cornwall that overlooks the ocean. It's in the trust as well. But I thought you and I could spend holidays there together."

"You did not have to do that." She held on to his lapels and stared into his eyes. "My place is beside the most wonderful man in the entire British Isles."

He frowned slightly. "Shouldn't you have said the entire world?"

Before she could reply, the vicar cleared his throat. "Your Grace? I hate to interrupt, but I am expected at the bishop's home in a half hour for dinner."

Dane rolled his eyes. "He has forgotten who his largest benefactor is. Yet, I suppose he is as anxious as I am."

"Ready if you are," Grace murmured.

"I have been ready all my life." Dane took her hand, and they walked to stand in front of the vicar.

Honoria and Pippa stood beside Grace, while Ravenscroft and Trafford stood by Dane's side. As the vicar had them recite their vows, Grace said a silent prayer thanking the powers that be for Dane.

As soon as the vicar pronounced them husband and wife, Dane swept into her arms and gave her a kiss that stole her breath. She could barely hear the cheers that erupted from her family. All of her attention was focused on their kiss. It promised love, passion, and laughter for a lifetime.

"*Your Grace!*" the vicar scolded.

Dane ignored him and continued to kiss her. After a few minutes, he pulled away but didn't let go of her. "Our family wants to have dinner with us. We shall eat quickly. Then, I'll personally escort them out. I cannot wait to have you in my chambers tonight, and every other night we have together for the rest of our lives. You are stuck with me forever, Duchess."

"The very place I want to be." Grace tugged him closer and lowered her voice. "You have made all my dreams come true. You are the most wonderful and loving man in the *entire world*."

Dane hmphed and pulled her close. "I like that sentiment and am delighted you agree with me." Then, the charming man winked at her. "Just wait until you find out what I have planned for us and our future. I wouldn't want to ruin my scandalous reputation, so we should plan for a few simple ones."

Grace returned the wink. "I cannot wait."

Epilogue

Months later
Ardeerton House,
London home of the Duke and Duchess of Pelham

It never mattered to Dane whether people thought him arrogant and aloof. Truthfully, he enjoyed such a reputation. It allowed him leeway in all of his social obligations. Yet tonight, he was his most gracious and charming self as he welcomed all of the members of his Millionaires Club and the *ton* into his home—he stood corrected—*their home* for the first annual Duchess of Pelham ball.

Next to him, his duchess stood and warmly welcomed their guests. She looked stunning in the Pelham parure of emeralds. If others saw him as a lovesick fool, he embraced the title. He became more of one with every day spent with Grace. Finally, he understood what his best friends, Ravenscroft and Trafford, had tried to convey to him—the world did revolve around their wives. He would even dare to say the entire universe did, but he didn't want to get distracted—at least not tonight, as it was to honor his bride, his beautiful Grace.

"Welcome, Grayson." He shook the marquess's hand. "Grace and

I are delighted you and your marchioness could join us this evening." The Marquess of Grayson was an old friend from Eton who had recently become his newest member of the Millionaires Club.

"Beth and I wouldn't miss this for the world." The marquess leaned in. "We had to meet the woman who brought the mighty Duke of Pelham to his knees."

Dane laughed. "Let me share a secret, old man. She was destined to be my duchess all along."

Grayson looked fondly at his wife. "I feel the same." He turned to Dane and smiled. "We're lucky men."

Dane nodded in agreement as the marquess stepped away to join his marchioness.

"It seems as if Pippa is enjoying herself even if she isn't dancing," Grace murmured in between welcoming guests.

Dane quickly located his youngest sister and smiled fondly. In several months, Pippa would deliver her and Ravenscroft's first child. Pippa ignored society's strict rule that a woman shouldn't appear at events late in their pregnancy. Nothing would keep her from celebrating tonight.

The same was true for his eldest sister, Honoria. She was waltzing with her husband and laughing at something he said. He'd never seen his sister so joyful and full of life. And it was because of Trafford.

"Look at Honoria," Grace pointed to the dance floor and smiled. "She's glowing." Grace's warm laugh echoed around him like Christmas bells. "Trafford, too."

"Indeed." Dane pulled her close and kissed her on the cheek. "Our family is growing."

"Do you think there's room for one more?" Grace asked, then turned her attention to their next guest.

Dane tilted his head as he contemplated his duchess's words. He continued to greet the next rush of guests but didn't linger in conversation. He had to get to the bottom of this mystery before he and Grace descended the ballroom steps and danced together for their guests. Then, the ball would begin in earnest.

He smiled at a young viscount and his viscountess but couldn't remember their names. As soon as they passed, Dane leaned near his wife and whispered, "What did you mean?"

"I'll tell you in a bit," she murmured in return, then her face broke into a huge smile. "Welcome, Lord and Lady Marbury."

Athena grinned as she placed a protective hand over her stomach. "It's so good to see you both." Athena's gaze bounced between the two of them. "I can tell marriage agrees with both of you."

"It does." Grace leaned in and hugged her. "It seems to agree with you as well. How's the baby?"

Athena blushed prettily. "Relentless in his kicking."

"He must take after you, wife." Marbury beamed. The earl leaned toward Dane as Grace and Athena continued chatting. "I can never repay you for coming to see me that day. She's my world, and I almost lost her."

Dane gripped his shoulder and squeezed. "Later, let us toast to our good fortune."

Marbury nodded. "I would like that."

Dane greeted Athena and kissed her on her cheek. "You look happy, my dear."

"I am," she said. "Thank you."

"For?" Dane's brow furrowed.

"For ignoring Jasper's matchmaking efforts." She glanced fondly at her husband.

"It was my pleasure." Dane offered an elegant bow.

As the last guests arrived, Dane took Grace's hand and escorted her to the top of the stairs. "Now, what was that about adding another?"

Grace turned to him and took his hands in hers. "We're going to have a baby."

Few things could make him speechless, but his wife's announcement topped the list.

"Darling, close your mouth," Grace whispered. "People are staring."

"I don't care about them." Dane dropped a hand on her flat stomach. "Are you sure?"

Grace nodded. "The midwife stopped by today and confirmed it. In about seven or eight months, you'll become a father."

Dane's breath accelerated as his heart pounded in joy. "Grace," he whispered, squeezing her hands. "Are you happy?"

She nodded.

Tears welled in his eyes. "Gracie, we will be parents. I cannot wait to hold her or him in my arms."

"Neither can I." Her smile was filled with love.

"Thank you for making me the happiest man alive." He pulled her close and tipped her chin to look into her eyes.

"Your brothers-in-law might argue that they are the happiest men in the world," she argued.

"I can share the title," Dane said with a laugh, then swept his wife close and delivered a searing kiss.

Murmurs spread through the ballroom as everyone stared at them.

"Dane," Grace admonished softly. "People will gossip at our own ball."

"I am a duke. You are a duchess. Do you care if we cause a scandal?" he asked with an arched eyebrow.

She shook her head, then shrugged. "We've been through far worse, wouldn't you agree?"

He tilted back his head and laughed heartily. "Yes, I do. But I've learned a valuable lesson. Simple scandals are the best kind."

If you're not ready to say goodbye to Grace and Dane, point your camera **here for a bonus epilogue!**

Have you read A Simple Marriage, the second book in the Millionaires of Mayfair series?

Read on for an excerpt.

A Simple Marriage – Chapter One

London, 1819

Only the thought of dresses could compel Lady Phillipa 'Pippa' Ardeerton to consider marriage. More specifically, a dress shop was the reason Pippa stood in Hyde Park, pretending to admire the lush trees before her as she waited for the first gentleman she had invited to meet her so they could discuss marriage.

The dress shop in question belonged to Mademoiselle Mignon, who was soon to marry. Like a fairy godmother, she had offered to sell her dress shop to Pippa. When they'd first met, Mignon had taken Pippa under her wing and taught her the business of running an exclusive dress shop. It was an opportunity of a lifetime to own her shop. Mademoiselle Mignon's gowns were legendary as women from all over the British Isles traveled to London to visit the talented modiste. To don one of her dresses for a *ton* event ensured that the wearer would be the center of attention. It was an understatement to say that her dresses were works of art.

But so were Pippa's creations. To own this shop was her destiny.

To buy it, she needed her trust fund. To receive her trust fund, she had to reach the age of thirty and still be unmarried. Waiting six years was out of the question. But the trust provided that if she married, the funds became hers on the day she said her vows. And she'd only consider marriage to a gentleman *if* he'd agreed to marry her quickly and leave her trust fund alone after they exchanged "I dos."

Her lady's maid, Alice Roberts, stepped closer and looked over her shoulder. The movement reminded Pippa of a spy, one in the midst of some clandestine affair waiting for the enemy.

Well, this was a clandestine affair, but Pippa didn't want to marry her enemy. All she wanted was one man, and she wasn't picky. Practically any man would meet her requirements if he agreed that she would control her trust fund.

And he must not mind that his wife was involved in trade.

"My lady, your first appointment should have been here by now," Alice murmured.

"There's no need to whisper. No one can hear us." Pippa bit her lip to keep from laughing. Alice was a little sensitive at times if teased about being too dramatic. She patted her maid's arm in comfort. "He's only five minutes late."

Alice pointed to her elbow. "You know how my elbow can predict things. Right now, it's stiffening up on me. That's a warning, my lady. It's telling me that your idea to fetch a husband by writing him a letter isn't going to work." Alice shook her head in disapproval.

Pippa normally adored the antics of her lady's maid. It helped keep the loneliness at bay. An affliction that had only worsened when her older sister, Lady Honoria Ardeerton, had married Marcus Kirkland, the Earl of Trafford, and had moved to his estate in Amesbury.

However, today was not the day for Alice's elbow to start acting out. Uncannily, it regularly predicted when it would rain or if there was a change in the weather. But Pippa very much doubted that it could predict when things were set to go awry.

"Sweet Alice, it's a perfectly conceived plan." Taller than an average woman, Pippa smiled down at her maid.

The maid shook her head and looked about the park again. "Don't you think your brother will think it's a little suspicious that you're going to Hyde Park for the next five mornings for exercise? His Grace is a wily thinker." Alice tapped her finger against her temple. "His mind is always working. He'll smell it. Mark my words."

"Well, it's a good thing he has the sniffles," Pippa retorted. Her brother, Dane Ardeerton, the Duke of Pelham, was a *problem*. Uncommonly astute, he was the one who had sole discretion over her trust fund. She'd already asked him to release her funds early, and he'd declined.

While her brother was her biggest supporter of her art, he didn't particularly care for her going into trade. He'd always declared, "*A duke's sister is a rare creature. To lower oneself into mixing with the masses and handling money is unseemly. Unheard of for the Duke of Pelham's youngest sister.*"

However, Pippa considered his thinking to be a tad myopic. His focus was running his millionaire's club and his gambling hell disguised as a coaching inn, the Jolly Rooster. Pelham created the millionaire's club one day at Eton to develop a group where men and women with self-made wealth had a place to discuss business.

In Pippa's opinion, there wasn't much difference between a modiste shop and a gambling hell coaching inn. All were created to deliver a fantasy of sorts. The gambling hell promised that a man might win a fortune if Lady Luck sat beside him for the night.

A dress offered something just as thrilling. The perfect gown could turn even the most ordinary event into something spectacular. It could also turn that same event into something magical just by the way it could make a woman feel. Pippa considered it an honor to create such fantasies. Heaven knew her need to design was as vital to her well-being as her next breath.

Frankly, her plan was flawless and rather ingenious if she did say so herself. She'd picked five men from her brother's millionaires club to meet and discuss her proposal of marriage. Once she picked a man, her brother wouldn't object. He'd personally approved each of the members. It made little difference if they were titled or not. The only requirements? They had to have assets worth over a million pounds, be trustworthy, and, last but not least, be honorable. Pelham didn't allow riffraff into his club even if they did possess fortunes. If the men were part of the club, then Pelham would approve them as eligible men to marry. She was certain of it.

"My lady, look over there." Alice threw a furtive nod of her head in the direction of the paved walkway. "He's coming."

Pippa lifted her gaze. The man walking toward them wore a striking blue morning coat that fit him like a glove and emphasized his broad shoulders. She had little doubt that underneath his apparel, his body was fit and trim. Her eyes swept over his buff-colored breeches, another immaculate fit as they framed his muscular legs. Even from this distance, his clothes were expensive and of the highest quality. She could always recognize such clothing. It was her special power.

Yet, Pippa couldn't tell if it was Lord Bedford or not. She'd invited him to be her first bachelor to interview. She'd always found the viscount to be delightful. But she'd never remembered him being that muscular or tall. However, when they'd danced together at an event, he'd always found a way to amuse her. Humor was important in a marriage, more so than love.

As the man came closer, her confidence wilted like a cheese soufflé. The viscount possessed hair a tad darker than Pippa's blonde mane. The man strolling toward her had locks the color of obsidian. Too long, it fell across his brow and brushed his shoulders. It was so dark that it blended into the black of his hat. She still didn't recognize him as the brim shaded his face.

Alice clapped her hands together in glee. "Look, Lady Pippa, it's Lord Ravenscroft."

As her maid laughed in pure, unadulterated joy, Pippa gasped in horror.

Of all the men to meet in the park, it was just her luck it was Hugh Calthorpe, the Marquess of Ravenscroft.

He was her brother's best friend. He was also confident, intelligent, and funny. When he shared something with you, he'd lean close and lower his voice. His green-eyed gaze always held yours. He made you feel as if he were sharing something extraordinary only with you. That made him dangerous.

Pippa didn't need intimacy with a man.

She needed friendship, and that was all.

Pippa patted her hair to ensure everything was in place, then smoothed her dress. She would not let the appearance of the marquess deter her. She had every right to be in this park. Women of her stature went for walks every day.

She stood tall and tilted her chin slightly when Ravenscroft drew to a stop in front of them.

"Good morning, my lady." His gravelly voice reminded her of a cat's tongue against the skin, a sign of affection that was unexpected.

Or an unanticipated taste before a bite.

"Good morning, my lord," she answered as he bowed before her.

A man in possession of consummate manners, Ravenscroft turned to Alice. "Good morning, Miss Roberts."

"Oh, my lord, good morning," Alice cooed. "Imagine meeting you here."

That was the problem with her fifty-year-old maid. She adored Lord Ravenscroft and always tried to find a way to see him when he visited Pelham, which was practically an everyday occurrence. For heaven's sake, the man had even bought an estate close to the Jolly Rooster just to be near her brother and their other best friend, the Earl of Trafford, her sister's husband.

"Yes, imagine meeting me here." Ravenscroft slowly turned his gaze to Pippa's, then smiled. The mirth in his eyes made them twinkle. It reminded her of pure mischief, the aggravating kind. The earl was a master at provoking her brother. Simply throwing out a barb disguised as an observation was his modus operandi.

Whatever he said, she'd not take the bait. She smiled in return. "Are you just arriving?"

"Indeed," he answered, never taking his gaze from hers.

"Such a shame that we're leaving." She nodded again in a show of manners. "Enjoy your walk, my lord."

"My lady, how unfortunate that you're departing. I wanted to join you." A wicked smile that emphasized his full lips tugged at one corner of his mouth. Fine lines fanned the skin surrounding his striking green eyes.

No doubt they were a direct result of his constant exultant temperament. Truly, she'd never seen him angry or bored. Everything seemed to amuse him, which suited him. It enhanced his extraordinary handsomeness, if that were possible. In all her life, she'd only seen a few beautiful men, and the Marquess of Ravenscroft was one of those rare individuals. His features were masculine and attractive. Sharp angles framed his cheekbones and square jaw. The only thing that wasn't sharp about his features were his full lips.

Making her wonder if they were as soft as they appeared. She shook her head slightly to clear such thoughts. She had no business considering the man's mouth. He was her brother's best friend.

"How do you know I'm here for a walk?" His voice broke her out of her reverie. "Perhaps I'm here for an assignation of some sort...or another."

The scoundrel winked at her.

"Seems to be the popular thing today," Alice added unhelpfully.

Pippa drew a deep breath and released it. She'd learned early in life that it was best to put your adversaries on the defensive. "Well, we don't want to keep you from your appointment." She waved a gloved hand in the air. "Or tryst or rendezvous," she said under her breath.

"It's my lucky day. It just happens that my assignation is with *you*." He held up his arm. "Walk with me."

"I can't..." She turned toward the entrance of the park. Bedford was nowhere in sight. Where was the blasted man? It wasn't a good omen. Perhaps he wasn't interested in her proposal.

The subtle fragrance of sandalwood mixed with a heavenly masculine scent wafted her way. Ravenscroft always smelled divine. That's why he was one of her favorite dance partners at an event.

He leaned near, almost close enough to kiss her. Then, his whisky-dark voice teased her ear. "He's not coming."

It was a wonder that Lady Pippa didn't injure herself when she whipped her head to face him.

Hugh didn't mince words this time. "You should walk with me. I think you'll find it highly enlightening."

Her eyes narrowed in wariness, then blazed into anger. She wasn't pleased. Normally, he never involved himself in others' business, but this wasn't anyone ordinary. It was Lady Pippa Ardeerton, his best friend's little sister.

Honestly, she was also one of the most interesting people he'd ever met. Uncommonly beautiful with a rare wit, she could make anyone feel at ease, even Bedford, who was a nervous nelly.

Simply put, Lady Pippa was perfect. She'd make a perfect wife and partner.

If someone were looking for such a thing.

Slowly, she took his arm. As they strolled down the path, he chuckled to himself. They must appear as if they were two friends who, by happenstance, met at the park for an early bout of exercise. How wrong that observation would be. He'd purposely arrived at the exact time she was supposed to meet with Bedford.

When Hugh stole a glance at Lady Pippa, her eyes met his. They were royal blue, the same as her older brother's. But he'd noticed that hers had flecks of gold sprinkled throughout the irises. When he'd first met her, he'd been taken aback at her beauty. Even today, she could steal his breath. In a silken green morning gown with a jaunty little hat with peacock feathers, she was confident, assured, and carried herself with a grace that others could only wish to possess.

As much as he enjoyed counting her attributes, now was not the time. They had business to discuss.

With a quick glimpse, Hugh ensured that Lady Pippa's maid was behind them. She was still within proper chaperoning distance but couldn't hear their conversation. With his free hand, he pulled Bedford's letter from the inside pocket of his waistcoat. "The reason your beau isn't coming is because your letter was delivered to me."

She stumbled, and instantly, he tightened his arm around hers to keep her steady. They'd stopped their casual stroll, and Pippa's defiant chin lifted as she stared straight into his eyes. How uniquely refreshing for him. He didn't have to strain his neck when conversing. Normally, women peered up at him, but Pippa was only a half-foot shorter than him. The censorious look in her eyes was also refreshing. Most women, particularly ones looking for a husband, simpered and whispered around him as if he thought such behavior was enticing.

They were all utterly boring. But he would never consider Lady

Pippa boring, particularly when sparks of outrage flashed in her brilliant blue eyes.

"For your information, he isn't my beau." She snatched the letter from his hand and examined it. Her eyes widened in horror. "The seal is broken. You opened it?"

He winced at the incredulity in her voice.

"Not on purpose." He closed the distance between them until a mere six inches were between them.

Alice loudly cleared her throat in warning that he was too intimately close. He nodded his acknowledgment and stepped away until a respectable foot separated them.

"When my mail arrives, my butler organizes it on a silver salver and then places it on my desk. All the correspondence is presented with the wax seal facing me. It makes it quicker to open the stack." He shrugged slightly. "When I opened your letter and read it, I realized that it wasn't addressed to me."

"You even read it?" Heat bludgeoned her cheeks, and her voice had softened.

"I did." Honestly, it didn't feel as if he had anything to apologize for. She was on a fool's errand that could end with her being ruined.

She flinched slightly before a mask of indifference fell across her features. With a stalwart gaze, she slowly surveyed the park, completely ignoring him for a moment. Ramrod straight and with a determined demeanor, she reminded him of Diana, the goddess of the hunt. An appropriate comparison since, no doubt, Pippa would like to shoot him with an arrow about now.

Eventually, she turned to him with a pleasant smile on her face. It was as bogus as the calves of the men who wore padded stockings to give the impression of muscular legs.

"I trust that you will be discreet and keep that letter secret." She chewed on her lip, and her delicate brow furrowed into perfect lines. "As an honorable gentleman, you should do that."

He wanted to roll his eyes at that statement. As an honorable gentleman, he should have gone straight to her brother.

But out of respect for her, he decided to keep the appointment this morning. As an honorable man, he had to warn her about Lord

Bedford. More importantly, as an honorable man, he couldn't allow her to ruin herself.

Bloody hell, she'd asked the man to marry her.

And if that wasn't enough, she'd written to four more men asking the same.

Ready for more? You can pick up your copy **here.**

Have you read A Simple Seduction, the first in the Millionaires of Mayfair series? You can pick up your copy here.

Want to find out when my next book releases? Be sure to sign up for my newsletter **here.**

About the Author

Janna MacGregor pens romance novels with "Austen's spirit" (*Entertainment Weekly*) from her dual residences in the fast-paced Twin Cities and her native home in Kansas City. But she spends most of her time in Regency England, the setting for her beloved Cavensham Heiresses and the Widow Rules series. Her new series is The Millionaires of Mayfair. **For the latest news, sign up for her Newsletter.**

Connect with Janna MacGregor Online
Langham Hall Facebook Group
Instagram
BookBub
TikTok

facebook.com/jannamacgregor

instagram.com/jannamacgregor

bookbub.com/authors/janna-macgregor

tiktok.com/@jannamacgregor

Made in the USA
Monee, IL
03 March 2025

12910176R00173